OUTSIDE IN

A Cameron Andrews Mystery by

Nanisi Barrett D'Arnuk

New Victoria Publishers

Published by New Victoria Publishers, Inc., a feminist literary and cultural organization, PO Box 27, Norwich, VT 05055-0027

1 2 3 4 5   2000 1999 1998 1997 1996

Acknowledgements:
Thank you to Robie who read and reread and helped me think it through, to Joyce, Connie, Debbie, and Lisa for their comments and encouragement and to ReBecca for being patient.

Library of Congress Cataloging-in-Publication Data

D'Arnuk, Nanisi Barrett, 1948-
    Outside In : A Cameron Andrews mystery / by Nanisi Barrett
D'Arnuk.
        p.   cm.
    ISBN 0-934678-75-8   (pbk,)
    I. Title.
PS3554.A729098   1996
813' .54--dc20

96-18719
CIP

Printed in Canada

This is for Leslie who was always there and who took the first step.

Chapter One

Cameron didn't move as the door of the van opened beside her. She steeled herself for what was going to happen next, realizing how tensely she'd sat during the long ride. This was the real beginning! Her stomach jumped with excitement and exhilaration, but there was one little part of her, centered right below her esophagus that was scared to death. And though she hadn't been inside a church since her parents' funeral nine years earlier, she suddenly wanted to pray, *Dear God, don't let me forget anything I've been taught!*

They were inside the garage. The huge steel door was lowered behind the van and the heavy clank of the locks sliding into place was all too loud. It still didn't seal out the oppressive heat and humidity of the late July day. The stale air of the oil-smeared cavern held the heat and magnified its misery.

Silently, she stared forward, unconsciously fingering the short loop of chain that shackled her wrists to the chain around her waist, her one sign of nervousness.

"Come on, hot shot, move it out. We ain't got all day." The guard stood back, her hand resting loosely on her holstered revolver, waiting for Cam to exit the police van that had just brought her and two other women from the city of Baltimore to their new home, Hagerville State Correctional Facility for Women.

Cameron swung her legs over the side of the bench seat and hopped to the ground, careful not to trip on her ankle chains. She stretched her back slightly to release the tension. After the two other women had alighted from the van, the second guard, the driver, motioned them through the first set of steel-barred doors, his shotgun securely in hand.

Cam let the two other women go before her. The first one strode forward as best she could with the ankle shackles confining her movements. Her attitude seemed to imply there was nothing to worry about. Cam could tell that this wasn't her first time in prison. The second woman, though, was more tentative, her eyes wide. She was scared. Cam gave her a reassuring wink, then followed her as the guards nudged them forward. When the three were all inside the small entry way, the doors immediately slammed and locked with a heavy clang behind them. Then the iron door in front slid open to where three more guards waited for them.

"Small litter this time," the first guard inside observed, eyeing the three women who stood before him in blue coveralls marked with a City of Baltimore logo. "Any trouble makers?" he asked, taking the set of files that the van driver handed him through the glassed window next to the gate.

"Nah, gentle as lambs," the driver replied, watching the guard sign the transfer papers that released Cameron, Sharon and Donna into prison custody. "But this one," he continued, pointing toward Cameron with the butt of his rifle, "seems to have an attitude."

Shit, she thought, here it comes. It's starting already. Cameron checked her reaction, trying to keep her expression impassive as she continued to stare straight ahead.

"This a tough one?" the prison guard asked, thumbing through the files. He stopped as he came to the one with Cam's picture stapled to the front. Next to the picture, someone had handwritten a large capital "L" in red marker pen.

"Oh, another bulldyke," he chuckled as he opened the file, knowing the "L" stood for "Lesbian," and scanned her rap sheet. Surprised by what he read, he let out a low whistle as he brought his gaze up to Cam's face. "A cop!" he smiled, "We don't get many bad lady cops in here. Oh, we're gonna have a good time." He closed the file and handed them to his partner. "Well, *Detective Sergeant* Andrews," he sneered, walking up to Cam, so close that she could smell the cup of coffee he'd just chugged. "Welcome to Hagerville's House of Ladies. I think you're going to be very happy here." He waited. Cam just stood there, stolidly, hoping that her silence would keep him from pushing harder, but knowing that it probably wouldn't.

"Well, don't you want to be happy here?" he continued.

Cam finally looked him in the eye. "I'd rather be happy somewhere else," she said, her voice low.

"Oh, you'll change your mind," he promised. "You'll learn to love it here. You won't be able to imagine being anywhere else. I should think you'd be real excited to be shacked up with three-hundred and fifty other girls." He stepped back with a broad smirk on his face and motioned down the corridor that ended at a thick iron-barred gate. "Now, you three little ladies just move your pretty butts down there and we'll see that you get a nice little welcome party." He pressed a button, one of several on a long wall panel. It sounded a warning buzzer further inside the prison. "Here," he said, putting out his hand to stop Cam as she started past. "You take these with you," he said, handing her the files, "and be real careful not to damage them. No telling what might happen if one of these precious files got all bent out of shape." He smiled broadly as Cam took the files and started after her two companions.

2

"Bastard," Donna whispered under her breath as they neared the end of the hall.

"I'm prepared for it." Cam answered.

"No talking!" came as an order from behind Cameron.

At the end of the corridor, they were met by three stern and bored looking guards, all female.

"Well, well, well. If it isn't Donna Trachner," The first guard greeted them, looking happily at Donna, from behind the gate. "Welcome back, girl. I knew you couldn't bear to be away from us. What you in for this time?"

"Same ol' same old," Donna acknowledged. She had been arrested for prostitution and for robbing the johns she picked up. This was her third or fourth time in prison. "How you doing, Dee? Miss me?"

"Oh, you bet, Sugar Bumps," Dee smiled. "Missed you a lot. Things are really quiet without you. I'm glad you're back. Who'd you bring with you?"

Donna shrugged.

"Hand me the files!" the second guard ordered, obviously not in the mood for casual conversation. "Sorry we can't spend more time on this blessed reunion." Cam held out the files as far as the shackles would allow her to stretch her arm. As the guard took them, she acknowledged the male guard who had escorted the women, then pushed yet another button that slid the heavy door back. "Come on inside, ladies." As it slid back, Donna led the way through into the next corridor, which was painted in the same gun metal grey as the last hallway, with it's grey cement floors. The door slid closed behind them with another heavy thud.

Without taking her eyes off the files she was now perusing, the guard, whose name badge read "M. Emerson," addressed the other two guards. "Take them and get their processing started. See if Dr. Keystone is ready to examine them, yet."

As Cam started past her, Emerson put out a hand to stop her. Not any taller than Cam, Emerson outweighed her by a good sixty pounds and whether Cam wanted to or not, she felt intimidated by the cold, hard authoritarian look on her face. Cam waited as Emerson's eyes ran the full length of her, from her head to her feet. Having obviously passed the inspection, Cam was allowed to continue on.

"Be wary of this one," Emerson warned the guard who waited to escort Cam, "ex-cop." Cam sighed as the guard took her forcefully by the arm and pushed her forward. This was not going to be a good day.

The processing took a lot longer than it should have, but no one seemed in a rush to finish any of the paperwork. The pouches containing their few personal belongings were inventoried and they signed receipts for storage. Cameron read down the short list of her property: the shirt and trousers she'd worn to court to plead guilty and a wallet containing her driver's license and sixteen dollars and thirty-seven cents. Maggie had warned her not to take anything valuable with her, that if she pleaded guilty, she'd immediately be taken into custody again, her bail revoked.

Now, after being stripped and ordered to take a rather short, but hot shower with an abrasive soap, Cam sat on the cold metal chair wrapped only in the short, thin examining gown. Cam had tried to do what she was told without hesitating or balking, but no matter how co-operative she was, the guards always found something she hadn't done quite right, quite fast enough, or quite enthusiastically enough to suit them. Charlie had said they'd push her, that ex-police were viewed as scum inside a prison, both by the guards and by the inmates. She'd believed him, but the experience was almost more than he'd prepared her for. At least she wasn't sprayed with de-lousing disinfectant like on her first day in the city jail. Her skin still burned from that harsh treatment.

Looking at the other two, Cam almost was glad she'd attracted so much attention during this introduction to prison life. Donna seemed bored, but Sharon looked like she was on the verge of tears, even though most of the attention was centered on Cam. Donna stepped forward first to have her physical exam, but Sharon was more hesitant when her turn came. As she was escorted into the examining room, Cam could see that she was shaking slightly.

Cam watched her go, wondering if maybe she was anxious because she was trying to hide something. Or was there something about her, physical-ly, that she was embarrassed about? No. She hadn't really looked at Sharon when they were all in the shower together, but nothing seemed out of place. Maybe Sharon was just high-strung. Or maybe she's just cold, like me, Cam thought, trying to adjust the thin gown she now wore.

"Come on, sweetheart. Move your ass." The words, accompanied by a sharp rap on the shoulder, shook Cam from her reverie. Before she could react, Emerson had grabbed her by the arm and thrown her forward, shov-ing Cam toward the open door of the examining room. "Now the real fun starts. Just sit there." Emerson pointed to the doctor's examining table. Cam hoisted herself onto the table as the doctor walked into the room followed by his nurse.

"This the last one today?" Dr. Jerry Keystone asked.

"Saved the best 'til last, Doc," Emerson smiled. "This one gets the full treatment."

The doctor contemplated Cam for a minute. She began to chafe under his gaze.

"Step onto the scale," was the first order.

Cam did as she was told and waited while he adjusted the weights and height bar.

"Height, 5'7," Weight 129," the doctor told the nurse who wrote down his answers. "Hair, brown, eyes, brown. Do you wear corrective lenses?"

"No," Cam answered.

"Good. Sit down on the table."

Cam did as she was told. He began by asking her full medical history, year by year, childhood disease by childhood disease. Then, as she sat naked before him, he examined her.

"Where'd you get that?" he asked pointing to the bullet wound scar just below her left collarbone as he shined his examination probe into her left ear.

"Convenience store robbery," Cam answered curtly, "Rookie year."

"Perp get away?" Emerson asked scornfully.

Cam looked her in the eye. "No," she replied coldly, "I killed him."

Keystone shook his head. Was that disgust he felt? Or admiration? Cam couldn't tell for sure.

"Those, too?" he pointed to the other bullet wound scars on her left thigh and hip.

"No. Hostage situation. I rescued a child."

The doctor turned to Emerson who was leaning against the wall in the corner. He smiled. "We've got ourselves a hero."

Emerson just sniffed, uninterested. "Not too careful, though, with all them scars." she added with a shrug. "And she couldn't be too good, or she wouldn't be here."

The doctor adjusted his stethoscope in his ears and began his physical exam, listening to her chest, then peering into her eyes and inspecting her mouth, tapping her fillings and the gold cap on the back molar. That tooth, he wiggled and tried to see if it could be easily removed. "Make a note," he instructed the nurse who recorded all his findings, "There are two crowns in here, they'll have to be x-rayed, just in case." Then he stepped back and reached for a new pair of rubber surgical gloves from the shelf behind him.

"Ever had a full body cavity search before?" Emerson asked with a wry grin as Keystone pulled the gloves on.

Cam shook her head. "Not by a doctor," she grinned. She glanced from Keystone to Emerson as they exchanged bored but knowing looks.

"Then, you're in for a treat." Emerson sneered.

The doctor cleared his throat. "Turn around and bend over."

Cam stoically turned around and leaned over the table. Closing her eyes, she waited, as patiently as possible for the doctor to begin, ready to give her body up to his prodding and probing of her most private places, knowing that if she objected in any way, it would become even worse. She'd been warned that this would happen, that they'd try the most degrading forms of treatment, that she had to remain above and beyond whatever they threw at her. She'd known coming into this, that there were easier things than being in prison. But this was the choice she'd made.

Cam winced as the doctor's fingers explored her. She tried to keep a wall of detachment around her, trying to keep her mind on something else, not the way his probing seemed: cold and hard. She slowly repeated Charlie's eight rules for life in prison to herself. "You are in prison now, whatever happened outside has to be forgotten. You have to keep focused. Rule number one: trust no one. Rule number two: stay alert."

Cam suddenly felt the urge to pee as the doctor pushed against her bladder. Before she could check her reaction, her body stiffened to object to the treatment. A heavy hand on the back of her neck forced her face into the table.

"You got a problem with what he's doing?" M. Emerson growled into her ear, pressing her harder into the table.

"No, ma'am," Cam wheezed as the pressure interfered with her breathing.

"Then watch yourself. I'd love an excuse to get to you."

"Yes, ma'am," Cam acquiesced.

After a brief pause for emphasis, Emerson gave Cam a quick shove and backed away. Hands on her rear told Cam that the doctor had resumed his exam. But then, at last, it was finally over…or she hoped it was. Already, her body felt battered by his prodding. She just had to keep her psyche from feeling the same way.

"All right," the doctor said, "Turn around." He waited until she was facing him. "You look pretty healthy."

"Thanks," Cam couldn't control just one comment, "Was it as good for you as it was for me?"

"Don't get wise, scum," Emerson sprang at her and gave her a hard shove against the table. Cam was bent backwards over the table with the guard leaning heavily on her. "You think that's funny? You think you're the first one who ever said that? Now, just apologize to the good doctor and thank him for his *kind examination*." She gave Cam a hard shove and took a step back.

Cam straightened up slowly. "Sorry," she muttered to the doctor.

"Thank him. Nicely." It was an order.

Cam slowly raised her eyes to the doctor. "Thanks for the exam," was all she said.

"You keep running your smart mouth like that and we're gonna be seeing a lot of each other. And if it comes down to which one of us is tougher, I don't think you'd get very good odds. Do you understand me?" Emerson's threat held quite a bit of venom.

Cam looked at the floor and nodded. "Yes. I understand."

Emerson pointed toward the door. "Let's go get your new wardrobe and housewarming gifts."

Cam reached for the gown where it lay on the examining table, but Emerson stopped her.

"You don't need that," was all she said.

Cam wanted to object, but knew it would be useless. With a resigned sigh, she walked, naked, out through the back entrance of the room. Looking down the corridor, she could see a sign marked 'Supply Room.' She hoped that was as far as she'd have to go to be issued her prison clothes.

The intake interview and the rest of the paperwork were still ahead, another several hours work, before she would even come in contact with the other prisoners. Thank God Charlie had prepared her for what she'd have to go through. Now, if she could just keep her mind focused on everything else Charlie and Michael had taught her and not let the situation get to her, she'd be all right. And she might even live to tell about it.

As she waited for the bored supply room clerk to issue her clothing, her mind slid back four months...God, was it only four months?!...just to remind herself why she was here and reassure herself that she'd made the right decision. Today was the first day of a three year prison sentence for dealing drugs. It had seemed like such a good idea at that time...

Chapter Two

The turning point in her life had been early March, 1980. In little more than a month, Cameron would celebrate her thirtieth birthday. It was time for her to make a decision. As she'd sat back, evaluating her life, she had the feeling that she would come up short. Ten years before she had been the golden girl, near the top of her class, one of only three women taking the special joint courses being offered at Radcliffe and Harvard. A bachelor's degree, summa cum laude, in International Affairs with offers of scholarships for graduate school flowing in like water, the special opportunity to start her graduate work as one of five U.S. students invited to study at Universidad de Barcelona with prospects of working in the Diplomatic Corps almost assured. After that, she had been recruited by the State Department and opted to work as a linguist/interpreter for the CIA. But where was she now?

It had been six years since she'd moved to Baltimore; five years since she'd quit the CIA and enrolled in the Baltimore Police Academy and four years since Karen had kicked her out. Now on the Baltimore Police Force, she'd risen to the rank of Detective Sergeant in the Narcotics Division in record time. She was the first woman of rank in the division and on a fast-track for promotions. But how much longer was she going to run around playing cops and robbers? When did all this education and achievement begin to mean something?

She'd just been appointed to a new International Task Force on Drug Traffic Control. International? Yes, International. United States and Canada. Two countries. That made "International." And Drug Traffic Control? They'd probably just end up writing "How To" books for police agencies and catchy little jingles on "What-To-Do-If-Your-Child-Is-Toking-Weed-But-Won't-Share-With-You."

"You know your problem, Andrews?" she'd chided herself. "You've got a bad attitude. And you haven't been laid since before Thanksgiving. What kind of life is this?!"

She'd leaned back into the big overstuffed chair that dominated her living room. She loved that chair, bought at a junk shop when she was starting to set up her own apartment. It had reminded her of the chair in her mother's study, the one where she used to curl up and watch Mom pound away at the typewriter as she wrote all those speeches and articles for the League of Women Voters Newsletter. Even then, she'd known that Mom was doing something special, that people were listening to her ideas and politicians were using her words to convince voters about the things that were really important! Cameron would wrap up in her Mom's quilt, nestle into that chair, and let the rhythmic sound of the typing rock her to sleep. It had been her security blanket. This chair...well actually, any big overstuffed chair...had the same effect.

What a time she and her friend, Paul, had getting it up the stairs and into the apartment! They almost had to take the door off to get it in! And the hours she had spent, carefully measuring and fitting material to reupholster it by herself. Damn! Was this what her life was reduced to?

She'd gotten up out of the chair and walked into the kitchen. She'd looked around, opened the refrigerator and the cabinets, then turned back toward the living room. Somehow, nothing looked right to her. She wanted something but couldn't identify what.

Just then, the phone had rung. Had it been that phone call that had changed her life? It seemed so innocent at the time. And it still felt that way, but Cam knew that it had been a turning point. What would have happened if she hadn't answered it?

It was an interesting hypothesis. But she had answered it:

"Hey, Dahlin," had come an all-too-cheery voice from the other end of the line. "Have you had dinner yet?"

"Hi, Pauly." Cam had smiled at the sound of her best friend's voice. "No. I thought I'd just sit here and eat my heart out. What do you have in mind?" Cam leaned back against the kitchen cabinet and reached for a cigarette.

"There's a new gay bar just opened over near Fells Point. Want to check it out? I'll even spring for dinner on the way."

"Hey, have you ever known me to turn down a free meal?"

"As long as you remember that there's no such thing as a free lunch." He chuckled at his own joke. "I'll be right over to pick you up." With that, the line went dead.

Good old Pauly. They'd met at the Police Academy. Being two of the oldest in the class (she at the over-the-hill age of twenty-six and he after an eight year stint in the Army), they'd immediately struck up a friendship, which became even stronger when they learned that they were both gay. Since that time, they'd seen each other through devastating break-ups and lost lovers and had managed to keep each other on a balanced track even though they'd eventually been assigned to different precincts.

Cameron had walked into the bedroom and opened the closet door. Nothing in it looked comfortable or even appropriate to wear to a bar opening. And there was nothing in any drawer or shelf. It just wasn't a good night to find anything. Shit, she thought, What difference will it make? It'll probably be all men anyway.

She hadn't dated in several months. Not out of a lack of opportunity. It just didn't seem worth it. Most of the women she met were either turned off because she was a police officer or turned on because she wore a uniform. Go figure.

She had finally chose a white cotton shirt and brown corduroy vest that looked good with her jeans, then pulled on a pair of boots.

It would be a lot easier if I knew what I wanted to be when I grew up, she thought. Even her little sister Lori had found her niche and was very happy to fit neatly into the role of housewife and mother. But being the oldest, the smartest, the one most likely to make the right decisions for everyone involved, had finally taken its toll. Cameron had come to a place where she had to make decisions for herself. And that wasn't something she was good at.

"Well, who knows? Maybe I'll meet someone tonight." She tucked her wallet into her back pocket as the doorbell rang.

The bar, The Oak Tavern, was almost a museum with a long heavy dark oak bar and antique fixtures and wall hangings that had obviously been there since it had first opened as a neighborhood pub nearly a century ago. There was the glass-doored ice box cooler which held imported bottled beer in neat rows. And along the floor at the base of the bar, there was still the tin trough that ran into the drain so that the men who drank there wouldn't have to give up their places to go and relieve themselves. It spoke of another era when women entered bars through a back door and stayed out of sight in another room to sip their little glasses of whiskey where they wouldn't be bothersome to the men, that was, if they had any morals at all.

But now, the two men who owned it lived upstairs and were well on their way to making it a homey neighborhood place that members of the gay community could feel comfortable in without bright lights and blaring music.

As she'd anticipated, most of the bar's inhabitants had been men and the few women who were there had been neatly paired. She played a couple games of pool in the back room while Pauly danced and flirted with someone he obviously knew but didn't introduce. She had a few casual conversations, but there was no one who seemed either interested or interesting.

As the bar started to clear out, well after midnight, Cam sat on a bar stool nursing her scotch and soda. Sorting through some ideas and bouncing a few thoughts off Pauly, Cameron made a decision, or at least came to a place where she felt comfortable.

She would just have to see how it felt in the cold light of the next morning. What had Mom always said? "If you really want to do something badly enough, you'll do it. And if you're not sure; sleep on it. If it hasn't given you nightmares and it still seems good in the morning, it's probably the right choice."

It wasn't that Cameron didn't enjoy her job; it just wasn't quite enough, somehow. Enough what? Challenge? Excitement? What? What was making her so restless? She had been responsible for the arrests of dozens of small time dealers and had busted a lot of college kids who thought that the one hundred dollars for a quick rush wasn't a high price to pay, but then she'd been in on the joint bust that the Department had co-operated with the Feds on. They'd seized over a ton of the powdery white stuff and another ton of grass aboard a luxury yacht in the harbor before it ever had a chance to make its way into the city. Cam had felt that she'd finally made a difference in this war they were fighting.

And Craig Roberson, who'd been in charge of the big bust, had remembered her from her days at the Agency and had complimented her on her work with the Force. She'd been proud when he also mentioned that he'd been following her career. Now she was going to take him up on his offer: "Give me a call if there's ever anything I can do for you." Cam hoped it hadn't just been polite conversation.

The next morning, Cam reached for the telephone and dialed the number on the dog-eared business card she'd carried in her wallet since that night. After a few minutes, Craig's secretary answered and after taking her name, put her on hold. Cam expected that she'd get the I'm-sorry-he's-in-a-meeting-right-now,-can-I-take-a-message routine, so when the secretary returned to the phone and Cam heard, "I'm sorry but he's in a meeting right now," her heart sank. But the voice continued. "He wants to know if you can come see him here tomorrow at three p.m."

"I'd love to," Cam's stomach was rolling, "but I'm on the four to midnight shift tomorrow. Can he see me earlier?"

There was silence except for the flipping of some papers.

"What about nine-forty-five a.m? I think he can fit you in then."

Cam wanted to reach through the phone and kiss her. "I'll be there. Thank you." As Cam placed the phone back in its cradle she let out a wild yell. Yes! He was willing to see her, the second to the top man in the Agency wanted to talk to her! Maybe it hadn't been polite conversation. Tomorrow would tell.

What should she wear to the interview? Nothing too casual but still nothing too formal. This was a job interview of sorts, but she knew the interviewer and he knew her. It wasn't like she had to make a stunning first impression. She wanted to appear business-like and strong, so nothing too femmy or frilly, yet nothing too powerful that would make her look, well, like what? Okay. What she was going after was a competent, I-can-handle-anything image. She must have stared into the closet for a full ten minutes before she settled on a grey lightweight wool suit with a peach silk shirt.

She looked at her watch. It was three-thirty already. Shit, she had to get to work. She pulled on her jeans, a heavy wool sweater, and her tennis shoes, grabbed her Orioles baseball jacket and went out the door.

The alarm clock rang at six a.m. and shocked Cam out of deep sleep. She'd been dreaming of running, chasing a person she couldn't quite see, but knew she had to catch. Knew that her life depended on catching up with the runner ahead of her who was always just rounding the next corner. It took her a minute to realize why the clock was blasting when it was still dark out.

"Damn," she said to herself sitting up. "Hit the showers, lady, this day has just begun." She glanced out her bedroom window to the quiet yards that stretched behind the abutting apartment buildings. At least it wasn't snowing. That was a plus. But the traffic around the Beltway would be heavy with rush-hour commuters and it took over an hour to get from Baltimore to the Virginia border even on the lightest of days. She'd best leave by seven-forty-five to make sure she had enough time. Didn't want to be late for this one.

The tepid shower water took longer to wake her than usual. She stood there and let it course down her back, trying to decide if she had the courage to flip the faucet over to the cold setting. Just as she thought she might be able to take the freezing water that came directly out of the pipes in March, she decided she was awake enough to forgo it and turned the knob to off instead.

She knew the way to the Langley, Virginia facility, even though the signs directing traffic to the Agency's headquarters had long ago been removed by executive order.

It was just nine-thirty when she pulled into the driveway. Stopping at the guard station, she showed her driver's license and, after checking her name against the list on his clipboard, he pressed a button and the gate swung back. Cam guided her car down the long drive that ended in front of a large grey concrete and glass building. She almost turned into the employees' parking lot out of habit, but edged her car neatly into a visitor's space just a few feet from the front door.

Entering this building again after nearly five years astonished her. Nothing had changed; the tile floors were still the same color, the paintings on the walls the same, still clean, not dingier. It was as if time stood still here. She was shocked that the face behind the glassed-in reception area was unfamiliar. She had almost expected to see Beth Williams still sitting there.

She gave her name and the reason for her visit to the new face. This person had probably worked here longer than Cam ever had, but Cam still thought of her as new. She stood and waited while the receptionist typed her name into the computer to verify the appointment. Cam knew that there'd also be an on-screen identification photo of her as a security check.

"Thank you, Ms Andrews," the receptionist said, pushing a visitor's badge under the glass panel. "You may go right up to the sixth floor. Please take that second elevator."

Cam clipped the ID badge to her lapel. It was strange to see it there, to see it say "Visitor" and not have her name and photo printed on it. She walked into the elevator and pressed six.

When the door opened, she was directly across from a glass door that read "Craig Roberson, Regional Director." Craig was Director now? When had that happened? The card he'd handed her in October had said "Deputy Director." Her stomach started to roll and she hesitated. Finally, taking a deep breath, she nodded to the guard at the desk in the corridor and opened the door to enter a small waiting room. This one had been redecorated recently. The chair arms showed no signs of wear and the beige and rust colors were still bright and clean. A pretty young woman in a beige suit sat behind a desk, peering into a computer terminal.

"Ms Andrews, welcome." She stood and extended her hand. "I'm Martita Sanchez, Mr. Roberson's assistant. We spoke yesterday. We're very glad you could come today. May I take your coat?"

"Thank you." Cam slipped out of her trenchcoat and handed it to Martita. "This office is quite different from when Robert Page was here."

"Yes, Mr. Roberson insisted that it be redone when he took over. He said the old office was too impersonal."

"It's a nice change."

Martita smiled. "Have a seat. He'll be with you in just a moment."

Almost on cue, before Cam could sit, the door to Roberson's office opened and Craig stepped out.

"Cameron! I'm really glad you called. We must be on the same wave length. I was just talking about you a few days ago. I almost called you myself."

Cam almost replied, Why didn't you? It would have saved me a lot of agonizing hours.

But his hearty handshake drew her toward his office, his other hand on her shoulder. "Come in, come in," he continued, shutting the door behind them. He offered her a chair in front of his desk, then strode around and sat down facing her. He watched as she perused the office. Every piece of furniture here was new, just purchased three months ago when he'd taken over this division. It was all smooth and sleek. No rounded edges, just angles and sharp creases. A dark, heavy wood which, like the man who occupied this office, was meant for use, for business.

"I must apologize," Cam started, "I wasn't aware that you'd received this promotion. I still had the card you gave me last October."

"No big deal. I'm still me. I just got a bigger office and more headaches, that's all." He smiled. "There have been quite a few changes around here in the past few months. A lot of our people have been transferred to the Middle

East to deal with this Iranian hostage situation. It really caught everyone off guard. It's a real embarrassment for the Carter Administration, especially seeing that this is a presidential election year. There'll probably be a lot more changes before fall. Even more, if the Republicans get back into office." He spread his arm out to indicate the room. "I guess this office is just to impress those it's supposed to impress."

Cam liked his smile. They had been friendly when she'd worked here. He'd come down to the ciphering room late nights and bring her coffee as she worked on translations for him. They'd struck up a good friendship then, nothing very personal, but warm and comfortable. She realized now how little she knew about him.

"Shall I guess why you're here and show off my magnificent powers of deduction?" he asked.

"It probably takes very little deducing to figure why I'm here." Cam grinned. "I was going to ask you if you had any pull in getting me back into the Department. I guess that's a stupid question."

"I was hoping that's why you were here," He leaned forward onto his elbows. "Let's cut the bullshit. I told you last fall that I've been following your career. I have. I caught your name in the papers when you got that medal of honor a couple of years ago and I've been keeping my eye on you ever since. I have to be honest. At first it was just curiosity, you know, because we'd worked together but you've impressed the hell out of me. You've turned into one tough cop and I really liked the way you handled yourself on the Harbor Boat case. I'm glad you were assigned to it. If I'd been smarter, I probably would have recruited you then. Now I'm glad I didn't."

"Why?" Cam was puzzled by his last statement.

Craig hesitated just a fraction of a second. "You really serious about coming back to work here?"

"It's a long drive down the Beltway in eight o'clock rush hour traffic after getting off a midnight shift. I think if I were going on pure whim here, I'd have stayed in bed." She straightened her grey skirt and carefully smoothed the silk scarf she'd added to the ensemble this morning.

"Why do you want to come back?"

Cam took a breath. "Well… Cutting the bullshit, as you said, I just want to do more. I don't want another family to have to lose anyone." She knew he'd read through her file. Even if he didn't remember that she'd mentioned Ben or her parents, her whole family history was part of her old personnel file. "I'm not sure I'm doing any good where I am. Besides, I may be coming to the end of my effectiveness there. Too many people know my face now. It sort of blows the 'undercover' stuff. The next step would probably be a promotion upstairs into administration." She smiled. "And we both know how effective I am behind a desk." Yes, put her in front of a computer or a mixed-cipher coded message and she'd have it sorted out in no time, but ask her to write a letter or a report, and she'd stare at the blank page for hours on end. She just didn't have the patience for it. It was the one part of her college career she didn't miss.

Craig studied her carefully. She just looked steadily back into his eyes. "You want a cup of coffee or something?"

"Yes, coffee would be great." What I probably need is a neat scotch, she thought. What am I getting myself into?

"How do you take it?"

Cam looked up, she'd almost forgotten he'd asked about the coffee. "Oh, uh, black, one sugar."

Craig went to the door and stuck his head out to ask Martita for two cups of coffee. "I don't usually ask Martita to get coffee for me," he apologized, "but, I don't want to break our train of thought here. Now tell me. What do you want me to do?"

Cam took a breath. "I'm not really sure. I just know that I want to do more than I'm doing. I'm not unhappy in my job, but it's getting stale. I'd probably be happier if this led to some action."

Craig smiled. "What kind of action?"

"Getting some arrests made, shutting the border to drug traffic. You know that a lot of stuff comes in that way." Their eyes locked for a few seconds.

At that point, Martita knocked softly on the door and entered with two mugs of coffee, both black, one with a spoon sticking out. That one she placed on the desk in front of Cam. The other, she handed to Craig then turned and left.

Craig watched as Cam took a sip of the black liquid, assessing her. Finally, he sat back in his chair. "Cameron, I waste very little time these days. We just don't have it." He stood and began pacing. "Have you told anyone about this meeting today? Does anyone know you came here? It's very important."

"No. No one. I didn't know if I had anything to tell them. Why? Is this important?" She was just a bit apprehensive. "Not even your partner?"

"No, not even Russ. Why?"

"If you come back to the department, the way I'd like you to come back, it has to be under deep cover. Not even your grandmother's cat can know about it. It could mean life or death." He watched as she took it all in. "That scare you?"

"Should it?"

"I'd tell you to get out now if it didn't." He sat in the chair next to hers. "Look, we have several cases pending right now that we just can't nail. We've got some ideas on how to work this, but we can't quite fit the right person to it. But I'll tell you, every one has your name tacked to it. We need someone like you here." He took a deep breath. "Because of all the changes going on, I'm under orders not to recruit anyone right now. That's why I didn't call you. But you called me, so my hands are untied." He rose and paced again. "Look, I want to scare the shit out of you."

"You're doing a good job." Cam smiled. "This is not exactly the way I had pictured this meeting."

He sat back down beside her. "If all goes the way I'd like it to, this will mean a big change in your life. I can't say any more about the cases or the plans. But I can tell you that if you pass all the tests, and I see no reason why you wouldn't, you may be asked to take some difficult, very dangerous assignments."

"Why me? Why not someone already in the Department?"

"I can't explain fully. It just has to be someone with no apparent connection to the Agency. From now on, we'll do all your testing elsewhere. You and I will meet somewhere else. I don't even want to see your car in the Commonwealth of Virginia. I'm talking total secrecy, total disassociation. I also must ask that you adhere to a full oath of secrecy about this conversation. It never happened." He hesitated for a moment. "Do you realize that our interview is being taped?"

This last question took Cam by surprise. She hadn't even thought of the possibility. She kept her composure, though.

"No, I wasn't," she admitted, "but it doesn't really astound me. Craig, you still haven't answered my question. Why me? Why not someone else."

"Let's just say it's the right person in the right place at the right time. Look Cam, as a person, I like you a lot, I always have. As a cop, I respect you a great deal. You know that I've always marvelled at the way you crawled though those stupid codes and made sense out of sheer gibberish. I'll still never understand how it's done.

"This is not a job I'd want to offer to a friend and I do think of you as a friend, but I'm offering it anyway, because I think you're the perfect person to do it. Think this over hard. Take a few days to live with it. If you want to come back, there's a place for you, and it won't be a cushy desk job, you can count on that." He stood and walked around his desk, then hesitated slightly. "Do you have any vacation time coming to you?"

"A couple weeks, maybe three."

"Good. The beginning of May would be a good time to take it." He turned back from the window and flipped a switch just inside his top desk drawer. Then he handed her a business card with just a telephone number printed on it. "Let me walk you out."

Cam set the empty coffee cup on the desk and stood, trying not to show how wobbly her knees felt. "That's it?" she asked. "That was a short job interview." Then in an attempt to break the tension, "Don't you want to see how fast I can type?"

Craig let out a big laugh and his body relaxed. "Don't worry, the interviews will get longer...and harder."

He put his arm around her shoulder. Cam wasn't sure whether it was to show physical or moral support.

Martita handed Cam her coat and Craig walked her to the elevators. They rode to the first floor and walked out of the building in silence.

"This is a lot to think about." Cam admitted as she put the key into the lock of her car door.

"Good, I'll expect a call from you in four or five days. Don't forget to use my private line." He tapped the card she still held in her hand. "Oh, and Cam. One other thing. Uh, about your sexual lifestyle…Don't even make it look like you're trying to hide it." He winked at her and turned and strode back into the building.

Now what in hell did he mean by that?

Cam didn't remember driving back to Baltimore, but there she was, parking her car near her apartment. Her mind was buzzing with questions. It had happened too fast. She'd expected to go in there, have a nice chat and maybe, just maybe, get a "We'll call you in a few months, or years," but not, "Make up your mind and call me in four or five days."

And what they had spoken about raised more questions than it answered. What had he meant when he picked up on the word "action" and why should she "not make it look" like she was trying to hide her lifestyle? Didn't the Federal government still have its "no queers here" policy? What was she getting herself into? How much did she really want this job? And exactly what job was she being offered?

Cam understood the need for secrecy, but she'd sure like to go in with her eyes open, especially if her life was going to be put on the line.

Her life on the line? Why in hell was she even considering it?

She unlocked the door to her apartment. Had she just walked up the long flight of stairs without noticing it? And her mail was in her hand. She had no recollection of stopping at the mailbox next to the gate.

"You'd better get your head on straight before you go out into the streets tonight, kiddo, or you won't have to worry about being alive to have to make this decision," she told herself.

She stopped. She put her life on the line every night. Maybe she should just go for it and make it count. But was she playing against the odds now? How big was the safety net the Agency could provide for her. At least out on the street, she knew that her partner, Russ, was right beside her, or, at most, just a few doors away. Come to think of it, Craig hadn't even mentioned back-up. She couldn't believe they'd let someone go out without a safety net. But then, hadn't he said "deep cover?" Maybe, just maybe…

Chapter Three

C am didn't wait a full four days to call Craig back. Wednesday, when she'd first made the call to Craig, had been the thirteenth, and Cameron took that to be a good omen. So, on Sunday afternoon, St. Patrick's Day, just one month before her birthday, she called the number on the plain white card.

"Yes." Craig's voice answered the phone.

"Hi. It's me. I want in."

"Great. I'll get back to you." And the phone went dead.

Cam looked at the receiver in her hand. She hadn't expected a brass band but at least more than, "I'll get back to you." Had he lost interest in her? Had something turned up in her background report that had turned them off? *Damn* this secrecy shit! Well, might as well get used to it.

Russ, her partner, was beginning to suspect something. Twice last night, she hadn't even known he was talking to her; her mind was miles away. She hated being secretive around him.

They'd been partners for almost three years. They trusted their lives to each other. There'd never been anything she'd hidden from him.

"Just tired, I guess," was her response to his inquiry.

"Hey, Radcliffe, don't get burned out on me," he warned. "Why don't you take a few days off. You've been going at this full press for a while now."

"Maybe," she'd said, chuckling to herself. Theirs was a good relationship. Radcliffe and Russ. When had that nickname started? The first day they'd worked together, she'd gone off on a long analysis of the situation and Russ had just stared at her, laughing that she sure talked a lot. It must be the expensive education she had, you got the amount of words you paid for. He had gone to a State college. It was cheap, so he never had much to say. "Radcliffe." The nickname had stuck.

When Cam walked to her desk the next afternoon, there was a message for her to return a phone call to a Maggie Thomason. She picked up her phone and dialed the number. A sweet, young voice answered. "Dr. Thomason's office."

"Maggie Thomason, please."

"One moment. May I tell her who's calling?"

"Cameron Andrews, returning her call." The line clicked to dead air, but within a few moments, Cam heard a warm rich voice.

"Cameron, thanks for calling back so quickly. We have a mutual friend who thinks we should meet. I was wondering if we could have dinner tomorrow evening."

"A mutual friend? May I ask who?" Might this be her first connection?

"He said you dropped in to see him a few days ago. Really thought we'd hit it off. I'd love to get together."

So, Craig! Yes! Cam's mind and heart raced.

"Yes. Sure. I think that'd be great. I'll look forward to it."

"Why don't I pick you up there at the station. What time are you through?"

"My shift is over at seven."

"Then I'll be there at seven."

"Yes, fine. Can I ask one question? What're you a doctor of?"

"Psychiatry."

"Uh huh." Cam said. She heard a chuckle from the other end of the line.

"You can look me up in the phone book," Maggie admitted, "I have a legitimate practice. But you can just tell your friends there that you have a date."

"Sure."

"Until tomorrow, then." And the phone went dead. Cam looked at the phone, then back to the office. Russ was sitting on his desk, legs dangling over the edge when she hung up.

"Problem?" he queried.

"No. Not at all." Cam looked at him with a puzzled expression. "I just got asked out on a blind date."

"Sounds promising." He looked at her with a wry smile on his face. "I have to hand it to you, Radcliffe. I never have women calling me for dates. How do you do it?"

"Just living well," she smiled. "Besides, you're already married."

He nodded, with a warm smile. "Yeh. Now, that's the way you should go. Marie thinks you don't get out enough. If you dated more, maybe you'd find someone to settle down with."

Cam looked at him, incredulously. "You've been discussing my love life with your wife? What? Don't you have one of your own? You gotta dissect mine?"

"There's a lot I can't tell her. You know that. We got to have something to talk about. Besides, it makes her feel more secure to know that you and I aren't fooling around when we stay out all night on a stakeout."

"Maybe I should call her and have a long talk," Cam threatened, drawing out the word "long" as far as she could.

"Oh no!" Russ feigned horror. Then his mood changed and he shook his head. "We got a tough one tonight. Are you up to it?"

"Yeh, I'm up to it. What's the deal?"

"Some coke laced with strychnine showed up over by Johns Hopkins last night. Two kids dead. Another in the hospital."

"Whew! As if the coke itself wasn't deadly enough. Now they're adding strychnine! Witnesses?"

"Just the one woman, in Hopkins. Still in intensive. Freaked out of her mind. Won't talk to anyone."

"Maybe I should see her."

"Hoped you would." Russ hesitated, "Now, Radcliffe, are you sure your mind's on this one? You've been looking kind of strange lately. Something else bothering you?"

Cam looked into Russ' concerned face. They'd always been honest with each other, knew they could count on each other for anything. She took a deep breath and lied to him outright for the first time. "No, I'm fine. There's nothing else on my mind. I'm fine. Let's go have a talk with this lady."

Russ slid off the desk, handed Cam a file and strode out toward his car. Cam looked at the file in her hand, then followed.

The next evening, Cameron looked up from her desk as a handsome woman, in her mid to late thirties, in a flowing magenta dress with a short, tailored beige wool jacket, walked into the outer office, precisely at seven o'clock. Her dark hair, lightly sprinkled with grey, was swept back in a neat shag that fell just below her collar. The woman had an elegance about her that was highlighted by the expensive clothing. A hint of gold jewelry added just the right touch.

"That her?" Russ asked, his eyes wide. "Not bad. How do you do it? Women that good never threw themselves at *me*."

"You got the best one there is. I told you, I'll swap you anytime."

"Fat chance." Russ laughed as Cam took her blazer from the coat rack and walked out of their enclosed cubicle. As she approached, Maggie extended her hand and Cam took it, looking into warm grey eyes that wrinkled slightly at the corners.

"Maggie? I'm happy to meet you. I'm sorry I'm not dressed up. We had a lot of running around to do today. I could stop home and change if you like. I hope wherever we're going doesn't have a dress code."

"No. It's not a problem. I'm still dressed from the office. We'll be going someplace *very* casual. You should be comfortable." Maggie examined Cam's neat grey slacks and red rayon shirt. "I see nothing at all wrong, in any way, with how you're dressed. Let's go. I'm parked out front and I really don't want to get a ticket," she added with a light laugh that made Cam smile.

They walked out into the cold evening air and got into a late model yellow Mercedes.

"I was a little confused at first," Cam admitted as Maggie pulled away from the curb. "This is part of Craig's interview process?"

Maggie laughed quietly. "In a way, yes," she said in a lowered voice, "but it wouldn't look good to have you going to see a psychiatrist, now, would it?" She reached into her purse without taking her eyes off the road and handed Cam a small leather wallet. "That's my ID so you'll know for sure, going in, what this is all about. I have to officially inform you that what we may talk about and what may be revealed to you is of a highly confidential nature. Revealing any of this may be a breach of national security which may carry a very heavy fine and penalty. Do you understand?"

Cameron nodded.

"Don't nod. I have to hear it out loud," Maggie said, a smile in her voice.

"I understand." Cameron replied.

"Good." Maggie reached under the dash board and switched off a tape recorder which she dropped into her purse. "That's done." she sighed. "I hate this legal stuff, but it's regulations. I help Craig out with special assignments, you know, psychiatric evaluations. I'm the one that gets called when they think an agent has been out in the field too long. No one in the department knows me, so I get a chance to size people up without them realizing what's happening. And I really do have my own practice."

"Yes, I know. I did look you up."

"Good. I like that. Good initiative. Never take anything at face value."

"You've been in practice for ten years. Graduated from Temple. Spent two years in Viet Nam as a Paramedic. You do a lot of community service work, especially at drug half-way houses. You've been divorced for five years, have no children and currently no romantic involvements. Have I done my homework correctly?"

"Excellent!" Maggie beamed at her. "Craig said you were good. But you did miss the mole on my right shoulder blade."

Cameron almost blushed. "Should I be fooled into thinking you're really going to be a friend?"

"I hope we will be. In fact, Craig thinks we should even make it look like we're more than just friends. I'm glad I like you."

"You just met me." Cam watched Maggie as she maneuvered through the evening traffic going into City Center.

"You don't believe in *like* at first sight?"

Cameron smiled. "Yeh. I do. It's just that I expected you to be more conservative. It did take you almost three months to decide on which condo you were going to buy."

Maggie glanced at her with a small amount of amazement. "Well, we have done our homework. I'm usually slow in making up my mind about inanimate objects, but I'm well trained in sizing up the human factor. Would you like to see the condo I finally chose? Or do you already have pictures of it?"

"No pictures. But do you think you should take me to your home already? This is our first date."

Maggie chuckled once again, that beautiful warm chuckle that pleased Cameron very much. "Actually, I have every intention of taking you to my place. It's much more quiet there and we don't have to worry about eavesdroppers. We do need to stop and get a bottle of scotch, though. I'm afraid I don't have any in the house. I never developed the taste for it. It's Dewar's, right?"

"This is turning into an 'I know more about you than you know about me' contest. Doesn't that take all the mystery out of our relationship?" Cam asked.

"You're right. This could get too embarrassing. We should stop. You know I've read your file. I know you've done your homework. Let's stop at that. I'm sure there are lots of things that we don't know about each other."

"Right. What do you usually drink?"

"A good vodka stinger or white wine depending on whether I need to keep my mind on straight."

"Which are you drinking tonight?"

"I haven't decided yet." There was that chuckle again. They pulled into a liquor store parking lot and Maggie got out of the car. When she returned, she was carrying large bottles each of scotch and vodka.

"I hope that's not all for tonight." Cam commented.

"Let's just say I'm looking ahead to the future." she turned to Cameron. "Tonight is just getting-to-know-you night. Relax. I'm not fully on duty. That will come later. I just want to know you as a person before I start dissecting you as a potential agent. I'm a little nervous, myself. I usually come in at a cocktail party or meeting or I watch some seasoned agent get grilled and make my evaluations from behind a two-way mirror. I seldom get to meet people one on one and hardly ever before they've been given an assignment. Craig thinks that you're too top secret for the regular shrinks to work with. And he thinks you're very special."

"Do you know what my assignment will be?"

"Yes. But I'm not at liberty to tell you until you've gone through some evaluation and training. I'm sorry."

"I understand." Cameron stared ahead through the traffic.

"Relax, Cameron. Let's get to know each other before I have to get tough. It'll be a lot easier that way."

When Cameron walked into the office the next afternoon, Russ gave her a raised-eyebrow look.

"I noticed that your car didn't move all night," he said, keeping his eyes focused on the report in his typewriter.

"You my mother?" Cam asked. She sat down and thought back. It had been a very pleasurable night. After a wonderful pasta dish that Maggie swore she'd picked up at a deli, Cam and Maggie had talked about everything they could think of; their families, where they grew up, who they'd dated in high school, what college had been like for them, why they were doing what they were doing. Cameron was still aware that she was being interviewed, tested, evaluated, but Maggie was so open with her life that Cameron had almost no qualms about being open and honest in return. This woman was good at her job and knew how to draw the most out of people. They'd both been surprised to discover it was almost three in the morning, at which time, Maggie had declared that it was too late, and they were both slightly too inebriated, to drive around town. She'd shown Cam to her guest room and kissed her lightly on the lips then disappeared into her own room, shutting the door behind her.

"Well?" Russ broke into her train of thought.

"Well, what?"

"Your date." Russ always wanted details. "Well?" he demanded.

"I like her. Nothing happened."

"You didn't spend the night with her?"

"I didn't say that. I said nothing happened."

Russ shook his head. "Radcliffe, dear. You're either getting slow in your old age or there's something wrong with this picture."

"Nothing wrong. Just taking it slow. She's a classy lady."

"Slow, huh. When you seeing her again?"

Cameron smiled sweetly at him. "Tonight."

The two weeks after she had first met Maggie passed quickly. For Cameron, it was a time of burning the candle at both ends. Each night, when her shift was over at the precinct, she'd immediately grab a quick bite to eat, then meet with either Maggie or with Craig's assistant, Wendell Adreopolous at some predetermined place for a training session. And each night, from the different meeting places, she'd been taken by some circuitous route to a safe house where she'd undergo several hours of training or testing. The nights with Wendell were never the same. One night it'd be investigation techniques; another, technical surveillance devices; the next, a review of pertinent laws and prior case studies until he finally dropped her back where she'd left her car and she crawled home to bed. Her mind was reeling. She hadn't worked this hard in graduate school, but then, she hadn't had a full-time job at the same time either.

Her sessions with Maggie had gotten harder and had filled every other night. Question after question after question. And then begin all over at the first one. What was Maggie looking for with her questions? Why ask the same ones over and over again? Cam couldn't figure out what this was all

23

leading to. The only thing that made it seem easier was the bed in the guest room of Maggie's apartment, which had become her second home.

She was weary. She'd explained her family, she'd explained her education, she'd explained her job, she'd explained her relationships…well, most of her relationships. She'd never be able to explain Karen.

Beautiful Doctor Karen Amos. They'd met while Cam was working in Virginia and Karen was in her last year of medical school. A gorgeous blond with a body that left most fashion models in the dust. Men immediately assumed she was straight and fair game and that they'd found an easy mark. That was, until she unleashed her magnificent mind on them and left them with their mouths hanging open. Karen was more intelligent than anyone Cam had ever met. She inhaled the written word and could spit it back out fully digested and defined at a moment's notice. She adored opera and ballet and loved to jog and play volleyball. She loved living and she savored the day that she could find a cure for something or make someone's life easier.

Karen and Cam had lived together for over three years. Cam had even made the commute every day from outside Baltimore to Langley, Virginia just because Karen had been accepted to do her residency at Johns Hopkins Hospital. Cam thought it better for her to commute on her regular nine to five schedule, than for Karen to have to worry about driving home after late night or double duty shifts at the hospital.

It was Karen who had brought Cam to Baltimore. And it was then that she'd decided to apply to the Police Academy rather than sit behind a desk and stare at cryptic notes day after day.

Karen. Cam hadn't thought about her for a long time. Oh, she'd passed through Cam's mind now and then, but Cam had learned not to let her dwell there. She'd spent two years trying to decipher *that* relationship and still hadn't gotten past square one.

She'd probably never be able to forget that day:

It had been a hard afternoon. Cameron laid her crutches against the wall as she lowered herself onto the couch. Something was wrong. Karen had been distant, quiet, ever since they'd returned from the ceremony.

Cameron had just been decorated with the city's Medal of Valor. The newspaper and TV reporters had been buzzing around, trying to get her to say a few words; trying to analyze who this new hero was, this woman who had saved the life of a child being held at gun-point by his mother's crazed boyfriend. Karen had helped her weave her way through the crowd of well-wishers and finally get to a place where she could sit and relax without someone snapping a flash bulb in her face.

That was three days ago. Cameron still couldn't figure out what was wrong. But now Karen wanted to talk.

"What is it, honey. What's up?" Cam asked as Karen sat down across from her in the overstuffed chair.

Karen took a breath, her eyes still not meeting Cam's. "I can't do this anymore," was all she'd said.

Cam rolled it around in her mind. "I don't understand."

"I can't be there for you. I can't go on like this. I need you to move out."

The words hit Cam right between the eyes. She was totally unprepared. Three weeks ago they'd been making plans to go up to Provincetown for a couple weeks later in the summer. Then there'd been that hostage situation and Cam had ended up in the hospital with two bullets in her. One in her backside, another in her leg.

"I know this is a bad time for you, but it's something I have to do. I'd move out, but this is hospital subsidized. You'll have to go. I can't put it off any more." Karen pushed on. She still hadn't looked at Cam. "I'm going to D.C. for a couple days. I'd really appreciate it if you could be gone when I get back."

"What?! I don't understand. Is it something I did? If it is, I'm sorry. I could try to fix it." Cam could already feel herself breaking out in a cold sweat.

"It's not something you did, Cameron. It's who you are. I can't live worrying if the next time the doorbell rings, it'll be some clergy telling me I have to go and identify your body. Every time the police radio in the ER reports that a policeman has been hurt, I start to shake. I can't do that anymore. I don't want to have to be there for you."

"You don't need to worry so much," Cam pleaded. "I'm careful. I'm not going to get hurt again."

Karen's anger flared. "You can't promise me that!" she spat at Cam. "You've been on the force for less than two years and you've been shot twice. Either time could have been fatal. You put yourself in danger without ever giving it a second thought. It's who you are. It's how you think." Karen finally looked Cam in the eyes. "I don't want to be on duty in the ER the next time they bring you in."

"Well…maybe I can get a desk job, at least for a while. I can't go back out on the street, yet, anyway. Maybe there's something."

"Cam, you can't!" Karen stopped her. "I've known this ever since you talked about joining the police force. I've dreaded it. I thought I could handle it. I can't."

Cam let the silence stretch on for a few minutes.

"I could be more careful, maybe go into forensics. I don't plan on being a street cop all my life."

"Please." Karen put her hand up to stop her. "If I thought you could do that, I'd jump at the chance." She shook her head "I've known you too long… And too well. There's a lot of anger inside you. It's who you are. It eats at you when you sit behind a desk. One of these days it's going to erupt and swallow you. I can't be around when that happens."

Cam wiped her hand across her mouth, as if she could reach inside and find the right word to make this all go away.

"I'm sorry, Cameron. Please don't make this harder than it already is. I'll expect you out by next Thursday."

With that Karen got up and walked out of the apartment.

Maggie's question interrupted Cam's reflection. "So what happened?"

"That was it. She wouldn't return my calls, wouldn't answer the door, my letters came back marked "Return to Sender." Cam got up and started pacing again. She could feel herself perspire. "I understand her words. I just can't, maybe I just won't understand her actions. I'd just gotten out of the hospital. I was still on crutches. There I was. The whole city of Baltimore is turning inside out to honor me with the City's Medal of Valor for saving that kid's life. They think I'm the hottest thing going. Imaging that! A *woman*, doing what the men were standing around only talking about. I'd been wounded rescuing this little kid from a hostage situation, and my lover tells me she can't stand it when I get hurt, so we'll have to end our relationship."

"Why? What made her do that?" Maggie pushed, "Don't you think, perhaps, that she was afraid?"

"Afraid?! I was the one that was out there in the street getting shot at."

"And she was in the emergency room both times that you were shot while on duty. Maybe she was afraid of losing you."

"Losing me? She pushed me away."

"Losing you. As in 'watching you die.' Do you think that maybe it was easier for her to push you away on her own terms than risk the chance that one day they'd bring you in on a stretcher and she'd have to be an unwilling, and perhaps helpless, witness to your death."

Cam stopped. Maggie made it all seem so logical. So easy to understand. She sat on the couch. The clock above Maggie's desk said two a.m.

"Maybe you should get some sleep," Maggie suggested. She knew that Cam was practically out on her feet.

"In a minute." Cam shook her head. "I want to think this through. All she ever said to me was 'I don't want to have to be there for you'. Maybe she wasn't talking emotional support. Maybe she was talking as my doctor." Cam put her head in her hands.

Maggie watched her with admiration. This was a courageous young woman. Maggie knew she'd pushed a lot of Cam's buttons and yet, every time she did, Cam took the challenge and came out a stronger person.

It was Maggie's job to find the weak spots. To push and prod until she and Cam both knew where they were. Then to shore them up and strengthen them.

It was also her job to help Cam break down walls so that when she had to put up new ones, she'd be able to do it without bumping into herself.

In the past two weeks, she'd put Cam through many years' worth of psychoanalysis. She'd known people who'd seen their psychiatrists twice a week for seven or eight years and hadn't made the strides Cam had in seven or eight sessions.

"What do you fear most?" Maggie's question seemed to come out of the blue, but Cam knew that it was the last question of the night. Maggie always ended with that question to give her something to think about until they met again.

"Tonight? Tonight I fear…what my family is going to think. If I can't tell them what I'm doing, well, I've never kept anything from them. Hell, the night I came out, I went right home and told my grandmother that I was a lesbian."

Maggie smiled. "How'd she take it?"

Cam was embarrassed. "I don't remember. I was drunk at the time." She laughed with Maggie. "I vomited in her rose bushes. I think she was more angry at that than anything."

"Well, that's one way of sidestepping a confrontation. A good avoidance technique is sometimes the best method."

Cam smiled under Maggie's dubious praise.

"What else are you afraid of?"

"What else? You mean two fears in one night?"

"This is the graduate level course, twice the work."

Cameron hesitated, thinking it over.

"What about your sister?" Maggie asked. "From what you've told me, I think she looks up to you. You took over as mother. How will she handle this? What if it looks like you're doing something terribly wrong?"

Cam frowned. "I don't know, Maggie. I have to believe that what I'm doing is more important. She'll still have David and the boys, and our grandmothers. They have a very tight family. I miss being with them sometimes. I just have to believe that they'll be there for me, no matter what." Cam stopped. "You know, sometimes I think that Mom's still around, looking after us. I think she'll keep everything together."

"Maybe. Think about it."

That was always the assignment Maggie left her with. "Actually, from what you've just said, you have thought about it. Try to feel it. How do you feel about it?" For Cameron that may have been the hardest assignment of all.

Chapter Four

I t was the end of April. Six weeks of grilling and study had passed. Cam stood in the shadows near the street corner where she'd been told to meet her ride. A block away, laughter erupted as two young men emerged from the quiet corner bar. The usual black unmarked sedan pulled up to the curb in front of her. Leaning down to look inside, Cam was surprised to see Craig there. Usually, it was Wendell who picked her up.

As she'd done for the past, how many nights, on how many different street corners, she quickly slid into the passenger seat. Tonight, however, there was a hesitation. "Want to stop somewhere for a drink?" Craig asked.

"I thought you didn't want to be seen in public with me."

He laughed.

"It's almost one," she continued. "Everything's closing." She didn't want to add that the quiet corner tavern he'd pointed to was a gay bar, the same bar Pauly had taken her to when it first opened.

"You're right. Besides, there is a lot to do tonight." He didn't add that he'd spent the last eight hours going over her file with Wendell and Maggie and with Richard C. Deems, Head of Internal Covert Operations of the DEA. They'd read and discussed Maggie's and Wendell's reports on her progress and abilities and finally agreed with him that she'd be the perfect person to handle this assignment. It had been a hard discussion. Tonight they'd lay it all on the table and see if the pieces fit. In his heart he knew that Cameron could, should do this assignment, but he also knew that if there were any other way, he'd never offer this to anyone, let alone someone he knew and liked.

Deems had been against it at first. He'd put up good arguments against her: "Why'd she say she called you again?" he had said, going back over the transcript of the tape of Cam's original interview.

Craig and Wendell had looked at the man with scraggly grey hair and thick glasses. "You heard her. She's bored. And she knows that the life expectancy of an undercover cop is limited."

"You believe her?"

"Yes, I do. Cam's always been square with me." Craig had definitely been on her side.

"What about her lesbianism. Did she tell you about that when she was working for you before?"

"No. She knew we'd have to fire her. But she's never tried to lie about it. She's been real good about sidestepping the issue."

"She have a lover now?"

"No." Maggie smiled, "She really hasn't had time. We've been working her too hard."

"Doesn't she...date?"

"No," Maggie answered, "Not seriously. A night out with the girls every now and then. There's been no one steady for the last four years."

"Is there any way she'd let your conversations slip to anyone else? You know how pillow-talk can be."

"I highly doubt it," Craig answered. "Cameron has always been very, very good about keeping things confidential. You know how we always plant things with new staff just to check. Nothing we ever told her got back. She had a top priority security clearance."

"I don't know. This is highly irregular. Totally against policy." Richard C. Deems closed the file in front of him. Wendell and Craig exchanged glances.

"You really think she can do this?" Richard asked, looking at Maggie.

"Yes," she said without hesitation. "She works hard. I think she'd be very valuable. You read my report. And you know I wouldn't recommend this if I had any doubts."

"It's a good idea," Wendell interjected. "If we were trying to infiltrate a black neighborhood we wouldn't send in a white man. We've tried a straight woman and look what happened, poor girl." Wendell thought of the promising young agent who now sat staring into space in a mental hospital, her brain fried in a drug overdose.

"No saying that it won't happen to this one, too." Richard C. Deems didn't want to be convinced.

"No, but she's got a head start on the territory. She'll better know how to handle herself there," Craig offered. "Aside from that, I think this one's a better agent."

"She's green."

"No, she isn't. I saw her work on that Baltimore bust. She was the front person with Sanderson. Walked right up the dock like two star struck lovers and got right into position to close up any back door escape. When everything busted loose, she kept her head, even when bullets were flying right around her. I saw a .48 hit the wall about two feet from her head and she didn't even jump. She's got a lot of street experience."

Richard C. Deems still shook his head.

"It's better than anything else we've ever come up with. It's almost too good." Wendell sat back.

Craig looked around the table. He knew that Wendell and Maggie were sold but this was, technically, Deems' case. This was an internal, not an international, operation. This was the one flaw with the DEA: limbo land somewhere between the CIA and the FBI. Craig walked that line every day.

"Well," Deems said slowly, pushing the files closer together, "If Maggie is for this and will agree to continue as counselor and control, I'll go along. But..." He was quiet for a moment, then looked up for emphasis. "...the first thing I see that doesn't fit, I pull the plug. Understood?"

Craig smiled. "Totally."

Cameron remained silent as they drove through the city. The last six weeks had been grueling. She'd been getting tired of answering the same questions or trying to find different ways to solve the same problems or proving her abilities in self defense and marksmanship. She felt she'd done well, but no one had said a word, one way or the other.

But tonight was different. It was Craig who picked her up. That must mean that something was about to change.

Craig broke the silence. "Look, Cam, if you don't like what you hear tonight and you want to pull out, just say so. No one will look down on it, everyone will understand."

Cam looked at Craig's face in the dim light from the street and glow of the dashboard. "Why? What am I gonna hear tonight?"

Craig hesitated, then smiled. "Your first assignment." He pulled out into the flow of traffic and headed away from the center of the city.

Cam was suddenly wide awake. "Then I'm in? I passed?"

Craig nodded in the darkened car. "Yes."

Cam smiled and mentally hugged herself. She'd suspected that that was why Craig was here.

"But," Craig continued, "if you don't want this particular assignment, there'll be others. So don't take this if you have *any* reservations. I want you to be assured that we're not just offering you a desk job."

Cam rode in silence, hundreds of scenarios running through her head and excitement warming her blood. Yes! This was what she wanted.

At last, they pulled into the driveway of a darkened house that looked just like every other house on that block. All had quiet yards surrounded by wrought-iron fences and hedges and all looked asleep, although one or two had soft glows of light coming from upstairs windows. This house had no lights, the drapes all firmly closed. It was a typical residential house in a typical suburban neighborhood.

As they pulled in back of the house, Craig turned off the lights and motor. "Well, we're home," he said.

Cameron followed him up the back stairs which were lit solely by the light of the half moon, and through the back door into the kitchen of the house.

Three people were already there. "You know Maggie and Wendell," Craig said. Cam smiled at Maggie and nodded to Wendell, grasping the hand he extended to her. It was strong and firm, almost painful in its grasp, but familiar and reassuring.

"And this is Richard C. Deems, Head of Covert Internal Operations, DEA. Your new boss." Deems stood and shook her hand politely, much less firmly than Wendell. Cam had never considered that Craig might not be her boss and she suddenly wasn't sure she liked the situation. Deems was just standing there, silently inspecting every part of her.

"Sit down and have some coffee." Maggie was almost motherly. As a psychiatrist, she was trained to read people's body language and knew that Cam was suddenly uneasy under Deems' glare. "Don't let these bullies intimidate you." She gently pushed Cam into a chair at the end of the table. Everyone else sat as Maggie poured coffee into the five mugs that were already there. "Cream and sugar anyone?"

All three men declined but Cam said, "Sugar, please. Unless it's laced with something."

That broke the ice and Wendell laughed loudly.

Maggie made a big show of pouring two teaspoons of sugar into her own mug, then pushed to bowl to Cameron as she took a seat just to Cam's left. Cam put one small spoon of sugar into her mug and stirred it slowly.

It was Deems who spoke. "Well, I say let's lay the cards out. You ready?" He looked at Cam.

"As I'll ever be."

"Good. These three people have convinced me that you're the person we need. I think it only fair to let you know that I've had, maybe still have, reservations regarding your…uh…lifestyle. I'm a 'by the book' man and I don't need to tell you what that means. I'm straight forward and at times brusk. I'm not easy to work with but I get things done and I like people who get things done. There's too much bullshit happening these days. Too much pampering. Too much 'making nice.' I'm not a diplomat. I don't pretend to be. I'll always tell you what I think and I expect the same from the people I work with. I won't put up with brown-nosers. Enough said.

"Here's our problem. There's a big drug ring operating into and out of the women's prison facility at Hagerville. We don't know who or how but it's happening. There've been three ODs in the last six months inside the prison and the women coming out are so strung out that we're overloading the detox centers. Whoever's doing it is smart. They know we know what's happening, we couldn't miss it, but even though the Warden's given us her full support, we can't find the key. There have been lockdowns after lockdowns, searches after searches, but they never find anything. No one will talk. Not the guards. Not the inmates. Either they don't know or are afraid to talk.

Which means there's someone on the outside keeping tabs." He stopped and took a sip of his coffee. "Yes, I know there's always drugs in prisons, no matter what we do, but this seems out of the ordinary. There's something more there. We just can't get a handle on it. This isn't just a friend or a corrections officer sneaking a joint or a hit of coke in to a prisoner."

Cam searched each face. They weren't telling her everything. When had she ever heard the government worrying about what happened to women? Never mind women convicts!

Craig read her mind. "It's not just the women inside. The drug traffic has escalated in that part of the state to such a high level that we know there's something else happening. We suspect that it's a pipeline, probably into Pittsburgh and beyond. We know that there's a lot of traffic in the western part of Pennsylvania but we can't find where it's coming in. At first we thought it was coming in across the lakes but Canada has really sealed off the border there. Then we realized how much traffic we had around Hagerville. We've scoured everything in a hundred mile radius of Hagerville but all the pushers we've arrested in that part of the state are just small time and none knew anyone else involved. Or at least, no one they'd roll over on. Whoever's got the trade there has it sown up real tight. The only connection that keeps popping up is the prison."

Cam looked from Deems to Wendell to Craig. None of the three were looking at her but Maggie was watching her like a hawk hunting dinner.

"What aren't you telling me?" Cam asked looking directly at Deems.

He met her eyes strongly. "We've put two agents inside. One as an inmate. She's in a coma at Walton. OD on coke and bad alcohol. She'll never come out of it. Too much brain damage. We couldn't get to her fast enough."

"And the other?" Cam asked.

"Put her in there as a guard." There was a short pause. "Knife through the heart." Cam willed herself to continue her stare into Deems' eyes as she tried to calm her own heartbeat. Then, finally, she took a sip of her coffee and put the mug back down on the table thoughtfully.

"And what makes us think you'll do better?" Maggie read her mind.

Cam smiled. Thank God that Maggie was there.

It was Wendell who answered. "We want to approach this with such deep cover it can't leak. Obviously there are moles all over the place on this one. We want as little exposure as possible. We can't use someone already in the department. If there's a mole here, she'd be too easily recognized. We're so blind on this case that we don't even know if there's some of our own people in on it. The only people who'll know you're working for us are in this room."

"And I should trust all of you?" Cam looked across the faces, stopping at Deems. He sat back under her stare.

"Yes," was all he said.

Cameron thought about it for a minute, taking another sip of coffee. She trusted Craig, and she liked Maggie, but Wendell she was unsure of, although she had a good feeling about him. He'd been a good teacher and she knew that he was close to Craig. If Craig trusted him, why should she question it? But, what about Deems? Could she trust her life to him?

Finally she put her empty coffee cup back on the table. "What's the protocol? Who has the final word on what I say or do?"

Deems looked at his associates. "Dr. Thomason will be your control. If she says no then we pull the plug. You will have a certain amount of autonomy, but she will keep an eye on everything to make sure it doesn't get out of hand."

Cameron smiled into the table, then up at Maggie. Maggie patted her hand reassuringly.

"We need you to go through some more training," Craig stated. "It will be hard inside a prison. We want you fully skilled. I know you've done some work at the department and some more these past weeks with Wendell but you'll need more. Did you put in for three weeks vacation like we discussed?"

Cam nodded.

"You sending her down to Quantico?" Deems asked.

"No. That's taking a bigger risk that someone will see her there and recognize her later. Also, we really don't have time for her to go through a twelve week course. This calls for personal training. I'm sending her to the Caribbean."

Deems nodded his head thoughtfully. "Who's training her?"

"Charlie Harris is available," Wendell answered.

Deems nodded again, impressed. "Good choice. Strong man."

"Charlie Harris?" Maggie sat forward. "I haven't seen him in a couple years. Not since he left Pennsylvania."

"I didn't know you knew him," Wendell said congenially. "He's been on, well, a sabbatical. Said he was facing burn out. Moved to Canada. He raises and trains guard dogs now. How do you know him?"

"I worked with him when we were trying to deprogram Tommy Wallace five years ago. I really like the way Charlie works. He'll be a good challenge for Cam." Maggie gave Cam's hand a reassuring pat.

Wendell turned back to Deems. "When I explained the situation and the secrecy needed, Charlie also suggested Michael Gauchet for martial arts training."

"Who's he?" asked Deems.

"No, *She*. Michelle Gauchet. She pronounces it 'Michael.' She's Canadian, from Montreal. Sixth degree black belt in judo or jujitsu or one of those disciplines. One of the best. She's the supervisor in charge of the training program for the upper ranking Mounties. They say she's been asked to do a lot of the stunts in those new Kung Fu movies. I've heard that there's not a man in the Royal Canadian Mounted Police that can beat her."

"We saw a demonstration she did at that seminar in Ontario, last year. She is impressive," Craig said. He looked Cameron. "What do you think?"

"I'll leave that part up to you. You tell me what I need to learn. I'll trust that."

Everyone around the table concurred.

"Okay. Next step. How do I get in? What's the plan?" Cam asked

"Well, we could set you up with a new identity. You've still got a Boston accent. We could say you were transferred in from somewhere in New England—" Deems said.

Wendell interrupted. "I'm sorry. I know we discussed this but I still don't like it. That's the way we set up Kathy and look what happened."

A thought flashed through Cam's mind and she said, "And what if I run into someone I arrested? What if someone inside knows me. I'm sure there are several women in Hagerville that I arrested. Or, what if someone gets suspicious that I'm a plant. You said you don't know who's on the outside. What if someone starts checking? If I go in, I have to go in as me. Not even a hint of a cover."

"I agree," Craig said. "I'd hoped you'd see it that way. But, it is risky. Cam, we have discussed this part, but we're not fully in agreement. You know that cops, and some security guards for that matter, look down on cops that burn the law. They'll give you a hard time. The inmates won't trust you. It'll be difficult. This part will have to be your decision."

"But won't it be safer than taking the chance that there's someone outside who can find out I'm not who I'm supposed to be, or that someone inside remembers me? It might take a little longer to establish their trust, but won't it be better?"

"It'll mean that your friends and family will think you're a criminal. It will completely ruin your reputation."

Cam took a deep breath, tapping her coffee spoon in a rhythmic pattern on the table. She ran her fingers across her chin as she contemplated the enormity of the situation. Everyone waited silently for her to think it through. Finally she said, looking Deems in the eye, "If that's what it takes... You did say deep cover."

The other four exchanged glances. Had she just convinced them? Or had they just manipulated her into convincing herself?

"Then you'll want to get convicted of a crime. Not just sent there with the 'right' papers. That's another mistake we made with Kathy. She had no background. You'd have to actually break the law, get arrested and convicted."

"How? Hold up a liquor store or steal some old guy's Social Security check?"

Wendell smiled. "No. Seriously. It should be drug related or something that has to do with your job. We need to pin it down. But you're the one that has to feel comfortable with it. We want to kick around some ideas and see what sits right. We've come up with a lot of ideas among ourselves but nothing seems to gel. One of the first ideas we had was to have you go off on a 'brutality' rap but that'd put you in jeopardy once you got inside. Besides, with the system here, you'd have to get pretty mean even to get put in jail. You'd probably only get a wrist slapped and a couple weeks off with pay." He stopped and smiled to himself.

"We've thought of having you caught at a party using Coke, but that'd involve a lot of other people. If they're in on the scam, you're in trouble. If not, we've just set up a lot of people."

"We've thought of you buying, off duty, for your own personal use." Deems interjected.

"That won't work. My partner and just about everyone in my department knows how I feel about drugs. Hell, I bitch enough when I have to use for an undercover bust. I hate using the stuff."

"Maybe that's exactly why it will work," Maggie added. "You know, the old I-think-the-lady-doth-protest-too-much routine."

Cam shook her head. "No. I don't think so. There's got to be some other way. I've worked undercover for too long to think some of this would work. I don't—*won't* use, except when I'm making a buy to bust someone. But you're right." She looked at Wendell. "Let's kick some more ideas around. It *is* my life we're playing with. If I get inside, I don't want anybody to be suspicious."

For the first time, the cold wall of hardness melted from Deems face and he smiled.

"I better make more coffee." Maggie rose and went to the sink to fill the coffee pot.

It was almost five a.m. before they had what they thought was a plan. There were still details to work out, but all felt it was the most plausible idea they'd come up with. Deems had stiffened when Cameron brought up the idea of bringing one other person onto the team but all saw the logic in it and if it made Cameron more at ease...well, it was worth a shot.

"Are you working tomorrow? I guess I should say today?" Craig asked as he drove her back to her car.

"No. I've got the next two days off. We've got a big weekend coming up. You know, end of the semester—just before finals. Every student in town will be out trying to find something to get them through."

"Good. Sleep in tomorrow. You earned it. Call me Thursday morning so we can work out the terms of your employment."

"You mean you're going to pay me to do this?" Cam laughed, feigning surprise, "I thought this was just for the fun of it. You know, old time's sake and all."

Craig returned her smile and chuckled as he pulled up next to her Toyota. "You did some damn fine work tonight," he said, throwing the car into park and turning toward her. "He didn't show it but I know you knocked Deems' socks off. I'll make sure that Maggie gets the files we had from Kathy and Fran's investigations. Read them carefully." He stopped for just a moment, studying her. Finally he said, "You'll be okay with this. I can feel it."

"Thanks, Craig. It means a lot to hear you say that." She closed his car door and walked to her own car. She was exhausted but her mind was racing, imagining all the possibilities. Yes. She knew she'd made the right decision. This was what it was supposed to feel like! God, she thought, I hope it feels this good once I've slept on it.

Chapter Five

Cameron had just turned off the *Nightly News* when there was a knock at her door. She peeked through the peep hole of her door but could only see the top of a police hat in the darkness outside.

"Who is it?" She asked though the door.

"Me. Pauly."

Cam opened the door and greeted him with a big hug. "Welcome, stranger. Haven't seen you in a while."

He handed her a small package as he walked past her into the living room. "Happy Birthday. I know it was two weeks ago. Sorry I missed it."

Cam ripped the wrapping off the package and opened the small box. Inside was a pair of silver earrings with cabochon amethysts.

"Pauly. These are beautiful. I'd say you didn't have to, but I'm glad you did. Thank you." She hugged him once again.

"I heard you've been busy," he said, the smile gone from his face as he sank down onto the couch. Tossing his police cap onto the coffee table, he sat back, loosening his tie. "Got anything to drink? I'm off duty."

Cameron went to the cabinet over the refrigerator and retrieved a bottle of Dewar's. With two glasses, a cold bottle of soda water from the refrigerator, and the scotch, she returned to the living room. Setting it all on the coffee table, she sat back, inserting the earrings into her earlobes as Pauly poured them each a drink, then took a good swig of his.

"You sure you want to do this?" he asked turning to her.

"Drink scotch or wear my earrings?" she teased.

"Don't play," he said fiercely. "This is not a funny situation. You know what I'm talking about." He watched as Cam eyed him warily. "I had a discrete visitor this morning. Scared the shit out of me. I haven't been any good all day. Do you know what he told me?" He waited for Cam to answer.

"Hell, I stopped trying to analyze your love life years ago," she joked.

His stare stopped her. Pauly was not in a jovial mood.

She looked down into her drink. So they'd contacted Pauly and asked him to come in on the plan with her. She hadn't quite expected this reaction, though. She took a sip of her scotch and felt it warm its way to her stomach. "Yes, I know. It's true. I asked for you to help me."

Pauly just stared at her. "I wasn't sure." he admitted, "He didn't use names. But after what we talked about that night at the Oak Tavern, it just had to be you. Thanks for confirming it."

"And if I hadn't?"

"I had a great joke lined up." Pauly smiled for the first time since he'd sat down. He ran his hand back through his close cropped sandy hair. "But I don't know anyone else as loco as you that would do this sort of thing."

"What? You think I'm crazy? We talked about this years ago, when we'd kick back after shift was over and share our dreams over a bottle of scotch. We both said we'd love to have the opportunity to make a real difference, no matter what it took. Remember that?" The silence from the other end of the couch lengthened. "This is it, Pauly. The chance for my dream to come true. I know it's not like we planned, no big banners and medals of commendation for a job well done. No ticker tape parades. But I have a chance to make something happen. Even if no one ever knows it was me. I'll be doing something."

"Or getting yourself killed."

Cam stopped for a moment. "Maybe." She looked into his eyes. "Not if I have the kind of help and support I need while I'm there."

"What can I do? I'm not a hot shot, Cam. That's why I'm still walking a beat. I'm just some silly faggot who let his father push him into the police academy as soon as he got home from 'Nam. You know, follow in the old man's foot steps. When we used to talk about dreams, they were just that: dreams. All I want is to wear this badge, uneventfully, for thirty years and collect a pension so I can move to Key West."

"You think I'm crazy?" she asked.

"I'm not sure."

"Who talked to you?"

"Richard C. Deems. Pompous little ass. Probably a closet case."

Cameron laughed and relaxed, a little. "Hadn't considered that. Maybe that's why he was so upset when I wanted to bring you in with us. Probably worried we'd move in on his territory."

"He knows we're gay?"

"Definitely knows I am. Probably figured you out, too. They do a lot of checking before they recruit someone."

"Oh shit, oh shit. This is getting worse all the time. What if someone else finds out. What if this goes on my record? I could get blown off the force, lose my pension. I haven't had a serious lover in three years because I'm afraid someone will find out! Maybe I should just save everyone a lot of time and trouble and kill you myself." He shook his head as his whole body slumped farther down into the couch.

"Relax, son. The deed is done." She reached out and patted his knee. "I'm sorry I had to put you in this spot, but you were the only one I could think of that fit into the picture. How much did he tell you?"

"Not very much. He just said that a good friend of mine was about to take on a difficult and dangerous undercover assignment and would need my help. And that it had to be completely confidential. Made me swear an oath that I wouldn't discuss it with anyone."

"Then, what the hell are you doing here?"

"I had to find out if it was you. I didn't mention anything until you brought it up."

Cam grinned at him. Yes, she'd noticed that. "Good work. See, you're a born undercover investigator. Wasted on a beat."

Pauly just shook his head.

"I'm sorry if I've put you between the rocks, but I really need your help. We need someone on the force, who's a close friend, to feed me information. Someone that I've known for years."

"What about Russ, why not him? He's your partner."

"No. He's got to be completely outside. I need his honest reaction to what's gonna happen. My life is on the line if someone doesn't believe him."

"Why? What's going to happen? What are you going to do?" Pauly set his empty glass on the coffee table and leaned toward her.

Cameron finished her drink and took a deep breath. "I can't tell you any more until you're clear. Call Deems back and tell him you're in, then I can tell you everything." She sat back. "I know I've asked a lot from you. You took me in when Karen threw me out and let me cry on your shoulder when I couldn't tell anyone else. You've been the best friend I've ever had. I need you again. You won't be in any danger, but you sure could save my neck and it'd mean a lot to me to know I've got at least one person that I can really trust."

Pauly shook his head. "I don't know how I let you talk me into these things. Can I use your phone?"

Chapter Six

The flight to San Juan out of Baltimore/Washington International was on time leaving the gate, but before they were in the air, even before they'd taxied very far, Cameron saw the difference. She had never flown first class before—always thought the difference in price wasn't worth the difference in seating, but she was amazed at the contrast from coach to first class. Not only were the seats wider, but there was more leg room and the food service much more personal. Before they were in the air, the flight attendant had offered them champagne and orange juice on a small tray with linen napkins, rather than pouring from a pushcart parked in the aisle. Now that they were in the air, Cam gave her order for scotch and soda as she stretched back and looked at Maggie, engrossed in a magazine in the seat next to her. She'd never seen Maggie in such casual attire before. To see her wearing tan walking shorts and brightly colored shirt, you could believe that she was off to the Caribbean for a nice vacation. She looked like the average tourist who had enough money to fly better than coach. Cam never failed to be amazed at how Maggie always looked so fresh and neat. There was never a wrinkle in her clothes, not a hair out of place, not so much as a smudge on her shoe. This woman had class.

"Nervous?" Maggie asked, without looking up.

"Some," was Cam's answer. In the slacks and shirt Maggie had picked out for her, she, too, would be easily mistaken for a vacationer off for a few weeks in the tropics.

Maggie looked over as the attendant handed Cam her drink. A smile formed on her lips. "Relax. No, it won't be easy, but you'll do fine."

Cam smiled in gratitude for the reassurance.

"I guess it's just not knowing what to expect."

Maggie nodded her understanding. "You'll do well. It will be a little different from what you've been doing with Wendell, but there won't be anything you can't handle. Now relax."

Cam took another sip of her drink and stretched back to look out the window at the white fluffy clouds that flew by. This might be the last chance she had to just relax and enjoy her freedom. Doubts had been creeping into her mind since that last night at the safe house. Could she really do what she'd convinced everyone else she could? Oh well, she had to trust Maggie and Craig not to let her get killed. They knew what they were doing. Didn't they?

Cam must have dozed off because the next thing she knew, Maggie was gently shaking her arm and telling her to put her seat back up to prepare for landing. Out the window, Cam could see the bright sun light shining off aquamarine water as they descended on approach to the island of Puerto Rico. Although the light was very sharp, from the angle of the sun, Cam could see that it was late in the day. She hoped they were close to their destination, wherever that might be. Her stomach was beginning to feel empty. Had she slept through whatever they had served for lunch? Oh well, if she'd slept that hard, it was because she'd needed it and besides, airplane food had never been that satisfying. There'd probably be some really good food here on the island.

The landing was smooth. A quick taxi to the gates and they were exiting the plane. As they stepped onto the docking ramp, Cam felt the oppressive heat and humidity. What a difference from the chilly early spring in Baltimore. She was glad that she wore only a light cotton shirt and slacks.

After they had retrieved their luggage from the carousel, Maggie pointed to a local driver who stood just beyond the passenger area holding a card that read, *Thomason*.

"There's our ride."

After a brief word with the driver, who directed another man to take their luggage outside, they were led to a small grey car that took them less than a mile to the other side of the airport to a private hanger marked Aérea Rica. Several small private planes were parked on the tarmac. As Maggie and Cam got out of the car, two people, a grey-haired man that Cam judged to be in his mid to late forties and a tall woman, who looked not much older than Cam, stood up from the chairs in the small waiting room.

"Charlie! So good to see you again," Maggie greeted the man, giving him a warm friendly hug. "And you must be Michael," she extended her hand to the woman, who took it in both of hers. "It's so good to finally meet you. Charlie has told me so much about you. This is Cameron," she introduced Cam who shook hands first with Charlie whose hand was wide and strong, then with Michael. Cam stopped as the electricity of Michael's touch ran through her. Michael's broad smile and her strong grasp almost turned Cam to jelly.

Michael pushed her shoulder length, sandy-colored hair back behind her ear and looked down at Cam. "I am very happy to meet you. I know we will work nicely together."

Cam's breath almost stopped as she heard the heavy French Canadian accent in the deep, rich alto voice. What a gorgeous sound! And what a handsome woman. Cam hadn't expected this. From what she'd heard about this woman who held so many titles in martial arts, she'd expected a shorter, more compactly built, masculine looking woman, not this tall, elegant one who could easily be a model in a high fashion magazine. Even in her flat sandals she was almost six feet tall. A woman of that height could have been gangly, awkward in her movements, but Michael's movements were strong and fluid, not afraid of the space they'd take up.

"Were your flights all right? Have you been waiting long?" Maggie asked before Cam could formulate a response to Michael's comment. Cam had to concentrate to let go of Michael's hand.

"Mais, oui," Michael turned her attention back to Maggie, "The flight was fine, merci. I've only been here for about twenty minutes."

"I flew in last night." Charlie smiled, "Thought I'd go into old San Juan and get a good meal. I love Puerto Rican cooking. Nothing like it. The shrimp is the best in the world. And arroz con gandules. I love the way that sounds," he lowered his voice conspiratorially. "So much nicer than saying rice with pigeon peas."

"Maybe I will stop and try some on the way back. You know we can't get really good shrimp in Montreal," Michael added.

Maggie noticed that the pilot was waiting a few feet away. "Come on, troops. I think our flight is ready," she said.

"Oui, allons. Let's go." Michael smiled and wound her arm through Charlie's and leaned toward him as they sauntered to the waiting plane.

"You'll have to give me directions to your favorite restaurant," Cam heard as they walked away. "Is this the one you talked about…?"

Cam took a deep breath as she observed the way Michael held Charlie's arm. A straight woman, she thought as she followed them toward the small twin-engine prop plane. Just as well. This is no time to develop a crush. Self consciously, she wiped her sweaty hand on her slacks, then picked up her carry-on and followed Maggie.

****

There were sandwiches and cookies waiting for them on the plane which could have held eighteen or twenty people instead of only the four of them along with the pilot and co-pilot. The flight from San Juan lasted almost an hour and Cam felt the plane bank into several turns so it was impossible to determine which direction they went and exactly how far. For all she knew, their final destination was still in Puerto Rico, or even back on one of the Keys, but from the heat that still radiated from the land at nine that night, Cam ventured that they were farther south than that. During the flight, Michael was congenial, talking to both Cam and Maggie, but mainly to Charlie. It seemed that they were good friends, perhaps lovers?

On the plane Cam was completely mesmerized by Michael's hands—the long slender fingers, the strong palms. She'd found herself staring at Michael several times and had to force herself to look away. Michael's long, muscular legs, bare and smooth beneath her flowing cotton skirt, were engrossing as they stretched out into the aisle. Cam realized she was sweating quite heavily. Was it really that hot in the plane? She consciously took her eyes away from the graceful arch of the foot that slowly dangled the beige sandal rhythmically back and forth as Michael talked. Would this flight never end? Was this what she had to contend with for the next three weeks?

It was dark by the time they arrived at the small private airfield. When they landed, there was one car parked at the airstrip. Only one person waited for them there: a young, thin, black man who looked Caribbean. He immediately loaded their luggage into the waiting car, then handed the keys to Charlie. That was the last Cam saw of him. It was Charlie who drove them a short distance to a large beach house. She could hear the roar of the plane taking off again as she got out of the car.

The bedrooms were on the second floor of the main house. Each had a private bath much like any hotel room and, to Cam's delight, a firm king sized bed. The wall farthest away from the door was covered with drapes. She carefully pulled the drapes aside, then opened the sliding glass door behind them and walked out onto a wooden balcony. A stretch of sand was dimly lit by some small lamps along a walkway below. From there, she could make out the movement of the ocean waves and hear them beat against the beach. Down the beach, she could see other buildings in the dim moonlight, but couldn't tell what they were. Stairs led down from the balcony to the walkway, but Cam decided to wait until morning to explore. She turned back into her room and closed the door and drapes behind her.

It took her several minutes to drift off, the excitement of this adventure made it hard for her to clear her mind long enough to fall sleep. And she kept thinking about Michael. Her mind kept reverting to a fantasy of how those hands would feel caressing her, how Michael's full lips would feel against hers... It was not the way she usually reacted to someone new. Especially a business associate! Damn!

* * * *

The next morning Cam discovered a magnificent view of the long white sand beach and the rolling waves of the clear, bright blue-green ocean. Walking out onto the deck, she could see five small cabins along the beach, although their purpose was unclear. They could be storage sheds or separate living quarters, but their windows were blocked and the sand around them seemed undisturbed by traffic.

Other than the cabins, there was just fine white sand, a few tall palm trees and clear blue sea as far as Cam could see. The sun bathed everything in a golden glow and was starting to heat the moist air already, even at that early hour. If she'd had more time, Cam would have walked along the beach, but her watch told her she'd better hurry or she'd be late for her first meeting.

After a quick breakfast of fruit and cereal that had been set out for her on the table in the kitchen, Cameron went to join the other three in the living room.

As Cam entered, Maggie looked up from the clipboard she'd been reading from. She smiled warmly at Cam. Both Charlie and Michael echoed her "Good Morning" from where they sat next to each other on the sofa.

"Did you sleep well?" Maggie asked as Cam slid into the big overstuffed chair. It reminded her of her chair at home and immediately made her feel comfortable and a little more secure.

Cam smiled. "Very well, thanks. Are you discussing my future?"

Maggie nodded with a smile. "Yes. Strategy. Are you ready to begin?"

"If I said no?" Cam asked.

"Then we could all go home." Charlie grinned. "Or back to San Juan for shrimp." He smiled at Michael who gave his arm a gentle shove.

Oh, God, thought Cam, it looks like they really are lovers. I wonder how long they've known each other. She looked back at Maggie's waiting face. "I'm ready. Throw it at me."

Maggie's face became serious. "All right. It will be a rigid schedule. You'll meet Michael at seven every morning for physical training, then with me from eleven 'til one. We'll include lunch in our session. Then Charlie will work with you from one 'til four and Michael again for martial arts until six. At six, we'll break for dinner and at eight, you and I will meet again unless Charlie feels you need more time with him. Any questions?"

Cam thought it over for a moment, then shook her head.

"Good. Charlie will be working with you on the mental and emotional aspects of your assignment. He's worked as a military drill sergeant and as director of several reform schools. He's trained corrections officers and he's been inside prisons. He knows what happens there. He will prepare you for almost anything you run into. He'll keep you from making the mental mistakes that will get you killed.

"Michael, as you know, is a martial arts instructor. I just found out that she was the youngest person in Quebec to reach sixth degree black belt in Hapkido." Maggie smiled broadly at Michael who bowed her head slightly, humbly. "It's her job to give you the skills to keep you alive."

"I will teach you a combination of different martial arts techniques," Michael offered. "Mostly some Japanese ju-jitsu and some Korean Hapkido. Unfortunately, we do not have the time to explore the spirituality of the moves, its most beautiful part, but you can learn enough to protect yourself.

I sure hope you do your jobs well, thought Cam.

"You and I have discussed this before, but I want to make it very clear in front of Charlie and Michael. This is all up to you. They can take you only as far as you're willing to go. They will not go easy on you, they will expect only the best. If you reach a point where you can't go on, we'll stop. That's it. The end. You've got a very difficult job ahead of you and if you don't feel fully trained, or one of us doesn't think you're ready, we'll pull the plug. Craig and Richard are adamant, and frankly, I fully agree. If there's any doubt, however small, by anyone, we stop. We'd rather try another approach entirely than see you end up the way those last two did. Do we agree?"

Cam looked her straight in the eye. "Totally."

Maggie relaxed back in her seat. "Good," she said. "Shall we begin? Charlie gets to start today."

Charlie looked at her appraisingly. Cam became agitated under his intense gaze. Finally he spoke. "This will be more intense than Marine boot camp. In boot camp you'd be only one out of forty or fifty people, so in twelve weeks, you'd get what amounted to maybe two days of personal attention. Unless, of course you were so friggin' incompetent that your sergeant had to be on you every minute. I don't think that would be the case. You're going to get twenty-one days of personal attention. We've got a lot of barriers to break down. In three weeks, we've got to turn you into a steel fighting machine that can withstand anything that's thrown at you. We can't miss any little chinks in the armor that could put you in danger. If you're going to be in prison for any length of time, you will be completely alone. There'll be no way to call anyone if you need help and even if you could, they wouldn't be able to reach you in time. You've got to be completely self-sufficient. Maggie's right. If you have any doubts, we stop. I'm not sure why anyone would volunteer for such an assignment, but seeing that you have, I'll make sure you make it. That's if you really want to. It's all up to you. Understood?"

At that, Charlie rose and walked over to Cam. "Stand up," he said. Cam got to her feet. "Are you sure you're ready?" he asked.

Cam nodded.

"Positive?" he asked again.

"Yes," Cam said, a little annoyed and indignant at his insistence.

"Good. Let's set some ground rules. First of all, don't nod. Speak up. Loudly. Don't take the chance that I won't hear you or I'll miss your gesture." He continued on as he paced in front of her. "Second, you will address me as Master Trainer. Master Trainer, SIR. And you will address Michael as Mistress." He turned to Michael with a grin, "As does everyone else."

Michael shook her head with a smile, at their private joke. Charlie turned back to Cam. "Thirdly: What we teach you here in the next three weeks could save your life. Remember that. Remember it always. Forgetting any part of this for even one moment could mean the difference between life and death. Now, are you sure you're ready?"

"Yes, sir. Master Trainer, sir." Cam smiled, starting to get into the role play.

Charlie leaned forward until he was just an inch away from Cam's face. "Then get rid of the attitude, maggot," he stated firmly, his voice suddenly hard, with a tone of contempt. "And wipe that stupid grin off your face. This is not fun. *It is not a game.* From now on, you belong to me. You are mine. And you belong to The Mistress. If we say jump, you say, '*Thank you, sir, Master Trainer, sir. How high?*' Do you understand me?"

Cam glanced at Maggie. This was a new twist. She didn't like being yelled at.

"Don't look at her, scum," Charlie's face was right in front of hers. "She's not going to be in prison for you. She's not going to fight your battles or wipe your ass for you. You're in this by yourself. It's just you…and me. Or you and The Mistress. Am I clear?"

Cam nodded. She wasn't use to being spoken to like that. Her first reaction was to tell him to go take a flying leap, but she knew she had to get used to it, no matter what.

"Am I clear?" Charlie repeated, his tone threateningly.

"Yes." Cam acknowledged, taking a mental breath and remembering to speak rather than nod.

"What?" he shouted in her face.

"Yes, sir. Very clear," she repeated firmly.

Charlie took a step back. "Now. Your skills. Number one: *Trust no one.* Is that clear? What's skill number one?"

"Trust no one." Cam repeated. "Does that include you?"

"Judge for yourself. You wouldn't need to ask such stupid questions if you used your brain. Think it through. Why are you here? Why am I telling you this? What's rule number one?"

"Trust no one." Cam repeated.

"Do you trust me?"

"I trust no one."

"Do you trust your Mistress?" he asked.

"I trust no one."

"What about Maggie? Do you trust her?"

Cam stopped. Her eyes went to Maggie who watched her from across the room.

"What about Maggie? Do you trust her?" Charlie repeated.

Cam looked him in the eye. "I trust no one," she said clearly.

"Do you believe that? Do you believe what you just said?"

Cam wet her lips. Didn't she trust Maggie? Did she believe that?

"Not yet," she admitted.

"Then you'd better give it some hard thought. Remember this: it's better to trust no one—to question everyone, than to trust the wrong person and end up with a shiv in your back. Do you understand that?"

Cam started to nod, but remembered in time. "Yes, sir. Master Trainer, sir."

"Skill number two: Always be alert. Don't ever let your guard down. Mistakes happen when you're not paying attention. What's skill number two?"

"Be alert." Cam stated.

"And number one?"

"Trust no one."

"Skill number three: Don't get into debt to anyone. Owe nothing. Don't *ever* put yourself in debt to anyone over anything because if you do, someday, damn it, they'll collect. Payback can be a real bitch. Stay loose. Always be alert. Mistakes happen when you're not paying attention. You can't afford to let anyone sneak up on you. Do you trust me?"

Cam looked at him, momentarily bewildered. It seemed like a non sequitur.

"Do you trust me?" he demanded.

"I trust no one." Cam repeated, determined.

"Do you trust these skills?"

Cam stopped. Was this a mixed message? Suddenly it made sense. The skills she learned could save her life. She just couldn't put her trust in the people who taught them.

"Yes. I owe you nothing. I'll be alert," she stated firmly.

"Do you trust Maggie?"

"I trust no one."

"Skill number two?" His questions were fast and furious.

"Be alert."

"Skill number three?"

"Owe no one."

"Skill number one?"

How many times was he going to ask this? "Trust no one." She could feel sweat breaking out around her eyes and over her upper lip.

"Skill number three?"

"Owe no one." And five times eight is forty and use 'i' before 'e' except after 'c' and all the other things you learned by rote.

"Do you owe me?"

"I owe no one."

"Skill number one?"

Yet again. "Trust no one."

"Go with your Mistress."

Cam was stunned, but she just turned and followed Michael out of the room.

At eight that night, as Cam sank down into the big chair in the living room, she involuntarily let out a sigh of pain.

"Sore?" Maggie asked from her seat on the couch.

"Battered. I ache in places I didn't know I had," she answered, letting her head fall back.

"Don't worry, sweetie," Maggie smiled, "It'll get worse. How are you handling today?"

Cam looked at her for a moment. "So far, Michael's just been testing me on what I already know. We haven't started any new stuff yet. A lot of push-ups and crunches and running on the sand. My calves are killing me."

"What about Charlie?"

"Skill number one. I don't trust him. This afternoon, we got to skills four, five and six: Don't divulge information that isn't asked for, Keep your ears open, and Stay in control."

Maggie raised an eyebrow inquisitively. "Do you trust me?"

"Oh, fuck," Cam just let out a long exasperated sigh.

Maggie sat forward. "You know, down deep, that you *can* trust me, don't you? If you trust no one else, you can trust me."

"Maggie, I imagine that by the end of this I won't even trust my own grandmother."

Maggie watched as a very tired Cameron sank deeper into the chair. Cam and Michael had worked outdoors that afternoon and Maggie could see the glow of a wonderful sunburn shining off Cam's face. "Tell me about your grandmother." Maggie said, tossing a tube of aloe vera lotion to Cam.

"Which one?" Cam asked, opening the cream and smoothing it gingerly across her face.

"Your favorite."

"That would be Mom's mother," Cam said without hesitation. Being with Maggie and answering her questions seemed like a reality check. "Anne Bennett Loring." Cam stopped. She didn't want to talk about her grandmother. Not just yet. Not until she'd figured out what she was going to tell her about this. "Have I told you how we all got our names?" Cam asked, sliding away from the subject.

Maggie shook her head.

"We got all the maiden names. I was named for Dad's mom: Christina Cameron, Benny for Mom's mom, Anne Bennett, and Lori for Mom, Emily Loring. I probably should have been a Loring or a Bennett instead of a Cameron, but they didn't know if I'd be a boy or a girl and Grandma Chris wanted to have everything monogrammed, so they chose Cameron, either gender. From what I know, though, the women on Mom's side of the family have been real strong, independent women. Grandma Anne was a Wellesley graduate, 1918. She was a suffragette. I guess Mom and I got the political gene from her. Lori's not like that. She's more like Grandma Chris, a real homebody. She likes decorating the house and choosing china and planning parties and all that. I could never get into it. Grandma Anne and I have always been close, but especially so since Mom died."

"Tell me about your brother's death. We haven't touched that very deeply."

Cam curled her legs under her in the overstuffed chair, a gesture Maggie had learned was Cam's way of comforting herself when she had to face a difficult situation.

"He died. I was there. I had to tell my parents," was all she said.

Maggie waited a few moments, watching the turmoil build in Cam.

"Were you responsible?" she asked.

"No," Cam acknowledged. "For a while, I thought I was. I thought I hadn't watched out for him. But, no, I wasn't responsible for his death. It was February of my sophomore year. Benny was a freshman at Boston University. I got a call one night from his roommate..."

The mention flashed her back to that one night that was etched in her memory:

Cameron had been sitting in the far corner of the dorm study hall, by the window, totally engrossed in the large text open before her, her short dark hair hanging loosely over her forehead. Her only movement was writing short, terse notes on the pad to her right.

"Phone for you. It's another guy. Sounds like he can't keep his pants on. Got to speak to you right away." Her roommate, Andrea, whispered, leaning over the table. She emphasized the "right away" and leaned against the wall as Cam stretched back.

Cam looked up at her. "Who?" Andrea just shrugged as Cam pushed herself away from the table.

Andrea shook her head in resignation. There she'd been, practically sitting on the phone, waiting for Jimmy to call, and who was the first call for? Cameron.

Cam went grudgingly to the pay phone in the hallway where the receiver dangled and picked it up. "Hello."

"Cameron, it's George. You've got to come over here right away. Something's wrong with Benny. He's real sick. I don't know what to do."

Her brother's roommate sounded panicked.

Cam's shoulders tensed. "Slow down. What's happening?"

"I don't know. Honest, I don't. He just kinda collapsed. We can't get him to wake up!" Was George crying? "I...I think he took some drugs or something."

"What do you mean, you think."

"I don't know... Really. Please come over."

Cam took a deep breath. "Tell me his symptoms."

"His face is all red and he's breathing funny, you know, gasping. We can't get him to wake up."

"Damn." Cameron spit into the phone. "Take him to St. Elizabeth's right away."

"The hospital?"

"Yeh, St. E's."

"But they'll ask a lot of questions. Bob and I aren't really in any condition to go there."

Damn him! "Just get him there. Call 911 if you have to. I'll meet you in the parking lot by the Emergency entrance. Do it! Do you understand me?" She slammed the receiver back into its cradle. Her insides were starting to churn. George was high, too. Just what she needed—to go and get her little brother's stomach pumped on the night before a big test. She walked back to her room and took her jacket from the closet.

"Got a study date?" Andrea smiled with her all-too-shiny teeth.

"No, I got to go get my brother's head examined. Sounds like he's on a bad trip."

"I'll call you when I know."

As Cam walked from the dorm to where she'd parked the old '64 Ford, she thought, If he'd stayed in a dorm like Mom wanted instead of getting his own apartment with those other two idiots and trying to be Big-Man-On-Campus, I wouldn't have to be constantly bailing him out.

She got in the car and steered onto Western Avenue, the quickest way to St. Elizabeth's Hospital. The window steamed as soon as the heater hit it and she used her glove to clear a place to peer through until the defroster kicked in. The temperature was in the teens and would hit the single digits before morning. It was a lucky thing that it hadn't snowed earlier or the road would be sheer ice by now.

Western Avenue always seemed so long when she was in a rush, but there were few other cars on the road, so she pushed the pedal a little harder and prayed that a cop car wasn't hiding behind the Volkswagen showroom.

As she pulled into the Emergency entrance parking lot, a small VW bug blinked its lights from the far corner. She pulled up beside it and got out. Her brother, Ben was slumped in the passenger seat, George was behind the wheel and Bob was in the back seat. George glanced back at Bob as he reached across to roll down the window. Cam caught the odor of stale beer. Both boys' eyes were wide with fear or worry, she couldn't tell which.

"Drive him over to the Emergency Room door; I'll park my car and go in with him."

She slid back into the driver's seat of her car and pulled into a space near the door. She was out of the car and through the Emergency Room doors before George could turn off the motor. As the paramedics raced out with the gurney, George stepped away from the car and back into the shadows. Bob had hunched down in the back seat, trying to hide.

"Just get your asses back to the apartment and stay there." Cam ordered. "I'll call as soon as I know something." George moved quickly and was out of the parking lot before Cam had reached the nurse's desk. The paramedics pushed Ben directly into one of the examining rooms and people moved quickly.

Cameron was already filling out the forms when a young man, probably an intern, approached. "You're here with the OD?" he said, more a statement than a question, and he never looked up from the clipboard he was writing on. "Do you know what he's on?"

"I have no idea. Probably some grass and a few beers. I know the other guys were drinking beer."

"What else were you serving at the party? You his girlfriend?"

Cam was put off by the line of questioning, but tried to keep her cool and not tell this jerk where he could stick his stethoscope.

"No, I'm his sister, Doctor Walcott." She made a big show of reading his name off his nametag. "My name's Cameron Andrews. I just got a call from his roommates that he was sick and could I meet him here. If you need to pump his stomach or something, I know we've got insurance to cover it."

"I'll be back with you in a few minutes." The doctor escaped down the hall.

"Nice bedside manner," Cam commented as she turned back to the forms. The nurse behind the counter chuckled her agreement. Cam sat in the waiting room, leafing through some dog-eared magazines. Why hadn't she thought to bring her Economics book with her? Damn Ben. And George, and Bob. Those three had been best friends all since grade school. They'd always been inseparable. Dad called them the Three Musketeers. Now when Ben and Bob got accepted to Boston University and George got into Boston College, they'd decided to get an apartment together so they wouldn't have to split up. In the six months since school had started, Big Sister Cameron had been over there to bail them out three or four times. Nothing major, just little things like calming a neighbor when the boys partied 'til two, or calling the insurance people when Bob's car got rammed by a garbage truck because he'd parked too close to a dumpster. Just like in high school. They'd always come to her to square it away with a teacher, or Mom and Dad.

She thought back. It was a role she'd fallen into over the years, watching out for Ben and Lori while Mom was off on one of her political junkets as she called them. Yes, she'd learned to take care of herself, and half the other kids in the neighborhood.

Not that she disliked the role; she felt that it was her place to be in charge, to take care, and she liked it. Benny was more than her brother, he was her best friend and the one person she confided in. He was the 'planner'; she was the 'fixer'. They shared their hopes and dreams with each other. They always had. She'd been the first to know when he was selected by his coach to try out for the state swim team and he was her most ardent supporter when she decided she wanted to join the Diplomatic Corps after college. Everyone knew it. She had a gift for handling irate people. Her study of International Affairs was a natural. She'd make a great diplomat someday. She just hoped these guys would be around when she needed help. And she'd sure be glad when those three grew up.

She looked at her watch—almost nine o'clock. It had been almost an hour. Should she call Dad right now or just let Ben explain the insurance claim when it came. Probably serve him right. Especially if she flunked this test tomorrow. Well, she knew she wouldn't flunk but she did want to get a good enough grade that she didn't have to worry about this class the rest of the semester, or the fact that she was the only female in it.

A grey-haired man in a white lab coat was standing in front of her. "Miss Andrews?" he inquired. "I'm Dr. Harold Balforth. I believe you came in here with your brother Benjamin."

"Bennett," Cam corrected. "Yes, Bennett."

He checked the papers on the clipboard he held. "My mistake. May we talk in private?" He led the way past the nurses' station to a small conference room.

"May I inquire how old you are?" the doctor asked.

"Nineteen. I'll be twenty next month. But I'm sure there'll be no problem with me signing the insurance papers. I've done it before and they've never complained."

"No, I'm afraid it's more serious than that. Please sit down." Cam sat. Surely they weren't going to call the police just because Ben had had too much to drink. "Is your family near here?"

"Lexington. I haven't called them yet. I didn't want to worry them until I knew what to tell them."

"Well." The doctor took a long breath. "I'm afraid that your brother didn't make it." There was no other way to break it to her. There was no way to lead up to it. He searched her face, watching for a reaction.

Cameron just stared at him. Didn't make it? The words didn't make sense to her. Then it began to sink in and the complete meaning hit her full in the face. This man was trying to tell her that Ben was dead. This must be a joke!

But the doctor was talking again. "It was a mixture of barbiturates and speed along with the alcohol—an overdose. His heart just couldn't take it. I'm very sorry." Cameron was in shock. She rose without a word.

"Would you like some help in contacting your parents?" the doctor asked.

"No." She shook her head. "I can do that." Could she? She wasn't as sure as she sounded. Where to start? What to do first? "Where is Ben now?"

"He's still in the examining room. They haven't transferred him downstairs yet." It was a nice way of saying he hadn't been sent to the morgue.

"May I see him?"

"Yes, of course." He motioned for a nurse to come and escort Cam into the room where her brother was stretched out on the table.

"How did your parents take it? Did they blame you?" Maggie asked.

Cameron shook her head. "Everyone was devastated by Ben's death. Especially Dad. I guess it was hard losing his only son. Grampa Jon took it the worst, though. Especially the next year when Mom and Dad were killed in the car accident. Grampa Jon just couldn't handle losing his son and his grandson. He never fully got over it. He just went downhill until he died last year."

"And your parents' deaths?"

"It was so senseless: some young guy, high on LSD or grass, or a combination, drove onto Route Two using the off-ramp and struck their Ford head-on, It killed them both instantly. He walked away with just a few stitches."

"So Grandma Anne was the one you turned to for solace."

"I was ready to drop out of school, to stay home in Lexington, get a job and get Lori through high school. Grandma Anne wouldn't allow it." Cam let out a short laugh, shaking her head slowly. "You don't defy her when she's made up her mind. She closed up her own house, moved in with Lori and sent me back to Radcliffe. I'm not even sure how I got through that next year. I wouldn't have if she hadn't been there."

"How will she take your going to jail?" Cam closed her eyes. After a moment, she said, softly, "I don't know."

"Does she trust you enough to believe you might be doing something other than what it looks like? Do you think she'll believe you're a criminal? Will it hurt her?" Cam slumped down further into the chair. These were the questions Maggie somehow always found just the right ones that she hadn't wanted to have to answer.

Chapter Seven

Cameron leaned forward, her hands on her knees, trying to catch her breath. Today had been especially taxing and it seemed like she'd never get the hang of the combinations of jujitsu and Hapkido moves Michael was trying to teach her. She'd spent more time on the ground than on her feet.

"If I try to punch you, step into it," Michael was saying. "Deflect it, upwards—like this." She moved Cam's arm over hers and around and then back down and over her own arm to lock the elbow behind her. "See? Even if I were holding a knife, not just my fist, you can use the cross wrist block to deflect it, disarm me. Do not be afraid of being hit, you can counter it, use it. Use my momentum. Turn, meet my force with yours. Once again."

Cam took a step back and waited. Michael threw a punch at her face, but Cam sidestepped it turning, bringing her fist up to meet Michael's forward motion.

Michael's nose stopped just fragments of an inch from the back of Cam's fist. "Yes! That's it!! Oui!! Encore! Once again!!"

Michael threw another punch and Cam deflected it, but this time, as Michael pretended to fall backwards from what would have been a twisted arm and a blow to her face, her legs whipped out and swept Cam off her feet. Before Cam could draw a breath, Michael was over her and ready to land a quick, deadly blow to Cam's windpipe.

For a brief moment, they stared into each other's eyes. There was suddenly a tension between them, accentuated by their heavy breathing. Were they both really out of breath? Or was it something else?

Cam quickly shut her eyes. Being this close to Michael, to have Michael leaning over her, just inches from her made her shake. Why was she reacting like this? Michael was her teacher and, from Cam's observations, obviously straight. What power did Michael hold over her? She suddenly wanted to reach up and pull Michael to her, to hold her and beg forgiveness for being inept. She shook her head in frustration.

"Do not stop your own momentum," Michael was lecturing as she pulled Cam to her feet. "One move always causes another. Be aware. It is like a chess game. Plan your moves, anticipate your opponent. Know her moves before she does."

Cam knew that words were of no use. No matter how it was explained, no matter how many times she repeated the instructions back to Michael, doing it was a totally different matter. This was not very different from the training she'd had at the Academy, but Michael was so much better than anyone she'd ever faced. Would she ever be able to learn this? She braced herself for the next attack, but Michael relaxed her stance. "We do not have time to play. If you want to stay alive, you must work harder. You must stop being afraid of being harmed. Bruises will fade. Death will not." Michael reached out and caressed Cam's face. "You are such a sweet little lamb. It would be a shame to have something happen to you."

Cam's anger rose, but damn ! she was not about to show it to Michael.

"I wish only that I could be there to protect you," Michael added softly.

As Michael threw a punch, Cam stepped past it, turned and threw Michael over her hip, onto the beach, her arm twisted awkwardly behind her.

Michael let out a sharp laugh as she rolled onto the sand. "Oui!! Ah, ma cherie! Yes! Yes! Tres Bien! You have such anger inside you. Use it! Make it work for you! If you are going to explode, direct the energy! Make it work for you! It is who you are!!"

Cam stopped short. Michael's words... "You have such anger inside you... It is who you are." Those had been Karen's exact words.

"Use it," Michael continued, "Don't ignore it or deny it. Direct it in the right direction. It will be very good for you."

Maybe that was the secret Cameron needed to know. Just because Karen hadn't been able to handle it didn't make it bad. Maybe it could be her best asset...

But Michael was on her feet again. And this time Cameron was ready.

* * * *

"This is your job. If you let them get to you, if you let them push your buttons, you've lost the battle. You are dead. Do you understand me? You're playing a role, a part in a play. Stay in character." Charlie stood in front of her, as she balanced on one foot, on an overturned bucket, holding the other foot in her hand. She'd withstood his verbal abuse for nearly two hours, now. Today was, by far, the worst. And it was only Friday of the first week. "First of all: who are you? What is your name?" Charlie growled at her.

"Cameron Andrews."

"What? Who are you talking to?"

"You, sir." Cam tried to remember the drill she'd just gone through: how to address those with the power.

"*You, sir*? What's a 'you'? Do I look like a ewe? Do I have a white fuzzy coat and lots of tits? What's a ewe?"

"A ewe is a female sheep, sir." Couldn't she ever get anything right?

"Do I look like a ewe?"

"No, sir."

"Then who are you talking to?"

"To the Master Trainer, sir." Cam felt like her leg was about to give out, that she was about to fall from the bucket.

"Then, what is your name?"

"Cameron Andrews, sir." Cam was beginning to really respect the military inductees who went through this every day for twelve weeks.

"And what is a Cameron Andrews?"

Cam took a deep breath and regained her balance. Would this session never end? "Nothing, sir," she said, thinking she knew what he wanted. "A Cameron Andrews is a nothing, sir."

But once again, Charlie was a step ahead. "Wrong. She's a dyke. A lesbian. And a criminal. She's scum. Isn't that right?"

Cam let out an angry breath. "Yes, sir," she answered.

"What is she?"

"Scum, sir." Cam's voice was beginning to get louder, rising in pitch.

"You think lesbians are scum?"

"Yes, sir," she lied.

"Why do you think that?"

Cameron had stood there in that position, in the hot sun for the past half hour, listening to Charlie berate her, admonishing her, contradicting every answer she gave. She'd tried to second guess him, to give him the answers she thought he wanted, but he always came back with something different, something new.

"Because the Master Trainer told me that was so, sir," she threw back at him.

"Am I always right?"

"Yes, sir." Anger was beginning to creep into her voice.

"Why?"

"Because the Master Trainer told me he was, sir."

"Am I a god, then?" he asked.

"Yes, sir. The Master Trainer is God." Cameron conceded grudgingly.

"What would a dyke know about God?"

Cam stopped. "Sir?"

"And why would God have anything to do with such a heathen lowlife as a bulldyke? Especially one that took an honorable profession such as police work and corrupted it down to the worst level it could possibly attain. Only a *bulldagger*," his language getting more and more offensive, "would have such low regard for *good* society that she twisted and turned the trust the people put in her into nothing more than a way to steal and debase things that honest, god-fearing people have worked hard for, have shed tears and blood to attain. Only a god-damned dyke would be so devoid of morals that she could use her trusted position on the police force to shield her decadent crimes. It's no wonder that lesbians stick so close together. No one in their right mind would want to get close to one, would want to allow poor innocent children within their grasp…"

Cam was breathing harder as she listened to Charlie continue his ranting about gays and corrupt police officers. She knew in her gut that he was just goading her, just egging her on, but he was hitting close to home. How many times had she seen the disdain on the face of someone looking at a gay person, someone they didn't even know? How many times had she allowed such bigoted hatred to pass? As a police officer, she'd had to ignore it, or diffuse the situation diplomatically instead of expressing her views on the issue. How many times had she had to hide her sexual preference just to avoid that hatred? Charlie's words were too well placed.

Damn him. Don't trust anyone? She certainly didn't trust him enough to believe that he wasn't speaking what he really thought, that his words weren't coming from his heart. She was seething.

So, when she heard, "…exposing our children to figures of trust like police and teachers who in secret hide the sick perversion to corrupt…,"she blew.

"Fuck you!" she swore at him. Charlie wheeled around and pushed her from the bucket. She landed in the sand with a thud.

Charlie stood over her. "You're dead. We might as well tell Maggie right now that we can all go home. You have no control, you just let me get to you. You let me know where your weakness was. I know where your buttons are, now, and I can push them whenever I want. You have no control over it. You are one dead piece of meat. You are mine."

Cam sat on the ground, her head in her hands, shaking, both from the physical exertion of balancing on one leg and the anger she'd just vented.

Charlie watched her for a moment.

"What's the verdict?" he asked, finally. "Do we tell Maggie to pull the plug?"

Cam took a deep breath. "No, sir," she finally acquiesced, "I'll try harder."

"Try? *Try harder?*" Charlie was right back on her again. "Don't *try*. Be. Be harder. Put yourself in control. Do you understand?"

"Yes, sir," Cam was resigned to his abuse.

"What's skill number seven?"

"Stay detached."

"Get on your feet."

Cam dragged herself upright and stood at attention in front of him.

"Skill number eight?"

"Don't show emotions."

"Especially…?"

"Especially anger, sir."

Charlie just turned and walked back toward the main house. Cam waited, unsure if she'd been dismissed or abandoned, or if he expected her to wait until he came back. Charlie was one sick sadist, Cam thought, but she also felt that if she could live through this without trying to kill him, she could withstand just about anything. She shook her head in amazement. These skills could keep her alive. Up to now, he'd been absolutely right. Damn him!

Chapter Eight

The days stretched one into another and Cam completely lost track of time. Sitting at the table, during dinner, with the other three, was a chore. She ached. She was black and blue. She was tired. Tired physically. Tired emotionally. Tired mentally. As Charlie, Michael and Maggie cheerfully chatted, Cam only pushed the food around her plate, taking small bites that tasted good, but she was too tired to complete the whole chewing process.

Cam felt like she was making progress with the Judo, Jujitsu and other martial arts moves that Michael was teaching. She knew that Michael was still not fully reacting to her moves, but she was growing more confident and knew that Michael had to use more and more counter moves to thwart her. Cam felt confident, however, that by the end of this training, she'd be able to handle herself reasonably well in a tough situation. Michael was a good teacher, patient but persistent.

But her situation with Charlie...well, she had no way to judge that. He never responded to her except to point out her mistakes. He never acknowledged her achievements, if there were any.

Maggie watched as Cam slowly placed a few pieces of stroganoff in her mouth. Elbow on the table, her hand supported her head that rested wearily against it. "I think we're at a place where we deserve a 'Time Out'," Maggie announced.

All three just looked up at her.

"We've been working very hard for ten days now. We all deserve a break." Maggie turned around and reached into the cabinet and withdrew a large bottle of Cam's favorite scotch. "I'm serious," she continued as she placed the bottle ceremoniously in front of Cam. "Tonight you're off duty. No lessons, no drills, no questions. You can relax tonight, let your guard down. Tonight it doesn't matter who you trust or what you feel or say...or do. This is your first *shore leave*. This is a safe haven. Enjoy it. You deserve it."

Cam was surprised by Maggie's announcement. She looked across the table at Michael who smiled back at her and then at Charlie who was sitting next to her and, for the first time since she'd met him, he actually smiled at her and nodded in agreement.

"You're making progress," he stated flatly. "*That* you can trust. Tomorrow we begin again. There's still a lot to do. But tonight, you're on semester break." That was as close to any form of praise as Charlie had ever come.

The relief Cam felt as she let her guard down was like a multi-ton weight being taken off her back. She suddenly felt awake and alive. She poured a large shot of scotch into her empty water glass and held it up in toast to the others.

"Thank you," was all she said. Then she rose and walked out the door toward the beach.

Maggie watched her go. Then without looking at either of them, she asked, "Well? What do you think?"

"She'll be all right physically, Maggie. She's got a good natural rhythm. She could even reach second or third degree black belt if she trained well. I don't think she'll have a problem there."

"I think she needs to know that, Michael. Charlie?"

"She works hard. She wants to succeed, that's the most important part. I've had to push her pretty hard to reach her breaking points. We still have a way to go, there are still some issues we haven't touched, but she should be all right. Up 'til now, we've been viewing everything as black or white. Right or wrong. I think it's time I let her explore some of those grey areas...who to trust and how much, when to let anger show and why, what kind of debt to let yourself get into. Things like that. It's always easier to relax into the grey areas once you're firm in the blacks and whites."

Maggie nodded as she thought through their comments. She wanted very badly for Cam to succeed. And she wanted to know that nothing bad would happen to her. She knew there were no guarantees, but Charlie's and Michael's endorsements made a big difference.

"Are you serious that she is free to do anything she chooses tonight?" Michael asked.

"Yes, why?"

Michael smiled and winked at Charlie, who shook his head as he grinned back at her. "Oh, nothing," was all she said as she took the bottle of scotch from the table, leaned down to kiss Charlie on the forehead and left the room.

* * * *

Michael found her sitting on the beach. "Hi," she said, smiling as she walked up and held out the bottle of scotch to Cam. "Thought you might want a little more of this."

"Trying to get me drunk?"

"I judged you to be more than a two shot drunk," Michael laughed, sinking down beside Cam. They sat in silence, just listening to the waves beating on the shore for a minute.

Michael was the first to speak. "It is so beautiful here. I wish we had time to really enjoy it."

"Me, too. I'd like to just lie on the sand for once instead of landing on it. It is pretty hard to fall on."

"You're doing well," Michael patted Cam on the shoulder. "I have not told you that because I want you to continue to work hard, but seeing that tonight we can let our hair down, I thought you should know. I think you will be fine in your assignment."

Cam looked over at her. In the glow of the moonlight off the water, Michael's finely chiselled features glowed and her long legs stretched out in front of her made a graceful line that sent a chill through Cam, now that the first glass of scotch had relaxed her. Cam had felt very attracted to Michael throughout the week, but had kept her feelings in check. Michael was Cam's trainer, her teacher *and*, from the way she'd seen her act around Charlie, she was straight. Those were two barriers Cam didn't want to even try to cross. But she had no control over what her mind did while she was asleep.

Twice during the past week, she'd woken in a cold sweat, after having had dreams of being with Michael. Of holding her, caressing her, and having Michael return the affection. In one dream, Michael had been her teacher, her trainer, but this time, she was not learning martial arts...

Cam wrenched her thoughts from her dreams as Michael commented upon the moonlight and the heat. As ever, Cam became enthralled by the beautiful sound of her accent. Soon, Cam was asking questions just to hear Michael's voice. The conversation remained light and easy.

At first, they talked about the Olympic Games that had taken place that past winter in Lake Placid, New York.

Michael talked passionately about them. "It was so wonderful for them to be that close to where I live. It is too bad you did not get up to see them. I had to tear myself away from them to go back to work. Quel magnifique! I was actually there in the arena when your Eric Heiden won his fifth gold medal in the speed skating. No one could catch him. The roar was overwhelming. My brother, Jean-Rene, went crazy! He had tried speed skating when he was younger, but he didn't have the discipline to practice every day. Neither did I."

"Did you skate?" Cameron asked. A vision of Michael on skates flashed through her mind. The fluidity of Michael's movements would be incredible gliding and twirling across the ice.

But Michael shook her head. "Not really. I was too...hyper, I think you would say. I tried speed skating, but I didn't have the patience to pace myself for the long track and I am too tall for short track skating. I was always tripping someone or creating a foul. Do you skate?"

Cameron smiled. "Nothing like that. We skated on a pond near home, but just for fun. I never took lessons or anything. I played a little hockey with my brother."

"Oh, then he must have loved it when the U.S. won the gold medal in hockey!"

Cameron stopped. "My brother died. Ten years ago."

Michael reached across and laid her hand on Cameron's. "I am so sorry. He was your favorite brother?"

"My only brother. We were close. He was only fourteen months younger than me. He died of a drug overdose. That's what got me involved in drug enforcement."

Cameron talked of her parents and Ben and how they had died. Michael listened quietly.

In turn, Michael related how she'd never really thought of becoming a police officer until both of her older brothers had graduated from the same police academy that their father had attended and teased her about being the only Gauchet without a badge. "Except my mother. But, she always was so strict that we referred to her as The Warden. Same thing, no? I don't know if I could ever become a constable, but my talent in martial arts kept me from a street beat."

"I tried doing desk work after college. I worked as a translator." Cam omitted that it had been in the Decoding Section of the CIA.

"Then you are fluent in other languages." Michael brightened.

"Well, basically, Spanish. I did a year of graduate work at the University of Barcelona after I graduated from Radcliffe. I can read a little French and even less German."

"You should learn more of the French tongue. It is quite interesting."

Cameron wasn't quite sure how to take that. There was something in Michael's use of the English language that kept Cam a little off guard. In fact, there were several times when Cameron wasn't sure if it was just a language difference or if Michael was actually coming on to her.

"What about your little sister?" Michael asked, "Is she as vigorous as you?" Michael had one hand dangling over her knee, holding her wine glass that was now nearly empty. Her other hand caressed it in such a way that made Cam uneasy. Michael's long fingers traced the patterns made by the condensation. Back and forth across the glass, ever so slowly, gently.

Damned straight women, thought Cam, didn't they realize what they were doing? She forced herself to look away from those graceful hands.

"Lori? She's happily married with two little boys. Ben is four, Kevin just turned two."

"And her husband?"

"David's a nice guy. He was a college friend of one of Ben's buddies. The guys just stuck around after Benny died. David tagged along. That, as they say, was that. I like him. He's a lawyer."

"Ooh. I hate lawyers. They are so...so tricky. But if you like him, he must not act like a lawyer."

Cameron laughed. "I guess, since I knew him before he was a lawyer, I still see him as just one of the guys."

Michael set the wine glass in the sand and reached out with both hands to knead Cam's shoulders.

"Oooh, you are very tense. And I know you must be sore after all the work we have done this week."

How could Cam tell her that the tension came from her touch. That she couldn't really relax watching her movements and listening to her seductive innuendos.

Cam quickly finished the last half inch of scotch in her water glass.

"Come," Michael jumped to her feet and held her hand out. "We can go up to your deck where it is less sandy and I will give you a massage. You deserve to be pampered."

Against her better judgement—or was it the judgement of the scotch?—Cam took Michael's hand and stood to walk back toward the house.

* * * *

Cameron stretched out on the floor of her room, allowing herself to relax into Michael's massage. She tried hard not to allow herself to feel any hint of sexuality, but Michael's touch still felt like an electric shock. She tried to concentrate on the sound of the ocean through the open doors.

As Michael's kneading became more insistent, Cam began to relax.

"Roll over." Michael's softly spoken words were low and relaxed. Cameron languidly rolled over onto her back, aware that she had taken her shirt off, but not self conscious about her nakedness.

Softly, Michael's lips were on hers, gently, but insistently kissing her as her hand roamed the length of Cam's body.

Cam sat up suddenly, sliding back, putting some distance between her and Michael. She stared at Michael with a look of surprise and bewilderment.

"Have I misinterpreted?" Michael looked perplexed. "I thought…that you were attracted to me, as I am to you."

"But…" Cam searched for words. "I thought…I mean, I assumed…I am attracted to you…but I mean, well, I thought you were straight," she blurted. That's right, be articulate, express yourself succinctly.

Michael looked at her incredulously.

"Straight? Mais non. Why do you think that?"

"I…I just assumed. You're so…intimate…with Charlie…"

Michael smiled and relaxed back onto the floor. "Intimate." She shook her head. "Intimate with Charlie? Is that why you have been avoiding my advances?"

"I just thought…and you're my teacher. I just…" Cam stared at the floor.

"Intimate," Michael repeated. She smiled thoughtfully. "Oui. Charlie is

63

my friend. We know each other very well. He is my confidante. We were intimate, once," she admitted, "but only because we were dating the same woman. That is how I met him. She wanted us both at once. It was…interesting. But she dropped us both. Charlie and I have become great friends. And we now make it a point not to date the same women."

Cam laughed. "I guess I totally misjudged that one."

"But it is all right, now that we have figured it out, no? I love women. And I am very attracted to you." Michael moved closer. Caressing Cam's cheek, she added, "I think that maybe we can work as well together during the night as we do during the day." She leaned forward to kiss Cam and this time, Cam did not move away.

Cameron's arms circled Michael's lean body and felt strong muscles flex under her touch. As the tip of Michael's tongue gently probed her lips, she parted them slightly, allowing Michael to explore the inside of her mouth. Her body responded, pressing itself into Michael's, sucking in her tongue. As she engulfed Michael's mouth, their bodies began a slow grinding against each other.

Before Cameron realized they had moved, they were stretched out fully on the floor, Michael's body pressing down on hers. Cam matched Michael's passionate kiss with her own as she let her hands explore the curves of Michael's sides and hips and back. Her legs intertwined with Michael's as Michael finally pressed her upper thigh strongly into Cam's crotch. Cameron groaned as waves of heat ran through her.

"I like women who are strong as you are." Michael whispered as she placed her mouth over Cam's and began a new wave of sensation as her hand gently stroked the breast beneath it, caressing the hard erect nipple. Her fingers on Cam's breast mirrored the movements her tongue was making inside Cam's mouth until Cam's body was pushing up into hers. Michael slowly slid down Cam's body, stopping first to nuzzle her neck, then to slowly draw a line with her tongue from the base of Cam's throat to the other nipple. With slow, deliberate motions, she roused that nipple, sometimes drawing it into her mouth and holding it with her teeth while her tongue flicked it, other times barely touching it and letting her breath cool and warm it in turn.

"Michael," Cameron hissed and started to massage the strong shoulders that pressed against her.

Michael answered by attacking Cam's mouth and sucking both her tongue and breath from her. Taking Cam's wrists in her hands, she stretched her arms up until Cam was fully extended. Soon they were both writhing, body to body, mouth to mouth, Cam stretched along the floor beside the bed, arms over her head, Michael's body fully atop hers, grinding and rubbing strongly against her. Their breathing had become ragged.

Suddenly Michael sat back. "I want to make love to you. In my own way," she said, her voice husky.

Cam looked at her, perplexed, not understanding the meaning of Michael's words. "In your own way?" she asked.

Michael smiled, a dark, brooding smile. Cameron found it arousing, but dangerous in some mysterious way. Michael's eyes took on a new quality, as if she could look through Cam. She watched as Michael reached into the rear pocket of her shorts and withdrew a pair of handcuffs. "I wish to show you why Charlie calls me Mistress," Michael whispered.

Cameron stared at the handcuffs. Alarms in her head went off. What had she gotten into? Yet, something…what? the sense of danger, of the loss of control was thrilling. She could feel her heart speed up, her breathing become more erratic. "I don't do this, Michael," Cam whispered, trying to keep the panic from her still husky voice.

"But I think you will like to learn," Michael answered matter-of-factly as she drew Cam toward her and took Cam's earlobe between her teeth. Her tongue wound its way into Cam's ear.

Cam closed her eyes. The thought of handcuffs and bondage, any kind of kinky sex, frightened her, it always had. What was she afraid of? The loss of control? The fear of the unknown? She'd read about it in magazines. She'd seen traces of it in that old bar in Boston, The Other Side, where she'd gone once with friends. The dark bar where women played out butch and femme roles with great intensity. Where the butches took what they wanted and the femmes obeyed without question. Cam had been amazed at the scenes, and followed her friends down to another more 'politically correct' lesbian bar where the interaction between the women was more egalitarian, more 'vanilla,' as she'd heard it described.

Suddenly she flashed to a memory of that night in Baltimore when she's had to go into a leather bar in her police uniform to check on a disturbance. Women dressed in tight black leather, some very scantily, had tried to stare her down as she and her partner had made their inspection, checking ID's for underage patrons. There had been one couple that she remembered. One of the women had been obvious as she stared at Cam, rubbed her body against the door jamb directly in front of her, in suggestive and very seductive ways. Then, as the butch reached out and wrapped her hand into her femme's hair and pulled her to her, Cam had turned to meet a challenging stare from the larger woman. "If you want her, take her from me, if you can," the butch had challenged Cam softly. As Cam turned to walk past, she heard the butch chuckle, "or take her place if you dare."

Cam had followed her partner through the rest of the bar. It wasn't until they were outside, that she realized how heavily she was sweating, how aroused she'd become, or how erotic she'd found the entire experience.

Now, with Michael hovering dangerously close to her, Cam's body was reacting in ways she'd never experienced; thoughts she'd had this week, of

Michael overpowering her, of holding her helpless, were beginning to fall into place. A thrill worked its way up the back of her neck and she shivered.

"You will be wonderful at this," Michael said softly as she fastened the handcuff around Cam's wrist. She leaned into Cam and slowly reclined her onto the floor. Then, Michael's body was on top of hers, pressing and rubbing strongly against her. Their breathing became more and more ragged.

Then, Cameron felt like she was watching from another perspective as she let Michael wind the handcuff around the leg of the bed and lock it around her other wrist. Michael carefully adjusted the bracelets so that they were not too tight and set the locks so they wouldn't tighten further. Then she sat back. Slowly, she undid the button of Cam's shorts and even more slowly lowered the zipper.

Cam's old self was suddenly back and she protested. She tried to look over her head to see where her hands were shackled. She still wasn't convinced that she could go along with this, but Michael put her hand over her mouth, gently. "Shhh," she warned, sitting back on her heels. "Trust me, just for a moment. If you cannot, you cannot. But try. You may enjoy it. I believe you will."

Cam's eyes told Michael that she was still not totally convinced.

"Let us make a pact, then. If it is too much, if you cannot continue, Say...where do you call your home?"

Cameron thought a moment. "Baltimore," she answered.

"Good, then if it is too much, if you want me to stop, just say *"Baltimore,"* and I will stop. You will be safely home again. I promise. You will be safe. Will you agree?"

Cam wanted to object again, but the look in Michael's eyes held her riveted. She closed her eyes, suddenly embarrassed, as well as confused. Suddenly, she *wanted* to be under Michael's control. She wanted Michael to touch her, to take control of her. She wasn't sure how to react.

Taking Cameron's silence as concession, Michael's fingers slowly traced the soft line just inside the waistband of her bikinis. Cam dropped her head back and wallowed in the sensations.

She lifted her hips as Michael slowly coaxed the shorts and panties down, past her thighs, over her feet. Then kneeling between Cam's legs, Michael slowly and deliberately stroked her inner thighs, her pelvis and just the edges of the triangle of dark hair.

Cameron was becoming unglued. "Touch me. Now!" she wanted to yell as the tickling became torture. She pressed her body toward the hands, but Michael was always just barely within reach.

"Patience. We'll get to it." Michael hissed as Cameron's writhing became more intense. She pushed Cam's legs further apart and gently brushed the ends of the hair around her cunt. It was glistening with moisture.

Cam moaned, a suppressed scream.

"Oh, you are so beautiful. This will be very good." Michael whispered, brushing the hair a second time. Then she sat back.

Cam opened her eyes to see what Michael was doing and found her kneeling between her legs, slowly, deliberately, unbuttoning first one button, then the next, slowly, teasing until Michael's pale blue cotton shirt fell away to fully reveal her lithe, boyish body.

Cam licked her lips. The sight of Michael slowly removing her own shirt, then folding it carefully and laying it aside, had its desired effect. She wanted to reach out and touch, no, kiss, no, suck the small nipples and run her hands over the small, firm breasts. She pulled against the handcuffs, but Michael put her hand on her arm to stop her.

"Shhh," she purred. "Don't hurt yourself. You don't want to leave marks." She bent and kissed Cam gently on the mouth.

Cameron stopped her struggling and remained immobile.

Michael slid off to the side and took the handcuff key from her pocket and set it on the floor next to her folded shirt. Then she slowly started to remove her own shorts. Cameron turned to the side to look at her.

"No, no. You cannot move. I am in charge now and I have not given you permission." Michael pushed Cameron onto her back and raised her knees. She pushed Cam's legs apart. "And you cannot forbid me the sight of this." She brushed her hand lightly over Cam's cunt hair.

Cam sucked in a lung full of air as her back arched. "Michael…"

"You must not speak until you are given permission. Just watch."

This was becoming almost too exciting. And she was in new territory. Only the familiarity of this room that she'd occupied for the past week and a half made any sense to her. Where was this headed? "Michael…" she said, then paused. She had to stop herself from mentioning Baltimore.

"No. I am Mistress. That is what you shall call me." Michael was suddenly suspended above Cam, her naked body just out of reach. She looked deeply into Cam's eyes. "Now, what can you call me?"

Cam's mind started to revolt, but her senses overruled. She was flustered, unsure of what to do. "This is so silly. Let me out of these."

Michael's eyes bore into hers. "Do you really want that? Before you've even tried? I expected that you'd be a little more adventurous than that."

Cameron stopped. Why was this so strangely erotic? Maybe…all thoughts of escape quickly fled. Did Charlie's training work for this, too? Should she trust Michael? Should she trust no one?

"You are a police officer, n'est-ce pas? You ask people to put themselves in your hands every day, to trust you with their lives. Will you not do that yourself? Please. Trust me. Even if just for tonight." Michael's soft voice enticed as her hand again gently brushed the tips of Cam's cunt hair.

Cam closed her eyes in acquiescence. This was new. She was unsure. But something about Michael…well what? Wasn't this what she'd been imagining, craving since they arrived here? Was she suddenly willing to place her complete trust in this woman's hands? "Yes." she whispered, looking up into Michael's confident face.

Michael smiled, pleased. "Now, what can you call me?" she asked.

She searched Michael's eyes. There was no room for debate in Michael's expression. She had come this far. One more step? Softly, she submitted. "Mistress," she smiled demurely.

Michael rewarded her by lowering her body into Cam's and kissing her long and hard. The feeling of Michael's flesh against hers and the power of the kiss left her gasping for air as Michael released her.

Michael praised her. "I knew you would learn quickly." Cam responded by spreading her legs even farther apart.

Michael bent to kiss Cam's belly. Her hair lightly brushing Cam's flesh sent a shudder through Cam. Then, Michael's mouth began its slow descent. First, barely brushing Cam's pubic hair, then slowly circling to lick the inside of her thighs.

Suddenly, a quake racked her as Michael's breath found the small globe between Cam's legs. The warmth of her breath sent shock waves through Cam. She wasn't sure how much she could stand. She wanted Michael to just take her clit into her mouth and suck her life out, but Michael had her own timetable and would not be rushed.

"Michael…" Cam panted.

The kissing of the thighs and teasing of the clit stopped abruptly.

"What did you call me?" Michael's voice was stern.

Cam stopped, confused. This was a new situation and her mind fought between making a joke of it or letting the scene play itself out. She laughed, nervously. "Mistress," she finally managed.

"What do you want, my dear?" Michael asked, sweetly.

Cam couldn't put words to what her body was crying out for. Sex with her other lovers had always been so gentle, so tender, with her partners willingly taking every signal, every moan as a plea to go further. But now, Cam wanted more, and Michael was not responding to her. Michael was doing only what Michael wanted. And Cam was craving more. Her immobility, the power that Michael held over her, left her with totally new desires, thoughts she'd never entertained before. Finally, she breathed, "Touch me. Suck me hard."

"Please?" Michael teased.

"Please," groaned Cam.

"Please, *Mistress*?" Michael taunted.

"Please, Mistress."

"Please, Mistress, what? What do you want?"

Cam was on the verge of hysteria. "Please, Mistress, suck me. Eat me. Fuck me." she cried out, words she'd heard inside her head before, but never out loud.

Michael responded by running her tongue the length of Cam's cunt, from her wet vagina, up the smooth path between the lips to the hard round globe. She flicked it forcefully and felt Cam's body react with shivers and spasms, then sucked it into her mouth and her tongue began its forceful manipulation.

It was not long before Michael felt Cam's body tense, the muscles begin to quiver. She stopped.

"I have not given you permission to come, yet. I'm not finished." she warned.

Cam was frantic. Every cell in her body wanted to explode. Her mind was beginning to erupt.

"Please, Mistress," she begged, nearly crying.

But Michael stopped and slowly withdrew from between Cam's legs. Cameron had become completely unglued. She opened her eyes as she felt Michael unlocking the handcuff around her left wrist.

Yes, she thought, Now I can touch her, I can hold her—

But before the thought was complete, Michael had flipped her onto her stomach and her hands were now locked securely behind her back.

"Wait," she pleaded, not knowing what had happened, or worse still, what was going to happen. She felt Michael adjusting her arms into a more relaxed position and checking the cuffs to make sure they were comfortable and secure.

Then Michael was behind her, between her legs again. She reached around under Cam's hips and raised her pelvis until Cam was on her knees, but Michael's other hand on her back, kept her chest to the floor.

"I know you have observed my hands this week." Michael was slowly stroking the dripping opening of Cam's cunt. "You've watched my long fingers, haven't you? You've wondered how they will feel within you." Michael's teasing was starting to melt Cam's cunt into molten liquid. "You've imagined how deep within you they could go, how strong they could be."

Cam was beside herself. Yes, every one of Michael's accusations was completely true. She had imagined what those long glorious fingers would feel like. Why was Michael waiting? Why was she holding back? The teasing at the opening was almost more than she could stand.

"Please," Cam begged.

"What do you want, cherie," Michael asked softly, pressing just slightly harder. "Have you fantasized about my hands?"

"Oh yes," Cam gasped.

"Where were they?"

"In me," Cam's voice barely made it out of her throat.

"Where in you?"

"Deep in me. Please, please, deep in me. Fuck me hard." Cam rubbed her face on the carpet, trying to retain enough hold on reality to keep from coming.

"You mean, like this?" Michael slid two fingers into the wet pool that was now raised high in the air.

Cam gasped. "Ohhhh, yessss" she hissed between clenched teeth.

Michael slowly stroked the front inside wall of Cam's vagina and Cam's body responded by taking the rhythm and pulsing against Michael's hand. Her hardened nipples rubbed roughly against the carpet, creating yet another sensation.

"Not so fast, yet," Cam heard Michael whisper, "there is still a lot of time left." Michael slowed the rhythm of her strokes, driving Cam into a frenzy. "Control," Michael whispered. "Concentrate. You can restrain yourself. Enjoy this. Don't let an early orgasm end it too soon."

Cam listened to each of Michael's commands, wanting desperately to obey, wanting to have the control Michael demanded. Her mind grasped at any thought she could concentrate on long enough to maintain her composure: Charlie's rules? No. Not that. She was breaking at least three of them right now and was about to break number six. How much control did she have left?

Finally, just as Cam was losing her battle to maintain control, Michael's stroking became faster and faster, harder and harder. Now three of her fingers were in Cam.

"You may come now," was all she said as she added a fourth finger and pushed powerfully.

Cam didn't need to hear it a second time. She let go of the thin thread of sanity she'd clung to and let her body erupt. Spasms racked her and her muscles closed tightly around Michael's fingers. Her back arched as every muscle in her body tensed. Michael lengthened the response by continuing her stoking until Cam's body finally fell limp, covered with sweat.

"I knew you would be good at this," Michael whispered as she caressed Cam's body with her own. Cam still felt minor tremors running through her.

Finally, when Cameron's breathing had returned to normal, Michael unlocked the handcuffs and rolled Cam onto her back, stretching herself alongside Cam's still body.

"What about you?" Cam murmured languidly.

"Tomorrow," Michael whispered. "I have more to show you. But tonight, you must rest. Charlie will be angry if you are not in peak form in the morning."

Chapter Nine

Charlie stood behind her as she deftly slid the deadbolt of the mortise clock back into its housing. Wiping the sweat from her eyes, she sat back and reached for the glass of water that sat on the tray on the small wooden table. Today was hotter and more humid than any of the other days. Even sitting here on the covered porch of one of the small bungalows, there was no breeze to relieve the heat. The small buildings on the beach had proven to be storage sheds. One had contained beach chairs and tables, another electronic surveillance equipment, the others different kinds of equipment to be used in training.

"Very good. You pick locks well."

Cam looked back at him. It was the first time Charlie had complimented her for anything since they'd gotten here.

"You seem surprised," he said looking down at her.

She turned her head away from him. "You just never..."

"Praised you?" he asked sharply.

"Well, not exactly praise, but usually you just tell me if it was right or wrong, not good or bad."

Charlie slowly walked around in front of her.

"Stand up," he ordered, back to his normal tone.

"Who am I?" he asked as Cam snapped to attention.

"The Master Trainer, sir," was Cam's automatic, well rehearsed answer.

"What's skill number one?"

"Trust no one, sir."

"Number two?"

"Be alert."

They went through the list of Charlie's Eight Commandments. When she'd finished, Charlie took a step back.

"Those are all right," he said, "You've learned them correctly. In this past week, you've loaded, fired and taken care of your weapons correctly. You hit the target, which is what I expect you to do. That was correct. You've answered all my questions correctly and you've learned all I told you correctly. You've done everything I've asked you to do correctly. There was only right and wrong. Am I correct?"

"Yes, sir."

"When I ask for perfect, is less than perfect correct?"

"No, sir, less than perfect would be wrong."

"Then why would I compliment you on perfect? If it was not perfect, it was wrong. Am I right?"

"Yes, sir," Cam wanted to smile.

"You've picked locks before, haven't you?"

"Yes, sir."

"Have you always been successful?"

"Yes, sir."

"Then you've always been correct."

"Yes, sir,"

Charlie walked around beside her but Cam continued to stare forward as he had always ordered her to do.

"Today, however, when you picked the lock, you did it very quickly with a minimum of movement and without marring the apparatus. You did it well. Was it the same as before?"

"No, sir," Cam allowed herself a deep breath.

"Was it better than before?"

"Yes, sir."

"Then, when I tell you you did it well, was I correct?"

"Yes, sir."

"Do we agree that right and wrong is totally different from good or bad?"

"Yes, sir."

Charlie walked around her and stopped in front. "Good. I'm glad we agree. Now, something else." He stared deeply into her eyes. "Do you trust me?"

"No, sir," Cam replied. "I trust no one."

"Then how do you know what I teach you is correct?" He stood back.

Cam hesitated. Was this another trick question?

"I'll answer for you," Charlie continued. "You know it's correct because you've thought about it and analyzed it. You trust that. Yes?"

Cam still hadn't moved. "Yes, sir."

"There will be times when you will have to put a certain amount of trust in someone. Someone to watch your back. Someone to be on your side. Someone to help you play your part. Yes?"

Cam licked her lips. Was he telling her to ignore the rules?

"You've got to make friends, allies. You won't survive without them. But will you trust them?"

"No, sir."

"Yes, you will. You'll have to. But you'll be selective." He stopped and studied her face. "Think about this. Think about it hard. Very hard."

He leaned back against the table.

"Everything you've learned here is still completely true. But you'll break each and every one of the rules. Many times over."

Cam felt his gaze burning into her.

"What will keep you alive," he continued, his voice still hard, "will be how you break them. You'll have to trust someone sometime, but you'll select who and when. You'll have to, just to survive. But you'll never trust them completely. You'll never let them know who you really are. You'll lose control. But just to show that you're human. You'll show your anger. But just because everyone else will be angry. You'll be angry and you'll have to vent it or it'll eat you alive. You'll let someone do something for you, you'll fall in debt, but not to the extent that they own you." He stopped. "Do you understand?"

Cam swallowed. "Yes, sir," she said softly, slowly.

"But you won't forget those rules, will you." It was not a question.

"No, sir."

"Then what are they?" He stood up in front of her.

Cam recited the eight rules, confidently.

"Remember them. What are they?"

Cam repeated them.

"Now, there's one other thing we need to discuss." He stopped. He'd hoped that he wouldn't have to do this, that Michael would have done something, but he knew that Michael still did not sleep in her own room and he'd seen no change in the way Cameron reacted, or rather, deferred to Michael and that disturbed him. He knew he had to act. "You've been, well, I guess your term would be, 'having sex' with The Mistress, have you not?"

Cam looked at him. What business was it of his what she and Michael did together? What right did he have…

"Answer my questions, maggot," he demanded, stepping up into her face, "See where they're headed before you get your back up about what right I have to talk about such things. Answer my questions. Have you been 'having sex' with The Mistress? Yes or no?"

"Yes, I have." Cam answered, defiantly.

"*Sir*," Charlie reminded her.

"*Sir*," Cam threw back at him.

"You've let her fuck you?" Charlie began his incessant pacing.

"Yes, sir." Cam really did not like this line of questioning.

"The way she likes to fuck? With handcuffs and strap-ons and other toys?"

Cam swallowed. "Yes, sir."

"And you've enjoyed it." That was not a question.

"Yes, sir."

"Is it something that you'd tried before?"

"No, sir."

"Then, it was a new experience for you and you liked it."

Charlie wheeled around when Cameron did not answer.

"I will take your silence as an affirmation," he continued as he paced again. "And have you made love to her?"

"Yes, sir, and I've enjoyed it."

Charlie stopped and turned on her. "Have you made love to her? Or have you fucked her, the way she fucks you?"

Cam hesitated. She and Michael had spent every night together over the past week. Each night becoming more and more intense, their lovemaking taking on more and more power. But, no, her lovemaking to Michael had been nothing like Michael's lovemaking to her. She'd only been on the receiving end of Michael's paraphernalia. She thought back to yesterday, to the discomfort she'd had sitting through her training, her butt still tender from the spanking Michael had given her the night before.

"Let me assume, here, that your hesitancy to answer says that it hasn't been as reciprocal, power-wise, as it could be." Charlie added before she could answer, "Am I correct in my assumption?"

"Yes, sir," Cam's answer was less defiant.

"Then, taking the assumption one step further, we can say that she is your Mistress and you are her Slave." Charlie watched as the thought rolled through Cam's mind. "Can we then say that," he stepped up into her face again, "if some god-damned bulldyke," his voice was becoming harder and rougher, "walks up to you in prison and demands to have you, you belong to her?! You just go belly up to the first powerful butch that presents herself? Is that correct?"

"N-no, sir," Cam stammered.

"You simply surrender to the first dominant fist that rams your ass and let her own you? What have I been teaching you here? Have you listened to anything I've been saying? What the hell have we been doing for two and a half weeks? Are you so stupid that you're totally without a clue to anything we've talked about? Do I have to spell each and every step for you? Can you see no relation between things?"

More angry than she'd been in a long time, Cam whirled on her heel and stomped away.

"Wait, Cameron, don't go, yet."

Cam stopped. It was the first time Charlie had ever used her name and the first time she'd heard the softer tone of his voice.

Suddenly his voice was gentle. "Relax a minute. Come back and sit down."

Hesitantly, she turned and slowly walked back, dropping onto the bench. His accusations still ricocheted through her head.

"Have you fallen in love with Michael?" he asked softly.

Cam looked up into his face. It was a question she'd asked herself all week.

"I...I don't know," she admitted.

"Have you discussed this with Maggie?"

Cam shook her head.

Charlie sat down next to her and put his arm around her shoulder. "Cameron, I know I've been exceedingly rough on you. I haven't given you the luxury of knowing what my rules really are, but it's because I want you to be on top of everything. I want you thinking every minute. I want you to succeed. I...I don't want to have to attend your funeral. You know that, don't you?"

"Yes, sir." Cam's answer was soft.

"Michael and I have been friends for years," he said, "I know her power over women. Hell, I admire it! I wish *I* were half as lucky." He smiled as he released his hand from her shoulder. "I just want you to know what you're doing. I'm not asking you to change anything at all in your relationship with her, I just don't want you to fall into the same pattern inside a prison. It could be deadly. You don't want to become the property of anyone. You want to remain your own person. Yes?"

Cam nodded. "Yes," she replied, thoughtfully.

"Cam, You've done remarkable work these past two weeks. I've been amazed at the strides you've made."

Cam looked at him, surprised. "Thank you, Charlie," she smiled.

"Don't let down, kid," he was back to his old self, "There'll be no 'time out' in prison. It'll be twenty-four hours a day, seven days a week for as long as it takes. Be on your toes. Remember everything you've learned here."

"Charlie..." Cam started. He just waited for her to go on. "Charlie, has Michael said anything to you about this?"

"No, why?"

"I was just wondering..." She let her question hang in the silence.

"Ask her," Charlie was guessing what Cam wanted to know. "She doesn't always say what she wants, emotionally, but if it's just a nice diversion to her, she'll tell you. But, Cam, I have to warn you, she doesn't let many people get close. She has a best friend and me and her brother. Other than that, no one knows the real Michelle Gauchet."

"But I know she's had a lot of lovers."

"No, she's had a lot of *tricks*. One-nighters. Only one lover, eight years ago, no one since. I love her dearly, but I can't tell you to be hopeful. I keep hoping that one day, someone...someone with the same intensity, the same power..." He took a deep breath, "I would be very happy if it were someone like you."

"Thank you, Charlie," she patted his knee, "I appreciate your concern."

"Concern? Hell, I got a reputation to protect." He let his head fall back as his voice took on its boastful tone. "I haven't lost a trainee yet, I don't want to start with you. Get on your feet."

Cam stood at attention.

"What's skill number one?"

"Trust no one."

"Who told you that?"

"The Master Trainer, sir."

"The Master Trainer? And which one of us is The Master Trainer?"

Oh, shit, Cam thought, had he just backed her into another corner? "You are, sir," she answered tentatively.

"And what is a 'you'?" came the question Cam expected.

"It's a female sheep, sir."

Charlie stepped right up into her face, only this time, Cam saw a twinkle of humor in his eyes. "No, Ms Andrews," he said slyly, "it's a personal pronoun. Now, what's skill number two?"

* * * *

Maggie looked at the clipboard in her hands.

"Three more days. How do you feel?"

Cam lay back on the couch in the living room, watching the ceiling fan make it's slow revolutions above her.

"Maggie, I've never felt like this before. I'm sore but I'm happy. I'm sad but I'm excited. I want to get back and get started, but I don't want this to end."

"Charlie seems pleased. Has he spoken to you?"

Cam smiled. "Yes. We had a good talk today. I feel a lot better. I wasn't sure I liked him, but he's...he's wonderful. I underestimated him. He even warned me about Michael."

Maggie raised her eyebrows in question. "What about Michael?"

"About how she doesn't let anyone get close." Cam frowned. "About not expecting this to turn into a relationship."

Maggie shook her head. "Have you been?"

"No, I don't think I was expecting anything beyond this week."

"What about Michael? Has she?" Maggie asked.

"I doubt it. Especially after what Charlie said." Cam shook her head in amazement. "You know, if you'd told me a month ago that I'd willingly let myself get involved in strange sex, bondage of any kind, I'd have said that you were crazier than your patients."

A thought suddenly struck her and she sat up with a look of anger. "Is that part of the training, too?" she asked.

Maggie looked up in thought. "Have you asked Michael?"

Cam clasped her hands in front of her and pressed them against her mouth. "No. I didn't think to ask. I trusted her. Mistake number one. Trust no one."

"Do you really think she's doing it just to harden you? Do you think she

76

isn't sincere?"

"Oh, she's sincere. She's enjoying every minute of it." Cam rubbed her jaw thoughtfully. "Am I being paranoid?"

"Are you?" Why would Maggie never answer a question?

Cam stared at Maggie. "Have I been set up?"

Maggie looked at her thoughtfully.

"And don't answer my question with 'Do you think you have,' 'cause I'm not in the mood."

Maggie smiled at Cam's outburst and studied her before answering. "No," she said finally, "I don't think Michael would intentionally set you up, but maybe you're learning more than either of you thought. You should ask her."

"Maybe I should," Cam acknowledged.

Maggie watched as Cameron thought through her dilemma. Cam had changed during the past three weeks. There was a wariness that Maggie hadn't seen before, a level of control within her that hadn't been there. Maggie missed the small amount of innocence that she'd seen before, but the new Cameron, the self-assured, intense Cameron, was quickly becoming a solidly trained agent and Maggie was now assured that they had not made a mistake with her. She had a new confidence in Cameron Andrews. But part of her grieved for the young woman she'd first met three months ago. "Do you want to continue tonight? Or are you tired?"

Cam got up and started pacing. Maggie read that as the new level of anger being held in control.

"No, I'm not tired. But I need to think through some things by myself," Cam's voice was lower now, too. Much more forceful. "Maybe I should find out just what Michael's intentions really are."

* * * *

Cam poured herself a drink as she listened to the soft humming coming from the bathroom as Michael showered. Today, as yesterday and the days before, Michael had come to Cam's room as soon as Cam's final session with Maggie was over.

There had always been some conversation, perhaps over a glass of scotch or wine, and it always was the easiest, most effortless talk that Cam could remember. Even her banter with Pauly could be forced from time to time. She couldn't remember having a friend, never mind a lover, who was so easy to talk to.

Then there would be a new scene, some new situation Michael created as the setting for their sexual tryst. They'd tried new things that Cam had only read about and she found that the toys that Michael brought with her were wonderfully erotic and added even more pleasure to what Michael was teaching her. Cam found herself doing, and saying, things she wouldn't have even considered a week ago. This morning, she had found several small black and blue marks on her breasts and belly, where Michael's clips had tortured her the night before.

Last night, as they lay in bed, Cam had felt safe to admit, "You know, I always thought this type of sex was perverse and sick. My previous lovers have always been so gentle, so *loving*."

Michael had looked up at her from where she lay nestled against Cam's shoulder. "You don't enjoy being sick and perverse?" she asked.

"Is that what we really are?"

"So some say."

Cameron stared at the ceiling above the bed. Should she ask Michael what she was really thinking, or just let it go and chalk it up to a learning experience?

"Just when I think it can't get better, we turn a new corner," Michael had continued, resting her head back on Cam's chest. "Sometimes, I think we are going to explode. Maggie and Charlie will miss us and come to find us here in many tiny pieces."

They'd laughed about it and speculated on how their "pieces" would be identified. It had been one of the easiest, and enjoyable conversations they'd had.

Now, however, after her talks with Charlie and Maggie, Cam had decided that tonight had to be different. Tonight she would confront Michael and find out what was really happening. She would be the one to create the scenario.

She sat in the chair and waited for Michael to come out of the bathroom. Her drink was in her hand and she sipped it slowly, hoping that she'd have the courage to follow through on her plan, and that it wouldn't backfire in her face.

"Well, my sweet. Are you ready for tonight?" Michael walked into the room, clad only in a towel. "Perhaps you should begin by taking your clothes off for me."

"I don't think so." Cam said coolly, observing her over the rim of her glass.

Michael looked at her suspiciously. "What did you say?"

"I will not undress for you." Cam placed her glass on the table beside her.

"And is my little girl being a bad boy tonight?" Michael walked over and leaned down, placing her hands on the chair arms. "Is there some punishment that must be done?"

"Let's just say that I'm tired of playing *your* game. Let's play *mine* tonight." Cameron reached up and ripped the towel off Michael, leaving her standing naked in front of her.

"Oh, a very bad boy, indeed," Michael smiled.

Cameron put her bare foot on Michael's belly and pushed her back.

"I think that you're the one who's being bad tonight. In fact, you've been bad since we started all this. Perhaps I've let you get away with too much. Spare the rod, spoil the child. You have been behaving like a spoiled brat all week. This has been wonderful training, but I think *I'll* give the final exam this time."

Michael looked at her, perplexed. At first she showed a patronizing little smile which faded as she looked into Cam's face.

"I've had just about enough of it." Cam made her voice hard. "I've let you bully your way in here and I'm tired of it. I think you're the one that needs to be taught a lesson. You're the one that should be punished." Cam stood. "Get on your knees."

They were face to face. Michael's smile froze. She was suddenly unsure. She hadn't expected Cameron to try to take control. It had been years since someone had even tried to flip her, to make her switch roles. And even though she still stood a couple inches taller than Cam, the power in the woman standing in front of her made her stop. Had Charlie said something to Cam? Had he urged her to try this? What was happening?

"Very good, ma cherie. You make a wonderful attempt." She reached out to touch Cam's face.

Cam threw her hand aside. "I'm not playing, Michael. Get down on your knees. Now."

Michael hesitated. Cam's newly found power was exciting her.

"*Now*," Cameron repeated. "Don't make me say it again. What was it you said to me that first night? 'You ask people to put themselves in your hands every day, to trust you with their lives. Will you not do that yourself?'"

Michael hesitated still. No one had called her bluff like this in years. She knew that she was stronger than Cameron, but Cam's stance made her uncertain. This was a side of Cameron she hadn't anticipated. She looked into Cam's eyes and saw a determination she knew she couldn't, maybe didn't want to fight. Slowly she lowered herself to her knees.

"Very good." Cam strolled around in back of her. "A little slow, but I expect that will improve." She stroked Michael's hair. "That's being a good girl. Much better." She stood once more in front of Michael. "Now, down. On all fours."

Michael looked up at her incredulously but didn't move.

Cameron wove her hand into Michael's hair and pushed her head back to look straight into her eyes. "Can't you hear me? I said down. Hands on the floor, *garce*."

Michael looked at her with astonishment. Where had Cam picked *that* up, the French street slang for 'bitch?'

"Didn't think I knew French, did you. Well, I know that much. Now hit the floor before I get angry."

Michael slowly leaned forward. Cameron pushed her the final two inches until her palms were on the floor.

"Very good. Tres bien. Just stay like that." Cameron walked around behind Michael.

Michael was shell-shocked. What had come over Cameron? She hadn't expected any of this, but something in Cam's eyes made her afraid to disobey. Perhaps she had pushed too far, last night. Her mind raced. And her heart was beginning to pound. Her lips were dry. A combination of fear and excitement was overtaking her. No one had tried to dominate her in years. It was a new experience.

"I think you should spread your legs farther apart."

Michael glanced back over her shoulder, but couldn't quite see Cam. "Cam, I..."

"Quiet!" Cam's voice was harsh with authority. "You do not have permission to speak. *And* you do not have permission to address me in that fashion. Keep your eyes on your hands and keep your mouth shut unless I tell you to do something else with it."

Michael froze. She could hear Cam moving around behind her and heard dresser drawers open and close but she didn't move. She was aware that Cam was slowly walking toward her. Soon she was looking down at Cam's feet.

"I thought I told you to spread your legs, garce."

Michael attempted one last protest but Cam's foot on her shoulder stopped her. She acquiesced and widened the space between her knees.

"Excellent." Cam took her foot from Michael's shoulder and prodded Michael's left hand with her toe. "This hand. Play with yourself. Make yourself ready for me."

Michael slowly shifted her weight and tentatively reached down between her legs.

Cameron walked around her and sat on the chair directly in back of Michael. "Make it good. Make me want it. And don't make me wait all night."

Michael was starting to perspire. She wasn't used to being in this position. She'd given up control. She knew she could just stand up and walk away at any time, but something kept her riveted as she was. She reached into her crotch to rub herself. To her surprise, she was already wet.

Cameron watched for several minutes. Then finally she slowly knelt between Michael's legs and pushed them even further apart. "Don't stop now," she warned as she massaged Michael's buttocks and thighs. She reached around and her hands found the small nipples that were already hard and erect and rolled them between her fingers.

Michael's breath was beginning to become ragged and her body swayed in rhythm with Cam's stroking.

Cam reached back and took one of Michael's long, thick toys from her belt. Michael gasped as it sunk deep into her vagina.

"Fuck yourself on it. Take it all. Work for it." Cam demanded.

Michael began a slow rocking back and forth on the dildo that Cam held steady behind her.

"Slower," Cam demanded. "*I* set the tempo this time." She sat back on her haunches, placed one hand on Michael's ass and guided her back and forth along the smooth wand.

Cam felt the tension in Michael's body and increased the tempo. Soon Michael was humping back and forth with a frenzy.

Cameron pulled the stick away. Michael gasped.

"You made me beg. Can you beg?"

Michael's cunt was in spasms trying to grasp the emptiness. She swallowed hard.

"Please," she whispered.

"What? I didn't hear you."

"Please," Michael repeated, a little louder.

"Not good enough."

Michael shook her head back and forth. She was frantic.

Cameron smiled to herself. She knew what Michael was feeling. She'd been there every other night this week.

"Please, m…" she searched for the right word. She was The Mistress, not Cameron.

Cam smiled at Michael's distress.

"I am the dominatrix tonight. You will call me Mistress, tonight."

"Please, Mistress. Please. Fuck me." Michael's voice was still tentative.

"What?" Cameron demanded.

"*PLEASE FUCK ME!*" Michael's suppressed scream erupted.

Cameron laid the dildo on the floor and thrust all four fingers into Michael's cunt. Michael pushed back urgently. Cameron's own breath stopped as she felt the power of Michael's need surging against her. She felt her own body tense as she pushed and rubbed, then added her thumb to the part of her hand already emerged within Michael's wetness. With one last push from both of them, they gasped in surprise as Cam's whole fist sank into Michael.

Both gulped for air as Cam flexed and rotated her fist within Michael. Soon they were both pulsing at a frenetic pace. Both in spasms. Both women screamed and came together in a heap on the bedroom floor, gasping for air.

* * * *

Michael lay with her back to Cam. Both were still covered with sweat but not a word had been spoken in the last half hour. Michael had simply rolled away when their love making ended and, after the first few minutes, Cam had thought she'd fallen asleep. Now, from her breathing, Cam knew she was awake.

"Is something wrong?" Cam asked, softly.

Michael hesitated. "Maybe I'm just tired,"

Cameron sensed that that was not the full truth.

Something was wrong. Even in their morning workout and Hapkido training, Michael had been quiet, uncommunicative, as if her mind were elsewhere. Even their love making tonight had been a lot less energetic than usual. Michael seemed unwilling to set the scene and their conversation was strained. They'd fallen onto the bed almost out of habit, but the sex hadn't been inspired. Now, there was just silence.

Cam was puzzled. Since two nights ago, when Cam had topped her, Michael's attitude had changed. Was Michael angry because Cam had taken the lead? Tomorrow morning, the airplane would arrive to take them all back to San Juan to meet their flights to Baltimore and Montreal. There was so much to be said, but Cam didn't know where to begin and Michael wasn't helping.

Cam's emotions were in turmoil. All her training was telling her to just walk away, not to think about commitments, but her heart wanted very much to somehow secure the connection she'd made with Michael. It was a strange feeling she hadn't felt in a very long time. Why was this happening now?

"Will you be glad when all this is finished?" Michael broke the silence.

Cameron looked over at her. "Will you?"

Michael rolled onto her back and closed her eyes. "It's been a long three weeks. I am very tired."

Cameron studied her. What did Michael really mean by that? Was she longing to get out of here, away from her? Was she tired of Cameron? Damn, stay alert, keep in control.

"Well, only a half day more and we'll be through with this. It'll be back to the real world. Thank you for all you've taught me." The words were out before Cam had even thought about it.

Michael was silent.

The reality that this would all soon end was not something Cam wanted to think about. And there was this chasm between them, now, an obstacle that made talking very difficult.

"Cameron, I did not intend for it to come this far. I have—" Michael stopped herself.

Cam waited, hoping for a hint at what the rest of the sentence would have been. But Michael sat up and moved away from Cameron.

Perhaps Charlie had been right. She'd allowed herself to become too comfortable with Michael. She'd wondered, worried, how this would end. Now, she was unsure of herself. It was taking every ounce of her new self-control to keep from expressing her feelings for Michael.

"I have been very unprofessional," Michael said, as if she felt she should apologize for something. "I—" The sentence hung unfinished.

Unprofessional? thought Cam. The word made her bristle. "You don't always fuck your students?" The tone in Cam's voice cut harshly. More than she intended.

Part of Cameron wanted to hold Michael in her arms, be held in return and never let go. But she had become vividly aware, today, after her session with Maggie, that this was the beginning of her new assignment. There would be no liaisons, no comfortable relationships for quite a while. The prospect of being on her own had never scared her before, why was it bothering her now?

Cameron studied Michael's face which was turned slightly away from her, their eyes not meeting. How far had Michael wanted it to go? Did Michael have a hidden agenda? Suddenly, all the openness and trust she'd felt for Michael drained away. Maybe it was Charlie's training, maybe it was…maybe she was afraid of her own feelings.

"You surprised me with your power," Michael admitted softly.

"Really." Was that what she thought? Cam was suddenly sure that Michael had something else to say. "I thought that's what you'd want, for me to show you how much I learned."

Michael quickly glanced at Cam. "I was not testing you," she uttered, her voice still soft, but with a slight edge. "I just did not expect you to be so…powerful."

Cam stiffened. Had Michael expected her always to be a submissive? "Was it too much?" It was ironic that Michael had pushed her beyond her limits yet now seemed so reticent to let her enjoy it. "Don't you think I'll need that in prison?"

"No, not too much for prison. I…I applaud what you've learned." Michael was still unable to meet her eyes and her voice was becoming harsher.

"Charlie is very good at discussing power, but you have been excellent at teaching it." Cam suddenly wanted to lash out at her. Or did she just want to lash out at the situation? She'd been so well behaved, so compliant all week. What was she feeling? If she'd met Michael two months ago, would she have volunteered for this assignment?

Michael stiffened. Her own anger smoldered. "You learn quickly. I'm sure you will have no problems at all inside the prison. If you remember your lessons, I'm sure you'll be able to get anything you want."

"I just hope I can remember it all." A trace of sarcasm was sneaking into her tone.

"You *will* remember what you have learned these past weeks. I think your training will work well for you."

"All of my training?" Cam asked, letting the emphasis remain on the all.

Michael winced as if struck sharply. Cam felt the anger in her own question. Well, to hell with it, she thought. If this meant nothing to Michael, then it would mean nothing to her. She stared into Michael's eyes, but for the first time since they met, she was unable to read their meaning.

"I have always believed," Michael said with a bravado that seemed out of place, "that knowing your own power is the most valuable thing you can learn. If you know how much you have, how much you can use and even how much you can relinquish, you have a control that no one can take from you. I think you have learned that, Cameron. It will be your greatest asset in prison."

Cameron bristled. She knew that Michael was being complimentary, but it also sounded like Michael was classifying their lovemaking on the same scale as their martial arts training. Maybe it *was* just a casual fling to Michael. Damn! Why had she fallen for that?

"I have also believed," Michael continued, "that if you want something, you should just go after it. Too many people spend their lives worrying about the things they never do. They die regretting it. It is a waste of time. If you want it—do it. It is better to be sorry for something you have done than to regret something you haven't done. I wanted to…" Was she about to say 'make love?' "…be with you from the minute I first saw you. I am not sorry we have. Now I feel confident that you will succeed within the prison. You have the strength to survive."

Cam took notice of Michael's terminology. This time she had not misinterpreted Michael's meaning. It had been just that, having sex, not making love, not being intimate. And if Michael was so sure about just going after whatever you wanted, then obviously, she didn't want any more from Cameron or she'd just say so. "Does either of us have to ask forgiveness?"

Michael just shook her head, trying to keep her anger out of her voice. "I don't see why we should. You are a good…" Lover? What? "You are very good."

Cameron studied Michael's body language, aloof, withheld, distant. "I'm glad you don't have anything to regret," she heard herself say as she felt her stomach tighten. There were so many things she wanted to say to Michael. So many things to tell her. To ask her. But how? She was angry at Michael for not being able to handle that the tables had been turned, and at herself for feeling the need to turn them.

"Yes, you have been a very good student," Michael repeated.

Maybe, thought Cam, this is my biggest test. If I could go through this next night without telling Michael that I've fallen in love with her, then maybe I've become a good enough actor to pull off this undercover assignment.' She listened to her own thoughts. Where had that word love come from? Slowly the moment passed.

"Thank you for all you've taught me. You've done your job exceedingly well," Cameron muttered as she got out of bed and walked into the bathroom.

Chapter Ten

"Who's Harley out front?" Detective Steve Krakowsky asked as he walked into the Detectives' Office.

"Mine." Cameron smiled at him.

"Nice. Nice. Damned fine garbage truck," referring to the extra dash panel and hard sided saddle bags. "Must've cost a bundle."

"I got a good deal on it." Cam didn't look up from the report she was typing. She had a lot of paperwork to catch up on. Her workload hadn't stopped just because she'd taken the past three weeks off.

"You bought a Harley?" Russ stared at her with a look of suspicion in his eyes. "Come on, Radcliffe, where'd you get that kind of money?" He knew she didn't make that much unless she was getting a whole lot more than him. Of course, she didn't have a wife and two kids to take care of.

"I had it put away. Some money my folks left me. Just decided to spend it 'stead of letting it sit in a bank. Might as well enjoy life."

"Hell. You take a three week vacation in Puerto Rico, and then you buy new clothes *and* a Harley! Your folks must have been loaded."

"They had enough," was non-committal.

"Well, next time you want to blow some of it, take me along. Marie's always saying I dress like a slob." He went back to his report. Cam watched him for a moment. The "up front" money Deems had given her had paid for her new clothes and bike. And the vacation in Puerto Rico...well, she still couldn't prove she hadn't been there.

Poor Russ. Cam knew she was using him and she wanted to take him for a drink and spill her guts to him. She still didn't feel right lying to him. But he couldn't know what was really happening. Her life could depend on what he did or didn't say about what she was about to do.

She looked back at her report, beginning to feel guilty. She didn't want to leave too much for Russ to have to wade through when she was no longer his partner. Maybe tonight she'd take him out for a ride on the Harley. Now, she thought, I'd better get some use out of it before they have to take it away from me. I wish it really were mine.

* * * *

Russ had Bob Smythe (if that *was* his name) sweating. He and Cameron had scored a big bust. A level above what they usually reeled in. No nickel and dime bags this time. The guy had a trunk full of cocaine and enough cash to choke a mule. *And* they'd caught him dealing to three small time pushers. Four busts in one night, and almost by accident. They'd actually just been tailing one of the pushers, on a tip from an informant, hoping to catch him in the act. Now, here was this Bob guy, not answering a single question, just sitting here asking to talk to his lawyer. Maybe he should get Cameron in here and let her play "Good Cop," see if Bob would spill something.

"I want to talk to my lawyer," Bobby was saying for the umpteenth time when Cam walked into the interrogation room.

"Bob Smythe, or should we say R.J. Smith, or maybe Al Smith, Jr., or Allen Roberts, or maybe even Bobby Lee Allen."

Bobby looked up at her. Then repeated, "I want to talk to my lawyer."

"Your prints came up on the computer nice and neat. North Carolina was really interested," Cam continued as she placed a file in front of Russ. "We caught you holding eleven kilos of cocaine and ninety-six hundred dollars in cash. Two of the kids you sold to are willing to trade you for a suspended sentence. It's only their first offense. This is your, what, twenty-eighth, twenty-ninth? We're waiting for the report to come back from Raleigh/Durham. Want to add anything?"

Bobby was staring at her, trying to figure something out. Finally he said, "I want to talk to my lawyer."

"You should have stayed with that Berlitz course a little longer. They'd have taught you more than one sentence."

"I want…"

"Yes. We know," Cam interrupted. "Russ, you did remember to Mirandize him, didn't you?"

"Just as eloquently as possible."

"Good. Let's get a phone for him."

* * * *

Bobby sat with his lawyer in a tiny conference room outside the cell block where he'd been held for the last thirty-six hours.

"Well, Bobby, we're looking at twelve to twenty first off. They got an airtight case and with your record…well, I just wish we had something to trade."

Bobby had been thinking about it ever since she'd said it. It didn't add up. He'd kept good track of what he had; he was a good businessman. And they couldn't have overlooked it. It'd made him mad at first, but he knew enough to hold his tongue. Now he was too fidgety to sit still.

"Abe. Something's buggin' me. How much did they say I was holdin'?"

Abraham Siegel looked at the report copy in front of him. "Eleven kilos of cocaine and ninety-six hundred in cash."

"That's what I thought she said. It don't make sense. I keep good track of what I have. I should'a had thirteen ki's and almost twelve thousand dollars. Somebody must be holding."

"Think we got a bad cop?" Abe studied Bobby. Bobby had always been square with him in the past and Abe knew just how dirty Bobby really was. Abe had even gotten Bobby off on a couple charges he thought were airtight. But, he'd never seen Bobby this agitated.

"One of those two that busted me musta kept some for themselves. Probably figured I wouldn't complain. Who filed the report?"

Abe looked at the bottom line of the page in front of him.

"Cameron A. Andrews."

"That's the broad. I knew it. The guy was too dumb to stiff me. Unless they're in this together."

Abe brightened. "We may have an angle here," he muttered. "Don't mention this to anyone else. I'll talk to Internal Affairs tomorrow. Sit tight. We may have found the key to get you out of here."

* * * *

Steve sat on the edge of Cam's desk. "So, when you gonna let me borrow your bike?" He'd asked the same question at least twice a day since she'd gotten the Harley.

"Give it up, Krakowsky."

He leered. "I will when you will."

Cam smiled sweetly at him. "What's the temperature in Hades?"

"Then how about a ride? Tomorrow's Saturday, you and me. We'll go up through Pennsylvania, pack a picnic lunch and a blanket. Talk about powerful machines between our legs."

"Get off my desk." Cam had heard it all, and put up with most of it, even when she was seething underneath.

"Come on. You gave Russ a ride and I've seen you tooling around town with that pansy from the 7th Precinct on back. What? He's got something I ain't got?"

"Yeh, a brain," Cameron fumed. He was really pushing the limits now. "Get. Off. My. Desk." She articulated each word. "Is there some word here that you're not familiar with?"

"You molesting my partner?" Russ had just come through the office door.

"I wish." Steve sauntered back toward his desk. "Probably be the best she's had in a long time."

Cam turned and threw her stapler at him which missed his head by just a few inches, but clanked noisily against the file cabinet, leaving yet another pronounced dent.

"I wouldn't count on that, from what I've heard." Russ laughed at him as he dropped a white bakery box on Cam's desk. Definite grease stains were seeping though the bottom.

"These better be chocolate covered," Cam said ripping the tape off the box lid. She picked out the biggest donut and took a bite. Steve reached over her shoulder and grabbed one, but made his escape before she could pick up her letter opener.

"Who's the 'suit' in the Captain's office?" Russ asked, taking a cinnamon covered cruller.

"Someone from upstairs," Steve offered. "Word has it that the Captain's up for a promotion."

"God, I hope not," Cam said. "I just got used to him. I hate getting used to new bosses. It always means more paperwork." But she had a good idea who the person in Shafer's office was, or at least *why* he was there. She'd heard from Craig that his sources saw Bobby's lawyer talking to Internal Affairs yesterday afternoon.

The plan was getting in gear. Hopefully, it would kick in before she died from the suspense. The last two months of waiting were beginning to work on her nerves. She didn't know how many more nights of tossing and turning her body could withstand.

* * * *

Cam met with Maggie again late that night. The files lay open on the dining room table, the pages spread across the surface, just as she'd left them. Once again, as she had every night for the past two weeks, Cam had gone through the reports that had been compiled from Fran Wilson's and Kathy Sheldon's attempts at breaking the drug ring in Hagerville. Photos of the three people, two guards and one inmate, believed to be at the pinnacle of the ring, sat on the top. The faces, and their names, were burned into Cam's memory. They were the three people she had to watch most closely and they were the three she had to be most careful of. It wouldn't be long before Frank Briscoe, Antonia "Tony" Hernandez and Ruth Tarlow would be more than pictures in a file. So, each night she read every word of the reports, fearful that she'd miss something, that some clue she needed would slip past her.

She still spent most nights at Maggie's even though they'd both agreed that any training was now completed. Maggie had become the source of her confidence, her check with reality.

"How do you feel?" Maggie asked as she sat with her vodka in front of her. The lights were low in the room and the curtains opened to see the lights of the city around them.

"How should I feel?" Cam asked, standing at the window, not drinking the scotch in her hand.

"Why are you answering my questions with other questions?"

"Was I?"

Maggie laughed. "I'm glad this waiting is almost over. We're both nervous wrecks. Come sit down." Maggie patted the couch next to her. "We won't have many more nights like this, I'm afraid. I'll miss you."

Cameron walked around the couch and sat down, then turned her body and laid down with her head in Maggie's lap.

"I'll miss *this*." Cam's gesture took in the whole room. "You've been a great friend, Maggie. I feel closer to you than I've ever felt with anyone. Sometimes I wish we really were lovers, like all my friends think. I feel very much at home with you."

"Yes," was all Maggie replied.

"But I guess you're supposed to make me feel that way. That's your job."

Maggie took Cam's face in her hand and tilted it up to look at her. "Don't get carried away with your 'trust no one' philosophy. Yes, it is my job, but that doesn't make me any less sincere. I care about you a great deal. If I didn't honestly believe you were right for this, I'd pull you out so fast your teeth would clatter. I do worry about you. I'm…I..," she let the sentence drop.

Cameron closed her eyes, feeling the warmth from the lap under her head. Maggie's hand slowly brushed through Cam's hair. Silence emphasized the tension in the room and Cam melted into each touch of Maggie's hand, feeling herself drifting.

It was Maggie who spoke next. "Have you heard from Michael?"

Cam scowled. "No, I don't expect to," she answered evenly. "She did her job. I hope she was paid well."

Maggie looked at her with astonishment. "Cameron—"

"It's all right," Cam cut her off, "I got what I needed. I feel secure that I have skills to take with me. I've never been able to see the link between sex and power. The *take*, as well as the *give*. Michael sorted it out for me. There were parts of me I didn't know I had."

Maggie started to respond, but again Cam cut her off. "I really don't want to get into it. Not tonight. Especially not tonight."

Maggie thought this through. It was the first time that Cam had actually refused to discuss anything with her. Usually, when a difficult subject arose, Cam would sidestep or change the subject, but Maggie was usually able to lead her back on course. Tonight, she knew she couldn't. She had to consider that Cam was changing, was becoming more self-sufficient, more…what? hard?

It was a hard decision for her. And for Maggie, one of the few times she was at a loss. It had been several days since Michael had called. Maggie thought she had talked Michael into calling Cameron right away. There were many unresolved issues that she knew they needed to talk about and she'd encouraged Michael to make the first move. Obviously she hadn't. So now, should she tell Cam what she knew about Michael's feelings? Or should she let Cam and Michael sort it out themselves. And if Michael hadn't called Cameron, why? Had Michael changed her mind? And if Cam knew that Michael was a possibility, how would that effect her work? Would she still want to go through with this assignment? The professional CIA agent in Maggie said "Leave this alone. You're just asking for trouble," while the caring friend in Maggie said "Let her know that Michael really cares." The psychiatrist that was Maggie just sat back and shook her head.

Maggie finally decided it would be best to change the subject for the moment. "You haven't told me about your weekend in Boston." Cameron had gone home last weekend.

"It was hard. Lori and her family live in the house we grew up in. There's an old safe in the room that used to be Mom's study. I had her put some things in it, Mom's necklace, Dad's watch, Ben's medals, my medals. You know, things I don't want to get lost while I'm away. There's also an envelope with the instructions that it only be opened in the case of my death. It explains everything to her just in case. I hate holding anything back from her. I never have. I wanted to tell her everything"

"Did you?"

Cam shook her head. "I just told her that whatever she heard about me, she'd have to trust me and know that I knew what I was doing. It was asking a lot of her."

"I know. It is hard."

Cameron sat up and turned to look Maggie in the face. "Promise me one thing. Please, Maggie. As my friend, not as my shrink or my control." Cam was her former self again.

"What, honey?"

"If anything happens to either of my grandmothers, please, I don't want them to die thinking I'm a loser."

Maggie looked at the panic in Cam's face. "I can't promise that, Cameron. You know that."

"Please, Maggie."

She pushed the hair back off Cam's forehead and looked into pleading eyes. "I'll think of something. Hopefully the occasion won't arise."

"Thanks, Maggie. I know it's a lot to ask."

Maggie smiled. "It's okay. Relax. Everything will be taken care of."

"Am I supposed to be this scared?"

"I don't see why not. Your whole life is changing. A lot of things you took for granted will never be the same."

"I almost called Michael." Cam's confession surprised Maggie.

"And?" Maggie didn't want to push, but if Cam were really ready to talk…

"And what? What the hell would I say to her? She did her job. She did it very well."

Maggie remained silent.

"You saw her at the airport," Cam continued. "Just a handshake and a *good luck*. Nothing."

"What did you say to her?"

"I thanked her for the training."

"Do you think she might have expected more?"

"More?!" Cam's anger exploded. "I gave her everything she asked for. And then some."

"Do you want to see her again?"

"When, Maggie? When do I have time? I'm going to get arrested tomorrow night. I'll probably spend the next year of my life in prison. By the time I get out, I'll just be another rusted notch on her belt." Cam's level of frustration was getting higher and higher.

"Do you really think so?"

"Would it matter?" Cam sank back down onto Maggie's lap. "Yes, I would love to see her again. I just don't think Michael is an option." The silence stretched on for several minutes.

Cameron waffled. Should she ask the next question?

Maggie saw the hesitation in Cam's face. "What is it, sweetie?" she asked.

"Will you hold me? Just for tonight?" Cam whispered.

Maggie reached out and drew her into her arms.

Chapter Eleven

Cam cleaned and checked her police revolver for the third time. Since she'd left the office at seven, she hadn't known what to do with herself. She wanted to call Maggie or Pauly, but stopped herself every time she wanted to pick up the phone. She knew that tonight was The Night. The 'suits,' as Russ called them, had been around for two weeks and Cam knew they'd been watching her closely. She'd even seen a dark burgundy car parked on the corner when she came home and the restaurant on the next block suddenly had a new car parking valet. She knew her apartment was being watched. Her phone was probably tapped too. If she really were a thief, as they suspected, she'd just curl up at home with a good book for the next few weeks until this all blew over, but she had a job to do. Tonight was the perfect time. The eve of a big holiday when everyone wanted to celebrate, tonight was the night she had to get herself arrested.

She thought about driving over to Maggie's, but she and Maggie had finalized their parting this morning over breakfast and she didn't want Maggie to think she'd gotten cold feet. She knew Maggie still had confidence in her and didn't want to jeopardize that trust.

So. Here she was, walking around her apartment for what might be the last time. She stopped to touch each painting, each memento. She'd chosen every piece carefully since she'd found this apartment two years ago. Now she had to give it all up. Pauly had already asked if he could move in and she'd agreed, but this would never be *her* apartment again.

She took a deep breath as she opened the top drawer of her desk. There, neatly laid out, were a dozen small ziplock bags of cocaine, a gram each, a larger bag holding half the kilo she'd swiped from Bobby Lee's stash, razor blades, a small scale, some plastic straws and several small squares of aluminum foil. She reached into the back of the drawer and withdrew a five by eight manila envelope. From it she took two wrinkled hundred-dollar bills, four twenties and a fifty. It hardly deflated the envelope. She knew there was still three-thousand-seven-hundred and seventy dollars left plus the full kilo in the bottom drawer. After she'd reported her stolen stash to Craig, he'd deducted the price of the motorcycle, the new clothes she'd bought and a few other incidentals, then provided her with everything in the drawer in exchange for half the first kilo. It all looked so neat and clean, like she'd sold the first half, paid her bills and was about to sell the rest. She hoped it also looked like she might have been doing this on a smaller scale for quite a while.

Cameron looked at her watch. It was only ten o'clock. Not quite time to hit the road, yet. She picked up the new black leather jacket she'd bought just that afternoon. Holding it to her face, she inhaled the smell of the new leather and she smiled. The smell of leather had come to mean power to her and that also brought Michael to mind. Her body reacted with a quick surge of heat. The thought of Michael brought a frown to her face. Why wait until eleven? she thought. Now's as good a time as any to get this over with. She clipped her holstered gun in the back of her belt, put on her jacket, put some samples of coke repackaged in foil and money in her pockets, picked up her bike keys and left the apartment without looking back.

* * * *

As she rode down Lafayette Avenue, the chilled wind on her face shook her from her self pity and determination. Damn it! she thought, I don't need this. This is too much to ask of anyone. I should just turn around, grab the rest of the money and hit the highway for Montreal. I could be there in twelve hours. Shit, on this baby, I could be there in eleven. Even if Michael won't take me in, I'll be in another country! I can just keep going. No one'd ever find me. Look how many draft dodgers still haven't been found!"

But she rode on, without turning, toward the punk bar she'd explored earlier in the month.

* * *

She pulled into the parking lot beside the bar. It was poorly lit and one or two couples leaned against cars, talking, touching each other. Cameron was glad this was not a gay bar. Deems had chosen this bar himself. They knew that the owners did everything they could to keep drugs off the property and even called the police when they knew something was happening. But the clientele was young, just at the minimum drinking age, and other things besides drinks and phone numbers were exchanged there. The kids, though, knew that the bar would get closed down if any drugs were found there, so the traffic either went on in the back alley or behind closed bathroom stall doors. No one'd been busted there in over a year.

The bright strobe lights off the dance floor assaulted Cameron as she walked into the darkened room. Donna Summer was screaming from the overhead loud speakers as she approached the bar and ordered a beer. She pushed her hair back and realized she was sweating. It was hot in the bar and the smokey air was stale. She decided to take her jacket off. Before she did, she slipped her gun out of her belt and hid it in the jacket pocket. Checking to make sure that all the pockets were zipped, Cam let the jacket hang from her left hand as she turned and leaned back with her elbows on the bar. The foamy mug of beer was in her right hand. She searched the mangle of bodies that throbbed like one giant amoeba on the dance floor.

"Hi, hon," a sweet little voice said into her left ear after just a few minutes. "Where you been hiding?"

Cameron turned her head and looked into the face that couldn't possibly be in here without a fake ID. The face's name was Allison.

"Not hiding, just restocking." Cameron smiled. She'd been in this place three or four times in the last two weeks and on her first night here had met Ally and her friend Chris in the ladies room. After she'd shared her coke with them, they'd become her best friends and a few nights later had introduced her to their boyfriends Bill and Danny. She'd partied with them in the back alley and the boys had bought two or three grams from her. She'd also given the girls another gram to share.

"Ooh! Then let's party!" Ally squealed as she pranced past Cameron, her short miniskirt just hiding her thin young butt.

Cameron placed her half-empty beer mug back on the bar and followed Ally down the dark corridor, past the restrooms and out into the back alley. Even though it was still hot outside, Cam stopped in the hall and put her jacket back on. Making sure no one was behind her, she placed the gun back in her belt before she went through the door.

A lithe blond in a long flowing dress cheered as Cam emerged into the back alley. "Candy Lady's home, kiddies!" Chris beamed, "Line up for treats!" She ran up and threw her arms around Cam's neck and gave her a big kiss on the cheek.

Cam watched as Bill and Danny exchanged smiles. Had they been speculating between themselves that she was looking to hit on one of their girlfriends. Maybe they even hoped she'd let them watch.

Okay, little boys, she thought, You want to see this? I'll go for broke tonight. With that thought, she held Chris tightly against her and turned her face to catch Chris' mouth in hers. Her long, rough kiss forced Chris' lips open and Cam slipped her tongue into the young woman's mouth as she ran her hand up and over one firm young breast, stopping to take the erect nipple between her thumb and forefinger.

Chris pushed against her, but Cam held her very tightly. Finally Cam loosened her grip and Chris took a step back. Cam looked her squarely in the eyes, her own eyes fiercely challenging. Chris' seemed unsure, surprised by her own reaction to Cam's kiss.

Cam grinned knowingly and Chris rose to the challenge. Her look became defiant and coy. "Ooh," she purred, "and what will Momma give me if I'm really good?" She danced just out of reach, moving to the pulsing music coming from the bar.

Cam chuckled and unzipped her jacket pocket. "I don't know. Who deserves some of this?" She withdrew a small foil packet from her pocket.

"Me!"

"I do!"

The four held up their hands like hungry school children. They'd played this game the last time Cam had been there and been rewarded with two lines apiece, free of charge.

"Wait." Cam closed her fist around the packet. "Who's she?"

There was a new face in the crowd. A fifth face. This one just as young and fresh, dressed in the same way, but somehow, oddly out of place.

"This is Terry. She's our new friend." Chris was again at Cam's side, holding onto her arm.

Cameron studied Terry. A new kid on the beat, she thought. A rookie. Fresh out of the academy. It was written all over her. First undercover, first bust, scared out of her mind. Probably thought I'd recognize all the regulars. At first she was insulted that the department thought she'd fall for such an obvious setup. She decided to play with Terry for a while. At the very least, Terry needed to be taught how to act like a good undercover cop before she got blown away on a real bust.

"You a cop?" Cam asked outright. If the kid was wired, the guys on the other end must be shitting in their pants.

Terry's eyes opened wide. "N-no," she stammered. "What makes you think that?"

"You look like a cop." Cam continued her stare.

"How would you know? How do I look like a cop?" Terry's voice wavered slightly.

"I know cops when I see them. You just look like a cop. I'm not giving this to a cop." The other four were beginning to get scared and slowly started to back away.

Go ahead, thought Cam, Talk your way out of this one.

Terry's face softened as the initial shock of Cam's statement raced through her. "Don't be silly." she smiled. "You're being paranoid."

"Shouldn't I be?" Cam asked.

Terry tried a stall tactic to get the four kids back on her side. "She ain't got no more stuff. You guys are full of it. This is some kind of joke. I'm going back inside." She walked past Cam toward the bar.

"Come on, Terry," Ally said. "She's just kidding. Aren't you?" she turned to Cam. "This is movie shit. Tell her you're just kidding." She was trying to salvage the situation. She wanted the coke Cam had, but she also didn't want to lose this new friend who had been so generously buying them all drinks.

"I wasn't kidding." Cam said. "Cops can be anyone. You never know. What if I were a cop?"

Danny and Ally exchanged glances. Cam wondered if they had considered that, but had written it off to being too scared of being busted and bounced out of school.

"Don't be silly. You're no cop." Chris hugged even closer to Cam. "I never been kissed like that by a cop." She looked boldly into Cam's eyes.

"How many cops you been kissed by?" Cam asked. "Okay, okay, enough playing. We're all getting paranoid."

Bill was starting to get a little shook by the interplay between Cam and his girlfriend. "Come on back, Terry. We're all just a little uptight."

Cam realized she'd pushed about as far as she could without blowing Terry's resolve. "You're right, children. I just get a little suspicious with new people."

Terry looked like she'd been given a reprieve from a death sentence. She turned and rejoined the group.

"Terry's okay," Ally assured her. "She's been hanging out with us all week. If she were a cop she could have busted us a long time ago."

Unless she were waiting for bigger fish, Cam thought. "Okay, Okay." She said aloud. "Sorry, Terry. What's your last name?"

"Does it matter?" Terry asked. She was beginning to get her confidence back.

"You don't know *our* last names." Bill piped in.

"How do you know that?" Cam glanced at him out of the corner of her eye, but kept her attention focused on Terry.

"Does it really matter?" Terry asked again.

"Sometimes." Cam said. "I take big chances to get this. I like to know where it's going."

"Then why are you just giving it away?" Terry's confidence had gotten the best of her. She thought she was on solid ground now. "Trying to get us hooked so we'll buy more and more from you?"

"Who said I was selling?" Cam's eyes still bore into her. She wanted to say "Don't blow it now, kid. You're almost home free. Just keep your mouth shut. Don't ask stupid questions."

Terry wouldn't let it go. "Bill said he bought some from you."

"Bill said that? And you believed him?" Cam wondered how much the kids knew about what was really going on here.

"Don't be so uptight, hon." Chris was getting antsy.

Cam suspected that Chris either wanted to get some coke or get out of here and get laid. Maybe she was beginning to wonder how hard it would be to get Cam to ask her home, but Cam knew Chris was more than willing to go home with Bill and fuck his brains out. She wanted to get moving. She didn't want to spend the rest of the night standing in the alley.

"Come on, relax." Chris massaged Cam's neck.

Cam handed her the foil packet. Chris snatched it and opened it carefully. She licked the tip of her finger, dipped it in the snowy white powder and rubbed it across her upper gums.

"Soooo goooood," she crooned, handing the foil to Ally. "Thank you, Momma." She kissed Cam again on the cheek.

"Here." Cam tossed a second pack to Terry. "No hard feelings."

"What about us?" Danny asked.

"Don't get greedy. Learn to share."

Terry was still standing holding the foil. Danny took it from her hand. He opened the foil and sniffed up a noseful through the short straw he'd had ready in his pocket. "Here. Try it. She always has the best stuff." He held the straw out to Terry who took it hesitantly. Cam snickered and turned as if to go back into the bar. Let Terry get herself out of this one.

"Wait, don't go. Stay and party with us." Chris pleaded. Bill had just put a small pile of coke on the back of his hand and blown it quickly into Chris' open mouth. Now the tingling freeze at the back of her throat was clearly beginning to give her a rush. She walked over and stroked the leather down the front of Cam's jacket.

"Yeh, this is good." Terry piped up, brushing her nose where the small residue of white powder remained. "How much you want for more?"

Cam thought, Maybe you just blew it—entrapment. The guys on the other end of your wire must be having heart attacks. Your impatience may have just cost you this bust. Cam took as step toward her. "More what?"

"You know. More of this. Cocaine."

Cam was tired of playing. She wanted to end this before Terry blew this up in all their faces. "How much you got?"

Bill, Ally and Danny were busy dividing up the remainder of the packets and Chris was pouting because Terry was getting all Cam's attention.

"Fifty?" Terry offered.

"Make it a hundred and I'll eightball it."

Terry looked at her questioningly.

"Discount. Three for two." Cam added.

"Yeh, sure." Terry fumbled in the purse that hung from her shoulder and finally offered Cam two new fifty-dollar bills. Cam took them and placed three small bags in her hand.

"Okay, I'm police. You're under arrest. Put your hands in the air." Terry suddenly pulled a gun from her bag, she held her shield in the other. The coke dropped to the ground. She quickly put the shield into her skirt pocket and held onto the gun with two hands.

"What the hell?" Danny looked up from the coke. Four pair of eyes shone widely in the dark. None of them had expected this.

Terry shouted as the adrenaline and coke raced through her veins. "You…" She waved her gun at Cam. "Put your hands on that wall and step back." She reached out and pushed Cam toward the wall. In that split second, Cam knew she could have swung around, decked her and been out of there. But she knew she had to go along with this now.

"Shit," was all she said as she leaned forward onto the brick wall.

She heard running footsteps and the back door of the bar slam as a police car, lights flashing, but siren silent, turned into the alley.

Chapter Twelve

Cameron had been in the small dark room dozens of times, but never on this side of the table. Usually she sat at one of the two empty chairs across the wooden table. And never without the freedom to get up and leave.

The walls, once institutional green were dingier than she remembered, dirty with layers of stale smoke. The windows, painted shut a half dozen times, were covered with mesh and there was a single light bulb that hung directly overhead, surrounded by a large saucer shaped cage that was dimmed by smoke and dust. Cam wondered why she had never noticed the small details before, but then, she'd never just sat here for, how long was it? An hour? Two?

She looked at her wrist where her watch usually was, but all that was there was a thin red line where the handcuffs had dug into her. She wiped her hands on the table. Her fingers were still greasy from the fingerprinting ink.

A pack of cigarettes lying on the table was the only other thing in the room. Cam usually only smoked as part of a cover, or when she was very tired or upset. Now seemed like the perfect time.

She turned to the large mirror that formed one wall. "Anyone got a match? I'd like a smoke." She asked the mirror, knowing it was a two-way and that she was being watched.

After a few minutes, a uniformed officer entered and lit her cigarette. He exited without a word.

Keep cool, she told herself. You've played this game before. You know what's happening. Just relax and wait it out. She took a long drag on the cigarette and sat back to wait

* * *

Captain Shafer entered the small observation room and joined the two police officers who stood by the plate glass mirror.

"How's she doing?" he asked.

"Ice," the male officer grunted. Shafer watched Cam take a last drag on the cigarette and stamp it out on the floor. To his well trained eye, she looked a little scared, but her body language betrayed that. She lounged back, relaxed and still. He knew that something had changed since she'd come back from vacation, but he'd never expected this. What had happened? What had gone wrong?

Officer Terry Koffman couldn't take her eyes off Cameron. "She knew I was a cop. How? And if she knew, why didn't she run?" she wondered aloud.

Shafer looked at her. "We'll find that out in a minute. Keep your eyes open and watch what's happening. You may learn something."

"We got enough from her apartment to seal this up," said a voice behind Shafer's shoulder.

"Come on. Let's get this over with."

Shafer followed the two I.A. Detectives into the Interrogation Room.

* * * *

Cameron looked up as the door opened. The two men who had been in and out of Shafer's office all week entered, followed by the Captain himself. Cam couldn't read Shafer's expression.

"Detective Sergeant Cameron Andrews," the taller of the two addressed her. "I'm Lieutenant Hal Richards, Internal Affairs." He flashed his ID. "And this is Sergeant O'Brien." They each took a seat across from her. Shafer receded into the corner. Cam did not meet his eyes.

"I don't think I need to explain procedures to you." Richards opened a file in front of him. "Would you like to give a statement?"

"I wasn't selling cocaine. It was entrapment."

Richards and O'Brien exchanged looks and O'Brien glanced toward the mirror he knew that Terry Koffman stood behind.

"You knew she was a cop. Why did you let yourself be set up? Did you want to get caught?"

Cameron shook her head with an ironic smile on her face. "I couldn't believe a real cop would be that ludicrous. I second-guessed myself. I couldn't believe you'd let a bungler like that out on the street."

O'Brien cleared his throat. That was exactly what he'd said to his partner earlier that night.

"You wanted to get caught."

Cameron sat up and looked at him incredulously. "You've got to be kidding."

"No. *You* got to be kidding. Your record's too good to have fallen for that. What are you pulling here?" Richards leaned forward.

Cameron sat back. "I was stupid," she said flatly as she crossed her arms in front of her chest.

"Where'd you get the coke?" O'Brien asked.

"On the street."

Richards took a sheet of paper out of the folder and turned it toward her. "This your signature?" he asked.

It was the arrest report for Bobby Lee.

Cam remained silent and still, her eyes on the paper.

"You wrote here that he was in possession of eleven kilograms of cocaine and ninety-six hundred dollars." He waited but Cam didn't move. "Allen says he had thirteen kilos and almost twelve thousand."

Again, Cam remained unmoved except to lick her dry lips.

After a minute, O'Brien stood. "Recognize this?" He emptied the card-board box he'd been carrying onto the table. Out rolled the contents of Cameron's desk drawers.

Silence filled the room.

Finally Richards spoke. "We have enough here to convict you on Possession and Distribution. There's also fairly substantial evidence for 'Grand Larceny: Theft of Government Property,' He paused. "You *do* know that the cocaine became government property the minute you arrested Allen. And we have 'Falsifying Police Records.' Shall I keep going?"

"It might be better for you if you made a statement," O'Brien added. "Admit it all now. Save the city some time and money. It'll go down better for you."

Cameron still stared at the table.

"How long you been skimming?" Richards asked. "This can't be the first time. You started spending big money about two months ago." He leafed through some papers in the file. "Took a vacation in the Caribbean, bought a Harley Davidson, lots of minor purchases." He looked up at her. "Want to explain the sudden availability of cash? We've checked your bank accounts. There've been no major withdrawals in the past three months. There have, however, been several deposits."

Cameron shifted her position. So, they had checked everything.

"We *can* stay here all night, if you like," Richards continued. Again, silence.

"Your partner was in on this with you." Richards' short, flat statement brought Cam's eyes to his.

"No. He knew nothing about this." Her voice was raspy from the tension. She cleared her throat and sat up, her elbows on the table.

"Then, you'd better explain the whole thing so we get it straight."

"I should have a lawyer," Cam said. "Let me call a lawyer and I'll make a statement."

Richards and O'Brien exchanged glances. "We've got enough here to book you," O'Brien said. "Get it over with. Make the statement and we can all get some sleep."

Cam rubbed her forehead and pushed her hair back; a nervous habit. She knew that once she'd asked for a lawyer they couldn't force her to talk without one present, but that it was their form of intimidation to keep trying.

Only silence followed. O'Brien started placing the evidence back in the box.

Shafer stepped out of the corner. "Let me talk to her alone."

Richards glanced at O'Brien, then stood and left the room. O'Brien was only a few steps behind him.

"Why?" Shafer stepped up to the table, but didn't sit. Cameron still hadn't met his eyes. "Just tell me that. Why?" His voice was soft, but an anger burnt around the edges. He stood looking down at her.

"For Godsakes," he said after a minute, walking around the table toward her. "Why? You had everything going for you. You'd have made lieutenant in another year or so. Hell, you'd have taken *my* job in a few years. What do you think of that? The first woman to reach Captain in the department's history! You were being groomed. I tried to teach you everything I knew!" His pacing became quicker. He stood in back of her now. "Just explain this to me!" He leaned over the back of her chair to spit the last into her ear.

Cameron cringed at his fury. She tried to swallow, but her throat was dry and tense.

Shafer strode around and sat across from her.

"Are you using? Are you hooked on the coke? Did using it in the line of duty get you strung out?"

Cameron stared at her hands. She knew he was trying to find some handle to help her with.

Shafer slammed his hands on the table and Cam jumped.

"Look at me!" he said between clenched teeth.

Cameron forced herself to look into his eyes. They studied each other in silence. Finally, in exasperation, Shafer pushed himself away from the table and began to pace again.

"You're not the woman I knew," he stated. "I don't know what happened to you on your vacation, but you're not the woman who sat in my office two years ago and swore she'd get every drug dealer off the streets even if she died trying. You're not the daughter who…"

Cameron slammed her fists into the table. She had to stop him before he took this too far. She tapped into the anger he'd just unearthed and let it surface, full blown. But she used the words that she'd rehearsed with Maggie. "I've been paying for my parents' deaths for the last ten years. I wanted something for *me!*" She forced herself to stare straight into Shafer's eyes, fist clenched, eyes wild. "I'm not strung out. I knew what I was doing. I just wanted more than a fucking bronze medal!"

Cameron was shaking. The anger, on top of the terror she'd felt all night, brought her to the brink of madness Before she could stop them, tears coursed down her face and she sank back into the chair, burying her head in her hands.

Shafer watched her for a moment. Maybe he wanted to reach out and offer comfort. Maybe if he had done that sooner, they wouldn't be here now. But it was too late. Not knowing what else to do, he turned and left the room before his guilt got the best of him.

Cameron, however, cried because of the hurt and compassion she'd seen in the eyes that had just burned into hers.

Chapter Thirteen

Cameron walked through yet another steel gate and heard the gate clang shut behind her. She'd hadn't thought the slam of the door would sound so loud. They never had before, but then, she'd always had the ability to turn around and have them opened back up for her. The eyes of the closed circuit cameras that scanned each corridor also looked larger now that she knew that someone was watching her. Was paranoia one of the things Maggie hadn't warned her about?

Three years, she thought. That's what the judge had agreed on. Three years each for possession and theft, to run concurrently. The other charges had been dropped in exchange for her cooperation. The Harley-Davidson and the new leather clothing had been confiscated as had the newly deposited money in her savings account. Three years. Cam knew that she wouldn't have to serve that long, but the prospect that loomed in front of her seemed insurmountable at the moment.

She remembered looking around at the spectators that day in court. Her eyes had met Russ' briefly, but he'd averted his, out of embarrassment or disgust or both. She'd wanted to reach out to him, to be able to talk to him. The look of abandonment and betrayal on his face was very obvious.

Marie had sat next to him, holding his hand, trying to give her support.

When the judge had adjourned the proceedings, Cam had looked for Russ, but all she saw was the back of his head disappearing out the door.

Now, as she walked into the cell block followed by M. Emerson, who'd been her shadow the whole morning, she looked around. It was an old facility. As they climbed the stairs, Cam could see that each floor was lined on both sides with thick steel bars; barred doors slid back to show doorways that faced each other. Cold, grey, dingy walls separated the small cells, each containing a bed and a toilet and sink. Some of the cells had been decorated with belongings that made it look a little more personal.

In her arms were a blanket and sheets, several shirts and pairs of pants, some underwear and a pillow. That, along with a toothbrush and the stiff cotton shirt and jeans she wore were all she had now.

"Come on, come on. This ain't the sightseeing tour. Move your ass." Emerson stopped at one opening.

"This is it. Your new house is C-332. C-Block, third floor, cell thirty-two. A-Block is administration, that's where you've been all morning. B and C are residences. Think you can remember that?" There was no expression on her face and Cam thought that she must be as bored by what they'd gone through in the last four or five hours as she was. "Gina. Fill the new kid, here, in on the rules," Emerson said to a thin woman with long blond hair that leaned against the wall just outside the cell. "You can be her mother for a few days." Then she turned to Cam. "Keep your nose as clean as a whistle, sweetheart. In case you haven't figured it out by now, your kind isn't highly liked in here, by the inmates *or* the C.O.s." She turned and walked back toward the stairs.

Cam walked into the cell and looked around. The young woman was just staring at her from the door.

"Hi." Cameron nodded, looking around the cell. It was smaller than the closet she'd had at home. Just big enough for the single bed, a toilet and small sink.

The young woman didn't speak, so Cam laid her armful of belongings on the bed.

"Put your clothes up on the shelf." The voice was soft, yet rugged, like a child with a cold.

"Sure, thanks." Cam acknowledged her.

"What did Emerson mean by that? What kind are you?"

Cameron stopped and took a breathe. She and Maggie had worked on these answers for days. "I used to be a cop."

Silence and Gina's eyes followed her as she scanned the cell. "What kind of cop?"

Cameron didn't look up at her. "A Narc."

Gina remained silent, evaluating Cameron. "Whatcha in for?"

Cameron returned her gaze. After a minute, "Selling cocaine."

Gina burst out laughing. "A narc getting busted selling cocaine. That was stupid." Cam grinned.

"Yeh. That was stupid."

Gina smirked at her in silence.

"What are you here for?" Cam asked, finally.

Gina studied her for a moment. "I robbed a store."

Cameron just nodded.

"Well, well. New blood!" a voice came from behind Gina. "Looks like we got the pick of the litter."

Cameron looked up. Three women stood in the door, leaning against the bars pushing past Gina.

"Yeh, the other two they brought in this morning were real dogmeat," agreed the one farthest from Cam. "Looks like you lucked out, Gina."

"Don't count on it." Gina turned and pushed her way through them and sauntered off down the hall.

The first watched her go, then turned her attention back to Cam. "Looks like you didn't score very high on her list."

"Looks that way," Cam agreed with her.

"You don't look straight. You butch or femme?" the question was direct. Cam ignored her.

"I think she's deaf," the second one whispered to the first.

"Maybe she is." The first woman took a step into the cell and stood next to Cameron who was putting her clothes on the top shelf next to the one small window. "Hey, New Blood. You deaf?" she raised her voice. "I asked you a question. You butch or femme?"

Cameron looked at her. What she'd been through that morning had left her in a worse mood than she'd been prepared for and she'd missed lunch. But on second thought, she decided not to get too smartmouthed, first impressions and all. "I'm sorry. I didn't realize you were speaking to me."

Shirley turned and smiled at her two companions. "Oh. Pardon me. I was speaking to you."

"She don't look too femme," the second woman entered the cell and slowly approached Cam. "You a big baby butch, Baby?"

Cameron scrutinized her carefully. "Why?" she asked.

"She sure don't like to answer questions, now, does she?" the woman at the door shook her head.

"You looking for trouble?" the first asked.

"No." Cam looked straight at her, but kept her voice level.

"What are you looking for?" the second asked.

"Just a little space. I've been pushed kind of hard this morning."

"Oh, poor baby butch. Don't you like those nasty old guards? Did Miss Emerson bother you? She can be such a bitch." The second woman reached up to push Cam's hair behind her ear, but Cam ducked out of the way.

"Cut the shit, Joany." A fourth woman stood at the door. "Give the fish a break. The C.O.s did push her hard this morning."

The three women took a mental step backward as the new woman pushed her way into the small room.

"My name's Lou." She extended her hand.

"Cameron," Cam acknowledged as she shook the firm rough fist. It was large and fleshy like it's owner.

"First or last?"

"What?" Cam didn't understand the question.

"Cameron. First name or last name."

"Oh. First. Cameron Andrews."

"Nice name." Lou turned to the other three. "See. She answers questions when they're asked right. You three turkeys, you need to be somewhere else, don't you?" It wasn't a question.

Joany and her two companions took the cue and left.

"Our welcoming committee needs a little work."

"They *are* a piece of work." Cam stood with her hands on her hips.

Lou smiled and snorted. "Yeh, I guess they are. You'll get used to them. They'll give you a hard time at first, but their attention span is short. They'll forget all about you when the next new blood comes in."

"Thanks for the warning." Cam licked her lips and looked around. "What's the protocol here? What's off limits?"

Lou dropped her five foot five inches of bulk onto the bed. "Free time is free time. You can go to the library or watch TV or just hang out. What's your work assignment?"

"Library. Eight to noon." Cam had been assigned to help with the reading program.

"Are you a teacher?"

"No. But I got a college degree so they thought I'd know how to read."

"Do you?"

"Read?"

"Have a college degree."

"Radcliffe, 1972"

"Nice school. You musta had money. I graduated City U., New York. Forget what year. It was a while ago."

Cam wanted to ask more questions, but knew she'd better back off for the moment. She sat down on the countertop that ran the length of the back wall of the cell behind the toilet.

Lou sized her up. "Lunch is at noon. The yard's open from one to four. Dinner's at five-thirty. Evening's are free time. Warning bell at nine-forty-five, Doors close at ten. Lights out at ten-thirty. It all starts all over again at six-thirty a.m. Breakfast's at seven. Make sure you're where you're supposed to be when you're supposed to be there. If you're not there when they take 'count', everyone has to wait 'til you show up. It pisses a lot of people off. Be late too often and you get bounced into solitary for a month or two. Keep your nose clean and watch your back. It's a pretty simple existence."

"Thanks."

"There's also a lot of things scheduled in the afternoon. There are different kinds of teachers that come in each week. You know, Community-do-gooders. There's a whole bunch of stuff: dance classes, aerobics, theater, music. All sorts of things to get you rehabilitated. Turn you back into a solid citizen again."

Cam took a deep breathe and rubbed her neck.

"Three ways to work off tension around here. One, if you're a jock, there's always a good ball game in the yard, or two, you can use the exercise room if you got enough points."

"Points?"

"Merit points. For keeping out of trouble. You gotta earn the right to use the exercise room. Don't try to brownnose your way in, though. It's not worth the hassle."

Cameron nodded her understanding. "What's the third way?" she asked.

Lou chuckled. "Get in good with one of the femmes, like Gina. Make a friend who'll keep watch: give you some privacy. Otherwise it's a long lonely time."

Cameron smiled. "I think I blew that already."

"Don't worry. Gina's ice at first, but she warms up quickly." Lou hefted herself off the bed. "Come on. I'll show you around."

Cam stopped. "Why are you doing this?"

"What? Being nice? I'm just a nice person."

Cameron looked at her in silence. "And 'cause I know you're an ex-cop. You'll have to fight your way upright here. It won't be easy. Let's just say I like rooting for the underdog. Although, I may give you even money now that I met you."

"How'd you know I was an ex-cop."

Lou looked at her, with disgust. "You're not the only one who can read. We do get newspapers here, you know. I like to keep up with current affairs. Yours was an interesting little item; a highly decorated narcotics agent skimming off the top of the stuff she takes in busts and resells it on the street." Lou shook her head appreciatively. "Imaginative. Too bad it didn't work."

Cameron lowered her eyes, chastened.

"Come on, Harvard, let's go."

"Radcliffe. It was Radcliffe."

"Big fucking deal." Lou turned and walked out of the cell.

****

The cafeteria was crowded and noisy. Clumps of women congregated around the long tables. Some laughed and joked. Others talked softly and seriously. Several turned to inspect the "new blood" as she walked in.

Cameron was aware of the eyes on her and more than a little self conscious as she followed the others through the food line to get her dinner. The food looked monochromatic to her, the vegetables—at least that's what she assumed they were—and meat—what little of it she was given—all had an overwhelming grayish tint, just like the rest of the prison. All had cooked so long that any nutritional value they might once have had was long washed away.

She took her tray of food and sat at a long table where the two other women who had been admitted with her that morning were already eating. "How you doing?" Cam asked them.

"This place sucks." Donna's mood hadn't changed since this morning. "I've been in better joints than this. It's even worse than when I was here last time. At least the C.O.s are laid back."

"C.O.s?" Sharon asked.

"Corrections Officers," Donna smirked. "Think they're too good to be called guards." She turned her attention to Cam. "What house are you in?"

Cam had already learned that no one called them cells, they were houses. "C-332," she answered.

Donna brightened. "I was in C-block last time I was here. They got good families there. Try to get in Ruth's or Lou's. Stay away from Jay's. No one likes them. They're real dogs. What did you get for work assignment?"

"Library, reading program," Cam answered. "You?"

"Prison store, same as the last time I was here. I guess they figure if I'm gonna sell something, it might as well be toothpaste and cigarettes."

Cam joined her in a friendly laugh.

Sharon just sat with her head down, slowly pushing the food around the tray.

"What about you?" Cam asked.

"I'm all right." She didn't raise her head, but Cam could see that her eyes were red. She'd been crying.

"Don't let them get to you. They'll push you just to see where you'll break. Don't give them the satisfaction," Donna warned her.

"That's easy for you. You've been here before." She leaned forward. "The woman I'm supposed to be next to asked if I would…would…" She didn't finish.

"What? Fuck her?" Donna was to the point.

Sharon just nodded. Then she looked at Cam. "I know you said you're one, but is everyone here a…?"

"A lesbian? I don't know. I tend to doubt it," Cam answered.

"What do I do?" Sharon asked.

"Tell her no. You don't have to do anything you don't want to do," Cam advised her.

"What if she attacks me?"

"Then scream bloody murder. Call for a C.O.!"

"But all the C.O.s are women! Are they all lesbians, too? Where are the male guards?" Sharon was almost frantic.

"Relax, hon," Donna brushed her worries away with a wave of her fork. "The guys are all outside. Only bitches inside. The guys are on the wall, in the admin building, outside the gates. There are plenty around. You just have to find a way to get to them." Donna placed a piece of grey meat in her mouth, chuckling.

"But what if—?" Sharon started to say.

"Listen. Rape is rape no matter where it's committed and no matter who tries it." Cam looked at her. She felt sorry for this woman who seemed too young and fragile to be in a place like this.

"She could kill me."

"She won't." Cam wished she were as sure as she sounded. "Just let her know where you stand and what you want. Or don't want."

"Everything all right?"

Cam looked up at Lou who stood over her with three other women behind her.

Cam smiled. "Yes. Thanks. These are the two who…"

"Yes, I know. More new bloods. Sorry to see you back again, Donna. Anyone giving you trouble?"

Donna shook her head, but Sharon just looked down at her tray.

Lou walked over behind Sharon and leaned down to whisper in her ear. Sharon's eyes opened wide as Lou slowly walked away followed by her entourage.

"What she say to you?" Donna asked as soon as Lou was out of earshot.

Sharon looked from Donna to Cameron and back. "She said to tell her to sell it to the night C.O. like she used to."

Donna sat back and laughed heartily. "Same ol' same old!" she chuckled.

"Did she mean what I think she meant?" Sharon was dumfounded.

"Sounds like it. Lou seems to know everything about everyone. She knew all about me and I hadn't been here ten minutes." Cam smiled. "You'll do okay. Just don't let anyone push you around."

As she said it, Cameron caught someone staring at her from across the room. It was a woman with intense black eyes and close cropped hair. Cam recognized her at once—Janet Lacey. She had put this woman in prison two years ago for armed robbery. Cam remembered how Lacey had looked at her with hate seething in her eyes at the trial. Cam made a mental note to steer clear of her. This could be trouble she didn't want.

* * * *

Cam's job in the library seemed like it would be easy for a few days. The woman who worked there as the librarian had explained that there were several inmates who had asked for help with their reading. Some had just never learned, others had English only as their second language. She had been very pleased when she learned that Cam was fluent in Spanish and promised that she would have Cam's schedule lined up by the beginning of the next week. Until that time, Cam could help by reshelving books.

So, now that all the books were neatly back in their assigned places on the shelves, Cam sat at one of the study desks with a pad of paper, writing a letter to her sister. It was a hard letter to write. An apology that wasn't an apology. An explanation to explain what she wasn't able to explain:

As soon as she had been released on bond, Cam had first called her sister to tell her that she'd been arrested, but not to worry. Lori seemed to take it very well, had even agreed not to ask any questions, but it was only the calm before the storm. Two hours later, Lori called back. "I'll be on US Air flight 2318. Tonight. It arrives at seven-twenty-nine. Pick me up at BWI," was all she said before the line went dead. Cam remembered that evening vividly.

All the way to the airport, Cam had worried about what Lori had to say. The tone of her voice had been terse, much like Dad's when he was getting ready to issue a stiff reprimand.

As Lori emerged from the plane with just a small overnight bag on her shoulder, Cam had seen from her sister's expression that this was not going to be an easy visit. The quick hug hello was just a mere formality, and all the way back to Baltimore Lori's silence made Cam feel like a naughty child waiting to be spanked.

It wasn't until they had been safely back at Cam's apartment and Cam placed two cups of tea on the coffee table that Lori had at last spoken. "I don't believe you."

Cam looked at her, slightly taken aback. "About what?"

"I don't believe you were arrested for selling cocaine," Lori stated flatly.

Cam reached over and took a newspaper from the other end of the coffee table. Folded out was an article with the headline *Decorated Police Officer Caught in Drug Sting*. It didn't have a picture, but clearly stated, *Cameron A. Andrews, who was honored with the City's Medal of Valor four years ago, was arrested last night after allegedly selling cocaine to another undercover officer...*

Lori just looked at the article without picking the paper up. She scanned it, then looked back at Cam. "I still don't believe you."

Cam just heaved a sigh. "I have a good lawyer. He's trying to arrange a deal for me. I may get off with just a year or two.

Lori studied her, much the way Dad used to when he expected more of an explanation. Cam just sat there, trying to avoid her eyes. Everyone said they looked a lot alike, that you could tell they were sisters, but Cam never could see the resemblance. To her, it was Mom looking back at her, using Dad's expressions. It made her uncomfortable.

"What aren't you telling me?" Lori finally asked.

"What makes you think I'm not telling you something?"

Lori just looked at her, took a sip of her tea, then carefully placed the cup back in the saucer. "I know there's something you're not telling me, Cameron. I know you're hiding something. Please don't make me try to guess what it is. I've already gone through list after list of things that might have happened. This isn't you...it just isn't you. Tell me what I'm missing."

"There isn't anything, Lor, please don't push me," Cam pleaded, trying to find a way around her sister's questions. Deep inside she wanted to tell Lori everything, to be completely honest, as she'd always been, but she knew she couldn't. Why hadn't she expected it to be this hard?

"Don't push you?" Loring asked, in an outraged tone. "My parents and my brother have died because of drugs and now I'm told that my sister has been caught selling them. And not just any sister, a sister that has dedicated her own life to working to get drugs off the streets, to arresting pushers and buyers alike. A sister that was recruited by the CIA because of her out-standing scholastic achievements. And all she can say to me is, 'Don't push me.' Am I missing something here? I know I don't have the IQ or the edu-cation that you have, but I'm not stupid, Cameron."

"I know that, Lori, I know you're not stupid—"

"Then why are you treating me like an imbecile? Explain it to me. If you're in some kind of financial trouble, tell me. We still have some money from Mom and Dad's estate in the bank. Half of it's yours. All of it if you need it. Or if you're being blackmailed, or you're in some other kind of trou-ble, tell me. I can help you. I know you've had to use cocaine when you've done undercover work. Is this related? Are you hooked and don't know how to handle it? There are programs that can help. I'm sure that your lawyer can get you off on something like that. I know that David can't practice in Maryland, but he's a good lawyer, maybe he could assist your lawyer—"

"Lori, stop, please," Cam interrupted. "I know that your husband is a good lawyer, but he can't help. I wish he could. I'm sorry."

Lori sat back. Her eyes closed. "Grandma Anne's first response was that this must be some kind of undercover thing you're doing. Is it?"

Cam was surprised by the statement. Her first response was to say, 'Yes, she's right! I knew I could never get anything past her!' But she checked her-self. She said only, "Why would she think that?"

Lori took a deep breath. "Because she has always had more faith in you than she's had in God. In her eyes you could never do anything wrong. You're the first born daughter of the first born daughter of the first born daughter, et cetera, ad nauseam."

Cam also took a deep breath. Was that resentment in her sister's voice? "Honey, I'm sorry."

But Lori held up her hand. "I don't mean to sound resentful. I'm not real-ly," she said softly. The coldness drained from her voice. "Sometimes I've thought it would be nice to have someone feel that way about me, but it must be a heavy burden. I saw you take over when Benny died. And when Mom and Dad died. I know you felt that you should have dropped out of school to take care of me. You've always been the one everyone turned to when they needed help." She reached out and took Cam's hand. Her voice was softer still, pleading, "Let me help you, now. Turn to me."

Cam closed her eyes. Of course it would be so much easier if she could just say, Yes, Grandma Anne is right. This is an undercover thing. I don't need help, but thanks anyway. I really appreciate it. But she couldn't. She couldn't tell anyone. She knew that Lori could be trusted, but what if she let something slip to David, and what if he let it slip to one of his colleagues.

Who knew who was involved in the drug trade. She could wind up dead before she even got started. With all her heart she wanted to tell Lori the truth, but with all her brain, she knew she couldn't.

Cam took Lori's hand in both of hers. "Lori, I wish I could make you feel better by telling you that Grandma Anne was right, or that I lost a lot of money that I can't repay, or that this is all a big misunderstanding, but I can't. I broke the law and now I have to pay for it."

"Have you been planning this for a long time?" Lori asked.

"No." Cam shrugged. "It just came up and I did it on the spur of the moment. I didn't think it through."

Lori pulled her hand back. Her look changed to one of suspicion. "Then why did you stop wearing Mom's locket and Benny's swimming medal? Why is Dad's watch sitting in the safe in Mom's library? You have never been without them. I know how much they meant to you. And your wonderful Medal of Valor. Why is it locked away in my house? What were you planning?"

Cam's eyes snapped open. "Why did you look in that box? You promised me you wouldn't. And you ask me to trust you?" Her voice was harsher than she wanted, but she was unprepared for Lori's admission. "You broke your promise! Did you open the envelope, too?"

"No. Should I?"

"Please don't. Lori, please, at least that."

"Cameron." Lori's voice was back to the harshness it had before. "You call me and tell me that you have been arrested for selling cocaine. In the safe in a room that used to be our mother's study, you have placed a box that you've asked me not to open. Under normal circumstances, I would gladly honor that request. But what am I to think? That maybe it contains more drugs, or drug related money? That if it is found, that I could become an accessory, that my husband and my sons might be implicated? What do you expect of me?!"

Cam rose to her feet. "I expected you to know that I wouldn't harm you. That I would never involve you in something like this!"

Lori's voice rose even higher. "I never thought that you would involve yourself in something like this! You want me to promise you anything, but you cannot be honest with me?! You ask for my trust, but you don't trust me?!" Lori accusations were becoming louder and quicker. "What am I supposed to tell my sons? 'Why didn't Aunt Cameron come for Thanksgiving, Mom?' 'Oh, it's nothing much, sweetie. She's in prison right now, but she'll probably be out by *next* Thanksgiving.'"

"Lori—" Cam started.

"'Oh, don't worry, Kevin,'" Lori continued, her voice full of anger and sarcasm, "'Your Aunt Cameron would never do anything really wrong. That's why she's in prison.'"

"Lori, stop." Cam turned toward her. "I'm sorry. I know this is hard for you. I wish I had something different I could tell you. I'm sorry you had to open the box, but I had to leave them with you. I didn't want you to worry, but I couldn't let someone else find them. They're the things I value most. I had to know they were safe."

"Then you *were* being blackmailed. You were afraid that someone would steal them from you."

Lori was grasping at straws, trying to find the explanation. "No." Cam said, then changed her mind, "Yes, yes, I was afraid they'd get ripped off." Let Lori believe something.

But Lori just stared at her. "This *is* an undercover thing, isn't it? Please tell me it is. Please trust me, Cameron. Tell me you didn't do this."

Cam turned away, her hands covering her mouth. Please, she was thinking, let me find the right words so I don't blow this!

She felt Lori's hands on her shoulders. "I'm frightened for you, Cam. I'm your sister. I'll be here for you no matter what, but I'm scared. I don't want this to be happening to you."

Cam turned and looked into Lori's worried face. Then, as Lori drew her into a soothing embrace, tears streamed out of Cam's eyes, for the second time in four days.

Now, sitting in the prison library, Cam was trying to compose a letter to somehow let Lori know that everything was all right. She was so absorbed in it that it took several minutes for her to realize she was being watched. She finally felt eyes upon her and looked up.

A short, slender woman with long flowing black hair leaned against the bookcase, her arms crossed.

Cam turned her notepad over. "Something I can do for you?" she asked.

"I'd say so." The woman took a step toward her. Her eyes were a beautiful almond shape and she used them to her advantage whenever possible. Right now, they were focused directly on Cam.

Cam cleared her throat. She'd seen this woman before and they'd locked eyes several times, but Cam's inquiries had revealed that Jenny was Ruth Tarlow's girlfriend so she kept her distance.

Ruth, Cam had learned, was one of the 'family' gang leaders in C-block, the 'Daddy' of the clan. She was a couple inches shorter than Cam, but sturdily built and out-weighed Cam by a good thirty pounds, something the files hadn't disclosed. She wasn't that old, perhaps forty, but she had a reputation for being the strong, silent type and few were willing to cross her.

Jenny walked over slowly and perched on the edge of Cam's desk. It was a quiet morning. Only one or two other women were in the library.

"I hear you were a cop." She waited, but Cam refused to answer. "I did a cop once. Said if I fucked him, he wouldn't bust me. Lied. He was a lousy fuck and he busted me anyway. Are you a liar?"

Cam sat back and looked up at her.

"Then, are you a good fuck?"

"What do you want here? This *is* a library. Ever been in one before?"

Jenny smiled and pointed to herself. "And this is a jewel thief. Ever been in one before?"

Cameron let out a breath and shook her head. "I don't want any trouble."

Jenny smirked and walked around the desk toward the book cases. "I also hear you're a college grad."

"You hear a lot," Cam said, watching the way Jenny's ass eased it's way across the room.

Jenny looked back over her shoulder. "Yeh, but my ears aren't the only things I keep open." She winked at Cam.

Cam watched as Jenny inspected several shelves. "You know what's in all these books?" Jenny called.

"Some of them."

"What's in the ones on the top shelf? I can't reach them."

Against her better judgement, Cam got up and went over to the shelves. "Which ones?" she asked. Jenny pointed. "That one."

Cam reached up to get the book and as she did, Jenny reached over and ran her hand down Cam's chest.

Cam brought her arm down quickly.

"Ticklish?" Jenny smiled.

Cam frowned at her. "Do you want to look at a book or not?"

"I want to look at something that won't hurt my eyes." Jenny smiled. "And I find you much more interesting than any book."

Cam smiled in spite of herself.

"See? You have a beautiful smile. You should use it more often. Now, what else can you do with your mouth?" She was standing as close to Cam as she could without touching.

"This is a library," Cam reminded her.

"Then we'll do it quietly."

Before Cam could object, Jenny was kissing her. It was a slow gentle kiss, but smoldering with promise. She pulled Cam to her as she leaned back against the bookcase. After a moment, Cam pulled away and looked around. They were well hidden by the tall bookcases.

"See? I don't bite. And I promise not to scream when I come."

Cam knew this was trouble, but considered allowing Jenny to lure her into her web. Maybe this was an introduction into the right circle of people. Jenny's eyes were eager as she pulled Cam against her back into the bookcase. Her hands circled Cam's head as she drew Cam into a second kiss. Cam's hands drifted down Jenny's sides almost without her willing them to, and around her back to stop on her firm ass. The pressure of her touch became harder until Jenny raised one leg and wrapped it around Cam's waist. Jenny's grip on Cam's head tightened as their kiss became more passionate.

Suddenly, a hand gripped Cam's shoulder and spun her around. Cam immediately started to react, but in the split second, assessing who was now in front of her, she stopped her reaction. She jerked her head back in time to absorb most of the force as a hard fist connected with her face. She went reeling backward into the book stacks as several books crashed, with her, to the floor.

Sprawling there, Cam looked up into one of the faces that had haunted her memory since she'd first seen the picture: Ruth Tarlow.

"What the fuck are you doing?" The look of venom in Ruth's eyes as she stared into Jenny's stopped Cameron's breath. She'd seen that look only once before, on a maniac who'd just killed four people.

Ruth turned her attention to Cam. Behind Ruth stood her lieutenant, Tuck.

"What the hell are you doing with my woman?" Ruth demanded of Cam through clenched teeth. She towered over Cam daring her to get to her feet.

"What's going on here?" Jo, the guard, stood at the end of the stacks. She walked her heavy frame toward them. "Get up," she ordered Cam. "What's the story, here?"

Cam got to her feet.

"Well?" Jo demanded as no one answered. Ruth's eyes were burning into Cam.

Cam looked at Jo, daring her to dispute her statement. "I tripped. Just knocked all the books over. I'll sort them. No problem."

Jo took Cam's face in her hand and turned it to look at the red blotch on Cam's jaw. Cam winced as Jo's thumb dug into the spot Ruth's fist had struck.

"Struck it on the shelf when I fell," she ad-libbed.

Jo seemed satisfied. "Be more careful." She looked at Ruth and at Jenny. "If I thought you were causing trouble, I'd be all over you." She leered at Cam. "I'd love to be the first to bounce you into solitary." She guessed what had happened, but if it was over now, it was none of her business. She walked away.

Ruth continued to stare at Cam.

"Sorry. I didn't know she was yours," Cam lied.

"Now you do. Keep your distance." Ruth turned and took Jenny's arm and led her out of the library.

Tuck stopped. "Watch yourself. That one can get you in a whole lot of trouble."

Cam nodded as Tuck turned and followed after Ruth. Cam took a deep breath. Damn, Michael had trained her well. If she hadn't realized it was Ruth that had attacked her, she would have let her training take over and Ruth would have been the one on the floor. But that would have embarrassed Ruth in front of her lover and her friend. It also would have made

Cam one more enemy, and a very powerful one at that. It was one enemy she couldn't afford. And what would that have proven? What would have happened if she'd allowed herself to be drawn into a fight? Would she be on her way to solitary now?

* * * *

By the next Sunday, Cam was still brooding over her clash with Ruth. She was not certain of the effects of allowing herself to fall into Jenny's trap, but at least she'd made a first impression on Ruth. But now she may have created a bigger problem. She'd been biding her time, trying not to appear anxious, but she needed to get in with one of the families to find out what was happening. Her tryst with Jenny may have cost her the chance to get next to Ruth. She knew enough to keep her distance, at least for a while. She'd have to come up with some other way or get in with another gang. From what she'd learned, however, Ruth's family was the most powerful and that was the one she needed to get into.

"Andrews!" she heard the guard call. "You got a visitor."

Cam hoisted herself up off the bed and walked down the corridor.

Maggie's eyes opened wide in shock when Cam entered and sat down across the table from her. "What happened to you?" she asked.

"Walked into a wall." Cam gingerly touched the side of her face that was slightly black and blue and still swollen. "I'm all right. Don't worry."

"How's the other gal look?"

"Not a scratch on her," Cam boasted. "I was really careful not to hurt her."

Maggie smiled and Cam laughed.

"It took all my will power not to deck her. I've been trained too well. How's the outside world?" Cam asked. "Are you getting my letters?"

"Delivery's fine." Maggie assured her. (*In other words: Your letters come without anything being censored.*) "But I get them all at once. None all week, then three on Friday. Maybe you should number them so I know which one to read first."

Cam nodded. She understood. Because they were delivered out of sequence, Maggie was having a hard time deciphering the code.

"Dickie sends his love." (*Deems was waiting for news.*)

"Tell Dickie the feeling's mutual. (*There was nothing to tell yet.*) Have you seen Pauly? Is he watering my plants? I don't want them to die." (*Has Pauly heard anything on the street that could give her a lead?*)

"He's taking care of your plants, but nothing's blooming right now. He may have to do some pruning." (*Nothing on the street. He may have to find new informants.*)

"You look tired." (*No more news.*)

Cam sat back. "It's been a very long four weeks."

115

Chapter Fourteen

Cam had just come in from the yard. It was a miserable Maryland day at the end of the summer. The temperature was over ninety degrees with humidity around ninety percent. The dampness off Chesapeake Bay permeated the air even this far inland and made it heavy. Moving was an effort. Even breathing caused everyone to sweat.

Despite the heat, Cam felt a small amount of self-satisfaction. Today, in the yard, she'd been with a group of women standing close to the far wall when someone had produced a small amount of cocaine. Unlike other days when she'd been shielded from any transaction like that, she'd watched as three of the women had inhaled the powdery white stuff. And they'd known she was there, too. They hadn't even tried to hide it from her. Maybe they were beginning to trust her, or at least had grown tired of being careful around her.

Cam stepped into the bathroom next to the shower room. She ran her hand under the faucet and splashed her face, allowing the tepid water to run down her chest.

Cam was suddenly aware of someone behind her. She turned around, wiping her face with her sleeve. Three women stood blocking the door. Except for them, the shower room was empty.

The tallest of the three entered the room, slowly striding, studying Cam as she circled her, nodding her head. "You sure look a lot smaller without that badge," Lacey said.

Cam didn't move, but every muscle tensed. She'd been waiting since her first day here, since they'd locked eyes in the cafeteria, for Lacey to make some move toward her. She'd almost begun to hope that Lacey hadn't recognized her, but knew that was too much to wish for.

"Roni, did I tell you what a Wonder Woman we got here?" Lacey called back to one of her two friends without taking her eyes off Cam. "Super Cop. Busted five people in one night! All by herself. Of course, she had to kill one and maim another." She stopped, assessing Cam. Then she spoke. "You like arresting people? Liked it so much you decided to arrest yourself!" She threw her head back and laughed. The sound rumbled all the way from the bottom of her belly. "Or d'you like shootin' them better?"

Cam shifted her weight to a more relaxed-looking stance, but was still ready to move. This was obviously a situation she didn't want to come up on the short end of. Allowing Ruth to slug her was one thing, this could be something entirely different.

Lacey glared at Cam. "This *bitch*, shot my sister. Busted her leg so bad, she'll never walk right again. Shot clear through the bone."

Cam didn't lower her eyes from Lacey's face, but she remembered. Remembered a young girl running down the alley, ignoring their shouts to halt, turning, raising her hands, a gun pointed straight at her and Russ. Cam had brought her own gun up and fired, intentionally aiming low. She'd seen the girl crumble to the asphalt and heard the gun discharge, the bullet hitting the brick wall across the street behind them.

"Maybe you'd prefer I'd aimed higher and killed her."

"It might have been more humane. You'd have done that much for a dog."

"Dogs don't fire guns at me."

Lacey brought both her hands up and jolted Cam hard in the chest. Cam was tensed and stood her ground, not allowing herself to be pushed back. She had to stop herself from throwing Lacey to the floor. Let's see if this could be settled without resorting to aggression, she thought.

"You wasted my whole family, man. Shot Rashi, put me here. My poor mama's stuck with taking care of my three kids. And Rashi's son."

Cam stood face to face with her. "Maybe she should have thought of that before she brought you into this world."

Lacey took a wild swing, but Cam sidestepped and blocked the punch, using Lacey's weight against her. She threw Lacey off balance against the wall. Grabbing her by the throat, Cam held her there, preventing her fall.

Cam's voice was low and intimidating. "We've both got bad times here. Why don't we just call a truce. We can settle this when we're both back on the street. No sense getting bounced down the hole over some silly misunderstanding."

Lacey grabbed Cam's wrist with both of her hands. "I'll waste you right here," she threatened. "It'll be worth the extra time."

She threw all her strength at Cam and pushed her back. The two began to circle. Lacey lunged at Cam, but again, Cam sidestepped. For several minutes, Lacey tried her best to hit, punch, bat, or scratch Cam, but Michael's training had been good and Cam was responding well. At last, when Lacey threw a punch which Cam sidestepped as Michael had taught, Cam caught the Lacey's arm and, using the momentum, wrapped the arm back behind her and held it there.

"Sure you don't want a truce?" Cam asked softly.

Lacey let fly a string of expletives that Cam wasn't sure she understood all of. Loosening her grasp on Lacey's arm, she stepped back. But Lacey wasn't to be stopped. Her face reddening, she threw her body at Cam, trying to ram her midsection. At that moment, Roni's foot flew out and tripped Cam as she sidestepped, off balance and Cam tottered backward. The third woman grabbed Cam's arm and yanked her back as she fell, keeping her from rolling with her own momentum. Lacey seized the opportunity and pulled Cam's other leg out from under her and Cam fell back, helped by the heavy hand that held her arm and slammed her against the wall, banging her head against the cement.

Cam was dazed by the blow. She felt hands pulling her to her feet, her legs watery.

Lacey finally had the upper hand. Her first blow caught Cam in the stomach and knocked some of the wind out of her, doubling her over. Before Cam could fight to inhale, Lacey's knee connected with her face and the taste of blood filled her mouth.

Cam gulped for air. The only thing keeping her on her feet were the hands around each of her upper arms and the wall behind her back.

A second blow caught her in the lower ribcage.

"Well, ain't that a pretty sight. Three against one. Takes a lot of courage with those odds."

Lou stood in the doorway.

Lacey stopped as she was about to deliver a third blow and turned to face the newcomer. Roni and Tony released their grip on Cam who sagged to her knees, putting her left arm out to prevent herself from falling to the floor. Her right arm went up to hold the bump that was starting to swell on the back of her head.

"This fucker deserves it. She put me in this joint," Lacey cursed.

"Looks like she put herself here, too," Lou observed.

"I'll kill her." Lacey was breathing hard with anger.

Cam tried to lift her head to see who was in the room, but nausea overcame her and she nearly fell forward.

Lou stared her challenge at Lacey. "Yeh. You *could* kill her. Seems to me, though, that it'd take a whole lot more guts to let her live."

Lacey stepped back. She exchanged glances with her two friends. Resentfully, they backed down.

"Now," said Lou, knowing she had the situation under control, "you need to be somewhere else, don't you?"

The three sullenly pushed past her out the door.

* * * *

Where had Cam heard that phrase before? She wasn't sure just how much she was really hearing. Her ears were ringing and she wasn't fully conscious. She fought not to pass out.

"How're you doin', Harvard?" Lou's face drifted out of the haze.

Cam got up as Lou's and another pair of hands helped her. Before she was fully on her feet, nausea gripped her and she lurched toward the toilet stall.

Lou stood by the stall door as Cam emptied her lunch into the john. She stood back as Cam came out of the stall, wiping her mouth with the back of her hand. Blood was still running from her nose. She staggered to the sink and splashed water onto her face and the back of her neck.

Just then Emerson appeared in the doorway. "What's going on in here?"

Lou looked at Cam. "Oh, she's just been out in the sun too long. You know how that can turn your stomach some times," she answered before Cam could even understand the question.

"She all right?" Emerson's question could almost be taken as concern.

"Yeh. Cold water will help."

"I saw Lacey and her buddies coming out of here. You sure that's all it is? Heat stroke?" Emerson had recovered from her bout of compassion.

"Sure." Lou smiled. "You know Lacey'd never try to pull anything with me around."

Emerson studied both of them, then turned and walked away.

As soon as she was sure that Emerson was out of hearing range, she turned to the short woman who had slipped off to the side as Emerson had entered.

"Run down to the kitchen and tell Judith I need some ice," Lou ordered her. "I'll walk Harvard back to her room." For the first time, it registered in Cam's mind that the person who just disappeared out the door was the small woman she'd seen at Lou's table at dinner.

Lou put her hand on Cam's shoulder to steady her. "Look at me," she gently ordered. She inspected Cam's eyes, visually measuring the size of the pupils. They were slightly dilated, but at least both were the same size. Lou knew that was a good sign. She held up one finger in front of Cam's face."How many fingers I got?"

Cam tried to focus, but started to fall backward. Lou's hand on her shoulder steadied her. "All of them, I hope," Cam tried to smart-mouth her way out of the embarrassing situation.

"Cute. Can you focus across the room?"

Cam blinked her eyes and tried, but it took an enormous effort. She was at least partly successful. "Yeh," was her reply. "How'd you get them to stop so quickly? They had me and they knew it."

Lou reached for a paper towel from the stack on the shelf. "Everyone needs old Lou on her side at some time or another. I don't get much flack from anyone. It comes with the seniority." She gently wiped the remaining blood from Cam's face. Cam reached out and leaned against the wall with one hand while she rubbed her neck with the other. Gingerly, she examined the lump that had already formed on the back of her head while her tongue explored the cut on her lip.

"Think Emerson believed you?"

"No," Lou answered. "But, like I said, I don't get much flack from any-one." She still looked into Cam's eyes. "You're gonna have quite a headache. That was a good flip you took. It mighta killed you even if Lacey couldn't."

Cam focused on Lou's face for the first time. She saw a genuine look of concern there. She tried to laugh it off. "I think I'm okay. Pretty clumsy of me. I'm just thankful Lacey wasn't stronger." She wiped at the blood that was still coming from her nose.

"Let's get back to your house, then. Walk slow. Right beside me. I can't support you. You gotta walk by yourself." Lou bent toward her and looked her straight in the eye. She lowered her voice. "You better not let Lacey think she hurt you at all or she owns you. Let her think you're backing down now and you crawl for the rest of your time here, which won't be very long. Comprende, Amiga?"

Cam stared back. She understood. It was exactly what Charlie had warned her about.

"If anyone thinks you're easy to get to, you'll have to fight everyone in the whole joint. Now, just take it one step at a time. Do you understand?"

Cam started to nod, but her head felt as if she'd just rolled a bowling ball through it.

"One step at a time," was all Lou said.

Cam gathered all her strength and stood as tall as she could. She let her arms hang loosely at her sides, ready to reach out for the wall if she needed the balance. She tried as best she could to walk and look straight ahead and not stagger. God, she thought, Michael would shit if she knew how I just let myself get beaten. Suddenly, for a split second, the pain in her head was replaced by a sharp pain in her heart. Then the headache returned in force.

Lou walked beside her, chatting away as if nothing were wrong. The length of the corridor between the shower room and her cell seemed to stretch on forever. Cam felt eyes watching her from every cell they passed.

"Okay. Good work," Lou said encouragingly as they reached Cam's cell. "Sit down real easy. And don't lose the rest of your lunch."

"Thanks, Lou," she uttered, sinking slowly down onto her bunk. The sound of her own voice boomed inside her head. She realized that she'd bro-ken Charlie's rule number three. "I guess I owe you one," she whispered.

"Hell, you owe me a couple," Lou told her. "We'll talk about payback later."

At least it was Lou that she owed, and not someone else who she trusted even less. Cam just wanted to lie down and pass out, but she leaned forward and put her head in her hands, resting her elbows on her knees.

"Actually, I was coming looking for you. I guess it was a good thing I found you when I did." Lou chuckled. "I was going to ask you to teach Lourdes how to read."

"Who?"

"Lourdes. The young kid that just ran off to get you some ice for that bump. She's not a stupid kid, just never had the opportunity to learn to read and write. Can't teach her myself. Haven't got the patience."

Cam's head was throbbing. "Sure, Lou, I'd love to teach her. Just as soon as my head stops hurting…in about three years." She leaned back as if to lie down.

"Hey. Don't lie back. Sit up. You can't fall asleep before dinner time. Might never wake up. How're the ribs?"

"They're just sore, nothing serious. Lacey doesn't really know how to throw a punch, thank God."

"Probably should'a marched you right down to the infirmary…"

"I'm okay," Cam interrupted.

Lou shook her head. "Yeh, sure. You're fine…and you'd better make everyone else here believe you are, too." Her voice was ominous.

Cam tried to focus on her.

Lourdes was suddenly standing next to Lou. She handed Lou a towel wrapped tightly around a handful of ice cubes.

"Judith said you will need these, too." Lourdes handed Cam two white tablets. "Aspirinas." She turned to Lou. "Everyone in the kitchen already knew that Lacey tried to kill her. They're taking bets on who will survive." She went to the sink to get Cam a cup of water.

Lou sat down on the bed next to Cam. "See what I mean? You got an hour to get it together before dinner. You'd better be ready to walk into that dinner room as if nothing happened."

Cam reached up and took the cup Lourdes held out for her. She swallowed the two pills and finished the water. "Gracias," she said to Lourdes. Then she turned her head slowly and looked at Lou. "I'll be there. I may not wake up tomorrow, but I'll be there tonight."

Lou nodded in acknowledgement at the look of determination she saw in Cam's eyes. As Cam gingerly applied the ice pack to the back of her head, Lou also saw the pain.

* * * *

Cam walked into the cafeteria slowly, after the others from her cell block. Every eye in the room turned and looked at her, although there were some who tried to hide their curiosity. Her head still pounded and her ribs and face ached, but she'd sworn to herself that she was going to get an academy award for the performance she'd give tonight. She had her shoulders back and walked tall as she got her tray full of food, food she couldn't even imagine eating.

Leaving the food line, she deliberately walked past the table where Lacey sat. Stopping beside Lacey's chair, she slowly bent forward. "Next time. One on one. Face to face. Just you and me. No trying to hide behind two other women's skirts," Cam challenged in a low voice. Only Lacey, and perhaps one other person at that table heard her words.

As she straightened up, she intentionally knocked Lacey's coffee over into her plate of food. "Oh, sorry." She smiled. "How clumsy of me."

She took her own tray and walked to a table near the wall and sat down to eat.

Lou was seated directly in back of her. "I don't know if you're the smartest or the most stupid person I've ever met, but you sure got guts," Lou whispered over her shoulder. Her eyes were on Lacey who still sat, unmoved, at the table, seething, as whispers went around the room.

All knew that this would not be the last time Cameron Andrews would come up against Janet Lacey.

Chapter Fifteen

Cameron stood at the door to the cell looking out into the silent, empty corridor. The glow of the amber safety lights that lit the prison at night gave an eerie feel to the place. More eerie than usual. Cam didn't know the exact time, but figured it was just after midnight; the guard had made her bed-check rounds a few minutes ago. Not everyone was asleep, yet. Cam could hear low voices and soft moans coming from the other cells down the corridor.

Gina still wasn't friendly, but at least she didn't ignore Cam anymore. Her cell was right next to Cam's and Gina had even asked her a few questions tonight as they stood in the corridor before lock down. Gina was part of Ruth's family and something told Cam that if she were going to get into that group it would be through Gina. No one else in the family even acknowledged her, except Tuck who Cam saw in the gym every now and then.

Cam had accepted a small hit of coke in the shower room tonight, but it wasn't the drugs that were keeping her awake. Usually, Cam would be asleep by this time, either from exhaustion or boredom, but tonight, sleep was the furthest thing from her mind. She'd tossed and turned for quite a while after lights out, but finally had gotten out of bed.

A letter had come from Michael today. Just one page, short, but to the point:

Dear Cameron,

  I am sorry I have not contacted you sooner. I have been a coward. Please do not think I misled you intentionally. I was not being honest with either of us. I was more upset about the time ending than I realized and more involved than I was ready to be. So, I tried to ignore it. I can't. I do have regrets. Maybe there will be time for us to reconsider. Charlie said I should apologize for my actions. I do. But Charlie was wrong about one thing: you can trust me. I hope things are going as you hoped and that your lessons are serving you well. Maybe one day I can ask for forgiveness. I think of you often.

  Michael.

"You can trust me." It had been that phrase that had caught Cam. Trust her?! What kind of a joke was this? Deep inside, one of the things Cam wanted most was to trust Michael. But why hadn't Michael said something before this? Why had she waited all these months? Why now, when Cam had other things on her mind. Why not sooner when she could have done something about it?

Cam's frustration level was running high and her tolerance level low. She'd torn the page into little pieces and flushed them down the toilet before she'd even finished reading it the second time.

She took a deep breath. The reality of her imprisonment was starting to chafe. The frustration, the loneliness and despair that effected almost everyone there was closing in on her. The total lack of privacy hadn't bothered her at first. She'd expected as much, but the strip searches that the C.O.s seemed to enjoy every time they were bored were eating away at her. Every few days, she'd return to find her cell in shambles, having been ransacked by the guards and at least once a week she again went through the indignity of being stripped and searched, sometimes in her most private places. She suspected that Emerson really leaned on her more than the others. It seemed that she was put through it more than most of the others, but who could she complain to?

She'd tried every tactic she could think of, short of openly asking, 'okay, who's selling drugs?' to find out what was happening where and still wasn't any closer to finding a source than when she walked into this place. Sure, she'd seen coke passing hands in the library and in the yard and had even snorted a hit or two, but everyone was close-lipped about it. No one seemed willing to share any information, especially with someone who used to be a cop.

Why did every movie or TV program about law enforcement show the detectives closing out a case like this in three or four days? Why hadn't she been able to do it in three or four months? How long was she going to be in here before she could get a handle on something? She'd known that it would take time to gain anyone's trust so she could get an "in" with whoever was dealing the coke, but it was just dragging on. Was she a failure? Should she let Maggie pull the plug?

After all, she'd already failed at following all the training she'd spent so much time on. She'd let her guard down long enough to get herself beaten up, hell, almost killed, in a fight she should have won. She'd let herself fall into Lou's debt. And, still, no matter how hard she tried to keep her ears open, she still hadn't heard a thing that could give her a clue to anything she was supposed to find out. On top of all that, she still had Janet Lacey to contend with. Just a couple days ago, Lacey had stopped her in the shower room. They probably would have ended up in another fight if one of the guards hadn't come in just then.

So much for Michael's training and Charlie's skills number two, three, and five. Now, Michael was asking her to forget skill number one. Trust her?! Cam shook her head. She was about to violate number six: she was on the verge of losing control! Damn, and if there were someone here right now that she could talk to, she'd break number eight, too, because her emotions were getting close to the surface.

Suddenly, there was a loud cry from down the hall.

"Guards! Help!" came the shout, "Somebody call the C.O.s! Hurry!" The voice was frantic. Cam heard running feet in the hall as the screaming continued. The full bank of lights in the hall came on brightly and two guards ran by, one fumbling on her belt for the coil of keys. Loud voices now rang from the other cells, some concerned, most angry at being woken by the noise and the lights. A third guard ran up, but stopped and turned as she heard the order, "Call a medic! Get a doctor in here, quick!"

"What's happening?" came a concerned, but sleepy voice from the cell to Cam's right.

Cam shook her head. "Someone's sick," she answered.

"Jezzus," she heard Gina exclaim, softly, "not again. Not another one! Did you see which cell they went into?"

"Just a couple down," Cam answered, leaning back against the wall. As the third guard loped down the hall, one of the first guards walked by, leading an inmate who cried loudly into her hands.

"Cheryl," Gina called out, recognizing the other inmate, "what happened? Who's sick?"

Without stopping, the guard answered, "Just go back to bed. Mind your own business."

"It's Libby," Cheryl sobbed as the guard led her away.

Voices called out from other cells for information.

"Everyone!" It was the booming voice of the head guard as she strode down the hall. "Ladies! Just remain calm! And keep quiet! We'll let you know when there's something to tell you."

The voices quieted a bit, but there was still a high level of talk along the length of the corridor. The buzz and the crackle of the guards' walkie-talkies could be heard through it all.

Suddenly, more people raced by carrying medical equipment, two pushing a stretcher. Concerned voices could be heard in the cell as everyone quieted to try and hear what was being said. Suddenly, the order, "Clear!" was heard, followed by the buzz and thud of the portable defibrillator. Then a short silence, and, "Again! Clear!"

There was a deafening silence after the second defibrillator shock.

Cam could hear sobs from Gina's cell. "Not another one!" Gina whimpered. "Not Libby!"

Before Cam could speak to comfort Gina, she heard Gina throw herself onto the bed and the sobbing became muffled.

Cameron stepped back up to the door and waited. In her gut, she knew what had happened. Someone had just OD'd, someone who lived just three cells away. And she hadn't even known that drugs were on this floor. Cam's self-confidence took a nose dive. She'd been put here to prevent just such a thing from happening and she hadn't done a damned thing! This woman's death was her fault. She'd better get her ass in gear and get something done soon. She knew she'd just broken rule number seven. She wasn't detached. She was taking this very personally.

* * * *

Now that the days were growing shorter and colder, the outdoor ball games weren't as frequent and an aerobics instructor from the community YWCA came to the prison three times a week to lead the women in exercises and stretching to loud disco music. The hardcore jocks stayed in the weight room, while the music and loud encouraging shouts from the instructor boomed from the adjacent room.

Several days had passed since Libby's death, but Cam still hadn't quieted any of the worries she'd had that night. In fact, she now found it easier to exercise with the loud music coming from the adjacent room than to sit in the library or common room obsessing about her failure. During the week, she'd somehow fallen into the role of 'soft shoulder' for some of the women who wanted to vent their grief. It wasn't a role *she* would have sought, but at least she felt like she was doing something. She just wished that she had a shoulder to lean on.

As Cameron was warming down from a particularly long set of situps and push-ups, her attention turned to three women who clustered by the weight bench. At first, she thought nothing of it, as their demeanor and light laughter seemed to indicate a cheerful comraderie and the two guards who viewed the room from their glassed-in booth seemed unconcerned.

But now that the music in the next room had stopped, Cam heard phrases that caught her attention. The first words were, "short changed," the next, "crush your skull."

Cam looked more carefully, and in horror saw that it was Tuck who reclined on the weight bench, the barbell in a full press, extended over her. As Cam watched, one of the two women added a ten pound weight to the already overloaded bar, which, Cam estimated, held at least one hundred and twenty pounds. Two of the weights, one a twenty pounder, were outside the weight locks, and had been added after the exercise had begun.

Tuck tried to guide the barbell back onto the rack, but the second woman put her hand out to prevent it. Their talk was too low for Cam to hear what they were saying, but she saw the frown and tension on Tuck's face.

As she saw Tuck's arms start to shake under the weight, Cam stepped up quickly to the head of the weight bench and grasped the barbell.

"Don't try to be so butch, Tuck," she smiled, jokingly, as she stared at the other two in challenge. Both stepped back, glaring at Cam as she helped Tuck guide the barbell onto the rack.

Tuck sat up as soon as the weights were secured.

"Just remember how important accurate weight is," warned one of the women as she and her friend turned and walked out of the room.

"You okay?" Cam asked as Tuck rubbed her shaking biceps.

"Yeh." Tuck nodded. She drew her gaze away from the door the two women had just exited through and looked up at Cam. "Thanks," she said, softly, "you didn't have to step in. I…I appreciate it."

"Not a problem." Cam smiled. "I just hate the sight of blood. It's hard to get it out of exercise mats."

Tuck chuckled as she stood up. Gesturing toward the door, she added, "You know you just made an enemy."

Cam shrugged. "What's one more. I got plenty in here already."

Tuck sized her up. "I wouldn't say that. You got a lot of respect, too…the way you stood up to Lacey, how you've been there for some of the women this week, how you handle yourself. Now this." She extended her hand. "You're okay, Andrews."

Cam accepted the solid handshake. "Thanks," she said.

Well, now you owe me one, she thought, maybe this will be worth an introduction to the right people.

Tuck was still watching her closely. "You're not even going to ask what that was about."

Cam took the weights off the barbell and return them to their rack. "If it's my business, you'll tell me. Some things I figure it's best not to know."

Tuck nodded thoughtfully, as she handed Cam the last free weight. "Come on," she placed her hand on Cam's shoulder as she turned back from the weight rack, "time to get cleaned up for dinner."

Chapter Sixteen

Cameron leaned against the door of her cell, just as she had every night for the past several weeks. She'd had more trouble sleeping and, rather than toss and turn, had taken to standing at the door, waiting, watching, talking to the C.O. as she made her rounds and just trying to work her way through the mysteries surrounding her.

She'd found herself becoming more and more violent, more abrupt, much less considerate, definitely less sensitive. Had found herself reveling in the knowledge that she could get just about what she wanted from anyone in the prison just by being tougher, by standing up for herself. Charlie would be proud. She could get anything. Anything, that is, except the information she needed to get this job done and get out of here.

She knew it must be well past midnight. The C.O. had made her rounds three times already and the talk between the cells had long ago sunk into silence. She leaned against the door, wishing she had a flashlight so she could read, or at least a cigarette. Maybe she'd ask the guard when she came around again.

Pacing back and forth, she thought down the list of things she had to do: find the source of the cocaine, where it came in, how it went out, who was really responsible, where the moles were, and on and on. Finally leaning against the door again, she heard the bed creak in the next cell.

"Need something to help you sleep?" she heard Gina ask in a low voice.

Cam didn't answer.

"She ain't worth it." Gina took a stab at what might be bothering Cam.

"What?"

"She ain't worth it. Your doctor friend. She's out there, you're in here. Ain't no way."

Silence filled the hallway.

Cam stared down at her hands. She knew that Gina'd been watching her for the past several days, but hadn't realized she knew Cam was awake.

"That's not what I'm thinking," Cam answered after a moment. Actually, it *was* what she was thinking, but not *who* she was thinking about. The thought of Michael still lay heavily on her heart and still was a major item on her to-do list.

"Look, she's out there. You know she ain't saving it for you." Cam's shoulders tensed. "Sure, she comes to see you every other week. Soon, it'll be every month, then just once in a while. What's a high class doctor want with a convict for a lover?"

Cam wished she could stop Gina's words, but stopped herself instead. Why was she having this reaction?

"You got a lot of anger," Gina tried again.

"Everyone does." Damn, couldn't people just let her be angry without reminding her about it!?

"Not like it's eatin' you. Maybe tomorrow I can help you with it."

"Maybe. Maybe not." Cam wanted to be in a mood to make this connection, but the fatigue and frustration were coiling her into a tight ball.

"Come on, Mama. Loosen up. I *can* help." Her voice took on a seductive tone. "You're as tight as a rock."

Cam really didn't want to talk to anyone. The words in Michael's letter still flashed into her eyes. "Go back to bed," she ordered. She didn't want to be bothered. In the past few days she'd begun to revel in her anger and had stopped caring about how her actions or words affected other people. She knew that there were several who made a conscious effort to steer clear of her.

"We'll talk tomorrow," Gina whispered.

Cam closed her eyes as the silence stretched. Was this what she needed, or was this just another problem to deal with?

* * * *

Cam wiped the sweat out of her eyes. Even though the temperature was in the mid-fifties, the basketball game was really heated up.

She hadn't gotten involved in any of the games before that week, but when Tuck tossed the ball to her as she stood along the fence, Cam accepted the invitation and joined in.

They'd been playing, five on five, for almost a half-hour and were still tied.

"Come on, Andrews," Tuck called as she in-bounded the ball to Cam. "Show them how it's really done." She lowered her voice as she slid past Cam. "Pass it to Reggie and get over in the left corner."

Cam dribbled to her right, then passed the ball to the tall redheaded center. Cam drifted back to the left corner as Reggie faked a few moves then handed the ball off to Tuck who ran down the lane and leaped to toss the ball, right handed, into the hoop. As her feet left the ground, so did four others and she found herself with four hands between her and the basket. At the top of her jump, she suddenly threw the ball to her left, right into Cam's hands. Cameron didn't even stop to think, but put the ball once to the ground as she went forward, then jumped to toss the ball toward the basket.

As she released the ball, a hard shoulder met her mid-body and threw her backward onto the pavement. She didn't see the ball slide neatly through the hoop.

Cam hit the concrete with such force that her entire body was shaken. The first reaction she had was pure anger and she jumped to her feet to attack the woman who had flattened her.

"Easy." Tuck was suddenly directly in front of her, blocking Cam from the other woman. "C.O.s watching," she hissed between her teeth.

All movement around the court had come to a halt, all eyes were on Cam. The other woman stood a few feet beyond Tuck, a smile on her face.

Cam stood, her body tensed to move. Several long moments passed. Cam took a deep breath and relaxed her shoulders.

Reggie broke the silence as she shepherded the others from the court. "Yeh, come on, take a break. Nice shot. We won!" Cam's attacker sniffed a laugh, then turned and joined her friends as they walked toward the fence. Cam saw that one of the women in that group was Janet Lacey.

Tuck was still in Cameron's face. "You proved you can play. We know you're tough. Don't be stupid when there are C.O.s watching. If you want her, there are other places, but personally, I don't think it's worth it."

"It was a cheap shot."

"Yeh. So what. You made your basket. Get her back next time we play."

Cam shook the rest of the tension from her body and smiled.

"Or, you can take it out on Gina. That'll make *her* happy."

Cam looked into Tuck's face. "Gina?" she asked.

Tuck chuckled. "Yeh, she's hot for you. Asked me to fix her up with you."

Cam just watched as Tuck assessed her reaction.

"She's pretty hot in bed." Tuck smiled. "Likes it heavy and strong and she can take a lot. She's really good to work frustrations out on." Tuck turned to look around the yard. There were few who were still watching. Everyone was going about their own business now. "You do the heavy stuff? You know, fisting, spanking…"

Cam swallowed. "Just with Michael," was what she wanted to reply. Instead she just nodded.

"Good. Thought you were the type. Gina's what you want."

"In here? How do you get away with it?" Cam was surprised. She knew that there was a lot of surreptitious sex happening. But Tuck was talking S&M.

"It can be arranged. Tony Hernandez is on duty tonight. She's real easy to make look the other way. I can fix it up for you."

Cam was leery. "What'll it cost me?"

"Hell, I owe you one. No charge this time."

Cam nodded. "Tonight?"

Tuck smiled and clapped her on the shoulder. "Yeh. Tonight. Consider it a date."

Tuck turned and walked beside Cam off the court.

"You play pretty good. Did you play in school?" Tuck's tone was much friendlier.

"No, I rowed."

"Rode? Horses?"

"No. Sculls" Cam smiled, pantomiming the pulling of oars, "Boats. I was on the crew team."

"Oh, yeh. One of those rich school sports." Tuck grinned as she thought about that for a minute. "Makes sense, though. Shows in your shoulders."

"What about you?" Cam was beginning to like Tuck.

"Just street ball. I was the only girl on the block that could play with the guys. Not well, but I held my own. I was crushed when I found out they only gave scholarships for guys to play."

"Did you go to college?"

"Hell, no. Where would I get that kind of money, or the brains?"

"You seem smart enough," Cam countered.

"Street smart ain't book smart. Not everyone's like you."

She walked on ahead, leaving Cam somewhat relieved and very encouraged.

* * * *

That evening, after dinner, Cam lounged against the wall outside her cell. She could see Gina talking with Tuck and two other women down the hall and saw that Tuck cast glances in her direction several times. Part of her still wasn't sure that this was the road she wanted to take, but, well, she needed *something*. Another part of her just wanted to be left alone. Just wanted to get the job over with and get the hell out of this place.

The life in here was beginning to eat at her. Every time a C.O. stopped her and wanted to know where she was going or what she was doing; each time she passed an intrusive camera, every ring she heard of a warning bell and every slam of a gate; something inside her was beginning to break.

She still felt the anger she'd held onto since the ball game. Why couldn't she let this go? It had been no big deal! But it was gnawing at her stomach and had made it difficult to swallow the tasteless meal they'd served at dinner. Why was she taking it so personally? What had Charlie and Maggie missed in their preparations? Or was it just the drawn out time that was getting to her?

She stood there, chatting briefly with one of the other women on the floor until, finally, the four from down the hall approached her.

"Come with me." Gina waited. After a minute Cam again turned her head to look at her.

"Why would I do that?" Cam asked.

"I can make you relax. It'll be reeeeal good. Won't it, Tuck?" Cam looked at Tuck whose grin broadcast the fun she was having with this situation.

"Go on," Tuck said, glancing around. "You've got forty-five minutes 'til warning bell. Think you can do it in that time? Use my house. We'll keep the C.O.s occupied. You'll have privacy. Everyone'll know to keep away."

Without waiting for an answer, Tuck and her two friends sauntered off in the direction of the guard who stood at the beginning of the corridor.

"Come on, Mama," Gina cajoled, pulling Cam toward Tuck's cell. "Come to bed. I know you want to. I know you need to. You haven't had anyone in soooo long."

Cam tried to shake Gina away. Yes, she wanted to be in bed, wrapped in someone's arms, between someone's legs, but it wasn't Gina she wanted. But the more Gina spoke, the more she moved her body sensuously and gave Cam her seductive little pouty smile, the more Cam wanted. She could feel the tension in her body tightening.

"It's okay Mama. I can take it. Whatever you need." Gina's voice was lower, more urgent.

Cam looked at her. Damn little masochist, she thought. Anger flashed in her eyes.

"Yeh, come on, Mama." Gina was egging her on.

"How the hell do you know what I need?" spat Cam.

"I can see it. You want to blow. Everyone's seen it. You're ready to explode."

"So the fuck what."

"So blow. Explode. It's okay. You need someone to take it out on? Come on. What are you afraid of?"

Cam turned and faced her, standing as tall as she could. Her five feet, seven inches towered over Gina's five-one.

Gina smiled seductively and placed her hands on Cam's shoulders, slowly stroking down over her breasts. Cam caught her wrists in her hands and held them tightly, like two vise grips. Pain showed in Gina's face, but she didn't struggle or whimper. She looked straight up into Cam's eyes.

"See? Feels better already," she purred. "Now come on, before the bell rings." She pulled back, then bounced off down the corridor and disappeared into the last cell on the right.

She was already stretched out, seductively, on the bed when Cam entered. Cam hesitated, still dealing with her own demons, her own personal morality pressing on her shoulder. Was this the way she wanted it to be? Or was this what the johns who picked up the prostitutes felt? Probably not, at least not after the first time. She looked down into imploring eyes.

"Relax, Mama," Gina whispered.

"Stop calling me Mama."

"I can call you Mistress."

Cam felt a twinge of…what? regret? longing?

"I can call you Daddy. Whatever you want." She reached up and took Cam's hand and placed it on her breast. "Anything you want."

"You're a little whore," Cam spit at her.

"Makes no difference." Gina was pressing harder. "Maybe that's what you need."

Cameron squeezed the tit under her hand and felt Gina's body react.

"Yes. See? I can take it." Her voice was eager. "I'm a whole lot better than that dried up piece of meat you think's gonna wait for you. She can't be that good in bed. Probably likes it soft and gentle." She rushed on. "That's not you. You don't wanna be nice and gentle. You wanna be rough. You want to take all you can." Gina waited. Cam didn't move. Maybe a different attack was needed. "Or are you really just a minty vanilla girl like they're saying. All attitude and no action. Afraid of your own shadow. Some are saying that the only reason you stood up to Lacey was because Lou put you up to it. That the reason you're in here was 'cause you couldn't handle it on the street. Maybe you need someone like Tuck or Ruth to protect you."

Cam sank down onto the bed and pulled Gina roughly against her, letting her hands dig deeply into the soft flesh of Gina's upper arms. Gina melted into her and Cam began to be seduced by the pliable body pushing into hers. It had been so long. But...Cam pushed her away. One last attempt at pushing her anger and her desires away. Of pushing the thought of Michael away.

Gina rubbed her lips with the back of her hand, calculating her next move. Then she reached down and pulled her T-shirt over her head. Throwing it to the floor, she lay back, in just her bikini panties.

"This is better than hers," She taunted. "You know you want it. Come on. *Mama*."

Finally, filled with anger, Cameron allowed Gina to pull her down to her. Then without stopping to worry about what she was doing, she ripped Gina's panties off and rolled Gina onto her stomach. Cam rammed her fingers violently into Gina's slippery, willing, cunt.

Gina's surprised gasp went unnoticed as Cameron began her exploration of Gina's cunt. Each stroke, each movement was strong and forceful. It was the heat, the tightness, the slippery juices that surrounded her fingers... That was what Cam concentrated on. Just the pure animal instinct, a release of every worry, every fear she'd been holding inside. Cameron took what she wanted without regard for the small woman who dug her face into the bed, chewing on the pillow to keep from screaming. Soon, however, Gina crawled to her knees, her face still buried in the pillows, but her ass high in the air. Cam continued, stroke after stoke as she held onto the small firm buttocks beneath her. It wasn't until she felt Gina's body shaking with the tension of a deep orgasm that Cam even became aware of what she was doing.

As Gina's body relaxed from it's quaking, Cam allowed herself to fall onto the bed and turned her face toward the wall. That hadn't been sex, that had been anger. And violence. Damn Michael! Damn this place! Cam closed her eyes as she felt the small body behind her move slowly to wrap itself against her. She reached back to hold the hip that pressed against hers.

****

When the morning alarm rang, Cam was in a deep sleep. She rubbed her face and was surprised by the smell of sex on her hand. She looked around, but she was alone in her own bed. She remembered walking back here, stopping to thank Tuck, remembered the bell ringing, but beyond that…well she hadn't slept this soundly in weeks.

She grimaced at the memories of what she had done last night. Where had she learned that? From Michael? No, one thing about Michael; she always formed a contract with her before she attempted any rough sex. There had always been a way out, always a safe word.

But last night, Cam hadn't even given Gina a chance to respond. She had taken out her anger and frustrations on Gina but, as promised, Gina relished the roughness she got.

Cam put her shirt on and walked to the sink without buttoning it. She leaned over the sink and splashed cold water on her face. She heard the locks release and the doors slide open behind her. When she turned around, Gina was standing there, already dressed, waiting to catch her attention.

"Good morning, Mama," she smiled shyly, sliding into the small cell. "You were soooo good last night."

"I might have killed you last night."

"I'll take my chances."

Cam looked at her, then began to put her jeans on.

"We can be very good together." Gina ran her hand up Cam's inner thigh.

"We'll see. No promises."

****

Cam couldn't keep last night out of her mind as she sat in the library. She kept replaying it in her mind. She was disgusted with herself for the way she had acted. For the first time in a long while, she thought of her mother.

Mom. Emily Loring Andrews. The dyed-in-the-wool Massachusetts liberal who preached political correctness before it was politically correct to be politically correct. The woman who brought her family to a weekend at World Fellowship Lodge in New Hampshire at least once a year. World Fellowship was a gathering place of the politically aware with a left wing perspective where one could combine the joys of camping, swimming and berry picking with political discussion and debate around the dinner table and evening campfire. Emily always insisted that her children pay their own fees there in work exchange programs, serving in the dining room or changing beds so they wouldn't grow up thinking they were too elite to do menial labor. Emily Andrews, who brought her children up to believe in the Bill of Rights, Walden Pond and the Golden Rule.

"I'm almost glad she's dead," Cam scolded herself. "She'd be so ashamed of me. I can explain why I'm in this prison; it was a decision I thought about and I made it knowing full well what I was doing. But how do I explain that I've become nasty and mean? That I mistreat other women...and I enjoy it?" She shook her head in remorse. "It's this place: the waiting. The frustrations are getting to me. I'm not handling it well." Yes, she'd been edgy, curt. And last night...had she really raped another woman? The thought made her nauseous.

Why had she done that? To get back at Michael? Well, partly. Or to get back at herself for being so stupid. Why had she taken her frustrations out on Gina? Rough sex with Michael had been tempered with...what? Love? Trust? There had never been anger. Not anger like there'd been last night.

There was no comparison between Michael and Gina. Gina was fragile, less able to give as well as take. Not that Gina wasn't willing. She'd been more than agreeable to try anything Cam wanted. But she didn't have the strength, the force that Michael had. Cam and Michael had been equally matched. Gina was much more pliant, more willing to let Cameron take command.

Cam finished rearranging the books on the top shelf, then sat down on the bench and rubbed her face with both hands. She stretched her back to get the stiffness out. Some of the muscles she'd used last night hadn't been exercised in a long time and she could feel their complaints.

Damn it! she thought. What have I become? When did I become such a sadist? Cam's thoughts were running the gamut from herself to Michael to Gina. She was deeply ashamed of what she'd done to Gina last night. And just because she was angry...or hurt...no, upset with Michael.

To hell with Michael. Why am I letting her get to me? Then her thoughts turned back to Gina. Well. She sighed. I'll talk to her tonight. She's got to know that last night was wrong. She caught me off guard. Every trite excuse in the world flew into her head.

Cam yawned. Sleep. That's what I need. If I could just get a good night's sleep, I could think all this through better. I know I'm missing something. It's probably right in front of my nose. If I weren't so damned tired, I know I'd be able to see it.

She looked up as the noon bell rang. Well, she thought, after lunch, a little fresh air in the yard, or even a good workout in the gym. That should be enough to make me sleep well tonight.

* * * *

Gina, however, had other ideas. Not long after they'd returned from dinner, Gina danced back into Cam's room from wherever she spent her evenings. She bounced down onto the bunk where Cam had been quietly reading.

"Did you miss me today?" she asked.

Cam folded the upper corner of the page down to mark her place as she closed the book. As she turned to talk to Gina, Gina leaned into her and planted a long wet kiss on her mouth.

"Doesn't matter," Gina continued without giving Cam time to speak. She lowered her voice. "I missed *you*. I got you a present. We can have a party." From her back pocket, Gina pulled a small packet of white powder.

"Where'd this come from?" Cam asked. She was astounded.

"Better you don't know where it comes from. It'll be safer," Gina whispered, sliding the packet inside the pillow case. She winked at Cam. "I already asked Tuck. She'll run interference again. Tonight will be even better than last night," she giggled, then she rolled out of the bed and went to the sink to wash her face and hands.

Cam let her head fall back against the wall. This new development shed a whole new light on the situation. But where did it put her? Was she just prostituting herself? Wasn't this why she was hired?

"Come on, let's do the coke." Gina grinned.

"What if a C.O. comes by?" Cam asked.

"Silly. I told you Tuck was running interference! No one will walk by!"

Cam looked at the young blond who stood by the sink. The thought flashed through her mind that this was probably just the type of woman that Michael was bringing home.

She shook the thought from her mind. To hell with Michael! Cam had a job to do. If this was how it was going to get done, then she was going to take control and do it right. If Gina was the key to this puzzle, then Cam would use her. And if she found some carnal pleasure in it? Well, c'est la vie, n'est pas?

Gina snuggled onto the bed next to Cam and, using the long fingernail on her left pinky as a coke spoon, she fed two rather large portions to Cam, one into each nostril. Then she inhaled the rest, herself.

"See?" she whispered as she wrapped herself around Cam while she unbuttoned Cam's shirt and slid her hand inside to massage Cam's body. "Isn't this much better? Every night can be as good as last night. Better even. Let me show you."

Slowly, she wormed her way downward until her mouth touched Cam's crotch. Carefully, she pulled Cam's pants down and threw them to the floor, then she nuzzled her way between Cam's legs.

Cam laid her head back onto the pillow as she wound her fingers into Gina's hair, guiding her head to the places she wanted.

Okay, she thought as she felt stirrings within her, some flamed by the coke, some by Gina's tongue. If I've got to do this, I'm going to make the most of it. I'm not taking this personally and I'm in control. I can handle the coke. I just have to be careful. I just have to be aware of how much I'm doing. Maybe I can even protect Gina from doing too much. Suddenly, as she felt a pang of anxiety. Isn't that exactly what Michael had said? "I only wish that I could be there to protect you."

Cam moved her hips and forced Gina's face deeper into her. I'm in control here, she thought. I can take care of myself.

* * * *

"Michael, wait, we can do whatever you want, but this is unnecessary,' she pleaded. The sightless and soundless world was frightening. The black leather hood that Michael had zipped over her head held thick, soft pads of wool against her eyes and ears. No sound or touch answered her. She hung suspended from two chains attached to the ceiling with no idea where Michael was or what she was doing.

Cam broke out in a light sweat. She was a thousand miles from home, in the complete control of…what did she really know about Michael? This was Michael's territory: HER home. And it was obviously well equipped with God-knows-what. A lot could happen between a Friday night and a Monday morning. Why hadn't she told someone where she was going for the weekend? She could have at least told Pauly. "What a stupid idiot!" she scolded herself.

She jumped slightly as she felt Michael's hands, at least she hoped they were Michael's, running down her outer thigh. Two hands massaged her leg, from crotch to ankle and back up. Then her foot was lifted and a cold, pliant, probably leather, ring was slipped over her foot, then tightened around her ankle. As she placed her foot back on the floor, she could tell that the cuff was attached to something heavy.

Then her other foot was lifted and another cuff was slipped over that foot and tightened around the ankle. This time, before she could put her foot down, her legs were spread wide apart. She was now shackled to a bar or pole that held her legs several feet apart. She hung from the ceiling like a giant X.

Hands ran up and down her body, sometimes near her breasts, sometimes close to her pubic hair, but never quite touching. Then she felt a creamy substance being rubbed onto her nipples and a cool breath of air set them tingling as she smelled a cool whiff of eucalyptus. Her breasts felt like they were afire.

"What are you doing?" she asked as she took a sharp inhale.

The response was a sharp slap across her rear. She felt the slap reverberate throughout her entire body. At first she was stunned, but as the tremor rose through her body, so did a sensation of heat and desire. A second harsh slap sent an even harder tremor through her.

Cam let a weak whimper escape her lips as she felt the heat between her legs increase.

There was a moment of silence, then the hands began their exploration of her crotch. Cam tried, but failed to close her legs against them. A creamy substance was smoothed over her entire cunt. This time the tingling began even before the breath of air hit them. Cam squirmed, but was unable to relieve any of the sensations. Then the touching stopped.

It seemed like hours had passed and she still had no idea where Michael was or what she was doing.

"Michael..." she said, then waited. Still there was no response. "Michael!" She was becoming distressed. The cream on her breasts and cunt was sending shocks of sensations throughout her body. She wanted to rub them to stop the irritation.

Then, her mind quickly replayed Michael's words: "Just like in the Caribbean."

On the island, the one way to communicate with Michael was to play the game. Oh, shit. she thought, Not this. She licked her lips and acquiesced.

"Mistress..." she said, "Mistress, please..." But before she could continue she could feel Michael's body pressed against her back, Michael's hands lustily rubbing her body and breasts. She felt Michael's lips against her neck and she allowed her head to fall back against Michael's shoulder as she reveled in the sensations. Then, as her breathing became even more ragged, she felt the pinch of cold metal clamps being squeezed onto her nipples...

Cam woke suddenly, flailing to a seated position.

Still gasping for air, she tried to shake the dream from her mind.

Cam lay back, listening to the soft sounds from outside her cell. Please, Michael, don't do this to me. Not now. Stay out of my thoughts, stay out of my dreams. Let me get this job done. Then...maybe—

Chapter Seventeen

That Sunday, Maggie looked into Cam's eyes across the table. "Are you all right?" she asked. Was Cam even thinner than last week? She wasn't sure she liked the look in Cam's eyes. Something there was harder—meaner?—than she'd ever seen before.

Cam shifted her weight to lean forward on her elbow, careful not to lean too far across the table that divided them. She was aware of the guard that stood at the end of the row of tables, listening and watching. She shook her head. "I don't know." Cam ran her hand down her face. "I'm not sure I like what I'm turning into." She leaned a bit closer. "There was another OD here. I'm taking it personally. I didn't even know she was using the stuff and I saw her every day. We even talked a few times."

Maggie studied her. "Let this one go," she warned "It wasn't your fault. You can't be everywhere."

"But I've got to be *somewhere*," was Cam's reply.

Maggie sat back and waited. She knew there was more to this.

"I'm beginning to get real angry. And sadistic. I almost ripped a woman apart the other night and I nearly got into a fist fight in the yard." She took a deep breath, not wanting to look up at Maggie.

"People handle things differently," was Maggie's comment. "I was worried by your last letter. Do you want Dickie to send some mail?" (*Do you want to pull the plug?*)

"No!" Cam slammed her hand onto the table as she looked up at Maggie sharply. Then she softened. "No. I can handle it. I just haven't been sleeping well."

"Should I worry?" Maggie was concerned. This change in Cam was not unexpected, but still something that could mean trouble.

Cam forced her shoulders to relax. She shook her head.

"Has the food gotten any better?" (*Are you gaining any new information?*)

Cam relaxed a bit. She shook her head and nodded as she grinned back at Maggie. "There was a really tasty meal a couple nights ago."

Maggie returned her smile and relaxed a little. She was amused at what she knew was Cam's double entendre. At least Cam still had her sense of humor.

"Was it filling?" (*Good information?*)

"I could develop a taste for it." (*It looks hopeful.*)

"Don't get too fat on it." (*Be careful.*)

"Are you seeing *him* again?" Cam asked. (*What was Deems thinking?*)

"Yes. It's platonic, but I think he wants more than that." (*He was getting impatient.*)

"Make him wait. He'll get what he deserves. Maybe in the not too distant future. In fact, Christmas may be closer than he thinks." (*Tell him she was on to something. And it might break soon.*)

Maggie looked at her hopefully. "He'll wait 'til I'm good and ready," Maggie assured her.

"God, Maggie," Cam was too impatient for the secret code words. "It's so frustrating, being here. I wish we could talk like we used to. God, I miss it."

"Me, too, sweetie. Maybe you'll be out soon. Have you heard anything from the parole board?" (Another code: *How long did Cam think it would be?*)

"Not a word. I probably have to do another month or so before I even come up for that." (*Not soon enough!*)

Maggie read the frustration in Cam's voice and body language. But there was something else there, too. Something else that was adding to the turbulence.

"Is something else wrong?" Maggie folded her hands in front of her, the sign that the codes were finished.

Cam shifted her position. Maggie could see that there was a deeper turmoil happening than she'd anticipated.

"I got a letter from Michael. Two weeks ago," Cam answered after a long hesitation.

"And?"

"And what? What am I supposed to do about it? I can't call Canada from in here and I certainly can't write her. That's all we'd need is an address that can be traced! At least she thought enough to use an address that wasn't her own on the letter coming in." Maggie saw a flash of anger in Cam's eyes she'd seen only once before. She surmised the depth of conflict within Cam. Maggie stopped, trying to figure out how to address this problem.

Cam scratched her head and ran her hands violently through her hair. "There was so much…I don't know what…in her letter. What am I supposed to do, Maggie?" Her voice was lower, but no less agitated.

"What did she say?"

Cam leaned forward. The message was burned into Cam's memory. "It's like…I don't know if she wants me to be her lover or her friend or what. She wants me to trust her. Trust her? About what?" There was a look of desperation in Cam's eyes. "Maggie..I know I misjudged her, but I don't know what to do about it. There's so much hurt."

Maggie let this news sink in. She knew that Cam's assessment of her relationship with Michael was wrong. She'd spent too many hours on the phone with Michael recently. Now, how would this affect Cameron's performance? She decided that Cam should know everything.

"She called me." Maggie confessed.

"She called you?" Cam's voice raised slightly. "What did she want?"

"She was worried about you. She was worried about how you'd take her letter." Maggie studied the turmoil in Cam's eyes. "It can be all right," she finally said. "It can be whatever *you* want it to be. She knows you can't contact her. If you want, I'll let her know that when you get out of here, you'll talk to her. She's concerned about you...and what you think of her." Maggie sat back, thoughtfully, "She let herself get more deeply involved than she knew how to handle."

"What can I do about it now?" Cam asked.

"What do you want to do about it?" she asked quietly.

Cameron looked deeply into Maggie's eyes for a long minute. Then she turned her gaze to the ceiling. "There's nothing I *can* do," she said with resignation. "At least until I get paroled." It was the catch word. She stared back at Maggie. (*Please understand. I just needed to tell someone. Don't pull the plug now.*)

"That's a long time to wait," Maggie said, acknowledging her code.

"But I'll be a better person for it." (*Don't worry, Maggie. I'll be okay.*) "Besides I've found a new diversion. And this one may be just what I've been looking for." She smiled, knowing that Maggie had understood that.

Maggie acknowledged her with, "I know you're working hard to get rehabilitated. Maybe next month will be the turning point."

The visit over, Maggie walked out of the prison and got into her car. She was concerned about Cameron. She knew that this was not going as quickly as they'd hoped and she could see the toll it was taking on Cameron. There was a frustration level that could be dangerous. Cam had indicated that she might be on to something, but Maggie knew that it was not a guarantee. How many months now had the department thought they were on to something only to have it dead end? She just hoped and prayed that something would happen soon.

Maybe I should talk to Michael, she thought. Another letter at the wrong time could really spell trouble. She shook her head. Maggie was not the type of person to manipulate other's lives, but this might have to be the exception.

As she pulled out onto the highway with her mind still on Cameron, Maggie failed to notice the grey car that followed her back to Baltimore.

* * * *

"I hear you're making my baby very happy." Ruth was standing next to Cam in the food line. Cam and Gina had become an item in the prison.

Everyone respected the situation that Gina was now Cameron's Woman, and time after time, Cam kept the C.O.s occupied so that Tuck and A.J. could have their time together and, in exchange, Tuck did the same for Cam and Gina. Gina still showed up in the late evenings with cocaine and Cam was beginning to get more of a feel for what was really happening in the prison. This was the first time, however, that Ruth had spoken to her.

"Your baby?" Cam said.

"I think of all my girls as my babies. Gina in particular. She's not quite got her head on straight yet. I'm very protective of my family."

Cam nodded, either in agreement or understanding. Let Ruth figure it out.

"She also don't know her limits, yet. She's still a wild one. I'd hate to see her get hurt." It was a clear warning.

"You don't have to worry. I know the responsibility that goes with the territory," Cam assured her.

"I thought you would." Ruth took her tray and walked over to a table where her friends were seated.

Cam took a seat at a table near the wall. Gina was beside her in an instant. "I saw you talking to Ruth. She's really interested in you. She wants to meet with you."

"Why?"

"'Cause I told her how good you are in bed."

"She's not my type."

Gina gave her a playful shove. "Silly. She's my family. Family always wants to meet a new lover."

"We've met before. She just wants to make sure I don't hurt you. You have a very protective daddy."

Gina snorted. "She's jealous that she's not getting into my pants."

Cam looked at her.

"I let her once." Gina was like a little child sharing a secret. "But she's not as good as she thinks. You're a whole lot better." She twirled Cam's hair around her finger.

Cam brushed her hand away. "Will you stop that! I'm trying to eat." Gina turned away, pretending to pout.

Cam took a mouthful of food. Ruth, she thought, and the coke, right after we become intimate. Now, Ruth's really curious about me. This is the link I need to get closer to Ruth Tarlow.

Gina had turned back. "We could go hang out with Ruth after dinner."

"I really don't think Ruth wants me to hang out with her."

"Oh, it's all right, now. Jenny's not around. She got out last week. I thought Ruth might take me as her woman…"

"But she didn't, so you jumped me." Cam looked at her.

Gina lowered her eyes. "I'm glad I did," she purred softly, stroking Cam's forearm. "Come on, let's go hang out. I know she'll like you once you get to know each other."

Cam didn't want to appear too eager. "I'm not all that sociable."

Gina looked at her with a big pout on her face.

Cam pretended to give in. "Okay, okay."

Gina kissed her on the cheek. "I'll owe you one."

"You bet your ass. And I'll collect, too."

Gina smiled and danced away. Cam saw her go over to Ruth's table and join in the talk.

* * * *

The television room at the end of the corridor on the second floor, had been commandeered by Ruth and her crowd. Few of the inmates not in that crowd risked disturbing Ruth when she was holding court. It was just easier, and safer, to go to another common room.

Ruth, Tuck and another woman that Cam knew was also Ruth's lieutenant were intensely watching the World Series as a half dozen other women lounged around the room. These were all women Cam had seen eating at Ruth's table

"Hi!" Gina bounced into the room ahead of Cam. She plopped herself down on the couch next to Ruth. "I brought Cameron with me."

The women all turned to look at Cam who stood in the door, her hands in her pockets.

"Come on in," Ruth beckoned. "Annie. Get up and let our guest have a good seat."

Annie looked Cam up and down and got up reluctantly.

"So you're the new fuck," Annie sneered as Cam sank down onto the vacated stool.

Cam just smiled at her.

"You know, the girls'd been wondering how good you were," Tuck said, "off the court, that is." She, Annie, and another woman exchanged knowing glances and smirked, making sure Ruth didn't see.

"She's *very* good," Gina boasted. "Wanna see my bruises?"

There were several chuckles around the room as Cam began to feel very uncomfortable. "Wait a minute..."

"Relax. We all know Gina. Hell, we've all *had* Gina. As long as she's happy and healthy, it's your business." Ruth brushed the incident aside.

"I hear you're teaching Lourdes Cruz how to read English," Annie said.

"How long you in for? That could take years!" Someone laughed.

Cam laughed with her. "She's doing pretty good. Considering she can't even read Spanish. She's a smart kid. Too bad she never had schooling."

Annie snorted. "Schooling ain't everything. You gotta have it up here." She tapped her temple. "*Education* don't mean a thing. Look where it got you." She leaned back against the wall smugly.

"Yes, I hear you went to Harvard?" Ruth asked.

"Radcliffe. They didn't allow women into Harvard when I was there."

"Shit. Your folks own a bank or something? Or were you selling cocaine back then?" Annie chuckled, sneaking a glance at Tuck as there were a couple other snickers heard.

Cam shifted uncomfortably. She felt like she was being baited.

"Enough. All of you." Ruth flicked the air with her hand. "Get off her back. We've all made mistakes or we wouldn't be here."

Annie turned and walked out of the room. "I just never liked cops. Even ex-cops," she threw back over her shoulder.

There was silence for a moment. "Forget it," Ruth finally said. "She's just on the rag tonight." She gestured toward the TV, "and the Phillies are losing."

"It's only their second loss," Tuck added, defensively.

"This will bring the Royals even in the series. Think the Phillies can pull it out?"

"I know they'll take the series. I got money on it." Tuck stated firmly. "What you think, Andrews? Baseball up to your standards or should we be watching something like polo?"

"Maybe I should just be going." Cam started to get up.

"Sit down," Ruth ordered. "Relax and enjoy the game. This is *my* party. I say who stays. You're my guest tonight. My little Gina brings a friend to visit, at least we can be hospitable." She put her arm around Gina and Gina whispered something in her ear. Ruth shook her head and mouthed "Thursday," then gave her a hug and settled back to watch the game.

* * * *

Now that she had observed Ruth up close, Cameron was certain that the reports had been right, that Ruth and her family were responsible for something underhanded happening in the prison, but Cam had to get even closer if she wanted to find out for sure. And Ruth was hard to get to. Even though Gina was in Ruth's good graces, Cam knew that Ruth and her family, especially Annie, didn't trust her yet, even though she was getting closer to Tuck. No mention of anything illicit was made in her presence, even though Gina still managed to acquire small bags of white powder on a regular basis.

Cam was baffled. She knew she couldn't push Gina too hard. Gina was just flaky enough to let it slip about Cam's curiosity. And Cam was using now, more than she wanted to, more than was safe. At first, it had been to make Gina think she was 'one of the gang'. Then, when she refused, Gina would sulk, so it became easier to join her than to cause a scene. Now it had just become something to do. She was beginning to like the rush and the sexual energy it gave her. Because of that, Gina was delivering more and more.

"How are you paying for this stuff?" Cam finally asked, one night as they shared several lines.

"It comes out of my account. The books say I buy a lot of toothpaste." She rolled over and flashed her teeth at Cam. "Don't it look that way?" She leaned close and kissed Cam on the mouth.

Cam smiled at her. "Tastes that way, too. Don't they get suspicious?"

"Who?"

"Whoever audits the accounts."

"Silly." Gina started to grind her body into Cam's. "Why would they get suspicious?"

"Seems like a lot of money for toothpaste." Cam tried to appear uninterested. "Maybe I should be paying for some of this."

"No need. I get enough. Besides, you pay in other ways."

In response, Cam rolled over onto her and nuzzled Gina's neck as her hand delved deeply between Gina's legs. As Gina's breathing started to become erratic, Cam's mouth worked it's way down Gina's body. But in the back of her mind, Cam began to calculate how the money transactions might be made. Gina let out a little squeal as Cam bit too hard on her nipple.

Chapter Eighteen

"Hey, Paul! Hold up a minute!" Mr. Watson, the landlord, called as Pauly went up the stairs to the apartment. The older man leaned his snow shovel against the garage and walked carefully across the trampled snow to where Pauly stood.

"How you doing, Mr. Watson?" Pauly greeted him. "Nice snow last night. Early for a first snow. If this keeps up, we'll have a white Thanksgiving."

"Well, it looks pretty, but these old bones of mine sure don't like to shovel it," Mr. Watson grumbled.

"Then just leave it. I can do it when I get home," Pauly offered. "There's no sense in hurting your back or risking a heart attack."

"Pssh." Mr. Watson brushed Pauly's words away. "No sense in leaving it to freeze. Get the shoveling done while the sun is still out and it makes it that much easier."

Paul chuckled to himself. This old geezer just loved to grouse about the work it took to manage the ten apartments, but if the truth be known, he'd be lost without the work to keep him busy.

"There was a man here this afternoon, asking questions about you." Mr. Watson continued, giving Pauly a sly wink. "A government man. Said he was from the FBI or CIA. One of those letter companies. I don't understand why they have to use initials for everything. Can't they come right out and say where they're from or are they afraid someone will remember the real name?"

"That's strange," Pauly chuckled. "Did he leave a name?"

"I don't remember. He was tall. Asked a lot of questions about Ms Cameron, too. I told him it was none of my business. She was paying for her mistake. Leave her alone when she got out. She'll have enough problems being an ex-con and all. Can't remember, but I think I've seen him out here on the street before, though."

Pauly stopped short. "Do you remember what he looked like?"

Mr. Watson thought it over. "No," he said, shaking his head, "Wait. He left his number in case I remembered anything about you or Ms Cameron." He searched through his pockets. "Asked me not to mention it to you that

146

he was here, but I hate the way these government people think they can just nose their way into people's lives. That's not what we fought all those wars for. If we wanted a Gestapo, we'd move to Russia."

Pauly chuckled. How lucky that Mr. Watson was a man who thought the government took too much power, even if he did get his foreign agencies mixed up. "What types of questions did he ask?" Pauly inquired.

"Just wanted to know who you were, what you did for a living, if you were the new tenant or if you were subleasing. Wanted to know if I really thought Ms Cameron was guilty or was she just doing one of her police jobs."

"What did you say?"

"I told him that the police had been the ones that caught her. I remember the night they came here and made me open her apartment. They took all that stuff out of her desk. I was really shocked. You think you can judge someone and then something like that comes up. I think she just got in with the wrong people. Wanted to buy all those extra things. It's a shame. Such a shame. Here it is." He handed Pauly a wrinkled business card.

"Did he say he'd be back?"

"No, didn't seem to. Just asked his questions and left."

Pauly's mind was racing. Was this someone Deems had put on to check Cam's cover or was this a mole within the department, checking to see if Cam's imprisonment was on the up and up.

"Hope I didn't answer any questions I shouldn't have," Mr. Watson said, seeing a look of concern on Pauly's face.

"Oh, no. No problem. I'm sure everything is all right." Paul turned back to the stairs. "Oh, Mr. Watson," he added. "If he comes back, tell me, but don't let on that you mentioned him to me. Okay? And next time it snows, let me do the shoveling? I need the exercise."

With that, Pauly bounded up the stairs and into the apartment. He had to call Maggie. This could be serious.

Chapter Nineteen

Cameron was walking down the corridor toward the Recreation Room to watch TV when, as she turned a corner, her eyes were diverted by movement down the other hallway. One of the C.O.s was unlocking a small storage closet and, as Cam watched, she ushered Gina inside and followed her, closing the door behind them.

Her first impulse was to rush to Gina's rescue, but she realized that Gina had appeared more than willing to go into the closet. Cam had no doubts about what was happening in there.

She continued on to the Rec. Room and joined some other women in front of the TV, but sat where she had a full view of the corridor. About fifteen minutes later, she saw the C.O. walk by with a huge smile on her face.

Shortly, Gina appeared and, seeing Cam in the Rec. Room, waved and came to join her, grinning from ear to ear. But Cam was on her feet and met her halfway up the hall.

"What the hell are you up to?" She grabbed Gina harshly by the arm and turned her around toward the stairs.

"What? What do you mean."

"Get your ass upstairs," Cam ordered. She pushed Gina ahead of her and remained in stony silence until they were alone in Cam's cell. By that time, Cam was furious.

"What's wrong, Mama?" Gina turned and raised her arms to hug Cam.

"Don't you call me that. Ever again. Do you understand me?"

Gina looked into the fury of Cam's face and meekly nodded.

"What's wrong? What did I do?" she pleaded.

"What did you do? I saw you go into the storage room with that C.O."

Gina's face softened with relief. She smiled, dismissing Cam's anger. "Oh, that. That was nothing."

"Nothing!" Cam exploded. "You fucked her."

"No, I didn't. I just licked her pussy. No big deal. I let her feel up my tits. That's all. She didn't touch anything else. The rest is still yours." Gina couldn't understand Cam's fury.

Cam stared at her in disbelief. "Why the hell did you do that?" she asked.

Gina stared at her as if she were stupid. "I do that all the time, Cameron," she whispered. "How do you think I pay for the stuff?"

Cam was dumfounded. "You're hooking for cocaine."

"To get *us* coke," Gina corrected her.

Cam exploded. She backhanded Gina across the face with all her force and sent her flying back onto the bunk.

Gina stared, wide-eyed, at Cam as she held her cheek. Tears ran down her face. "She didn't touch anything that was yours," she whimpered. "No one else gets what you get. Honest."

Cam turned and pounded her fist against the wall. She was seething. She'd never hit anyone before, at least not someone she had a relationship with. She'd never thought herself capable of resorting to physical violence in an argument. If she could control herself, she probably could learn a lot more about the network here, but her anger had control. It wasn't that she thought of Gina as her property, but the reality of prostitution in exchange for drugs sickened her stomach. She knew, on some intellectual level, that it happened, but being thrown up against it like this evoked responses she didn't know how to deal with. She had to do something to pull herself together.

"Please, Cameron, please talk to me. Don't be mad at me," Gina begged. She stood and wrapped her arms around Cam's back.

Cameron turned around and looked down into the tear-streaked face. She couldn't trust herself to speak.

"It doesn't mean anything!" Gina sobbed. "Everyone does it. That's the way it works. Please believe me. I only belong to you. I was just doing this for us."

That did it. Cam shoved Gina away and stalked out of the cell.

Tuck was standing in the hallway as Cam marched past.

* * * *

Cameron didn't know what to do. Outrage had taken complete command of her and she was afraid to speak to anyone. If she didn't regain her self-control, she could blow her cover and get herself killed or spend the rest of her three-year sentence in solitary.

She started toward the library, her one quiet refuge, but knew she had to vent some of her rage before she exploded so she headed for the gym.

Cam was too impatient to warm up correctly and immediately dropped down onto the mat to do a set of fifty situps. Those done, she rolled over and did fifty pushups. By that time, she was covered with sweat, but still far from calmed. She rested just a moment, then began a second set of situps and pushups. At the end of the second sets, she had worked off a lot of her anger.

She moved to the weight bench and lifted the barbells. She was on a second set of bench presses when two hands reached over and helped her replace the sixty pound barbell on their rack.

"Feeling better?"

Cam looked up at Tuck who stood behind her. She sat up and wiped her face with the tail of her shirt, which was already covered with sweat.

"Yeh." She wiped the sweat from her neck. "Gina okay?"

"She's resilient. She'll bounce back." Tuck cleared her throat and sat down on the bench next to Cam. "Look, Andrews. I understand your anger. I used to be that way about A.J. but they all do it. All our women. Shit. A.J.'s got a regular appointment twice a week with one of the night guards. I don't love it, but it keeps us toasted and it keeps the heat off us."

Cam looked at her and held her hand up to interrupt. "It's okay. I got it together, now. What I can't understand is why she didn't tell me before. How come I have to find out like this?"

Tuck sighed. "I told her to tell you, but Annie said *no*. She said you couldn't be trusted."

Cam jumped to her feet. "Trusted?!"

"Look, don't get all heated up again." Tuck stood, putting her hand on Cam's arm.

"I just don't handle surprises too well."

"So now we know. I *told* Annie she was wrong. Look. We all get real possessive of our women, and if it were some other inmate making a move, well, you know…"

Cam looked at her and smiled. "You'd flatten them, right?"

Tuck smiled. "Yeh. But this is just business. Look, Gina really is yours. She don't put out for no one anymore and I think you already know she used to slut around givin' it to anyone who wanted it."

Cam let her head hang forward. So…they thought she was just being possessive of Gina. At least she hadn't blown her cover with her outburst.

"She's more worried about you right now." Tuck's voice broke into her thoughts.

"I better see how she is." Cam started toward the door.

"She's in Ruth's room," Tuck volunteered as Cam walked out of the gym.

* * * *

Gina's eyes lit up when she saw Cameron standing in the doorway. She got up off the bed and walked tentatively to Cam, placing her hands, carefully, on Cam's shoulders. "I'm sorry I didn't tell you, Mama." she said.

Cam looked down into her face and immediately noticed that her eyes were dilated and her manner too exhilarated. "It's all right." Cam took Gina's wrists in her hands to remove them from around her neck. As she did, she looked down and noticed a fresh red needle mark on the inside of her right forearm. No! she screamed inside, Not this! She pulled Gina close and planted a light kiss on her cheek, holding her tightly.

Gina took this as a sign of Cam's forgiveness and pressed her body, seductively against Cam's.

"Hold on to it, Baby," Cam whispered in her ear. "In a little while," she promised. Gina stepped back with a smile on her face.

"Am I forgiven?" She was back in her childlike cajoling mode.

Cam smiled at her. "Yeh. You're forgiven." She brushed her hand over the reddened patch on Gina's cheek. "What about me? Am I forgiven for this."

"It's okay, Mama. You didn't mean it."

Cam winked at her. "Why don't you go back to my house and wait for me. I gotta talk to Ruth for just a second."

Gina reached up and kissed her on the cheek, then bounced away.

"What a lovely little scene. I may weep with joy," Ruth scoffed from her seat on the bunk. Cam grinned and sat down next to her on the bunk.

"Any other little secrets I should know about?" Cam asked, leaning forward, her elbows on her knees. "I hate being surprised. I almost stepped right into the middle of that. It could have been a mess."

Ruth studied her. "You handled it all right."

"What if I hadn't?"

"Then, you'd be in solitary for assaulting a C.O. I think you're too smart for that."

"Maybe. I still hate surprises."

"You're right, Andrews. You should have been told. That was a bad decision on my part. You'll know if anything else comes up."

Cam looked Ruth square in the eye. "When did she start mainlining?"

"Not long ago." Ruth didn't seem the least bit surprised that Cam had noticed. "We didn't have needles until about a month ago when Angie worked in the infirmary."

"How badly hooked is Gina?" Cam asked outright.

"I don't know." Cam doubted that Ruth was telling her the truth about this. "How much do you use?"

Cam looked at the wall. "Not nearly as much as she does. I'm not hooked."

"Yet."

"Ever." Cam looked back at her. "I feel sorry for those that are addicted, but they're not my business. I'd be real sorry to see Gina go that way." She hoped Ruth got her message.

Ruth nodded. "I know where you're coming from. You'll be told if anything else comes up."

"Thanks." Cam stood and exited the cell.

So you think you know where I'm coming from, she thought as she walked upstairs to her own cell. If you really knew where I was coming from, one of us would be dead. At that moment, she was more determined than ever to do anything, everything, to get to Ruth and her drug business.

* * * *

Pauly came to visit as usual on the last Sunday of the month.

At first, as usual, their conversation was light. Then, Cam led it to a subject she'd been thinking about all month. "I hear you're getting a new boss."

It took Pauly a moment to realize she was referring to the recent presidential election. "Yes," he acknowledged. "There was quite a big deal about it."

"Anyone worried?" she asked.

"Well, you know how it is. No one's ever completely sure until the takeover is complete, but the upper brass seems to think that there'll be too much concern about the overseas business to worry about the local stuff."

"What does Dickey have to say?"

Pauly laughed. "He says that the big guy probably doesn't even know we exist. He doesn't seemed concerned at all."

Cam sat back with a sigh of relief. She'd been fearful that the new Administration would take over and someone would pull the plug on this before she had a chance to complete the investigation. Finally, deciding that the time had come to take a definitive step, to push things into motion, Cam gave Pauly a cue and as rehearsed, he leaned forward and whispered in a low voice, just loud enough for whoever was sitting at the next table to barely overhear. "You'd better keep your nose clean this week. I hear there's going to be a visit from Santa Claus."

Cam just nodded her head and changed the subject, but after Pauly left, she went right to Ruth's room.

As usual, Annie and Tuck were there, as was Gail, Ruth's latest conquest. "Smells like old books, Andrews must be here," Annie snorted without looking up.

"Ruth, can I talk with you for a moment?"

No one made a move to leave.

"Alone?" she continued.

Ruth looked at her for a moment. "Sure," she agreed. Then she tapped her foot on the barrel Tuck was sitting on. "You guys go get lost for a while."

Annie and Tuck got up unwillingly. Gail didn't move. She cuddled closer to Ruth, but Ruth pushed her away. "You too, Sweetmeat. Give us a couple minutes together."

Gail sneered at Cam, but got up and followed Annie and Tuck from the cell.

"What's so important?" Ruth asked as soon as they were gone.

"I just had a visit from my friend Paul," Cam said.

"That's so secret you couldn't say it in front of them? I know you had company. That cute little faggot that comes in once a month. What's so special about that?" Ruth snorted in disdain.

"Okay. If you don't want to know..."

"Know what? What's so secret?" Ruth was obviously in a bad mood.

"He's a cop. And a friend. We used to share an apartment. He told me that Santa Claus was gonna make a visit…"

"Well, good for you, I hope you get both your stockings filled," Ruth interrupted her.

"No, wait. When we were in the academy together, it was a joke. Every time we'd practice a shakedown or a raid, we'd say it was like being the reverse of Santa Claus 'cause we'd just slide down the chimney and take everything out of people's stockings. We'd end up with the presents." Cam stopped. She had Ruth's attention. "I think he was trying to warn me that there's gonna be a shakedown this week."

"We have shakedowns every week. What's the big deal?"

"This one could be Federal."

Ruth frowned. "You got any contraband?" she asked.

"Not me. But Gina usually has some. I don't want to see her hurt."

Ruth thought about it. "We'll see. This Paul. Is he dependable?"

"Saved my ass a couple times."

"Where would he get that kind of info?"

"He's sleeping with a highway patrolman. They do a lot of pillow talk."

"Nice to know we got such macho men protecting our little state." Ruth stopped. "Okay. So, what do you want me to do with this info."

"Whatever you want. Like I said, I don't want to see Gina hurt."

Ruth nodded her head. She was deep in thought. Cam turned to go. Ruth's voice followed her out the door. "Hey, Harvard. Thanks. Thanks a lot."

* * * *

Cam left the library to take some books to the warden's secretary. As she entered the outer office, she could see through the partially closed blinds into Warden Spellman's office. Someone in prison garb was in the office with the warden, or at least she assumed it was her. The inmate was some-one short, but Cam couldn't see either face. Whoever it was appeared to be having a heated discussion although the voices were too soft to be heard.

"Yes?" The voice diverted her attention.

Cam handed the three books to the secretary who sat behind the desk. "You asked for these?"

The secretary took them from her. "Yes, thank you," she said looking at the titles on the spines. "No, wait. These two are right. This other isn't the one I wanted."

"That's the only one we have by that author."

"That's okay. Take it back. I'll get the one I want somewhere else. Did you sign these out in my name or Warden Spellman's?"

"Your name. Sarah Adrien."

"That's correct. Make sure I don't get charged for the third one if it shows up missing."

"Don't worry, I'll take care of it." Cam turned to go.

"What's your name?" Sarah asked.

"Andrews. Cameron Andrews."

"Thank you, Andrews." Sarah wrote her name down on a piece of paper. "You can go now."

Cameron glanced toward the warden's office as she opened the main office door, but still couldn't see who was in there. She walked back to the library.

* * * *

Craig leaned over the table which was spread with photos. "What do you think?" Ever since Maggie had called him with Pauly's report about his landlord's secret visitor, they'd been watching Bob Trumble as he was watching Pauly and Maggie.

"I can't believe it. Trumble is a good man." Wendell shook his head. It was hard to believe that this might be their mole, that someone he knew and trusted might be responsible for one agent's death and another's injuries.

All four men who stood around the table looked at each other in silence. "What are you going to do to him?" Pauly asked. Ever since he'd identified the DEA agent who was checking on Cam, Maggie and himself, he'd felt an overwhelming sensation of panic in his stomach.

"If we arrest him, I think that we can build a solid case here. Look at these photos; he's meeting with several guards from within Hagerville and several other known drug dealers. These are contacts he should have reported. I wouldn't have thought it, but he's our mole." Deems' certainty was solid.

"Will this jeopardize Cameron's cover?" Pauly asked.

"It might. But we should get him off the street." Deems hated the thought that one of his men was corrupt.

"No, wait." Craig was the voice of reason. "Let's not jeopardize Cameron's cover if we don't have to. We could use this to our advantage."

Deems stared at him with one raised eyebrow.

"Let's think this through. He's checking to see if Cam's cover is real, to see if she's really in prison for a felony. What has he found out?" Craig looked from man to man as he ticked off his points. "One: that the Internal Affairs report wasn't a fake, two: that the arrest was real, three: that the sentence was handed down by a real judge. It seems to me that it's only helped Cameron. Why blow that?"

"What does Dr. Thomason say?"

"I talked to her this morning," Wendell said. "She knows that Trumble is keeping tabs on her, so she's keeping as low a profile as possible. She thinks this could help Cam, too."

"It seems to me that as long as Trumble doesn't know we're on to him, we can make this work to our advantage. We can feed him information we want to get back to whoever is at the top of this. Info that we can trace once it's gone through the pipeline. And, we can really solidify Cameron's cover. As long as we keep him under surveillance and know what he's doing, we can always arrest him if we need to. In the mean time, he may lead us to something."

Much to his chagrin, Deems had to agree. He still wanted to root out the bad apple in his department, but he knew that Cameron Andrews was closing in on her prey and if this could help her, well, Trumble could wait.

Chapter Twenty

The whistles blew loudly. Everyone immediately stopped in their tracks. "This is Warden Spellman," a voice boomed over the intercom. "You are all to go to your cells. *Immediately*. You have four minutes to get here. Anyone not in her cell when the doors are locked will be immediately confined to solitary for not less than sixty days."

Suddenly, the walkways at the top of walls around the yard were lined with State Troopers.

As everyone shifted into high gear to get back to their cells, Cam looked over at Ruth who stood several tables away. Ruth glanced her way and motioned for her to join them. Cam slid in beside her as they all filed quickly back to their cell block.

"Looks like you were right, Andrews," Ruth said in a low voice.

"Unfortunately," Cam replied.

"How'd you know? Why were you so sure?" Annie glared at her from beyond Ruth.

"I got a friend on the outside."

Annie snorted.

"Never mind. She was right," Ruth frowned. "What we gotta do now is find out what's going wrong."

"You talked with *her* this morning. What'd she say?" Tuck asked.

"Said we were crazy. Said she didn't know anything about a Federal shakedown—"

As they filed back into the building, officers they didn't know were everywhere. Female state police officers and others, both male and female, in dark suits, who could only be Federal agents, lined the halls.

"I told you not to trust her," Annie interrupted.

"Forget it. Now we got bigger problems." She turned to Cam. "Andrews, what else do you know about this?"

Cam looked around. Every eye in the group was on her. "Nothing. Just that there was going to be a shakedown this week."

"Well, they sure didn't waste any time."

"There's something going wrong, Ruth." Tuck leaned toward her. "What are we going to do?" She reached over and pulled A.J. closer to her, whether for comfort or to protect her.

"Nothing. They won't find anything today. Just like they never found anything before. We just lay low for a while. It'll blow over." She looked at Cam. "Think your friend has any more info?"

"I'll see. He probably won't be back to visit for another couple weeks, though."

"Any way to get him up here?"

"I could try writing him. I gotta be careful, though. They read everything. I'd call, but he's never home when we can use the phones."

All nodded.

"Do what you can. See what else he knows." From Ruth, it was an order. "Until then, everyone be very cool. We don't want to get nervous and blow it. Now get back to your cell. We don't need any of you in solitary."

"What about *her?*" Tuck asked.

"I'll take care of it." Ruth threw back as they all rushed back to their cells.

Her, Cam thought, you talked with *her* this morning. Could that have been Ruth in Spellman's office? Was Spellman the missing link?

* * * *

"How'd you do in the shakedown?" Cam asked Tuck as they walked back from the gym that afternoon. She and Tuck had been working out together more often recently and Cam was enjoying the camaraderie that Tuck provided.

"Well, we're both here, so I guess they didn't find anything."

Cam shook her head. "Those Federal agents made our C.O.s seem gentle."

Tuck grinned. "Yeh, the Feds really got into it. You can tell they don't get the chance often. They bodysearch you?"

Cam nodded. "Made me almost long for Emerson," she laughed.

"I know what you mean. I hate that stuff. I hear they ripped the curtains in the shower room to pieces, making sure there was nothing between the pieces of velcro."

"They tore apart several of my books, checking in the bindings for contraband. I hear the library's such a mess, I'll be working my ass off for weeks replacing the books."

"We need to get you out of that place. Too bad you're so damned well-educated. You'd be real useful elsewhere," Tuck smiled, looking for Cam's reaction.

"For what?" Cam asked.

"We could use your brains *and* your muscle," was all Tuck replied.

"Listen, I want to buy some coke," Cam whispered, seizing the opportunity.

"Yeh," was all Tuck said.

"So how do I go about it?"

Tuck stopped and looked at her. "You don't know? I thought you used regularly."

"Gina always gets it. Now that I know how she's been paying for it, I don't want her to have to work that hard. I can pay for my share myself. I don't have to...you know...with one of them, do I?"

Tuck chuckled. "Hell, no. That's probably the easiest way to pay for it cause there's no transaction to track. The C.O. just gives the money to the one at the top and you find coke in your pocket the next day. But if you got the cash in your account here, it's no problem, either. How much you want?"

"Just a half gram for now."

"Easy. Just tell Donna in the store that you lost fifty dollars to me in a poker game."

"That's all?" Cam was skeptical.

"Easy as pie." Tuck took a small piece of paper from her pocket and handed it to Cam. "Write an I.O.U. and sign it. Donna will know what it means."

"Doesn't anyone check the accounts?"

Tuck put her hand on Cam's shoulder. "You got a lot to learn, sister." She shook her head and walked up the corridor.

****

The next day, Cam went to the prison store. Donna Trachner smiled at her from behind the counter. "Hi, stranger," she greeted Cam. "How's it going?"

Cam leaned forward against the counter. "I'm doing okay." She smiled. "What about you?"

"Oh, just fine. Same ol' same old."

Cam grinned at Donna's terminology. It seemed to be her basic comment on everything. "I haven't seen Sharon around much. Do you know how she's doing?" Donna asked

"I've seen her in the cafeteria. She looks okay, but she stays to herself," she answered.

Cam hadn't seen either of the two women she'd entered the prison with in several weeks. But she wasn't really in the mood to make small talk right now. "Listen, I need to transfer some money. Tuck said you could do it for me. I...uh...I lost fifty dollars to her in a poker game last night." She handed Donna the I.O.U.

Donna took a step back and looked at Cam with raised eyebrows. "I see," she said, knowingly.

"You can do that?" Cam asked.

"Of course." Donna smiled. "It'll be done tonight. I didn't know you were a player." She hesitated just a moment to emphasize her meaning. "A poker player, I mean."

Cam stared at her. "Sure, why not?"

"I should have guessed."

Cam leaned forward slightly. "This is her *special* account." she said softly.

Donna smiled patiently as she glanced back over her shoulder to check on the guard, who was talking to another inmate in the next aisle. Then she lowered her voice to a whisper. "A lot of people in here play poker. It's amazing how much money they lose!"

Cam nodded her understanding.

As she turned to go, Cam noticed a stack of journals piled on display. They were neatly bound in brightly colored cloth that was padded to create a soft exterior. "Are these some of the books they make in the bindery?" Cam asked, taking one from the top of the stack. It was set up and opened, the others were shrinkwrapped in tight plastic.

"Yeh," Donna smiled enthusiastically. "Ain't they nice? The girls do a real good job on them, don't they. They're blank inside. You can write whatever you want in them. They make neat Christmas presents if you got someone you want to buy for. If you put an order in, they can even be gift wrapped and shipped out from here." Donna straightened the pile and replaced the one Cam had picked up, open, on the top. "'Course, you don't get to pick out the one you send, it all has to be done through the bindery. You can specify a color, but you can't pick the material. That's so no one has a chance to slip anything illegal into one," she smirked in disgust at Cam. "They think they're so smart."

"Good idea," Cam said thoughtfully. "I got a sister I could send one to. She always used to keep a diary. She'd probably like it."

"You get a real good price on them, too. I've heard they do a hundred percent markup on them when they put them out in the stores."

Cam chuckled. The bindery and this little project was one of the few projects in the prison that both taught a skill and brought in money. Maybe she'd buy one for Maggie and for Grandma Anne. She stopped. It felt like the time she'd sent those little baskets made from popsicle sticks home from camp. Did everyone do that to show the family that they weren't just goofing off for the summer? Strange, how things pop up in your mind when you don't expect them.

"Thanks, Donna. I appreciate your help." Cam turned and walked back to her block.

That night, when she was going out of the cafeteria with a crowd of women, she felt a hand on her ass. Reaching into her rear pocket, she felt a small plastic bag of powder carefully placed there.

* * * *

"I got your letter, but I couldn't get away last weekend."

Cam smiled at Pauly. "No problem. It's good to see you."

159

There were several other inmates with their visitors in the reception room. Guards stood at each end of the long row of tables to insure that nothing was being handed between inmates and visitors. One of the inmates had obtained permission to hold her two-year-old daughter and the guard was watching closely as she hugged and bounced the youngster on her knee.

Pauly leaned as closely as he dared. "What's up?" he asked in a low voice.

Cam looked at him. "They want to know if you know anything else," she stated.

"Do I?"

"Maybe something. What can you come up with?"

Pauly looked around at the other people in the room. "I could probably come up with something. Did the last stuff work?"

"Like a charm. Check out the number one." She tried not to stare into his eyes, but hoping he'd get the code.

He nodded. "Think so?"

"Maybe. Just a hunch." She sat back. At that minute, the two-year-old started crying loudly and everyone's attention focused in that direction. The guard walked by in back of her, attention on the youngster and her mother.

Pauly sighed. "Must be hard. Both on the mother and the kid."

Cam nodded. "Glad it's not me."

"If you had a kid, you wouldn't be here."

Cam looked at him and smiled, ironically. "Right." Then she remembered and leaned forward a bit. "Listen, I need a little money. About two-hundred dollars. Will you ask Maggie to deposit it into my account here? For next week?"

Pauly looked at her with raised eyebrows.

Cam smiled. "Tell Maggie it's a business expense."

Pauly sat forward, concerned. "You using that much?" he asked.

Cam avoided his eyes.

"I'm close, Pauly. I'm okay. Don't worry."

Pauly hesitated. "You sure?"

Cam just nodded.

"By the way," Pauly leaned forward, "someone's been reading your file. I think we're gonna be all right."

Cam nodded. Maggie had briefed her about their friend and the files that Dickie had constructed that contained background info about the discrepancies in many of her earlier police reports. Hopefully, this would solidify her cover long enough for her to get the job done. Hopefully. As long as it didn't take too many more months. As much as she wanted to do her job well here and not leave any loose ends, there was still that one issue on the outside she wanted to tackle. She hadn't had another letter from Michael, but then, she hadn't answered the first one, either. Damn! She'd gone months without even a chance at a serious relationship. But now...why did things always come up when she had something else she should be thinking about?!

* * * *

"Well, did he have anything else?"

Cam was in Ruth's cell that evening. Just the two of them were there. Tuck and Annie were inexplicably absent.

"No. But he'll keep his ears open. He may be able to find out something, but he doesn't want to get caught."

"Can't say I blame him." Ruth paced back and forth in front of Cam who sat on the bunk. Cam couldn't read her expression.

"You got family?" Ruth stopped, looking at her.

Cam looked up, puzzled by the question. "Am I *in* a family?" she asked.

Ruth looked at her. "No, I know that Lou looks out for you, but you're becoming more a part of my family. Tuck looks out for you, too, you know. Not that you need looking out for. You hold your own okay." She continued, "I was asking about family outside; brothers, sister, parents..."

"None that want to admit it. Why?"

Ruth shook her head. "Christmas. Makes me sentimental." She plopped her bulk down on the far end of the bed.

"Well, I'm not expecting a lot of presents," Cam said. The question hit a hollow space in her gut. She still hadn't heard from Lori, although she had gotten a long letter from Grandma Anne the day before. It had the usual news about the family and some gossip about Lexington, but there was something more than just the usual monthly letter. This time, Grandma Anna had gotten a bit sentimental about all the people she wasn't spending Christmas with: Grandpa Josh, Cam's mother, Ben...and, of course, Cam. Had Grandma Anna written her off as dead, too?

"You like working in the library?" Ruth's question cut into her reverie.

"Why are you asking?" Cam couldn't figure out where Ruth's questions were headed.

"Annie's up for parole next week. I may need someone else to replace her on the loading dock. You mind physical labor?"

Cam tried to appear disinterested. Maybe this was what Tuck had alluded to. "Not at all. Sometimes I get bored in the library, but it's easy work."

Ruth nodded, but didn't say more. Finally, Ruth looked at her. "You know that Annie hates you."

"I understand that. Makes no difference to me."

"Tuck thinks you're okay. That was nice of you to help her out the way you did that day. Took some guts."

"I like her, too."

"I've had some good reports on you."

Cam looked into Ruth's face. So, Pauly'd been right, they had been checking on her. "Good reports? You checking up on me?"

161

Ruth smiled. "I'm a business woman. I like to know who I'm working with. I've been keeping my eye on you, that's all." Ruth nodded, thoughtfully. "I like your style. I like the way you treat Gina. Gives her some self respect. She looks up to you. I'm glad you look out for her."

"She's a good kid."

Ruth nodded her agreement. "You in love with her?"

"No," Cam answered truthfully without hesitation.

"Good. She is with you, you know. You're all she ever talks about."

Cameron nodded and made a mental note to be even more careful about what she said to Gina. "She'll get over it. One of us will get out of here and she'll forget all about me."

Ruth sat back and examined Cam for a long moment. "What makes you tick, Andrews? Why are you here?"

Cam was taken aback. Where was Ruth heading? "You wanted to know what Pauly knew," she stammered, buying time.

"No, I mean, why are you in this hellhole?"

Cam sat back. So Ruth was doing her own checking. "Does it make a difference?"

"I like to know people. I'd like to know your side of it." Ruth studied her.

Cam thought for a moment. "I don't know." She admitted, as she'd rehearsed. "I got greedy, cocky, thought I knew how to beat the system."

"You learn anything?" Ruth was grilling her. "If you want to tell me to mind my own business, go ahead. I'm a nosy old lady." Ruth chuckled.

"No," Cam said. "It's not that. I just, well,…I just haven't wanted to think about it."

Ruth sighed in agreement. "We all got our own story. I'm here 'cause I couldn't keep my hands off of other people's property. Annie was turning tricks to support a good-for-nothing boy friend. Tuck stabbed a man her lover was having an affair with. Gina was with her boyfriend when he shot a store clerk during a robbery attempt. Lou's here 'cause she caught her husband fucking their daughter and chopped his head off."

Cam sat forward. "I didn't know that."

"She don't talk about it. She's been here almost twenty years already, it'll be another ten before she even comes up for parole. People respect her 'cause she's been here longer than anyone else. She keeps her nose clean, but watches out for those who can't take care of themselves. She's a good family leader. Watches out for them that need it."

Cam nodded. "I know."

"She respects you."

Cameron nodded. Lou suddenly made sense to her, but the way she protected *her* children was a lot different from the way Ruth protected *hers*. Cam suddenly changed the subject. "I just want to get out of here."

"Don't everyone? But seeing we can't, we make do. Right?"

"Yeh, I guess." Cam almost wanted to like Ruth at that moment. Hopefully, her well-rehearsed act had been convincing enough for Ruth to begin to trust her. She just had to step back and wait.

* * * *

Ten days later, Cameron walked into the laundry after breakfast. Ruth had gotten her work assignment changed for the day. Annie was 'on hold' for her parole hearing, just waiting and pacing until they were ready to talk to her, and Cameron was to replace her for the day.

The DEA suspected that the laundry was the center for everything, but they'd searched it thoroughly several times and always come up empty handed. Maybe, just maybe, Cameron could find the key.

"Hey, Andrews. Welcome aboard," Tuck called. She was supervising several women who were separating sheets and blankets and putting them in bins to be washed. There were eight women in the laundry besides Cam and Tuck. Each went about her business of putting batches of laundry into the giant fifty pound washing machines and moving finished loads from those machines into the driers.

"What do you need me to do?" Cam asked, walking up to Tuck.

"Nothing right now, everyone's got a routine." Tuck smiled. "Have a seat. There's a delivery due in a half hour. We'll need your muscle when that arrives."

Cam hopped up onto the top of one of the machines and sat next to Tuck.

About forty-five minutes later the alarm sounded at the door of the laundry and the steel delivery door slowly slid up to the ceiling. Outside, two prison guards, with rifles in hand, casually leaned against the building as a truck marked Testa Laundry Service Supplies backed up to the loading dock.

Tuck walked out onto the dock and nodded to the guards as the driver hopped down from the cab and walked up the stairs to the platform.

"Hey, Mike, how's it going?" Tuck greeted him.

"Fine here. How're you?" Mike looked into the laundry. "Where's Annie today?"

"She's got her parole hearing today! With luck, she'll be out of here by Christmas."

"Good for her. Tell her I said Hi." He handed Tuck a clipboard with the delivery papers and unlocked the back doors of the truck, swinging them open. "Got quite a load for you today."

Tuck checked the list. "Great." She turned to Cam and nodded for her to join them. Another woman whom Cam knew only as Douglas had joined her. Cam had seen her several times in the gym. "We got to unload this stuff. Be real careful. Don't drop anything."

Cam walked over and picked up the hand truck that was lying at the back of the truck. Inside the truck were heavy fiberboard barrels, each marked Industrial Laundry Detergent Powder and several cartons of bleach and other laundry supplies.

"Put the detergent over next to the last washing machine 'til we inventory it," Tuck ordered. "Douglas knows the routine."

Cam and Douglas began the job of moving the fifty-pound drums. Tuck stood and talked to Mike and joked with the two guards until they were finished.

Finally, Mike closed and locked the truck doors, took the signed delivery slip from Tuck, giving her a copy, and drove out of the yard. The loading bay door was closed and locked.

"Okay, ladies!" Tuck called. "Let's do it in less than five!"

Suddenly everyone in the laundry snapped to life. Two of the women began shaking out newly washed sheets directly in front of the closed circuit camera, blocking the view of the rest of the room. Tuck tossed a ring of keys to Douglas who unlocked a metal tool box that was attached to the wall. From it, she took two large monkey wrenches and tossed one to another women who scrambled up next to her on top of the last washer.

Cam watched her as she tapped a brass water pipe that fed into that machine. She fit her monkey wrench onto the top joint as the other woman did the same at the bottom. Together, they unscrewed the five foot length of pipe which came away from the other plumbing completely dry.

"Andrews, I need you over here," Tuck's voice interrupted.

Cam turned her eyes away from Douglas and looked around. Two of the women were standing at the doorway, keeping guard. Cam moved from where she'd been standing to where Tuck and three others were prying the lids off the barrels of detergent. She helped Tuck slowly scoop the contents of one of the barrels, with her hands, into an already empty barrel. "Take it easy, do it real slow. Careful now," Tuck whispered as, about four inches into the barrel, a thin film of clear plastic appeared.

Tuck carefully brushed the detergent out of the way with a small clean paint brush. As the detergent was removed, Cam saw a small, round, thin, plastic pillow materialize. It was stretched to the circumference of the barrel and held in place by a thin strip of tape. Tuck took her thumb nail and carefully pried the tape from around the inside of the barrel, then slowly lifted the pillow out of its nest. The white powder inside the film was a bit shinier than the surrounding detergent. Tuck laid the pillow onto a sheet of paper that one of the women held out. Then it was rolled up and tied with a piece of string that had been glued inside the lip of the barrel. Quickly, but carefully, Tuck and Cam extracted three more pillows of cocaine from the barrel. Once the last thin layer of powder was bundled, Tuck smiled up at Cam. "Ingenious, ain't it?" Tuck tossed the packets up to Douglas who dropped them down into the pipe.

"Your turn." Tuck told Cam. "Those other three with the stars get the same treatment."

Within five minutes, four barrels, each marked with tiny red stars near the bottom rim, were emptied of their contents and the pipe was screwed back in place. Cam estimated that each of the barrels held about one-hundred grams of cocaine. The sheets were now being carefully folded and placed in the clean laundry hamper.

"Well, what d'you think?" Tuck was at Cam's elbow as they watched Douglas screw the pipe back in place.

Cam shook her head. "Incredible. Whoever set this up was a genius."

"No kidding. The pillows are rigged so they break if the barrel is just dumped out. Anyone digging into one of the barrels would just break the film and the coke would be so mixed up with the detergent, they'd never be able to trace it." As she spoke, she took several other small pieces of paper from her shirt pocket and wrote a series of numbers on them, then slipped them into her hip pocket.

"But what about the C.O.s? The cameras?" Cam asked.

"We share with the guards," Tuck smiled, using the term 'guards' in its most derogatory way. "Enough to make it worthwhile. They're on the take, they can't report it. The cameras aren't placed well enough to get anything happening over in that corner and they can't see the pipe at all. With the sheets flying around, there's not much anyone can see clearly."

Cam shook her head in amazement. She knew that the tapes from the cameras had been viewed. And no one had ever picked up anything? "Who thought of the pipe?" Cam asked.

"We had a woman in here about three years ago who was a plumber. No one has ever suspected that this pipe wasn't part of the water system."

"I am impressed."

Tuck offered her a cigarette and looked her straight in the eye. "You're also part of the process now. You know enough to keep your mouth shut."

"No one will find out from me," Cam lied, bending to light the cigarette from Tuck's match. She was in awe. No wonder no one had ever found anything. And there it had been all this time, no more that five feet above their heads.

Tuck, her back to the camera, carefully handed the remaining bag of powder to Douglas. "Put this where we can divie it up later. We got orders to fill."

* * * *

Maggie walked happily into the bi-weekly status report meeting and tossed her notepad on the table, blithely, as she slid into the chair. For the first time in months she hadn't dreaded coming to the meeting. At last she had some concrete information to report.

"It's coming in through the laundry with the detergent."

Deems looked at Maggie. "She's sure?"

Maggie smiled broadly. "She says the reason we never found anything was because it was in a fake pipe in the ceiling. It was right over your head all the time."

Deems laughed. "Damn her! That is good! Six months has been a long time to wait, but when she does something, she does it right."

"So, aren't you sorry you hired a 'God-damned Lesbian'?" Maggie threw back in his face.

"Who she sleeps with has nothing to do with this."

Maggie was surprised to hear Deems spout that type of philosophy. "Well, in this case, it had everything to do with it. It was her protection of her little 'next door neighbor' that got her into the family to begin with."

"So I was wrong. So, sue me." Deems glared at Maggie. "She'd be good anyway."

Maggie sat back. She knew when to stop pushing.

Wendell chuckled. "Not quite the image of the 'girl-next-door' I was brought up with," he smiled. Then he turned serious again. "We'll put a tail on the delivery company and the detergent manufacturer. Both look clean from the outside, but we'll check every angle. We want to be sure where this starts before we make a move," Wendell assured him.

Deems nodded. "Has she found out for sure who the conduit is yet? Or how it gets out of the prison?"

"She still suspects that the outside conduit is Spellman, but the only one who ever has contact with her is Ruth Tarlow. Cam hasn't been able to pin anything on Spellman, yet."

Wendell agreed with Maggie. "Neither have we. I've had men on her for the past month and she squeaks clean. Family, three grown kids, two grand-kids. Everyone goes to church AND Sunday School. Tithes to the church. Her husband's a Boy Scout leader. How am I going to pin anything on a woman like that?"

"Cam still doesn't know how it's going out of the prison, but she's very excited about this discovery. Leave it to Cameron. She'll find out more." Maggie assured them. "

"I bet she will. I just bet she will."

"She wants to make sure you'll wait until she has evidence on everyone before you make a move," Maggie reminded Deems. "She says that inside the prison the money is funneled through the prison store. Spellman administers the store herself. You'll have to figure out how the money is handled outside. "

"Yes," Deems agreed with Maggie. "I'll bet that her hunch is right about how people get paid inside, but proving it is another story."

"She's real nervous that someone will get missed. She doesn't want to get killed."

"Let her know that she's still calling the shots. We won't move until she's sure it'll be air-tight."

As the men left the room, Maggie let her buoyancy sag. Cam was much more relaxed and confident this weekend, but Maggie could tell from the topics Cam sidestepped that Michael was still a very sore issue. It didn't seem to be hindering Cam's performance right now, but if it escalated, if the time wore on and Cam let it eat at her…well, best be on the alert.

Chapter Twenty-One

The Rec. room was decorated with paper cutouts of Santa Claus and wreaths. There was a small tree in the corner, decorated with strings of popcorn and sponges shaped like reindeer and angels. Ladies from some community service organization had gone out of their way to try and bring some semblance of holiday cheer into the prison. They weren't allowed to have lights for the tree, but they'd made do as best they could. One fifth grade class in a nearby school had even gone to the trouble of tracing, cutting, and pasting a collage of a Nativity Scene to be hung on the wall.

Annie was holding court there. She'd had her parole approved and would be out on Wednesday, the day before Christmas, and she was celebrating. "I called my old man. He's picking me up at ten a.m. When I walk out of here I hope I never see any of your ugly faces ever again," she boasted.

"You'll be back," Tuck laughed. "You like the life here too much."

"Up yours," Annie retorted. "Maybe you like all these sweet young girls in your bed, but I like a good strong man in mine. I can't wait. I'm not letting him out of bed until after New Years!"

All the others laughed and added their comments, toasting her with their small glasses of boot-leg beer that someone had sneaked into the prison.

Ruth touched Cam's arm. "I want to talk a minute," she whispered. "Come up to my house in a little while. No rush."

Cam nodded. Ruth walked slowly away as Cam turned back to the celebration.

The party was warming up, the music getting louder and the talk more obscene. Tuck and A.J. stood just outside the door talking to two C.O.s, one, the short, dark haired woman named Tony whose picture had graced Maggie's table, the other a tall blond who A.J. met in a storage closet twice a week. Both women knew what the party was about, but wouldn't interrupt unless something got out of hand and there was trouble. It was their contribution to the holiday spirit to look the other way.

Cam turned to look for Gina, but Gina was dancing frenetically with some of the Latinas to loud music off the radio. She caught Cam looking at her and gave a little wave, then went back to her dancing, her eyes closed, caught up in the music.

Cam waited a few minutes, then slipped out of the room and slowly made her way toward Ruth's cell. As she rounded a corner, she nearly bumped into three women standing in the hallway. One was Janet Lacey.

Lacey gave her a shove. "Can't you just stay out of my face?" Lacey glared.

"I'd love to," Cam returned the stare. "It's just hard to get away from the stench."

Lacey pushed again. It took all of Cam's resolve not to throw Lacey to the ground.

"Hey, what's happening here?" A voice from the hall yelled.

Both Lacey and Cam looked up to see Emerson standing a few feet away. "Why nothing, Miss Emerson," Lacey smiled sweetly. "Just wishing my friend here a happy holiday."

"Cut the shit, Lacey. Everyone knows how you two feel about each other. Just keep it cool while I'm on duty. I'd get real angry if I had to do extra paperwork because of you two."

Cam took the opportunity to step away. "Happy Holidays, Janet," she said as she walked away.

"Same to you, Cameron, dear," Lacey's sickening sweet smile followed her, "And many, many more."

When Cam finally got to Ruth's room, Ruth was talking to Douglas. Ruth motioned for Cam to join them.

"Sit down, Andrews. Douglas and I have been discussing some business. You know now what really happens in the laundry. With Annie gone, I need more help." She paused as Cam sat on the edge of the bunk.

"Here's the story. Douglas, you've been with us for over a year now. I like your work. I like you. You got good influence with the straight women in this block. They seem to listen to you without being afraid, like they sometimes were of Annie." She turned her eyes to Cam. "Andrews, I know you're sort of in Lou's family, but I've had my eye on you since we first met," she paused and stifled a grin. "Let's just say I was impressed with your work."

"I didn't think I made a good first impression."

"You held your own and thought on your feet. I probably would have liked you right away if I hadn't been so damned mad. Anyway, you're smart." Ruth looked from one to the other. "I've spoken with Lou. She likes you a lot, but says it's your decision what family you're in. It'll be hard getting you out of the library, but I need you. I'll work it out. I want both of you to move up in the family, be the 'aunts', so to speak. Tuck is 'Mom'. She'll have final say, except for me, of course. You interested?"

"I think I could do it," Douglas said.

"Don't *think*. *Know* you can do it. I need strength here."

"I can do it," Douglas corrected herself.

Ruth turned to Cam. "What about you?"

"Do I have to call you Daddy?" Cam asked with a smile on her face.

Ruth sat back, appraising her. "Got a mouth on you, don't you?"

Cam grinned, to concede the point. "What exactly do I have to do?"

Ruth smiled and nodded her approval of the response. Never commit yourself to anything you don't know everything about.

"First, I need you permanently on the shipping dock. I'll take care of the money transfers. I want you to oversee the shipments, keep track of what comes in and what goes out. You got a head for figures. Be my shipping manager. Douglas, you'll be in charge of distribution inside here. Keep track of who gets what and make sure it's paid for."

"You need two of us to replace Annie?" Cam asked.

"Hell, no. Just time I took a step back. You know, semi-retirement." She smiled at them. "When I see people who can do the job as good as me, I let them. Tuck will take over the bindery. Jay's getting too squeamish for the job and besides, she's up for release in a few months." She looked at Cam. "Are you in or out?"

"I'm in."

"Good. Go back down and enjoy the party. We'll meet tomorrow to go over your new assignments. And be aware that there are several people who'll think they should have gotten your jobs. Especially yours." She directed that to Cam.

Both nodded and got up to leave.

"Andrews. Stay one more minute."

Ruth waited until Douglas had gotten to the end of the hall.

"I really need your eyes and ears more than anything," Ruth told her in a hushed voice. "Something's happening here I don't quite understand. If your friend Paul says anything else, let me know right away. We should have been told about that Federal shakedown and we weren't. I can't tell if our friend was lying to us or if she really didn't know it was coming. Just be on the alert."

"I understand," Cam told her. Ruth's slap on the back let her know that their meeting was over.

Walking back to the party, Cam felt a rush of adrenaline. Yes! She was in! She wished she could call Maggie and gloat a little about it. So, Ruth wanted her to watch and listen. Ruth didn't know how well, or how thoroughly she was going to do her job.

Chapter Twenty-Two
Two weeks later

"Happy New Year," Pauly greeted her as she took her seat across the table from him.

"God, I hope so," Cam smiled back at him. "I didn't expect to see you sober this early in the year."

Pauly shook his head in resignation. "I pulled traffic duty on New Years Eve. Spent the whole night getting drunks off the streets. Just a couple brawls, some verbal abuse. Nothing special."

"Sounds exciting. Why don't I miss it?" Cam grinned. "We had a nice little celebration here. In fact, I need you to ask Maggie to put another hundred-and-fifty into my account. It was an expensive little get together."

Pauly studied her, a frown across his face. "Is that wise?" he asked.

Cam knew she looked a little haggard and felt more edgy than usual. She sat back. The look she saw on Pauly's face disturbed her. She'd been worrying about her increased use of cocaine and especially about the fact that she was enjoying it. It was something she tried not to think about. But Pauly's expression stung like a sharp reprimand. She avoided his gaze.

"Probably not," she finally said, sighing. "But I hope it won't be for long. I've got to get out of here." She stared at her shoes—dirty not-so-white slippers that were beginning to fall apart. "I need something to happen."

Pauly leaned forward as far as he dared. "There won't be any snow this week," he whispered.

Cam looked up, at first not understanding his statement. Then her face suddenly became alive. "I'm impressed," she smiled at him. "Who thought of that?" The idea that a shipment would come in without any cocaine was a new twist.

Pauly smiled. "C'est moi," he gloated.

"Good work, son," Cam complimented him. "That should ruffle some feathers. Make a lot of people very unhappy."

"We'll see how good the hunting is then."

"Hopefully, we'll bag a whole flock!" Cam sat back. It was a perfect idea. Why hadn't she thought of it?

But Pauly's use of the French idiom had cut a deep hole in her stomach.

She hadn't thought of Michael in several weeks now. Maybe if they could close this case soon, she could make it up to Michael. Maybe. That is, if Michael would still want to talk to her again.

Pauly watched Cam carefully.

* * * *

"I tell you. It just wasn't there!" Tuck was practically yelling at Ruth. "I knew she was gonna pull something. Donna swears the money was transferred same as usual. Now we get a shipment without anything!"

"Keep your voice down," Ruth warned. Her face was red with anger. "I'll handle this. Whatever she's trying to pull…well, she won't get away with it. She's got more to lose than we do."

Cam watched as Ruth stalked out of her room. She, Tuck and Douglas stared at each other. The laundry supplies had been delivered as usual that morning, but none of the barrels held anything, but detergent. No one seemed to know what was happening.

Then Tuck looked squarely at Cam, trying to decide if, perhaps, her suspicions were ill directed.

"What?" Cam asked.

Tuck just shook her head. "Never mind," she said, "I still just get real paranoid."

Cameron willed herself to look calm and surprised, but Tuck's stare unsettled her. Did Tuck suspect it was Cam who had done something to interrupt the flow of drugs?

"I get a bit unnerved, too." Cam tried to steer the train of thought away from herself. "I don't want to do more time than I have to because of someone else's greed."

Tuck just nodded. Then, as Douglas walked away, she put her hand out to stop Cam from going.

"Level with me," Tuck looked her in the eyes. "You know that Ruth had her outside contact do a check on you."

Cam feigned surprise. "A check? What for?"

"We've had spies in here before, trying to figure out where the dope was coming from. We tend to get paranoid."

"So you checked on me 'cause I used to be a cop?" Cam let her anger show.

Tuck nodded. "We check on everyone. I just want to warn you to watch your back. A lot of people are getting really paranoid. I almost suspect you myself."

Cam stared at her. "And?"

"I said *almost*. I know you're a dyke and I can't believe, in my heart, that a dyke would rat on other dykes. Hell, we got enough to watch our backs for without suspecting each other, but something's wrong around here and I'm starting to suspect everyone. I'm trying to keep an open mind."

"If you suspect I'm a spy, why warn me? Why not just watch and see if I hang myself." Cam stared into Tuck's eyes.

Tuck looked at the floor. "I owe you because of that weight bench mess. Besides, I think of you as a buddy. I'm the one who worked to get you into this family. Just watch your back."

Cam studied her for a moment. "Thanks, Tuck. I appreciate your honesty."

As Tuck turned away, a feeling of fear ripped through Cam's belly. One dyke wouldn't rat on others? Her stomach turned. Her personal politics and her belief in the job she was doing were fighting. "Don't turn away from your own kind." vs. "Wrong is wrong, no matter who." What would Mom say if she knew? Or Grandma Anne? For a brief moment, Cam doubted her whole reason for being here. Sure, she'd known, going into this, that the reason she was here was because they suspected that there were lesbians at the top. She'd known this before she'd accepted the assignment. But now that Tuck had laid it out so black and white, what could she do?

If she backed off now, just because *family* was family, wasn't she letting Ben's memory down? Wasn't it more important to get the coke out of the prison? Wouldn't it be better, especially for lesbians like Gina, if the white stuff just never came in again? Anyway, it was too late to back off. She'd put not only her life, but her reputation on the line for this. There was no going back.

* * * *

Tony Hernandez paced the office. She couldn't figure out what had gone wrong. Shit, she didn't need this. Another few months and she'd have enough socked away to get out of here. Being a prison guard wasn't what she wanted to spend the rest of her life doing. Another few months and she could be long gone, from the prison, from Maryland, hell, even from the States. She could go back to the Islands with money enough to get her family set up in real houses, not the shacks they were in now.

The opening of the door interrupted her thoughts. In walked the one person she really hated. The person who held her fate neatly in a locked desk drawer somewhere. She knew when she'd gotten the summoning phone call this morning that this was not going to be a good day.

"The shipment came in this morning without anything in it." There was a pause, a cool evaluation anticipating Tony's reaction.

Tony was sweating. "I don't understand it. Everything was business as usual. I paid for two hundred grams. It was supposed to be in today's delivery."

"Well, someone's pulling a fast one. You have to contact your buddy and find out what's wrong. You're not trying to pull something on me, are you, Tony?"

"I wouldn't do that! You know it!" Tony could taste the hatred she felt. That voice grated on her nerves every time she heard it. "I do the same thing every time." Why was she explaining herself? "Donna gives me the account totals, I get the withdrawal, put half in your account and pay Mike."

"How much are you keeping for yourself?"

"Just the five percent we agreed on. I wouldn't try to stiff you!"

"Well, someone's getting real funny. If the lid blows on this, I'm taking you with me. Is that clear? I don't need to remind you that I still have those tapes."

Tony began breathing hard. Three years ago she'd let an old friend persuade her to sneak just a couple small packs of cocaine, not even a half gram, into the prison for her and she'd been fool enough to do it. The camera had picked up the transaction and was now the one obstacle between her island dream and hell.

It was perfectly clear to her. She was the go-between and she knew what a fine line she balanced on. Either side could be deadly for her and she didn't like the look in the eyes that bore into her at that moment. "I'll make a call tonight. Mike didn't say anything."

"Mike wasn't on the truck. The new driver said he was sick."

"Mike's never sick!" Tony's throat was closing with tension. "I'll call him." She reached for the phone on the desk.

"Not from here, you idiot."

Tony's hand stopped half-way. God, but this one person could make her feel like a complete fool. How she wanted to smash that face that sneered at her.

"And find out what your little G-man knows about this. I'm tired of paying him and then getting these big surprises."

"Yeh." Tony wasn't sure what to do now.

"I think you look sick. Why don't you go home now?"

"Yeh, Right. Good idea." Tony got up.

There was a pause. "Do you need to take Frank with you?"

Tony looked up alarm. "Frank?! Do we need that?"

"You tell me."

"No. No, I'll take care of everything."

"I'll be at home if you need me. You have my private number. But don't call if it's not important."

Tony nodded and walked out of the office.

* * * *

Pauly sat in the old station wagon just one door down and across the street from Mike's apartment. Poor little bastard, he thought. Mike had almost embarrassed himself when they'd stopped the truck a half mile from the prison. He'd started by being really cocky, but when he saw that the Feds knew exactly which barrels to take off his truck, he'd backed down and wept like a little child. Now he was inside his apartment, giving the show of his life for Tony Hernandez. And knowing all the time that the Feds were recording every word on their tape machines and watching every move on the video camera they'd hidden in his living room that afternoon. Mike wasn't stupid, he knew when to give up and was doing his best to cooperate in any way they asked.

"Okay, she's leaving," came over the walkie talkie on the seat next to Pauly. Sure enough, from the front door of the building emerged the short, compact woman fingered by Mike. Now, Pauly hoped, Tony would lead him to Spellman, or whoever was next up the ladder.

As the chevy van pulled away from the curb, Pauly pulled his car out of the alley and fell in line three cars behind.

* * * *

Cam helped two women from the bindery roll a dolly loaded with boxes of journals out onto the dock. This had to be the way the coke was being shipped out. She'd thought it through, gone over the shipments in her mind again and again. These were the only big shipments going out of the prison—the perfect set-up. She'd inspected the books themselves. It would be easy to slip a small bag of coke into the cover before it was shrinkwrapped. Maybe it was sewn right into the cover as part of the padding. There had to be a way to find out.

But, yesterday, on the pretense of getting this shipment ready, she'd hung around inside the bindery, watching each step of the process. The squares of paper were cut, stitched into small booklets, and then sewn together in stacks of six. The covers were cut, the fabric lined and fitted and all were glued together in a neat little assembly line. Each woman, all part of Jay's family, handled her part of the process with competence and agility. The process worked so smoothly that the books were made, shrinkwrapped and boxed before anything could be added. If the coke was hidden in the books, Cam hadn't found the way or the time it was done.

She took a couple small chits of paper from her shirt pocket and made a note of the number of boxes and destinations they were addressed to as she piled them on the dock. If she could get the addresses to Pauly or Maggie, maybe someone out there could check from the other end and find the next stop on the coke trail.

Sighing, she wrote down the address on the last box. Each carton had a different destination. Whoever was buying was doing only small quantities. There were only twenty-four journals in each carton, so there couldn't be enough in any one box to make a difference. Maybe this was just a red herring, maybe she was wrong about this. But there was still something that didn't feel right.

The red light above the door blinked and a buzzer sounded, signalling the arrival of the UPS truck. As the loading dock door raised, Cam stepped back and looked at the boxes one last time. What was she missing?

Two of the male C.O.s outside the loading dock entered with the UPS driver. They stood to the side, silently watching. All too willing to watch the women handle the heavy boxes.

"Hey, how you doing?" the UPS driver greeted her. "Small shipment today." He proceeded to check the addresses of the boxes with the shipping bill Cam handed him.

"You gals are doing pretty good with these books," he smiled offhandedly, "My wife bought one at that bookstore in town for my little girl. She loved it. She's using it as a diary. Won't let anyone see what's in it, though. All secret-secret, but then I guess you expect that from a twelve- year-old." He rambled on as he checked the shipping papers. Cam almost didn't hear him say "This bookstore in Pittsburgh must be your biggest customer. They get a shipment every week."

Cam looked at the address of the box he was loading onto the truck. "Briscoe Books" was the destination. Why was that name so familiar? Lost in thought, she almost didn't hear him say good-bye or realize he was handing her the copies of the bills of lading. With that, he and the two guards were gone and the door firmly shut. The other two women rolled the dolly back to the bindery as the lock bolts firmly, and loudly slammed into the door jamb. Cam just stood there looking at the shipping papers in her hand.

"You're really with it today," a voice whispered in her ear.

Cam turned to find Tuck standing behind her.

"Oh," she tried to regain her composure. "You scared me. I guess I was day-dreaming."

"Just don't let Ruth see you like that." Tuck nudged her. "Got to be on your toes. Did the shipment get out okay?" She stepped up to check through the peephole in the door to see who was outside.

Cam looked down at the pink shipping papers in her hand as she slipped the smaller papers and her pencils into her back pocket.

"Looks okay," she answered. "As long as they were addressed right, they'll get there."

"Good," Tuck smiled, clasping her on the shoulder, "Let's go pump some iron. I'm real tense, today. Maybe I pulled some muscles last night. AJ was real frisky." Tuck let out a deep laugh. "I don't know how you keep up with Gina. That's one lively little body she's got. I couldn't keep up with her. I know she was wired last night!"

Cam snorted. "It took me almost until the warning bell to get her off the ceiling. How much did she do last night?"

Tuck shook her head. "Gina and Gail went off somewhere. When they came back, they were both toasted." Tuck studied Cam for a moment. "You still bothered about the way she pays for it?"

Cam looked at the ground. "Could I stop her if I were?" she asked.

Tuck nodded thoughtfully. "You're right. Probably not. Come on. Finish up that paperwork and let's go to the gym." Cam watched her walk away, then folded the papers into the file and followed slowly.

Chapter Twenty-Three

I tell you, we've done it to her twenty-four hours a day and there's nothing there. No phone calls, no visits, nothing." Pauly kept his voice low. He knew that everyone in the prison was feeling the heat from last week's empty shipment. So far, they'd been able to identify Trumble, Tony Hernandez and Mike, the driver, as key players and they'd identified the warehouse where the coke was planted in the detergent, but they still hadn't been able to find out who was at the top.

"It's okay. Something will break." Cameron smiled back at him as if they'd just shared a cute little anecdote. "There's something here that might be the key to how it's going out, but I can't get a handle on it," she whispered. "There's something I'm missing. What's up on the other side?"

"Nothing for you to worry about. We planted a nice piece of shrubbery next to your fence. It should be blooming nicely in a couple of weeks."

Cam nodded, thoughtfully.

"Other than that, it couldn't be better. Our little friends outside are playing nicely. Dickey thinks it may be time to throw them a surprise party. What do you think? Do a little pruning while we're at it. See what crop we've really got."

Cam thought about it for a moment. No, she still hadn't gotten the identification of Ms Big, but maybe a real shakedown would stir things up just enough to get someone to start talking, or at the very least, make a mistake. If the middle level she'd identified were cleared out, maybe, just maybe, the top would be more visible.

"That might not be a bad idea," she conceded. "Maybe the garden needs pruning. I am getting antsy just waiting around. What has Maggie said?"

"She thinks it may be time, too. We'll invite everyone. Just to see who shows and who goes running home to Momma. It'll be a lot of fun. Will you want to be invited?"

"No, that's okay. Just give them all a big kiss for me."

"You want to come to the next party?"

Cameron looked at him. Should she allow herself to get busted and, therefore, transferred out of the prison, or should she stay behind? There was still so much work to do here.

"I'll let you know, but I think I'm partied out." Cam looked at him.

Pauly just nodded. He looked at Cam. She looked tired. He hoped this wouldn't have to go on too much longer.

"You gonna be all right with this?" he asked. Maggie had expressed concern to him that perhaps Cam had become too close to some of the people that were going to be hurt by this. It wasn't uncommon for someone to identify with their targets. It was one of the most prevalent reasons for pulling agents off cases.

Cam sighed. "I'll deal with it." She looked Pauly in the eye. "I'm still focused."

Pauly nodded. Cam seemed all right to him. "Do you need anything?" he asked.

Cam smiled. "I was going to ask for some pocket money, but there doesn't seem to be a good game in town lately."

"That's good," Pauly acknowledged. "All play and no work can give you a dull head."

Cam laughed. "I tell you, I'm all right."

"I know you are. I just worry. So does Maggie."

Cam smiled at him affectionately. "Thanks, son. One of these days, I owe you a drink."

* * * *

Cameron leaned against the brick wall in the yard and watched her breath steam from her mouth. The jackets they were given were hardly heavy enough to fight wind of a February afternoon. Few were butch enough to brave the cold anyway. But Cam had to get out of the building. The air inside was getting danker day by day and she wondered if she wasn't becoming a tad claustrophobic.

She finished her cigarette and ground it into the concrete with her shoe. She turned her collar up a little higher and rubbed her ears. They were burning from the cold, but she hesitated about going back inside just yet. The cold air was what she needed to keep her mind clear.

She had to think and the loneliness of the yard was the only place she could concentrate. Outside in the cold was the one place she knew Gina would not come to find her. And the library had become too busy since Lourdes had bragged how the gringa who spoke Spanish had taught her to read. Now, every inmate with less than a high school education wanted Cam's help. Even though she no longer officially worked in the library, women still found her, no matter where she tried to hide.

And she had to come up with a plan. Tomorrow was the day. The Federal agents would be on the truck that was supposed to make the laundry detergent delivery. Everyone in the laundry would be busted as soon as the delivery was accepted and checked. She couldn't be there. She needed to be as far away from that room as possible. But how?

If she'd thought sooner, she could have squirreled away a couple dozen aspirin and made herself sick enough to spend the day in the infirmary. Of course, when they diagnosed what was wrong with her, she'd probably end up in solitary or protective custody and people would begin to suspect that she'd known what was going to happen. No, it had to be better than that.

Please, she thought, there's got to be a way. I've got to come up with something. The only other thing she'd thought of was to make some tea out of a couple cigarettes and OD on the nicotine. It would be risky, though. Too much and she'd end up dead, too little and all she'd get would be a headache and an upset stomach. And this was not something she could fake. The medics in the infirmary would spot it a mile away and send her right back to work. She was at a loss.

She rubbed her hands together and realized that the feeling in her fingers was gone. Her feet and ears burned from the cold so she decided to go back inside. Pat, the afternoon C.O., acknowledged her as she stepped through the door. She unzipped her jacket and took it off, tossing it back over her shoulder.

She rounded the corner and headed down the corridor that led to the recreation room. She could hear loud voices and the TV wailing one of the afternoon soap operas in the room ahead. Deciding to stop first, she turned into the communal bathroom.

She was so lost in thought that she didn't notice the other two women who were in there. But as she approached, the taller of the two turned and rammed her fist into Cam's side. Stunned, Cam took a step back and felt a sharp searing pain. Her hand went to her side and touched warm, sticky wetness. She looked down. Blood.

"You're dead, Sweetheart." Lacey stood before her, a bloody piece of metal, sharpened into a blade, still in her hand. "I been waiting a long time for this."

Cam staggered back against the wall. Strength was already beginning to drain from her.

"This is where you say good-bye, amiga." Lacey took a step closer and Cam knew she had to act fast before Lacey slit her throat.

She lashed out with her foot and connected with Lacey's wrist. The blade flew up, bounced off the ceiling and landed just behind Lacey. Cam dove for it, and with it in her hand, rolled over just as Lacey pounced on her. The force of Lacey's body weight knocked the breath from her.

Their eyes locked for just a minute. One pair showing surprise, the other fear. Then Lacey's eyes dilated into a wide stare.

Cam pulled herself out from under the limp body and Lacey rolled back, the blade stuck firmly through her heart.

Just like that, in a brief instant, it was over.

Cam looked up to see the other woman running from the room. She didn't even register an identity to the person. She tried to get up, but lost her balance and slumped against the wall. Her strength was gone and a haze was encroaching on her awareness. As she slumped closer to the floor, she thought she could hear shouting voices and running feet, but as she lost consciousness, all she heard was her mother's voice saying, "Be careful what you wish for…"

* * * *

The next morning, Maggie arrived at the Hagerville City Hospital dressed in brown wool slacks and a cream-colored blouse under her beige wool coat. As Cameron's 'next-of-kin,' she'd been called late yesterday afternoon, but not allowed to visit until this morning. As she rode to the eighth floor, she looked at her reflection in the steel wall of the elevator. She wore no make-up and her hair was still a little tousled. She'd been up most of the night, meeting with Deems, trying to decide how to handle this.

As she got off the elevator, she saw a uniformed policeman standing near the nurse's desk. She approached him. "I'm Margaret Thomason." she presented her driver's license to him. "I'm here to see Cameron Andrews."

The policeman inspected her license then handed it back. "This way," he said as he turned and strode down the hallway to where a policewoman was sitting outside a closed door. "She's here to see the prisoner," he told the woman.

"Name?" she asked, picking up a clipboard that rested on the floor next to her chair.

"Margaret Thomason."

The policewoman checked her clipboard and nodded.

"I have to frisk you," she announced, unceremoniously.

"Go right ahead." Maggie spread her arms out to the side as the woman gave her a perfunctory pat-down.

"And I have to go in with you."

"I understand." Maggie passed her and pushed the door open.

Cameron lay in the bed, her left wrist handcuffed to the side bar of the bed. A bag of blood dripped slowly down through the long IV tube. Her eyes were closed.

The policewoman plopped herself down in the chair on the far side of the bed so she had a full view of both of them.

Maggie leaned over the bed and pushed Cam's hair off her forehead. Cam's skin was warm and moist.

The touch roused Cam and she opened her eyes. "Maggie," she uttered, then tried to swallow. Her mouth was dry.

Maggie took the paper cup of water from the bed table and held the straw to Cam's lips. Cam took a small sip. "How are you feeling, honey?" she asked gently.

"Probably like I look." Cam attempted a weak smile. Maggie could see that she was still sedated.

"Are you in much pain?"

"Only when I laugh." It was a poor attempt at levity.

Maggie pulled the other chair closer to the bed and sat down, taking Cam's hand in hers. "What happened?"

"The woman that's been giving me trouble jumped me in the bathroom."

Maggie nodded. She'd been told sketchy details, but she knew that Janet Lacey was dead.

"Dickie wants to know if there's anything he can do for you?" Maggie prayed that Cam was coherent enough to understand her message; should Deems pull her out now?

Cam's face wrinkled into a frown. It took her a minute to respond. "No. Tell him I'll be all right. There'll be no more trouble."

Good. Deems had been worried that her cover had been blown and he'd have to get her out of there just when they were so close to closing this case.

Maggie squeezed and stroked the weak hand in hers. "We...I...was so worried. They wouldn't let me see you last night."

"I wouldn't have been any fun." Cam managed a smile.

Maggie could see that Cam was beginning to drift off. "I'm going to let you sleep, sweetie. I'll be back a little later."

"Okay," Cam mumbled. She was almost asleep again.

Maggie kissed her hand, then got up and left.

* * * *

"But she'll be all right?" Deems asked. Maggie had called him from a pay phone the moment she got out of the hospital.

"The doctor said she'll be fine. She's lost a lot of blood. The knife or whatever she was stabbed with punctured her lung, but didn't do much more damage than that. It could have been a lot worse."

"And she killed a woman. Will she be charged?"

"I don't think so. I talked to the warden and she seems pretty satisfied that it was self-defense. There was a witness. And everyone in the prison knew that there was bad blood between them. Lacey'd made quite a few threats. Of course, none of the inmates are talking."

"Of course."

"From what I've been able to read into this, it had nothing to do with the drug case. Cameron busted Janet Lacey several years ago on an armed felony and also wounded her sister, who was crippled by Cam's bullet. So this looks like a revenge thing."

"You really think we should leave her there?"

Maggie thought it over carefully. "Yes, I do. At least for now. If we pulled her, everyone would know she was the one who blew the whistle. And we still don't know who's on the top, or more specifically, who's outside. That would make her a sitting target. She's probably in a better situation now to find out who's controlling this. Is the bust still on for today?"

"Yes. We already have our people in place."

"I'll let her know. It'll cheer her up."

"Thank you, Doctor. Let her know I think she's doing a good job."

"She'll appreciate that."

* * * *

That morning, Mike had made his delivery as usual. Tuck had signed the receipt, as usual, and the doors had closed and locked. As usual.

Within five minutes, nothing was 'as usual.'

Douglas was just starting to unscrew the pipe in the ceiling and the first packet of coke had been retrieved from the barrel when buzzers sounded and the whole laundry room was deluged with FBI agents in black commando outfits. Their submachine guns leveled at the workers.

Within fifteen minutes, it was over. The stash of cocaine was piled in a neat little mountain of plastic bags in the middle of the floor and all the women working there had been taken to solitary. Mounds of detergent and emptied barrels lay scattered across the floor of the laundry. It had all happened so fast that there'd been no time to react, nowhere to run, nowhere to try and hide anything. The coke, the keys, the plumbing, everything was seized by the Feds. The room was off limits to everyone until the agents had completed their investigation.

The laundry workers and the guards who were supposed to be monitoring laundry activities were now being interrogated while the DEA were unraveling who would be charged with what.

There was still no determination of who in the prison had been in charge of the cocaine traffic, but several inmates and some of the guards were very willing to tell everything they knew. It would just take time. The only definite outcome was that no more cocaine would be coming into the prison. At least through the laundry.

* * * *

Early Sunday morning, three men in dark suits got off the elevator. With them, was a fourth man, heavyset with wispy grey hair around his balding dome. He seemed out of place in his grey slacks and an old beat-up grey tweed jacket. They approached the uniformed officer who sat about half way down the first corridor on the left.

The officer stood as the men approached.

"How's the prisoner doing today?" The disheveled man asked, taking the lead.

"Seems fine, Lieutenant. Asked if I could get her a book or a deck of cards."

"Don't see why not." He looked back at the other men for concurrence. "Why don't you go get a cup of coffee," Lieutenant Erickson told the young officer. "These men are from the Federal Government. They have a few questions for our guest in there, so she won't need you for a while."

"Thank you, sir. I could use the break. Would fifteen minutes, or a half-hour be too long?"

"No. In fact, it will probably take the good part of an hour." The Federal agent who was obviously in charge told him.

"Thank you, Sir." The officer nodded and left.

Richard C. Deems turned to one of his companions. "Why don't you stay out here and keep Lieutenant Erickson company." he said. Then he pushed open the door without knocking and entered the room.

* * * *

Cameron was astounded to see her boss enter the room, but didn't recognize the second man who wore dark sunglasses to hide his eyes although something about him was familiar. Playing it cool until she knew what was happening, she said nothing, but looked back at the TV where cartoon characters were running back and forth, trying to beat each other with humongous wooden clubs.

Deems withdrew his badge and held it out for her to see.

"Richard C. Deems, D.E.A. We're here to ask you a few questions, Miss Andrews." Then he turned to make sure the door had closed completely behind him.

"About what?" Cam didn't look away from the TV.

"Have you ever been involved in drug trafficking?" Deems asked.

"I sold some aspirin to my sister once."

"Shit, I'll bet you did," said the second man, taking off his glasses and laughing loudly.

Cam started. It was Pauly! His hair was about five shades lighter and he'd shaved his mustache. No wonder she hadn't recognized him.

"Hey!" She exclaimed.

"Keep your voices down," Deems warned. "There's a police lieutenant from the city of Hagerville right outside your door."

"Sorry," Cam said. "I just didn't know how to react when you walked in. I didn't recognize this idiot at all." Cam smiled and winked at Pauly.

"Like it?" Pauly grinned as he ran his hand through his hair. "I'm really getting into this undercover stuff."

"What are you doing?" Cam was surprised.

"Well, the hair color is just temporary. I've been tailing some of your friends and I didn't want to be recognized. I have to tell you, though, this is a strange way to spend a vacation. If the guys at the precinct could see me now." He gave a sly snort as he fingered the handcuff that shackled Cameron to the bed. "Nice jewelry. I didn't realize they knew your sexual habits."

Cameron glared at him, then away from Deems, with a small look of embarrassment.

Deems either chose not to acknowledge the remark, or hadn't understood. "Look, you two catch up later. We've got work to do."

Cam sighed, "It's just so good to see someone who's not behind bars."

Deems sat down. "That's what I'm here to talk about. Of course, as far as anyone outside this room knows, we are interrogating you concerning the recent discovery of two kilos of cocaine and a well-constructed network of both prisoners and corrections officers engaged in the sale and use thereof. You are a suspect in the case as a known companion of one Ruth Tarlow who seems to be the ringleader of the group."

"I'm innocent. You can't prove anything," Cam said.

Deems smiled.

"Well, there's been quite a bit I know you haven't heard about. First of all, you don't have to worry about our little mole. He was stabbed in the back Friday night. Looks like whoever's in charge got kind of angry that they weren't warned about our little visit."

"They found him in an alley over past Fells Point. He's still alive, but in poor condition at Johns Hopkins. They don't expect him to pull through," Pauly added.

Deems continued. "There was a nice unexpected bonus: because you were here, your friend Ruth took your place in the laundry. So, we bagged her right along with all her family. It'll sure save building a case against her." Deems was starting to gloat. "Quite a few of them are trying to make deals so we'll have more before we're done, but no one seems to know who's really at the top, or at least no one's willing to tell. Right now, we're at a dead end at Ruth Tarlow and..." He checked a notepad from his pocket. "And Valerie Tucker."

"Tuck. I'm sorry about her. She was a friend."

"You have no friends in there, don't kid yourself. They'd all sell their mothers if they thought it would loosen the screws on them," Deems frowned at her. "We know there are more involved, but they haven't been fingered, yet."

"That worries me," Cam sighed.

"Yes, me, too. It means you're still vulnerable if you go back in."

"Isn't there some way of getting one of them to spill something?" Cam asked. Pauly looked at Deems who continued, "They also found Tony Hernandez' body Friday night. Shot through the head, small caliber. They're still doing an autopsy."

"She's the only one that Mike, the soap company driver, could finger," Pauly admitted. "We'd been following her, bugging her phone. We thought she'd lead us to the top."

"I guess I should feel lucky." Cam laid her head back and looked up at the ceiling. Suddenly, the ache in her side was almost welcome. "This seems to have been a bloody week. But this means that Tony was probably not that far away from Ms Big," she speculated.

"Yes," Deems agreed, "but nothing so far, except one short phone call. It may mean nothing, but we wanted you to hear it, see if you can identify the other voice."

Pauly pulled a small tape recorder out of his pocket, gave Cam the earplug, and pushed the play button, holding it so Cam could hear.

"Hola."

"We have to talk. There are unpleasant complications."

"Dios Mio"

"Same place. You know what time."

"Yeh." click!

Cam looked from Deems to Pauly. The second voice was a woman, that was expected, but not the cold crisp rasp of Ethel Spellman!

"Yeh, we weren't expecting that, either." Deems shook his head. "Makes the lack of dirt we dug up on Spellman look real."

"Maybe it was just Tony's girlfriend. Maybe she's sick or something." Cam still looked skeptical.

"Maybe."

"Let me hear it again."

Pauly pushed the rewind, then the play button. Cam listened, this time, with her eyes closed. Had she heard that voice before? Or did she just *want* to think she had? "I don't know. Maybe. I can't be sure."

"I wish I could leave you a copy to listen to, but that's too dangerous. Listen a couple more times. Get it planted in your mind."

Pauly handed her the recorder. She rewound and listened four or five times. Finally she looked up at Deems. "I think I'll remember it if I hear it again. She's got a sibilant 's' and a New York accent, the way she said 'Tawlk.' I'll listen for it. I don't think it's one of the inmates I've been hanging with."

"No, it couldn't be. This was recorded at ten o'clock Thursday morning. About twenty minutes after the bust went down. We weren't even out of the building."

"Any trace on where it came from? Have you checked the phone logs from the prison?"

"Too short for a trace. Haven't been able to access the phone records yet, but we're working on it. If it were someone smart, it'll be from a pay phone." Cam nodded. "When was Tony killed?"

"Coroner said she'd been dead about two hours, so sometime Friday night. Between seven and eight is as close as they can pinpoint it."

"Whoever it was sure didn't waste much time, did she?"

"We're checking personnel records and time cards right now to see who

185

was off duty."

Cam nodded, a frown still on her face. "Check wives and girlfriends, too. It could be a family affair, you know."

"Good idea. We're on it. We're auditing all the prison records now and by tomorrow afternoon, we'll probably have a court order to subpoena everyone's bank records. We might just find one small piece of information.

"We've also run into another dead end." Deems sighed as he sat in the chair next to the bed. "We busted the detergent company shortly after we were done at the prison, but everything was clean. Three of the employees hadn't come back after their morning coffee break. We've got a bulletin out for them, but we have nothing on them and when we checked out the garage where they keep their truck, it was all cleaned out, not a trace, no fingerprints, nothing." Deems stood and walked over to the window which faced the rear parking lot. "Not surprisingly, Mr. Testa, the owner, seems to have hired some illegal aliens."

"Well, at least you have him on that and if they still have the truck, it can be traced."

"Maybe. But his personnel records are well done. We can't even prove he knew they were illegal. He has everything on file including social security numbers. They've even been paying their taxes.

"Can you trace from that?"

Deems looked at her with chagrin. "It seems that all of the people that are working there have been dead for at least ten years. Even their addresses are bogus. I'm not even going to be surprised when the report comes back that says they're even all buried next to each other in some cemetery not far from here."

Cam shook her head in amazement.

"It does seem that we cleared out quite a bit. The only one we didn't get anything on was Frank Briscoe. He's checking out clean as a whistle."

Frank Briscoe! Cam sat up, oblivious to the pain in her side as she did. "That's it!" she exploded. "Briscoe Books! We shipped boxes of journals to Briscoe Books in Pittsburgh every week!"

Deems looked from her to Pauly. "I thought we checked the journals."

Cam nodded. "I don't know how it's being done. But we ship more journals to them than to anyone. There's got to be a connection."

"We're on it." Deems nodded.

"Good work." Pauly smiled, slapping her on the shoulder.

"How are they treating you here? Is there anything you need?" Deems asked turning back to the window.

"No, I'm doing all right for the time being. I could use a long walk on a beach."

Deems looked at her, a smile on his face for the first time that afternoon. "You deserve one. Hopefully, it won't be much longer. I hope Dr.

Thomason told you how pleased I am with what you've been doing."

"Yes, she did. Thank you, sir."

"I've been getting good reports from her, but I took this opportunity to come and see for myself. I'm sorry to see you get hurt."

"It's part of the territory, I guess." Cam lowered her eyes, "I'm sorry Lacey got killed. It was an accident. I'd been hoping that…well, I guess that's moot now."

"It's part of the job, Andrews. These things happen. They're never pleasant, but we learn to deal with them."

"I know that, sir. It's not the first time I've had to kill someone. I just don't like dealing with it."

"Do you need to talk to Dr. Thomason about it?"

Cam shook her head. "Not now, maybe when I get out." Cam looked Deems in the eye. "I can handle this for now. I know how to stay focused. I won't let you down."

"I know. I was tempted to pull you out, but we're so close to cracking this."

"We still haven't gotten the top dog at the prison and I want to shut them down completely." Cam was firm on this.

"Don't get greedy. Be thankful for one step at a time, Andrews."

"I am thankful," she assured him, "I'm just not satisfied. I know that some of those people were supposed to be my friends, but I can't feel sorry for them. There's one young woman in there that's so coked out, she may never be right." Cam turned her head and looked out the window.

"There are quite a few who are strung out. We're sending extra help into the prison to deal with it."

Cam looked at him. "Thank you." Then after a brief pause, "There is one other problem I'd like your help with."

"What is it?"

"There's a woman in the prison. Lou. Louise Holliston. She's been there a long time. I think her case needs to be reviewed."

Deems looked at her skeptically.

"She killed her husband. She caught him molesting their daughter. By today's standards that could be viewed as a crime of passion, self-defense, or something like that. At the very most, manslaughter. Twenty years ago, it got her Murder One and life."

Deems set his jaw. "We just can't re-open a case without cause. Besides, it might make someone suspicious."

Cam stared up at Pauly. "What if someone not in the department pressed for it?"

Pauly looked at her. "What are you thinking?" he asked.

"There's a lawyer. Over at the Women's Center at the University. Hunter, I think her name is. She's always working for good causes. I'll bet if this were brought to her attention…" she winked at Pauly.

"I've heard of her," Deems said. "She's the one who sued for that lesbian to get custody of her children."

"That's the one. Don't tell me you have a file on her."

Deems smiled at her. "That's privileged information."

"I know her, too. She's a good friend of Roger's," Pauly added. Cam didn't ask who Roger was. "I'll bet that if she somehow stumbled across the case, she'd snap at the chance."

"Thanks, Pauly. I'd really appreciate it."

"Why the interest?" Deems asked.

"She saved my neck," was Cam's response. "A couple of times."

"Okay, then. We'll see that Ms Hunter doesn't get too much resistance on this one."

Cam smiled broadly. "And one more thing."

"What now? I'm beginning to think I'm going to feel sorry I came to visit you." Deems scowled at her.

"When we close this one, I want to stay undercover," Cam stated flatly. "I know that this was as far as we talked about, but if I go back inside now, and finish my sentence, or I get paroled, I can have a cover that'll take me places we never thought we could get. I could possibly even get to the real importer."

"You've been watching too much television, Cam. This kind of stuff only works on film," Pauly interjected.

"No, I'm serious, Pauly. And in addition, I think I could be a great asset."

Deems looked at her. "Like…?"

"Well, there are a lot of doors that are never opened to the 'straight' people, and I don't mean that as a pun. I've learned things about the underground I could only guess at before. As an ex-con, there's a better chance I could infiltrate wherever needed. I've been lying here thinking. If I can get away with it inside a prison, think what I can get away with on the outside. It's a perfect cover."

"You really want to do that?" Pauly was astounded.

"Sure, why not? I just spent ten months setting up this cover. My former friends don't acknowledge they knew me and my family isn't even talking about it. That's some pretty heavy stuff. Why throw it away now? Even after I get to the bottom of this case—and I will." She looked Deems straight in the eye, "There's still some use in it."

"But if you go back to the prison now, there may be people there who suspect that you were the pigeon. You could be risking your life unnecessarily." Pauly looked to Deems for agreement.

"But if I don't go back, they'll *know* it was me. We don't know everyone on the outside, do we? At least inside I know who to look over my shoulder for. Outside, I'm flying blind."

"We can make it look like we charged you like the others and got you shipped to a maximum security—" Pauly said.

But Cam interrupted. "No. Someone can always trace the paper trail and find out I'm not where it says I am. And," she stopped for emphasis, "I'm not ready to do a twelve to twenty on a second offense."

Deems looked at her without saying a word.

"You know I'm right," Cam continued. "We've sunk too much time and money into this to throw it away now. Just let me go back into Hagerville now. With a parole, I can be out soon and still be useful." Cam put her head back on the pillow. She hoped he'd give in soon, she didn't have too much more strength to fight with.

Deems shook his head. He hated admitting when someone else was right and she'd pushed him to it more times than he wanted to count. "Let me think about it," he said finally. "If you get transferred back to the prison infirmary, you'll know you have my blessing on this." He stopped. "I don't want any grand-standing, though. Do you understand me? We'll keep this low key and use it only when we have to."

"Whatever you say, boss." Cam relaxed back into the bed.

He looked at her, thoughtfully. "I won't be able to get you out right away. It would attract too much suspicion. You might be in there another two or three months."

Cameron smiled. She knew she had his approval, whether he was ready to admit it or not.

He turned to leave, taking his coat from the back of the chair where he'd tossed it. "I'm going to keep Lieutenant Erickson busy for a few minutes," he said, smiling. "You two can visit for ten minutes or so. We may be back if we get any other clues. In the mean time, be more careful, will you?"

Chapter Twenty-Four

Gina sat in the cell, curled up on the back edge of the bunk. She hugged herself and gathered her sweater and jacket tightly around her, but she still couldn't stop shivering. Damn! She was cold. She was sweating, but she was shaking and couldn't feel any heat. She gathered her blanket around her.

"You need some help, little one?" Lou stood in the cell doorway.

Gina looked at her and burst into tears.

"Come on out of there where I can reach you." Lou held her arms out to offer help as Gina crawled out of the cell. Lou pulled her into her arms. She felt Gina's body shake as she held her tightly in her motherly embrace.

"Talk it out, little one," Lou whispered. "At least get the words out."

Gina took a deep breath. "Everyone's gone," she faltered. "It's all gone."

"Some are gone. I hear that Cameron will be back soon." Lou tried to lessen the pain.

Gina shook her head violently. "No. I know. They keep saying she'll be back, but she won't. She's dead."

Lou held her slightly away from her. "Where did you get an idea like that?"

"I saw her. She was all bloody. I saw them carry her away. She's dead."

"No, she's not, honey," Lou hugged her closely. "Cameron's very much alive. She'll be transferred back here to the infirmary this week. You get that idea out of your head. Cam's coming back."

"What about Ruth and Tuck? Are they coming back?"

"No, honey, they've been sent to another facility."

"And they took all the stuff with them. They didn't leave me any. Ruth promised there'd always be enough for me. She lied. Now I'm sick and she didn't leave any." Gina was starting to rant and become more agitated. She rocked back and forth in Lou's arms.

Finally she pushed Lou away and stood in the middle of the cell. "They all lied. Cameron said she'd take care of me, but she died instead. She was just selfish. She just wanted sex, she never wanted me. She never loved me!"

"Oh, sweetie, you can't say that. She cares about—"

"No!" Gina cut in. "She never loved me! She never kissed me!" Lou studied her a moment. "She kissed you, honey, I saw her kiss you."

"No!" Gina was determined. "If I kissed her, she'd kiss me back. But she never *started* a kiss." Gina spun around as if looking for something. "She never kissed me on the mouth. She'd kiss me everywhere else, but not on the mouth."

Lou sat back. That was an astute observation from someone who's mind wasn't exactly working at peak performance.

"There's nothing left!" Gina stopped her search of the room and turned back to Lou.

"What are you looking for, sweetie? Lou asked.

"Stuff! You know, *stuff*! Ruth said there'd always be enough for me as long as I was nice to the C.O.s, but she ran away, too."

Lou just watched as Gina's tirade grew more and more outrageous. She knew that Gina was a heavy cocaine user, but she hadn't expected this degree of withdrawal from her. She sat and watched as Gina disintegrated before her. Finally Gina collapsed into a small ball on the floor, holding herself and rocking back and forth as the tears streamed down her face. Gina was no longer aware that there was anyone else in the room.

Lou leaned back out of the doorway and motioned to Lourdes who, as usual, was not far away. "Keep an eye on her. She's having a bad time. I'm gonna see what can be done for her." She left Lourdes in charge and went to find a C.O. who at least could let someone stay the night with Gina, even if medical help was not available. Gina was not the first girl to go through these withdrawal symptoms since Ruth and her family had gotten busted and transferred to a Federal Facility. When the well of cocaine dried up, the authorities were unprepared for the number of inmates that needed help.

* * * *

Lourdes sat with a couple other women in one of the cells. It was late in the evening and the warning bell would ring in less than an hour. Talk was still of the bust and there was a lot of speculation on who had sold out to the Feds, and why.

"I still say it was Andrews. She's an ex-cop. Maybe she's still a cop. She knew what was happening. We never had this much trouble before she came here. Who's to say she wasn't planted here just to find that out?" one woman asked.

"I can't believe it was her," Lourdes said firmly.

"Why? Because she taught you to read? This is the real world, chica. She could still be a cop!"

"I thought Ruth had her checked out."

"So. It could still be her. Maybe she's trading info for a parole."

"If she comes back here from the hospital, we will know it was not her. If it was her, they would let her go home now. They wouldn't send her back here. If she were trading the information to reduce her sentence, they'd give her a parole and send her home, pronto, or at least transfer her."

"I think it was Annie," A.J. added. "I heard Ruth telling Tuck that Annie was trying to blackmail someone in here, that she'd gone to them after she got out and said if they didn't pay her, she'd tell everything she knew."

"Annie wouldn't be that stupid. Who'd believe her? It would be the word of an ex-con against the word of the prison employee. Besides, she was already on the outside! Why would she bother? We were all her family in here. Why would she want to hurt Ruth?"

Each looked around, searching. None had answers.

"It don't none of it make sense. Maybe it was someone else. It coulda been anyone."

"No, it had to be someone who really knew from the inside."

* * * *

It was Angie who found the article in the paper on Tuesday. "Hey! Look at this!" She shoved the opened newspaper onto the lunch table as people gathered around to look.

BALTIMORE—The body of a young woman, identified as twenty-nine-year-old Anne Gibson, was found behind the Pagoda in Patterson Park last night by two joggers. Police spokesperson Tracy Lyons said that the young woman had been killed by two bullets to the back of the head, in the fashion of a mob-related execution and that the murder was apparently drug related.

Gibson, who had been released from Hagerville Correctional Facility for Women less than two months ago, had been recently questioned by police concerning several drug and extortion-related incidents, but had not been charged.

Ms Gibson leaves a mother…

"See! I told you it was her." A.J. slammed her fist on the table. "I knew it! Whoever's on the outside knew it, too."

All around the table just sat back and let the news sink in. "Then it had to be Annie," someone said.

All nodded. "But why?" Angie asked.

"Who's to know?"

Chapter Twenty-Five

Cameron sat impatiently in Warden Spellman's outer office. She'd been transferred back to the prison. So, Deems must have finally decided to let her continue her cover.

She straightened up and winced as her side still ached. It was healing slowly. She still didn't have the strength she had before.

"It'll take a couple months to heal right," Carson, the city policeman who had escorted her back, observed. "I got shiv'd a few years ago. Still bothers me when it rains." The deputy laughed.

"Thanks a lot." Cam looked up at the stiff-backed cop who was waiting with her for the paperwork to be completed on her transfer. "Now I can always find a job as a weather vane."

At that moment, Spellman emerged from her office and handed the papers to Carson. "There you go, signed, sealed and delivered. Give my regards to Lieutenant Erickson."

"I sure will." Carson put his hat on and strode out of the office. Spellman turned to Cam.

"I know you were in with them." She looked her squarely in the eye. "You may have fooled the Federal Agents into thinking you had nothing to do with all this and you may have lucked out by being in the hospital when the bust went down, but you were Ruth Tarlow's lieutenant and I know it. I can't prove it, but I know it. I want you to know that I'll be watching you closely. You make one wrong move and I'll be all over you. Do I make myself clear?"

Cameron nodded.

"Lacey's death was self-defense. I'll give you that much, but that doesn't make you innocent of drug trafficking. I've been trying to crack this case for two years. It's cost a lot of lives. So, if I find so much as a trace of any kind of drug in this whole prison, I'm coming after *you*. You better be so clean, you squeak. Now, my secretary has some paperwork for you to fill out, then you have to report to the infirmary before you can be cleared." She stopped and drew herself up to her full height. "Don't think you're going to get away with anything. I'm watching you."

Sarah Adrien had been standing in Spellman's office doorway. She stepped aside to let her boss stalk by. Then, closing the office door behind her, she walked to her desk and sat down, opening the manila file with Cameron's name on the front.

"Welcome back. Quite a few changes around here while you were on vacation. You missed all the fun."

"So I've heard. Doesn't sound like my type of party, though."

Sarah placed a form on top of the file. The pleasantries were over. "I just need to get your statement about your injury. The official prison inquiry is over and there are no charges against you for Janet Lacey's death as long as your statement matches. Want to tell me what happened?"

Cam nodded and began her narrative. Sarah wrote down every word in shorthand. When Cam finished, Sarah placed her steno pad in the file. "I'll type this up and you can come in and sign it tomorrow."

"Did I pass the test? Did my story match up?" Cam asked.

"Word for word. You have a good memory."

"I don't think I'll forget it soon."

"There are several new counselors on staff if you feel a need to talk to anyone about it. They'll explain it all at the infirmary."

Cameron stared at her.

"You know, if you have any anxieties or whatever."

"Yes, well…uh, I'll consider it. Thanks." Cameron suddenly felt the need to keep Sarah talking. "What's my new work assignment?"

Sarah glanced at the file. "Janitorial."

"Shit," Cam spat.

"Yes, that, too." Sarah smiled. "But your friend Lou Holliston is your trustee now. She's responsible for you. Don't mess her up." Sarah handed her a chit with her work assignment hours on it. "I'll let the infirmary know you're on your way." Cam knew that she had been dismissed as Sarah picked up the phone to call the medical facility.

"Uh, Sarah—" she began.

"That's *Ms* Adrien." The stare was icy.

"I'm sorry," Cam said, recovering. "Can I ask you a question?"

"It depends on what it is."

"Where'd the others get transferred to?" Cam asked, hoping to start a conversation.

"That's none of your business, unless you want to join them. Now, do you know your way or should I get you an escort?"

Cam shook her head, got up and turned to walk out of the office. Once in the hall, she glanced at the huge clock near the end of the corridor, nine-thirty. She had three and a half hours before she could get to a phone and call Maggie. She had to let Deems know that she might have found the person they were looking for. The voice tone wasn't exactly what she remembered, but that could be the fault of either the telephone reception or the tape recording. But the way Sarah had said, "talk" and the slight hiss on the 's' in 'responsible' sure struck a chord. She'd be really interested to see what time Sarah Adrien got off work in the afternoon.

* * * *

"Hey, Harvard. How're you doing?"

The voice roused her. She'd been dozing since lunch. The food hadn't looked appetizing, although she had tried a few spoonfuls of the soup. The transfer from the hospital back to the prison had taken more energy than she'd realized and the medic wanted her to stay in the infirmary for two or three more days. She still was far from full strength.

Cam opened her eyes and looked up. There, in the doorway, stood Lou. She walked over and sat down in the chair next to the bed, shaking her head. "Well, well. Welcome back. How are you feeling?"

Cam smiled at her. "I'm still a little weak and I have a hard time catching my breath, but the doctors say I'm healing quite nicely."

"Good." Lou stopped. "We had a little scene here while you were gone. I guess you heard. Lots of changes here. Lots of changes!"

"How's Gina? Did she get caught up in it?"

Lou took a deep breath. "They transferred her to a mental facility. She was hooked on the coke really bad. When the source dried up, so did she. She thought you were dead, you know."

"Did you have a chance to talk to her?"

Lou nodded. "Lourdes and I took turns sitting with her. I think the transfer will be best for her."

"I'm glad she's getting help." What else could Cam say? That it was her fault that Gina used as much as she did? That she'd encouraged the use? That she was the pigeon who got the source dried up?

"This has been real hard on her. She's not all here, yet." Lou continued as she watched for Cam's reaction. "Did you know she was so hooked?"

Cam frowned and nodded. "I knew, but I couldn't stop her. There'd be nights she'd come back to her house at warning bell so high, I could hear her bouncing around in there until dawn."

"A lot of girls have had real problems since the connection dried up. At least they've been sending more counselors in. If that'll help." Lou stopped and studied Cam closely. "I thought you were going to report to work today. Or is pressing the sheets on that bed your new work assignment?"

Cam laughed. "I guess I overdid it this morning. I had a real lively conversation with Spellman. Or, I should say, she had a conversation with me."

"Yes, I know. E. K. was sweeping the hallway outside the office. She heard it all. News travels fast in here." Her gaze at Cam was a little unsettling.

"What, Lou?" Cam was becoming uncomfortable.

She took the folded section of newspaper from her pocket and handed it to Cam.

Cam read the item that was outlined in heavy blue ink. Then she looked up at Lou. "Annie?"

"I understand from the grapevine that our friend Annie was trying to blackmail someone. I hope they catch the killer soon. I think whoever it was also offed that C.O., Tony, too. Seems to be the popular opinion that Annie was the one who blew the whistle on the whole thing," Lou said.

Cam nodded. "I didn't know. Do you really think she was the one?" Cam wondered what the rest of the inmates thought.

"Saves your neck. A lot of people thought it was you."

"Why me?" Cam feigned a slight bit of surprise.

"Because you used to be a cop. A lot of people think 'once-a-cop, always-a-cop.' You know that."

"Did *you* think it was me?"

Lou leaned back. "I wasn't sure. Now... No. You're back here. If it had been me, I'd have blown the whistle and gotten out of this joint as fast as I could. Annie did you a big favor by getting herself killed. Now everyone knows it was her." Lou watched as Cam just lay there, her eyes closed so that Lou couldn't read the look of relief in them. "If they still thought it was you, you'd be dead in a week."

Cameron took a deep breath and laid her head back on the pillow. "Then, I'm not sorry Annie got killed," Cam whispered.

"No need to be. Some people get what they ask for."

How true! Cam thought. Any speculation who offed her? she asked aloud.

Lou shook her head. "As far as I know, Tony was part of the drug ring, but I know there've got to be more. Tony wasn't smart enough to run this. There was someone above her."

Cam shook her head.

"Oh," Lou said, reaching into her rear pocket and pulling out some envelopes, "I almost forgot. You got some mail." She tossed them onto the bed. "Looks like get-well cards. One's from quite a ways away." She leaned back as Cam picked them up and scanned the return addresses. One was from Grandma Anne, the second from Pauly, the third had a Korean postmark, but a return address in Seoul of M. Gauchet.

A letter from Michael?! In Korea? Cam inhaled sharply.

Lou watched as a range of emotions flashed across Cam's face. "Bad news?" she ventured.

Cam frowned. "Unfinished business," was her only comment as she returned Michael's envelope to the bottom of the pile. Without a second look, she pulled a card out of the already opened envelope from Pauly. Reading it, she gave a hearty laugh and handed it to Lou.

"Look at this," she laughed. "This boy is a mess!"

Lou took the card. On the front was the picture of a well proportioned woman scantily clad in black leather underwear. It read, "They tell me you've been sick in bed." Opening it, she read, "Funny. They say that about me, too."

"Great card," Lou chuckled, standing it on the table beside the bed. "He knows you too well." Then she motioned to the other two that lay untouched on the bed. "Want me to leave so you can read those?"

"One's from my grandmother. I'm not ready to read it yet. I'm not sure she knows I got hurt. I asked Maggie not to tell her. No sense in making her worry more than she already does." Cam still fingered Michael's envelope with mixed emotions, excitement that Michael still thought of her, yet dreading exactly *what* she thought.

"Must be pretty heavy business," Lou said. "I'll just come back later." She started to get up.

"No." Cam put out her hand to stop her. "Stay. I may need your support. The last time she wrote, I got so angry, I ripped it up and flushed it down the john."

Lou just looked at her, curious, but silent. Whatever this involved, she knew that Cam had to volunteer the information.

"It's from a woman I had an affair with just before I was busted." Cam just stared at the envelope, inspecting the stamp, but delaying in pulling out the letter. "We…we never really finished it."

"She's from Korea?" asked Lou.

Cam looked up for the first time. "No…" She hesitated, wanting to tell Lou more, but knowing she couldn't. "No. I don't know why she's there."

Lou shrugged. "One way to find out," she gestured toward the letter.

Cam looked back at the envelope, then slowly withdrew the letter and unfolded it.

Dear Cameron,

I'm very sorry to hear that you have been hurt, but Maggie says you are doing very well. When you are through there, I ask for a chance to talk about us, even if it is only to be friends. I'll be home at the beginning of May, hopefully with a new belt. I have tried to channel all my energy into my study here. It is the only thing that keeps my thoughts from you, although never for long.

Michael.

Cam laid the letter face down on the bed. After a moment contemplating it, she turned her attention back to Lou. "She's in Korea studying."

Lou studied Cam's face, trying to read what Cam wasn't saying. "And she wants to see you again." It was a statement, not a question.

Cam nodded. "When I get out."

"And you want to see her."

Cam wanted to shout, Yes!, but she only whispered it.

"Does your Maggie know about her?"

Cam smiled weakly, wishing that she could tell Lou everything, discuss the situation with her, with anyone, just to hear her own thoughts out loud. "Yes," she finally admitted, "but that's another story."

Lou shook her head. "Why am I not surprised? And why do I feel there's a whole lot more you're not telling me?"

Cam feigned innocence. "Haven't I always told you the truth?"

"I don't know. Have you?"

Cam smiled broadly and let her head fall back into the pillow.

"Get some rest, Harvard. We got lots of floors to sweep." Lou laughed as she left the room.

Chapter Twenty-Six

Cameron stood outside Gina's cell and looked at the blank walls. The corridor seemed empty now, without Gina bubbling around. There'd probably be someone new in there soon, but Gina's presence was still there, even though her personal belongings had been removed.

Now, it was show time. It hadn't dawned on her what today was until she'd gotten to breakfast. Today was March the thirteenth! Friday, the fuckin' thirteenth, she thought, Well, I guess this really will be someone's unlucky day. Let's just hope it's not mine.

What was it that Grandma Anna always said? "You make your own luck in life." Well, this better be a day for *good* luck. But Cameron had the feeling that luck would have nothing to do with it.

Was she ready? It was now three-thirty. At four o'clock, Warden Spellman had a private and confidential meeting with several Federal agents. At that time, the Deputy Warden would leave. Then, just before five, Sarah Adrien would also go home. Cam had just that one hour—sixty minutes to contact Sarah Adrien and get her to make some sort of mistake that could close this case. She took a breath.

"Well, I hope you guys are having a good time," she said softly. "If you can't hear me, I'm really fucked, so listen hard." Hopefully, somewhere, just outside the periphery of the prison, a truckload of FBI agents were monitoring her through a state-of-the-art bugging devise she had in her pants pocket.

Yesterday afternoon, Deems, Wendell and two other FBI agents she didn't know had sat with her and her lawyer in a private room under the pretense of questioning her further about the drugs. What anyone was told, from Warden Spellman to the other prisoners, was that the FBI was not satisfied with her answers to their investigation and would be interrogating her further regarding the Tarlow Ring, as it was being called. Only those in the room knew that Cameron was about to turn state's evidence and try to get information about who was really in charge of the drug traffic.

She'd been given a radio devise that looked like a short pencil. A thin wire ran from her pocket to wrap around inside the waistband of her trousers.

"Be careful," the FBI agent had said, laughing, "Make sure you have a good lunch. That wire is the most sensitive microphone made. It'll broadcast every rumble of your stomach. I hope you don't get gas easily when you're nervous."

She lightly tapped her belt and chuckled. "Sorry. Just keeping you from dozing off." She was picturing them jumping as the sound of her tapping was magnified through their earphones.

She reached into her pocket and took one of the small pieces of paper she always carried to make notes for herself. It always helped her to see her moves written out, even if she had to destroy them right away. If she could see the list of moves, she could remember them easier.

Suddenly, Cam just stared at the papers in her hand. Was this it? Had it been in her pocket all the time? Had Tuck waved it in front of her so many times?

The pieces of paper were all about the same size, about two by three inches and each stack, about a half inch thick, were uniform, if not precise. They hadn't been cut by a paper guillotine, but looked like they had been cut, freehand with a sharp knife. They were little stacks of paper that had been cut out of the middle of larger stacks. And the paper was the same as the pages of the journals.

Could it be that simple? It was an old trick, so obvious. Of course no one had considered it!

"They're cutting holes in the pages of the journals to hide the coke. *Then* they shrinkwrap them. No one ever checked! There must be some code on the label to identify them. Just like the stars on the detergent barrels!" Cam tapped her belt again. "Hear that, guys? It is in the journals. Check it out!"

This was it! She knew now exactly what had been happening. It was so simple, it was scary. Those nights, at least one a week, that Tuck and Douglas had been so mysteriously absent—had they been loading the journals and re-shrinkwrapping them?

Suddenly Cam was ready. "Okay, boys, it's show time."

Cam walked slowly, forcing herself to saunter, through several check points to the administration offices. The Deputy Warden passed her in the hall without any acknowledgment. She opened the door and entered the office.

Sarah sat at the desk, her head bent over some files. She looked up as Cameron entered. "What do you want? The Warden's busy," she said tersely.

"I wanted to talk to *you*," Cameron said, sitting in the chair next to Sarah's desk.

Sarah looked at her, her eyes questioning Cam's audacity at taking a seat without being told to.

"About what?" she asked.

"Well, Ruth said I should talk to you if I had..uh..problems."

"Ruth?"

"Tarlow."

"Why me?" Sarah said, going back to her paperwork. "There are counselors available, I'm sure."

"No, Tony and Ruth said you were definitely the one to talk to."

Sarah stopped and stared at her. "You must be mistaken."

"I don't think so," Cam countered. "Perhaps this isn't the best place to talk."

"What do you want?"

"I think you can figure that out." No entrapment, let Sarah set her own trap. This was what Cam was best at. She'd been undercover on the street long enough to know. She sat back. Let Sarah Adrien make the next move.

Sarah turned her attention back to the paperwork on her desk. "Why don't we talk a little later. I'll be finished with this work then and can fully devote my attention to you."

"Sure, I can come back."

Sarah stopped. "No, let's meet somewhere else. You're on janitorial detail now, right? I think the storage room behind the store needs to be cleaned out. I'll let them know you're on your way and I'll stop down in a half hour and see how you're doing." Her look was meant to challenge Cam.

"Sure, why not." Cam smiled, sweetly. She stood and exited the office, leaving Sarah tapping her pen thoughtfully on her paperwork.

"Well, boys," she whispered when she was in the hall. "At least she didn't throw me out. Stay tuned for the next exciting episode!"

* * * *

Cam paced the storeroom. It had been nearly an hour since she'd left Sarah's office and Cam's time was almost up. Hopefully, Deems could stall the Warden long enough for them to get something on tape. Now, Sarah was trying to psych her out by being late. She'd just have to be patient.

She stopped and leaned back against the table when she heard the door open. Sarah Adrien entered, follow by a tall muscular guard. Cam stared at him. Not only was it rare to see a male C.O. inside the prison walls, this was Frank Briscoe!

"Sorry we're late." Sarah smiled, too sweetly. "My associate was occupied with another problem."

"Not to worry. I wasn't going anywhere," Cam said. Had she just bagged two birds with one stone?

Sarah looked around the room. "You didn't get much swept up in here, I see."

"Didn't know exactly how much *cleaning up* you wanted me to do. I did bring a broom with me," indicating the one leaning against the wall, "just for appearances sake."

"Yes, well. What did you want to talk to me about?"

Cam looked at Frank as he stood behind Sarah. "Is it all right to talk in front of him?" This was an unexpected, but not un-agreeable development.

"I have nothing to hide from Frank. You can be very candid."

"Well," Cam said, "As I mentioned earlier, Tony said you'd be a great help if I ever needed it."

Sarah and Frank exchanged glances.

"Tony?" Sarah feigned innocence.

"Tony Hernandez. You remember her, don't you?"

Sarah scowled back at Frank.

"How come Tony never mentioned you?" Frank asked.

"Probably wanted an ace in the hole. Balance off those tapes." Mike, the driver, had confessed that Tony was afraid because someone had incriminating tapes on her, but didn't know anything more.

"And what might those tapes be?" Sarah asked.

Cam had run to the end of that bluff. "Look, let's not dance around. I come up for parole in a couple months. I'd sure be a lot less jumpy if I knew I had a little nest egg waiting when I got out. I hate being jumpy. I tend to ramble on about the most interesting things when I get nervous. You never know who might be listening."

"I guess you were right about Hernandez," Frank said, "Lousy little spick never could keep her mouth shut."

"Shut up, Frank. Tony's not our problem now. This one is. How should we handle it?"

"How much do you want?" Frank asked.

"Fifty-thousand in cash. I'll tell you how to deliver it."

"In exchange for?" Sarah looked at her with one raised eyebrow.

"My undying gratitude and silence."

Frank put his hand on Sarah's shoulder. "And how do we know someone else won't step up to take your place when you leave?" he asked. "Sarah, I'm getting tired of this. First Annie, now her. How many other people did that little shithead let in on this?" He turned to Sarah, "I knew I should have questioned her better before—"

Sarah cut him off with a curt wave of her hand. "Who else knows?" Sarah looked at Cam.

"No one. Everyone else got fried in the sting. I work alone, now."

"There. See, Frank? Our problems are solved. We pay this one off and we're home free."

Frank stepped away from Sarah's side as Sarah took a step closer to Cam.

"Give us a couple days to make arrangements and I think you'll be relaxed. But I think twenty-thousand would be closer to the real figure."

"No. Fifty." It was time to play the big card now. "I've seen what's come through in just the few months I've been here. Between what you're selling inside and what's being shipped to Briscoe Books," she said, staring at Frank, "fifty shouldn't make a dent in your share." Cam tried one last card. "Unless Warden Spellman wants to chip in." She knew that Deems and Adreapolous should be sitting in Spellman's office right now listening to every word that was being said. Richard C. Deems had wanted to see the look on Spellman's face when this went down.

Sarah and Frank exchanged yet another glance. "Spellman? Did Tony tell you Spellman was in on this?"

Cam stopped. "No, but she said it went straight to the top. I just figured—"

"Spellman? That little turd? She doesn't know how to find her own twat with both hands. I'm the top, sweetie." Sarah's voice was hard and angry now. "*I'm* the one who really runs this place. I have to do everything for her except wipe her ass. She doesn't know half the things that happen here. She didn't even know any of this was going on until the Feds told her. She's so out of touch with the real world, she might as well run for governor."

Frank stifled a smile.

"Let's get this over with," Sarah said. "When and where?"

"I'll have a friend call you and make arrangements. He'll be able to tell me when the transaction's complete."

"Does your friend already know about this?"

"No, I'll contact him tonight."

Sarah glanced at Frank. "Then I guess we have a deal."

"We might as well make the first installment now." Frank said as he rammed the broom handle into Cam's side.

****

The radio signal snapped and cracked loudly as the broom handle hit Cam. "She's in trouble. Let's go."

Wendell Adreopolous picked up his radio and spoke into it. "Move it out. We got trouble in here."

Deems turned to Spellman who sat, her face bright red from anger, her hands white from their grip on her chair arms. "Tell your guards to let our men through." To the C.O. who stood behind Spellman, he ordered, "Get us to that storeroom."

"Yes, sir," and the three raced off leaving Spellman to pick up the phone with trembling hands.

****

Cameron felt a searing, ripping pain in her side as the broom caught her just below her knife wound. She gasped and fell backward as she felt the not-quite-healed wound tear apart. The second swing of the broom handle caught her on the side of her head, but she was able to deflect it and wring the broom out of his hands, throwing it to the floor. She tried to duck and turn away as Frank lunged for her, but the re-opening of her wound slowed her reaction and Frank grabbed her by the collar. She twisted out of his grasp, but the pain in her side stopped her for just a fraction of a second and she never saw the hard fist that connected with her face. Frank grabbed her shirt and punched her again, just below her left eye. Cam slumped in his grasp, not quite conscious.

"How are you going to explain this one?" Sarah asked.

Frank looked around. "Those crates look pretty precarious to me." He pointed at the top shelf. "I'll bet if one of those were to accidentally fall, they'd smash someone's skull."

"I love the way you think. You are brilliant. It's too bad she had to be in here just when the shelf let go."

"Come on, sweetheart, let me make you more comfortable." He pulled Cameron over and let her sink to the floor, just below the shelf. He picked up a heavy metal can of soft drink syrup and held it above him, ready to smash it down into Cam's head. "Time to go night-night."

"*I wouldn't even consider that!*"

He turned toward the voice as Sarah took a step back. Lou and three other inmates were standing at the back of the storeroom. They'd come in, silently, through the back door.

"I'd put that down real gently if I were you," Lou warned.

There was a moment's hesitation. Then Frank flung the container at the women as he reached for his gun. At that moment, the main door flew open and Deems, Adreopolous and three C.O.s flew in, their guns drawn.

Lou and the other women dodged the container which clattered and split open against the back wall.

"I'm glad you're here," Sarah said, stepping forward to take control. She turned to the newly arrived guards, "Take all these women down to solitary…"

Deems stepped up to her with his badge and gun drawn. "You have the right to remain silent. Anything…"

Sarah's expression took on a look of indignant injury as Deems continued. Adreopolous and one of the other guards had grabbed Frank and handcuffed him.

"We're going to need a medic," Lou called as she bent over Cam. Blood had soaked through the bandage that was already there and the shirt on top. Her eye was swollen shut and turning a deep purple. Blood oozed from a small cut just over her left cheekbone.

* * * *

"And I hear that Frank and two other guards are peeing all over themselves, blaming everyone they can name for everything that happened. Sarah Adrien has been locked up. She was the head of all that. She and Frank are being charged with Annie's and Tony's deaths and for a guard's death that happened last year. I hear there might be a charge of attempted murder of a Federal agent that's still in a hospital. That is, if he lives. Oh, and also, attempted murder for what they did to you."

Lou sat beside Cam's bed in the prison infirmary. It was good to hear the side of the story that was running around inside the prison. Cam had spent another three days in the hospital before being transferred back to the infirmary. Pauly had reported all that had happened: that Spellman had sworn to keep Cam's involvement secret so she could continue undercover, that the journals being shipped to Briscoe Books, which was, in fact, owned by Frank's brother, did contain cocaine, that two of the women from the bindery had confessed that they had worked with Tuck during the evenings to unwrap the journals, cut the holes and insert the coke before shrinkwrapping them again.

Cam reached out to get the glass of water that sat on the table.

"Hey," Lou said, jumping to hand the glass to her. "Don't stretch like that. Want to rip those stitches out again?"

Cam smiled, or at least half smiled. The left side of her face was still swollen and bruised. A small bandage covered the two stitches it had taken to close the cut.

"Thanks." She took a sip and handed the glass back. "Do we know who actually pulled the trigger?"

Lou nodded. "Frank pulled the trigger, but he's swearing that Sarah Adrien ordered him to. I understand Spellman almost had a heart attack when all this happened. Things have been real tight around here. Not much leeway in anything. You even have to sign in with a C.O. when you go out into the yard."

Cam laughed. "And what were you doing in the storeroom?"

"Besides saving your life?" Lou smiled. "I got curious. I heard you'd been told to sweep up. Usually work assignments come through me. This one didn't. So, I went down to find out what was happening. Timing is everything, I guess. I heard the beginning of the conversation and figured I'd go get a little help. We got back just as Franky-boy was winding you up into a little pile. Sorry we were late."

Cam held her hand up to stop her. "You got there in plenty time."

"You missed the best part," Lou smiled. "Should have seen Miss High-and-Mighty try to have us all thrown into solitary for causing a riot. She was really indignant when they handcuffed her! Thought she would have a stroke! You were out cold for that."

"Yeh," Cam sighed, "Sorry I missed that."

"It was a real job cleaning up that cola syrup, though. I would've liked to have avoided that."

Cam chuckled and shifted positions slightly. The ache in her side was insistent, no matter which way she lay. It would be a week or more before she was up and around this time. "I'm still alive. That's the important thing. I was stupid not to be ready for his attack."

"One thing I don't understand. How did the Fed's get there when they did?" She looked deeply into Cam's eyes, searching for the truth.

"I don't know," Cam lied. "Maybe the room was bugged. I wouldn't be surprised if this whole place was wired."

Lou looked at her in silence. Both knew that Cam wasn't telling the whole truth, but would let it go for the time being.

"I understand you're up for parole next month."

Cam nodded. "That FBI guy said he'd put in a couple good words for me. I hope it helps." She looked at Lou for a reaction. "I told them everything that happened in the storeroom. I don't like it when someone tries to kill me. And I guess I'm still angry about Gina's condition."

"I don't blame you. Adrien and her cohorts deserve everything that gets thrown at them. I would love to see her sent back to this place. I know a lot of inmates here who'd be real happy to help her settle in!"

Both laughed.

"Oh," Lou changed the subject. "You're from Baltimore. You know a woman lawyer there named Hunter?"

"Hunter? Why?" Cam opened her eyes and looked at Lou.

"I got a letter from some lawyer named Hunter asked if I would talk with her. Something about re-opening my case."

Cam slid away from answering the question. "Re-open your case? Lou, that's wonderful!"

"Maybe." Lou mumbled. Cam had never seen Lou unsure before.

"Well, are you going to see her?"

Lou wiped her hands on her jeans. Her palms got sweaty when she talked about this. "I can't see why not. But it scares the hell out of me."

"Why?"

"I don't want to get any hopes up. I've been here eighteen years and nine months. Hell, Harvard, I got grandchildren I've never seen. Outside seems a long ways away."

Cam smiled. "Just take it one step at a time. A good friend told me that once."

Lou beamed.

Chapter Twenty-Seven

Cameron let her body sink lower into the hot sudsy bath water. The past eight weeks had seemed interminable, the longest eight weeks Cameron could remember. From the day she'd been released from the infirmary and set about her new schedule in the prison, until she was notified that the parole board would hear her petition for release, Cam had worked hard at her assigned tasks, read voraciously and worked out every day in the gym. She missed Gina's carefree banter and the camaraderie she'd had with Tuck, but they were both gone now. The new inmate who'd taken Gina's cell was nervous and cloying in her efforts not to offend anyone. And even the ball games that had begun again in the yard didn't seem to have the same energy. The only one, she'd really spoken to during that time, had been Lou who had met twice already with Attorney Gloria Hunter.

She leaned her head back against the plastic pillow that cradled her in the old, claw-foot white bath tub. She loved this old tub. It was large and deep enough to allow enough water to completely surround her, up to her chin. And it reminded her of the old tub in Grandma Chris' summer house in New Hampshire. All in all, it was the most comforting thing she could think of right now. A nice warm bath and privacy. God, she thought, I never realized what a luxury this was.

Earlier that morning, Maggie had driven to Hagerville Women's Correctional Facility and met her as she emerged from a year within its confines. Then after stopping to pick up Cam's favorite pastrami sandwich at Lenny's Deli, she had dropped Cam back at her old apartment then Maggie returned to her office to see her last two patients for the week.

There was a knock at the bathroom door. "Have you drowned, yet? Or would you like a drink to help you along?" Pauly's voice sounded from outside.

"I'm ready to kill for a good stiff scotch," Cameron called.

"Coming right up." Cam could hear Pauly rummaging around in the kitchen. Soon there was another knock on the bathroom door.

"Are you decent?" he asked.

Cam slid a little further under the abundant soap bubbles, letting her hair dip into the foam. "As decent as I ever was."

Pauly opened the bathroom door and entered with a tall glass filled with scotch and soda floating several ice cubes. "This is how you take it, isn't it?" he asked as he handed her the glass and sat down on the closed commode.

"Oh, Pauly," Cam sighed, as she took her first sip of the light amber liquid, "It's been so long since I had a drink, I can't even remember."

"Well, go slowly on that one, shweetheart," Pauly said in his best Bogart voice. "It won't do to have you shitfaced before three p.m. on your first day of freedom."

"Why not?" Cam asked, slowly savoring the taste of the hard, single malt. "I think I deserve to get good and drunk. This is my first day off in months. I don't have to worry about what I say and I don't have to worry about who might be sneaking up behind me. That is, unless you've done a radical one-hundred-eighty since we last spoke."

"My dear friend…" Pauly drew himself up to a regal position. "…I have been admiring your well defined muscles which you have developed of late and I love you dearly, but you are not endowed with the one piece of equipment over which I would lose sleep."

Cameron laughed and gave Pauly a big smile. "Son," she said, toasting him with her drink, "We have a beautiful friendship."

Pauly sat back and looked at his friend. "I am so glad to see you out of that place."

"You're not the only one. I never realized what little things meant. Like being able to take a bath, or sitting and talking to a friend. If I had stayed in there one more day, I would have been loony-tunes."

"Well, that part is over now. It's on to bigger and better things."

"Not yet! I need time off for bad behavior!" She let her head fall back in mock dismay, draping the back of her hand over her forehead.

Pauly chuckled at her theatrics. "Sweetheart," he admonished, "you act more like a queen than I ever did. You put me to shame. No one would ever believe that you were the butch and I was the femme. Now, let me get this place rearranged for you. I brought some of your clothes up from the storage unit. I'm sorry I didn't have time to have them cleaned for you. They must be nasty after being in storage so long."

"Don't worry about my old clothes." Cam smiled, feeling the tension in her muscles relaxing, both from the warm bath water and the scotch. "Most of them probably won't fit me anyway. I've lost quite a bit of weight. And I've put more muscle back in my shoulders. I need to just go out and buy a new wardrobe."

"Which we shall do as soon as Maggie gets here. And then, we'll start on fattening you up a bit. What's your choice for your first real dinner?"

Cam closed her eye, almost tasting her favorite food. "Anything in living color! Red meat, green vegetables, yellow corn… Actually, I've been thinking of rack of lamb and caesar salad with anchovies since I got the okay on my parole."

"Then that's what it shall be." Pauly rose to leave. "Now, don't splash water on the floor when you get out of there and hang up your towel when you're done. I've been careful to keep this place in good shape since I moved in. I won't have you messing it up in just one day, no, half a day back." With that admonition, he left the room, closing the door after him.

Cam laughed heartily. It did feel good to be home. Back with her best friend, in her own apartment among her own possessions. Well, at least among most of them. She'd noticed that Pauly had done quite a bit of redecorating since he'd been apartment sitting. It looked really comfortable and tidy. Not that it had been a pigsty when she lived alone here, but she had never taken the time to add little amenities, like the brightly colored shelf paper in the kitchen and the freshly painted shelves in the bathroom. She'd have to discuss it with him when they had time. She'd been thinking that perhaps she needed to live elsewhere. But for now, she was just grateful that the ten months she'd spent in prison were over and it was time to go on to the next case.

Cam downed a big gulp of the scotch and let her mind float on its easy wave. It was too good just to be out of the cold prison to worry about what would or wouldn't happen tomorrow.

* * * *

There was a knock at the front door as Cam was digging clean clothes out of the cardboard box Pauly had placed in the back sitting room. She heard Pauly go to the door and recognized a friendly, welcome voice as it sounded from the living room.

Zipping her jeans which hung well down on her hips, she went to greet her visitor. "Hey, lady," she grinned.

"Other people's problems are over for another week. Now I have time to pamper you and see that you enjoy your first day off." Maggie held her arms out and pulled Cameron into a tight hug.

"It sure feels good not to have a table between us," Cam mused.

Finally Maggie pulled back and surveyed Cameron. "You look a lot better out of those prison clothes, but we still need to update your wardrobe. Those don't fit as well as they used to," was her comment.

Cameron smiled. "I need to think about a whole lot of changes, I guess."

"Well, you two sit down and gush over each other while I get that other box out of the storage for you." Pauly shooed them toward the couch, then disappeared out the door.

"Dickie called the office to see how you were and says to tell you how pleased he is, too. Everything went very well. The driver from the detergent company has given some good leads that may close down quite a few routes. We've ascertained that Briscoe Books was getting about a half a kilo of coke in every carton. It was well done, and so simple no one ever suspected. All in all, this was more successful than we'd imagined. And your friend Frank has sworn that Trumble was the mole who blew the whistle that got Kathy's cover blown last year. Your cover is still very tight, by the way. Everyone believes that there was a hidden microphone in the storage room. No one knows it was on you except Warden Spellman and she was so upset by what was said there, that she's willing to do anything to put things back on track. The only thing we haven't nailed is Sarah Adrien's connection to the big dealers. It'll probably surface soon. There are a lot of people wanting to ask her a lot of questions. All in all, Dickie's very happy."

"Has Dickie said what's next?" Cam asked, hoping that he hadn't.

"Yes," was Maggie's reply. She took a breath and frowned as Cameron sank into the couch with a sigh of resignation.

"We still haven't answered all the questions on this case, have we?" Cam asked. "There are still things like how the money is being laundered and how the coke got to Testa's in the first place. We all know here's a lot more here than just what went on in the prison."

Maggie looked a Cam, her expression unreadable. Then she smiled. "Now we're not goin to talk about that. It can wait till later. First we are going shopping." Maggie had it all planned out. "Then, starting tomorrow, you're going to spend at least two weeks of well deserved R and R. You can stay at my new house out on the bay. Then we'll talk. Until then, you are to sit back and do absolutely nothing except relax." Maggie studied Cam for a moment. "Is there something special you want to do?"

"Well, I need to call my family, and I haven't seen a good movie in a long time And I know that Dickie expects a full written report too."

"Dickie's report can wait. He's not expecting anything for a few weeks. And there are movie theaters within driving distance. Anything else?"

"Not that I can think of at the moment, but I'm sure something will pop up."

Maggie waited a moment. "Have you thought about Michael?" she finally asked, her voice slightly lower.

"Every minute for the past two months. I don't even know what to begin to say to her." Cam sat forward, her elbows resting on her knees. Michael was the one piece of this puzzle that hadn't been settled. "Maybe I'm just chicken shit, Maggie. What would I say? What will she say? Do I just say, 'Hey, I want you to be my lover, but I have to go out and be a drug dealer so I'll probably be out of touch for months at a time and, oh, by the way, I'll probably have to sleep with a whole lot of other women, but don't worry, I'll always come back to you, that is, if I live to come home at all'."

"Well," Maggie smiled at Cam's chagrin, "I don't think that would be the best approach. But, the worst she could say is 'get lost.'" There was a lot that had to be worked through there, but at least she didn't have to worry that this would compromise an investigation. "Now, what do you want for dinner? I can't imagine the slop they've been feeding you and I know you can't be satisfied with just that pastrami sandwich. Paul and I will take you wherever you want to eat, tonight. Dickey's treat."

"You and Pauly." Cam shook her head. "I've been out of prison for…" she glanced at the clock, "…five and a half hours and all you two can think of is feeding me and getting me drunk." She smiled. "I think he's already made reservations." After Maggie's urging about Michael, Cameron suddenly wasn't sure she had a appetite, but another scotch sure wouldn't hurt.

* * * *

Cameron sank back into the wide, firm bed, letting her naked body feel the cool, smooth sheets. Another luxury she had never acknowledged. Part of her felt guilty as she heard the sofa bed creak under Pauly's weight in the living room, but then, he hadn't slept on a narrow, lumpy bunk for most of the last year.

Pauly and Maggie had made the evening very special for her, taking her to a mall just outside Baltimore and then, once she was dressed properly, with enough new clothes to last her for the next month, to one of the best restaurants in the city. The meal, the wine, the freedom felt wonderful.

Even as she tried not to think about tomorrow, she'd already started a list of "to dos" for the next day. She'd thought that the first item on the list would be, *Talk to Pauly about the habitation of this apartment*, but with Maggie offering her the bay house for a couple weeks, that pushed that decision onto a back burner. Now, near the top of the list, right after the note to call her sister, was *Call Michael*.

"Don't think about that," she warned herself. But the thousands of scenarios of what the call to Michael would turn into flashed through her mind. Luckily, the relief of being out of the prison combined with the alcohol she'd consumed thwarted her worries from keeping her awake for long.

Chapter Twenty-Eight

Cameron leaned on the railing of the back porch that looked out over one of the many fingers of Chesapeake Bay. Maggie's new summer house, which she'd just purchased in March, had been built three decades earlier. She'd immediately had it refurbished and landscaped to give her a bit of privacy. The house sat on the east side of a small inlet that ran off the main part of the bay. It was about an hour south of Baltimore, facing west over the water, thus getting the advantage of the late afternoon sun and later evening shadows. New, wider windows facing the water allowed for the side windows to be draped without losing the light. Shrubbery had been added along the side property lines which went to the water to keep the back yard secluded, even though her neighbors were still within hailing distance. Craig had made sure that special secret lights and scanning devices were installed that would immediately trigger warnings and keep any intruder under surveillance.

Cam had called her sister earlier that morning. Lori was very relieved that Cam called. The tension between them seemed to have faded as the conversation went along and they were laughing like they used to by the end of the call. Lori pressed her repeatedly to make sure she was all right and assured her that everyone there was fine. She made Cam promise to come home as soon as her parole officer allowed her to travel outside of Maryland. There was no mention of the envelope still tucked away in the safe. But although it felt like their relationship was back on track, Cam could tell that Lori still didn't believe the whole prison story. At least they were talking again.

She stepped off the deck and walked slowly to the dock that jutted out into the water. A small motorboat sped by, its occupants laughing and talking loudly as they cruised the inlet on their way to the larger bay, just a mile or so away. They looked like a couple of Naval cadets on leave from Annapolis, with their dates. For a moment, Cam envied them. Oh, if life were that simple again. Go to school, study hard, play just as hard, and don't worry about anything except making good grades and keeping out of trouble.

"Now that looks like freedom!" Cam sighed as the boat sped away.

Maggie looked up at her from the end of the dock where she squatted down and pulled on the rope that was tied there to pull the crab trap up out of the water. Two small crabs were caught inside, but she lowered the trap back into the water. They'd make a nice treat for tonight's dinner. Maybe by that time, there'd even be a few more.

"Well, I'm sorry, but a boat is the one thing I haven't bought yet, although I do have plans to build a small boat house by the edge of the property," she said, pointing to the water line as she stood up to meet Cam. "Maybe you can help me pick out a good boat. I haven't had a chance to research them yet."

Cam chuckled as she reached out and gave Maggie a hug. "Knowing you, it'll take at least another year before you make a decision on a boat. I'm surprised you bought this house so fast."

Maggie smiled. "I've actually had my eye on this area for about five years. When this went on the market in February, I knew I'd lose it if I waited, so I snapped it up."

"It's wonderful here, Maggie. Are you sure you don't mind me hanging out here for a few days?"

"Don't be silly! Stay as long as you want. I have to go back to the office this afternoon, but if I didn't have so much work piled up, I'd stay with you for a while, too."

Cam turned to her. "I wish you could, Maggie!"

Maggie returned the hug. "I think what you probably need the most right now is just some quiet time to yourself. I'm not sure I could have lasted as long as you did without a moment's privacy. Now, I do want you to think of this place as your second home. Please feel free to come here anytime you like, to relax, get away, hide out. You know all the codes to get into this place and Craig assures me it's the top of the line security. Even the water line and dock are rigged to watch for intruders."

Cam studied her for a moment. "It just dawned on me. Here I've been so involved in getting in and out of prison that I haven't even asked how you're doing. This was your first assignment as a controller, wasn't it?"

A strange look of introspection crossed Maggie's face. Then she shrugged off the feeling. "Yes, it was, now that you mention it. I was so concerned for you, and it felt so good, so…what's the feeling? It felt so *natural* that I haven't even given it a second thought. I guess we make a good team."

Their eyes studied each other for a moment until, finally, Cam shook her head. "You are a remarkable woman, Dr. Margaret Thomason," she said, smiling. "You liked this job, didn't you."

Maggie nodded. "Yes, I did. I wasn't sure at first, but I really enjoyed it. Richard wants me to stay on as your controller for a while longer."

"Wonderful!" Cam beamed. "And the people in the prison said you'd dump me as soon as I got out. What's a nice well-established doctor like you doing with a worn out ex-con like me?" Both laughed warmly.

Suddenly a voice rang out behind them. "Hey, lady! Where you want this stuff?"

Cam and Maggie turned to see Pauly standing on the deck by the back door, his arms loaded down with bags of groceries.

"Well, so much for security," Cam said, laughing as they walked back toward the house. Cam took one heavy sack out of his arms as Maggie opened the back door for them.

"What did you buy me?" Cam asked, peering into the sack as she set it on the kitchen counter.

"All your favorites." Pauly grinned as he took packages out of the bags and loading them into the refrigerator.

"Bagels...and cream cheese!" Cam exclaimed as she took them from the bag to hand to him. "This is great! I'm going to gain a hundred pounds! My new clothes won't fit me."

"I figured you could use the pampering," Pauly said, taking the items from her, "And the calories. There's also a pound of lox and a red onion in there, too."

Cam just grinned as she continued to examine each new item including the bottle of her favorite scotch, soda water, fresh oranges, and other foods she hadn't had in over a year.

The sound of the front doorbell didn't interrupt her as she continued to rummage through the sacks. Nor did she look up as Maggie murmured an apology and left the kitchen.

"Pauly!" Cam exclaimed as she emptied the contents of the fourth sack onto the counter. "There's enough coffee here to float an army!" She took a dark-colored can of ground dark roast coffee and set it next to a yellow tin, a plain brown sack and a tin of regular roast.

"I couldn't decide," Pauly smiled. "This was a special at that gourmet shop. It's Hawaiian blend. I know you like good coffee and I can't imagine the dishwater you drank in that prison, so I splurged. There's also a half pound of French vanilla in there, too."

"This is great!" Cam exclaimed.

"And I thought you liked your French a little stronger than vanilla!"

Cam froze as the voice sounded behind her. It was unmistakable: the deep contralto, the thick French Canadian lilt.

Cam glanced to the side at Pauly who was staring, wide-eyed toward the dining room door. Slowly, Cam turned around. Less than fifteen feet away from her, was one of the most stunning visions she'd seen in a very long time. There Michael stood in a full length black leather coat, a black turtle-neck and black leather trousers. The starkness of the form fitting outfit made her golden mane and hazel eyes stand out even more beautifully than Cam remembered. Even more that she imagined. She simply stared into the depth of the eyes that bore into hers.

Finally, it was Maggie who broke the silence.

"Michael, I don't think you've ever actually met Paul Tarelli. Paul,

Michael Gauchet."

Michael broke her gaze away from Cam and extended her hand to Pauly. "I am happy to finally meet you. I have heard very much about what a wonderful friend you are to Cameron."

"And I'm very happy to meet you, finally." Pauly smiled as he gripped her hand.

Cam still hadn't moved, hadn't taken her eyes from Michael.

"Am I interrupting?" Michael asked softly as she turned back to Cam.

Cam shook herself from her stupor. "Oh no," she stammered, "I'm..uh…it's good to see you."

Michael smiled at her. "And it is good to see you looking so well."

There was more silence as Pauly put the last of the groceries into the cupboard. Finally it was Maggie who again broke the silence.

"I hate to miss the rest of this stimulating conversation…" She laughed. "…but I really have to get back to town." She walked over to Cam and gave her an affectionate hug. "Call me if you need anything. All the numbers you need are next to the phone and if you go out, don't forget to set the alarm.

"Wait," Pauly interjected, "I have to catch a ride back with you." He dug a set of car keys out of his pocket and handed them to Cam. "Your car is freshly tuned, oil changed and the tank's full. Anything else you want?"

Cam shook her head, "No, I have everything," she managed.

Pauly glanced at Michael with a smile. "Call if you want anything else. I can come back out tomorrow…"

Maggie grinned. "Unless you're too busy for company." She patted Michael's arm. "I'm glad you're here." She smiled as Pauly followed her out.

As the door shut behind them, Cam crossed her arms as she leaned back against the counter. "Was this a set-up?" she asked, finally.

Michael smiled as she took her coat off and laid it over the back of one of the chairs. "Do not blame Maggie. It was my idea. You could never answer my letters and I was afraid you wouldn't take my calls. Maggie had already planned to bring you here to rest so I persuaded her to let me visit. I… I just thought we needed to talk about what happened between us. I had to take the chance. I won't stay if you wish me to leave."

Cam took a deep breath. "I'm sorry I couldn't answer your letters, but I had planned on calling you this week. I wasn't sure you were back from Korea."

"I returned last weekend."

"Did you get your belt?"

Michael nodded. "I am now seventh degree."

"I'm very proud of you."

Michael shook her head. "Not half as much as I am of you. Maggie has told me of your triumphs. Charlie also sends his congratulations," Michael had inched her way closer and was now only a few feet away.

Cam could feel her body reacting to Michael's closeness. She took another deep breath and tried to make her voice steady. "I wasn't that successful, I made a lot of mistakes."

"But you did succeed in your mission and you are alive. That is the important part," Michael interrupted, "We can always work on more skills later."

Cam gasped as Michael reached out and stroked her cheek, running her thumb over the small scar beside her left eye that Frank's ring had left.

Michael's words were soft, tentative. "I have thought of you constantly since last spring. I have been very good these past few years at being inaccessible, emotionally. It was a big shock to realize I could not erase you from my mind."

Cam stared back into the eyes that burned into hers, but didn't trust her voice not to break. "I...I'm still undercover. Legally, I'm on parole..."

"I know," Michael's eyes turned away. "Maggie explained it to me. I know that you must be free to play your part..." She hesitated slightly, "...and I understand that." Michael looked back at her, hesitantly. "But I...I want to be a part of your life, too. Even if I can't know everything that you do." Michael took a small step back and inhaled deeply. "Cameron, I need you to know...what happened in Puerto Rico...I was not playing. Maybe I was *too* serious. I did not make love to you to teach you a lesson. I made love to you because I wanted to make love to you. That is still what I want to do."

Was this too much to ask? It was much more than she had ever dared to hope for, but now... Did she have the right to ask this much of Michael?

Michael's eyes searched Cam's as Cam did not respond immediately. "Let me stay. Please. I know we need to talk through a lot of things. If you want me to leave, say so, I will. But I wish us to begin again."

Cam just stared into Michael's eyes. The rush of heat that rose in her as Michael took a tentative step closer was only overshadowed by the realization of the major risk Michael had just taken. Would she have had the courage? Could she have asked for so much? Now, it all seemed so clear. She managed to say, "Stay."

The word was barely out of her mouth before Michael's lips covered hers. Cam felt the rush through her entire body as Michael's arms encircled her and the kiss became stronger, less tentative. She allowed herself to melt into Michael as Michael's lips opened and her tongue began to trace lines across her lips.

Taking a deep breath as Michael released her, Cam placed her hands on Michael's shoulders, trying to clear her spinning head. "I would never ask you for something I couldn't give in return," she said softly.

"You haven't asked. I have offered," Michael stated flatly. "Cameron, I am in love with you. It hasn't happened often. I tried to get over it. I cannot." She gave a shrug. "Maybe you must tell me to go away. Or maybe you are just stuck with me."

Cameron studied her. Michael made it seem so simple. "I'll never tell you to go away," was all she said. Michael had her in an embrace again. This time she warmed to Michael's kiss and heated it with her own passion. Cam let Michael take the lead, let Michael's strong tongue enter her mouth and make its impassioned demands against her. It was the one feeling she'd missed these past few months, letting go, not being in charge, trusting someone else. Could she afford that? The more Michael asked, the more she wanted to give. Their bodies reacted together, pressing, rubbing, melting into each other. The heat between them, between Cam's legs, grew.

Finally, Cam pulled back to catch her breath. "Should we go upstairs?"

"I have waited so long, I'm not sure I could make it that far," Michael stated as she quickly undid the buttons down the front of Cam's shirt. Her eyes searched Cameron's, watching for permission or denial. Seeing the smile in Cam's eyes, she pushed the shirt open as her fingers slid across Cameron's breasts and softly caressed the erect nipples. Looking down, Michael saw the long, ragged scar, still bright on Cam's side. Stopping, she stepped back, gingerly touching the redness. "Does it bother you?"

Cam took Michael's hand from the scar and brought it back to her breast. "Only if it makes you stop what you were doing."

Michael immediately took both breasts in her hands. Cam wavered slightly as the pleasure surged through her. Michael backed her up against the sink as she slowly sank to her knees, leaving a trail of wet kisses down Cam's chest and stomach.

"Let me lie down," Cam said, feeling her knees begin to weaken.

"No, cherie. This will be better if you are standing. Brace your hands behind you, against the counter."

Cam smiled as her body reacted to the recognition of the dominating tone in Michael's voice. It was the authoritative emphasis she'd missed. She submitted without hesitation. "Yes, Mistress."

Michael stopped unzipping Cam's jeans to gaze up at her. The look of pure joy on Cam's face startled her. "No," she whispered. "Not Mistress. I am Michael. Just Michael. I do not want to control you. I just want to make love to you."

Their eyes met, briefly. They knew that whatever future they had, whatever had to be negotiated, would wait, at least a few more hours. Suddenly, they were both aware that their last words had meant more than anything else that could be said and had bound them tighter than any rope or chain possibly could.

Individuals order from : NEW VICTORIA PUBLISHERS
PO BOX 27 NORWICH VERMONT 05055
OR CALL 1-800 326 5297 email newvic@aol.com

FOUR MYSTERIES BY KATE ALLEN

TELL ME WHAT YOU LIKE An Alison Kaine Mystery
Alison Kaine, lesbian cop, enters the world of leather-dykes after a woman is brutally murdered at a Denver bar. She's fascinated, yet wary of her attraction to a dominatrix named Stacy. In this fast-paced, yet slyly humorous novel, Allen confronts the sensitive issues of S & M, queer-bashers and women-identified sex workers. $9.95

GIVE MY SECRETS BACK An Alison Kaine Mystery
A well-known author of steamy lesbian romances has just moved back to Denver when she is found dead in her bathtub. Suspecting foul play, cop Alison Kaine begins an off-duty investigation to find the chapters of her next book which are inexplicably missing, and may contain clues to her murder. $10.95

TAKES ONE TO KNOW ONE An Alison Kaine Mystery
This third Alison Kaine mystery finds the Denver cop and her delightfully eccentric circle of friends travelling to a women's spirituality retreat in New Mexico—and into an all too earthly mystery. Allen writes about the complexities and controversies of lesbian life with delightful wit and style. $10.95

I KNEW YOU WOULD CALL A Marta Goicochea Mystery
Kate Allen sets this new mystery series in the lesbian ghetto where the characters live 'close to the bone.' Written in Allen's humorous style, this book still manages to confront honestly issues of incest survival, abusive lesbian relationships, lesbian custody of children and community self-help. $10.95.

SIX MYSTERIES BY SARAH DREHER

STONER MCTAVISH
The first Stoner mystery introduces us to travel agent Stoner McTavish. On a trip to the Tetons, Stoner meets and falls in love with her dream lover, Gwen, whom she must rescue from danger and almost certain death. $9.95

SOMETHING SHADY
Investigating the mysterious disappearance of a nurse at a suspicious rest home on the coast of Maine, Stoner finds herself an inmate, trapped in the clutches of the evil psychiatrist Dr. Milicent Tunes. Can Gwen and Aunt Hermione charge to the rescue before it's too late? $8.95

GRAY MAGIC
After telling Gwen's grandmother that they are lovers, Stoner and Gwen set off to Arizona to escape the fallout. But a peaceful vacation turns frightening when Stoner finds herself an unwitting combatant in a struggle between the Hopi spirits of Good and Evil. $9.95

A CAPTIVE IN TIME
Stoner finds herself inexplicably transported to a town in Colorado Territory, time 1871. There she encounters Dot, the saloon keeper, Blue Mary, a local witch/healer, and an enigmatic teenage runaway named Billy. $9.95

OTHERWORLD
All your favorite characters—business partner Marylou, eccentric Aunt Hermione, psychiatrist, Edith Kesselbaum, and, devoted lover, Gwen, on vacation at Disney World. Marylou is kidnapped and held hostage in an underground tunnel. $10.95

BAD COMPANY
Stoner and Gwen investigate mysterious accidents, sabotage and menacing notes that threaten members of a feminist theater company. Sarah Dreher's endearing creation, Stoner McTavish, is on every list of beloved lesbian detectives.
$19.95 hardcover $10.95 paper

MORE MYSTERIES FROM NEW VICTORIA

I NEVER READ THOREAU A mystery novel by Karen Saum
From the author of the Brigid Donovan mystery series *(Murder Is Material, Murder Is Germane, Murder Is Relative)* comes a quirky murder mystery set on a remote Maine island, involving ex-nuns, political refugees, drifters, and eccentric locals. $10.95

DEATHS OF JOCASTA by J.M. Redmann
What was the body of a woman doing in the basement of the Cort Clinic? Could Dr. Cordelia James have performed the incompetent abortion that killed her? Micky Knight has to answer these questions before the police and the news media find their own solution. "Knight is witty, irreverent and very sexy." $10.95

DEATH BY THE RIVERSIDE by J.M. Redmann
Detective Micky Knight, hired to take a few pictures, finds herself slugging through thugs and slogging through swamps in an attempt to expose a dangerous drug ring. The investigation turns personal when her own well–hidden past is exposed. Featuring fabulously sexual, all too fiercely independent lady dick. $9.95

FIGHTING FOR AIR A Cal Meredith Mystery by Marsha Mildon
Jay's class of scuba students goes out for their first open water dive. All goes well until a young Ethiopian loses consciousness and drowns before the dive instructor can get him to the surface. $10.95

NUN IN THE CLOSET A Mystery by Joanna Michaels
Anne Hollis, the owner of a women's bar is charged with manslaughter in the death of a nun. Insisting she's innocent, Anne appeals to probation officer Callie Sinclair for help. The case grows more complex and puzzling when another nun is murdered, and Callie discovers that sex and money are involved. $9.95

IF LOOKS COULD KILL A Mystery by Frances Lucas
Diana Mendoza, a Latina lesbian lawyer, is a scriptwriter for a hot TV show featuring a woman detective. While on location in L.A., she meets blonde actress Lauren Lytch. Lauren is accused of murdering her husband and Diana rushes to her defense. $9.95

THE KALI CONNECTION A Lynn Evans Mystery by Claudia McKay
Lynn, an investigative reporter is checking on the connection of a mysterious Eastern cult with possible drug trafficking. Her attraction to Marta, a charming and earnest devotee challenges Lynn's skepticism and sparks her desire. Then Marta disappears. Was she kidnapped? Lynn travels to Nepal to find the answer. $9.95